It's High Noon for a Young Nation . . . and It All Depends on Dayle.

DAYLE DOBSON grew up in an orphanage to become one of America's first Lady Pinkerton detectives, and a damned good one at that. While once she ached for a family, now she's come to appreciate her lack of attachments, even to the point of convincing herself that love is a woman's worst option. She prefers the freedom to do what others don't dare.

HARRY BRYANT has never met a Pinkerton that he liked, and he isn't sure about Dayle Dobson, never mind the fact that he can't get her out of his mind or off his trail. He has a score to settle and for years he's been waiting for the right opportunity. No Lady Pinkerton, no matter how fascinating, is going to get in his way now. Or is she?

ALLAN PINKERTON is "America's Most Famous Detective." He invented the notion of a "private eye." Now aging, he'll do anything to protect his reputation, including breaking the law and betraying his own.

GARRICK BATEMAN is the big boss of White Springs, Wyoming. His job is to keep the mines open and the railroad running, and he'll stop at nothing to carry out that charge, even murder. He hired Dayle Dobson to keep his wife from learning too much about his affairs, but then things got complicated. Now both women have become a threat.

LOTTA BATEMAN is the high-society Bostonian bride that Garrick brought to this Wyoming outpost in order to give himself a little class. Now feeling trapped, and tottering on the edge of desperation, she has uncannily chosen to take up the one "charity" that could destroy her husband.

MARY STILLMAN DAVIES is the Presbyterian missionary who has set up an entire "underground railroad" to rescue some of the thousands of Chinese women being held as slaves in Chinatown brothels all over the West. Besides being a nuisance to the powers-that-be, her "good work" could get Lotta Bateman killed—not to mention the fact that her past could trip up Dayle Dobson's future.

Praise for Jerrie Hurd's
Kate Burke Shoots the Old West

"As a fifth-generation ranch woman, Jerrie Hurd knows the women who helped settle the West.... Her straightforward, descriptive style is engaging and interesting.... Her stories reveal real women."
—Linda Duval, *Colorado Springs Daily*

"A well-written, no-holds-barred novel . . . but it is the power of her storytelling that captures us. A truly interesting book with a unique heroine . . ."
—*Roundup* magazine

"Full of humor, fear, bravery, and conflict between the Indians and the whites. A very intriguing, touching, and interesting read."
—*Rendezvous*

"Interesting . . . her romantic outcome is a surprise. If you are in the mood for a western historical, this book should fill the bill."
—Becky Rotz, *Old Book Barn Gazette*

"Jerrie Hurd writes a well-defined study of the people and land of South Dakota. Kate is indeed a unique heroine. She's a little rough around the edges, but that's what makes her such a colorful, three-dimensional character. She has the strength of a true pioneer. We need more heroines like Kate Burke."
—Hollie Domiano, *Affaire de Coeur*

"Jerrie Hurd has concocted a tale of adventure and romance packed with action and intrigue."
—*Abilene Reporter-News (TX)*

Books by Jerrie Hurd

Kate Burke Shoots the Old West
Miss Ellie's Purple Sage Saloon
The Lady Pinkerton Gets Her Man

Published by POCKET BOOKS

For orders other than by individual consumers, Pocket Books grants a discount on the purchase of **10 or more** copies of single titles for special markets or premium use. For further details, please write to the Vice-President of Special Markets, Pocket Books, 1633 Broadway, New York, NY 10019-6785, 8th Floor.

For information on how individual consumers can place orders, please write to Mail Order Department, Simon & Schuster Inc., 200 Old Tappan Road, Old Tappan, NJ 07675.

JERRIE HURD

THE LADY PINKERTON GETS HER MAN

POCKET BOOKS
New York   London   Toronto   Sydney   Tokyo   Singapore

The sale of this book without its cover is unauthorized. If you purchased this book without a cover, you should be aware that it was reported to the publisher as "unsold and destroyed." Neither the author nor the publisher has received payment for the sale of this "stripped book."

This book is a work of fiction. Names, characters, places and incidents are products of the author's imagination or are used fictitiously. Any resemblance to actual events or locales or persons, living or dead, is entirely coincidental.

An *Original* Publication of POCKET BOOKS

POCKET BOOKS, a division of Simon & Schuster Inc.
1230 Avenue of the Americas, New York, NY 10020

Copyright © 1997 by Jerrie Hurd

All rights reserved, including the right to reproduce
this book or portions thereof in any form whatsoever.
For information address Pocket Books, 1230 Avenue
of the Americas, New York, NY 10020

ISBN: 0-671-51911-5

First Pocket Books printing December 1997

10 9 8 7 6 5 4 3 2 1

POCKET and colophon are registered trademarks of
Simon & Schuster Inc.

Cover art by Kam Mak

Printed in the U.S.A.

For Jon

Acknowledgments

The author wishes to thank Nancy Nordhoff and the Cottages at Hedgebrook for the lovely Pacific Northwest September. Every writer needs a retreat mid-book. As usual, Nat Sobel has shaped large parts of this story. "Thanks" may not adequately cover his contribution. And then there's my husband, Jon. For him, "thanks" is definitely not enough.

Author's Note

It's true that Lady Pinkerton detectives rode the West—mainly on trains. Some, indeed, became famous. Likewise Allan Pinkerton and his son, William, are historical persons. The rest of this story is based on a real event that happened in Wyoming Territory in the 1880s. For those reasons, care was exercised to faithfully recreate that time and place. However, the characterizations and actual incidents portrayed here are fiction.

THE LADY PINKERTON GETS HER MAN

*September 1882
Wyoming Territory*

Gutsy, Dayle thought as she teetered on the edge of a roof. The span in front of her was three feet, the drop two stories. She hated heights.

She hated worse the fact that Lotta had already made the leap, seemingly effortlessly. She and her Chinese cook were now running ahead over the next rooftop, not looking back.

Gutsy, Dayle thought again as she watched Lotta. It was begrudging praise of that other woman.

Normally, *gutsy* was a word Dayle reserved to describe herself. It allowed her to indulge a sense of superiority over a woman like Lotta Bateman. If you were gutsy, you didn't need a rich husband or Chinese servants. You didn't need Lotta's fair hair, pink cheeks, or blue eyes. Dayle's own beauty ran to a less fashionable sultriness—dark eyes, dark hair, and enough complexion to complement wearing bold colors.

She swallowed and studied the span in front of her. Then, drawing breath, she swore she'd make the leap

The Lady Pinkerton Gets Her Man

to the next roof, or she'd step off this one and be done with it. Having uncommon nerve meant that much to her. It was practically the badge of her being.

As part of her current disguise, Dayle was pretending to be a quiet, unassuming widowed seamstress who'd come to stay with her well-married second cousin, meaning Lotta. Dayle Dobson was no relation to Lotta. She was a Lady Pinkerton detective and gutsier than any woman she knew, or she was nothing.

Having touched on that determination, she took two steps back to give herself a running start, and then, at the last moment, she couldn't do it. She caught herself again, right at the edge, and teetered. *Don't look down.* She breathed and quickly glanced up and away, not that the broader perspective helped.

The scene was almost as dislocating as the height. In a quieter moment, she might have entertained the romantic notion that she'd been whisked away to some Cantonese village in old Cathay, complete with the smell of herb shops and opium dens. She knew better. This was the Chinatown of White Springs, Wyoming—a slaphappy collection of makeshift shacks, lining a maze of narrow alleyways and tiny garden plots. The structures, many of them two stories, had been thrown together from packing crates and black building paper. The roofs had been tiled with flattened tin cans.

Her foot slipped on one of those flattened cans, loosening it. She pitched forward, looked down. It was early, barely dawn. Ducks and geese and pigs rooted in the gutters below her. Not much else moved. Dayle hardly breathed until her foot caught something solid. Then she threw her shoulders back, and her balance steadied.

Not giving herself another moment to waver, Dayle jumped. Her foot tripped on one of the tin cans, snagging her momentum. The immediate sensation was not of forward movement but of falling. She flashed a mental picture of Sister Mary Julia, head teacher at the orphanage where she grew up. The older woman's finger was in Dayle's face, and her voice declared with a note of triumph, "I knew you'd come to a bad end." Only her idea of Dayle's descent into the gutter had been moral, not literal.

Then, to her relief, Dayle landed flat on the other roof with inches to spare. She rolled onto her feet and caught up with Lotta and her cook as they came to the edge of another roof with a trellis hanging off it and some kind of vine growing around it.

The cook, an older man wearing wire-rimmed glasses that hugged his face, lowered himself off the edge of the roof and began pushing the vine aside, clearing a path down the trellis.

"Hurry," Dayle heard Lotta say softly, an edge of impatience tingeing her usually lilting voice.

The cook, who Dayle observed always did as he pleased, mumbled, "Yes, ma'am," and continued as before.

Lotta's head came up. She looked around. "See anyone?" she asked Dayle. She meant Tong.

Dayle shook her head. The fact that it was getting lighter didn't help. Cocks had begun to crow all over Chinatown—a whole chorus of doodle-do's punctuated by barking dogs and the sound of a distant train.

Lotta leaned over the edge of the roof again. "Hurry," she told the cook. But he wasn't to be hurried. Voicing the vine's Chinese name, he said, "Very fine. Most fine plant like this I see," and then he continued as before gingerly clearing a path down the trellis.

Dayle stepped into the shadow of a chimney and studied the darkness under the eaves, behind barrels and clay pots, and in the latticework of rooftop chicken coops. She didn't see anything, but "Hop Alley" was a society unto itself where even the sheriff didn't come. Nothing happened here without the Tong knowing, and her skin crawled just thinking about Tong.

The Lady Pinkerton Gets Her Man

"You're quite sure you don't see anyone?" Lotta asked again as if she thought Dayle might be cavalier enough to forget where they were and slack off watching.

Dayle did glance over her shoulder briefly at the other woman. She was the "big boss's wife." The Tong would think twice before hurting her, but Dayle enjoyed no such privilege. They might even enjoy making an example out of a Lady Pinkerton. She had no doubt they suspected she was a Lady Pinkerton despite her pretense of being Lotta's relative. There was no fooling them. The Tong knew everything.

Meanwhile, Lotta had squatted near the edge of the roof, keeping low while she waited for the cook to clear the way. A short, slight woman, she was impeccably dressed for this outdoor adventure in an English tailored suit of fine brown cloth with velvet collar and cuffs. Her underskirts, visible when she leaped from roof to roof, were ruffled and French. Her overskirt was satin and bouffantly draped. Perched atop her head was a felt hat with the wing of an English blue jay stuck in the band.

The irony was that Dayle was supposed to protect Lotta and make sure she didn't get into "too much trouble." More like the woman was going to get Dayle killed without so much as mussing her clothes or breaking a sweat.

Dayle shook her head. She knew the popular parlor stories whispered among the ladies of Lotta's class—tales of white slavery, of women snatched by the Tong and carried off to richly textured opium dens where they were rumored to be kept naked and drugged. There were even lurid photographs supposedly taken in such dens of iniquity. It was said that white women had no resistance to the exotic herbs they were fed in such places. Not being able to help themselves, they begged to be repeatedly ravished. Of course, none of those stories was true, but such tales were usually enough to keep women like Lotta at home, minding their own business. Dayle still hadn't figured out what Lotta hoped to accomplish sneaking into Chinatown like this. That is, besides the obvious.

A noise. Dayle jumped. Her heart raced, but it was only the flutter of a bird finding the edge of the roof. Dayle breathed again and wished the cook would hurry. Meanwhile, she continued to search the shadows while she returned to the thought that it made no sense for a woman like Lotta to be dusting the rooftops of Chinatown with her expensive hems. It made even less sense for Dayle to be trailing behind her. The Pinkertons never investigated "matters of the heart." No spying on wives. No chasing errant husbands. No keeping lists of "pretty boys." But this was a matter of the heart as sure as she was balanced on the slant of this roof. Why else would her husband let her do something like this? Only some foolish misplaced passion could explain . . .

At the sound of splitting wood and breaking glass, Dayle suddenly grabbed the chimney to steady herself. Then, even though looking down was the last thing she wanted to do, she peered over the edge to see what was going on. Lotta's Chinese cook was kicking in a second-story window directly below them. Standing on a narrow balcony at the bottom of the trellis, his back braced against the rail, he made a couple more thrusts with the heel of his boot, smashing the last of the window. Brushing broken glass aside with his arm, he grabbed the frame, boosted himself to the windowsill, and dropped inside with an audible thud. That noise was immediately followed by half-whimpered screams—women's voices.

Thank God, he found the right place, Dayle thought. She considered finding the right place no small feat. She glanced back across the rooftops and wasn't sure how anyone found anything in this shantytown jumble.

Lotta was now climbing down the trellis. Dayle gave one more quick glance all around. Then she

The Lady Pinkerton Gets Her Man

grasped the top of the latticework, took a deep breath, and started down herself. She'd gone a third of the way when all hell broke loose.

It started with the sound of Chinese words mounting to shouts. Then the cook hopped back out the open window, his hands thrown over his head, warding off the blows of a younger, thinner Chinaman who jumped through the broken window brandishing a broom. The broom froze in midair, and the Chinese words died in a single guttural when the younger Chinaman spotted Lotta.

Absolutely unflappable, she stepped off the trellis, took time to correct the tilt of her hat, and told the younger Chinaman to put the broom down. She spoke in English using the same tones with which she ordered her servants, or Dayle.

The younger Chinaman stared, his mouth slightly open. From his expression, it looked as though he thought he'd encountered a ghost. That illusion was not unreasonable. Lotta was not only pale, but she wore a layer of face whitener over her cheeks, muting their color, which was the current style. Besides, he probably never imagined jumping out his window to discover a fashionably dressed white woman standing on his balcony.

Things hung suspended like that until the cook lowered his arms and said something in Chinese. The other Chinaman dropped his broom and jumped back through the window. A moment later, footsteps could be heard on stairs inside, going down, running away. Lotta put her hand out and waited until the cook took it and helped her through the window as if she were being helped into a carriage. He followed, disappearing through the same opening.

Dayle felt a wave of relief. Maybe things were going to work out fine, she thought, but her thought was premature. She made the mistake of looking up. Above her, she saw three Chinese men bending over the roof edge. Broad-shouldered thugs, they were obviously Tong. Seeing them, she caught her breath, gave herself a moment to wonder where they'd come from, and then decided it was time to get out of there.

She dropped to the balcony below. Poorly attached and already loosened by the cook's kicks, it swayed under her and broke away from the wall. She grabbed the windowsill and hung on as the balcony gave way, sending a dozen potted herbs crashing to the street below. The vine, rooted in one of those pots, now ripped away from the trellis, shedding its leaves as it fell.

The first of the Tong thugs had started down. Now, as the trellis began to pull away with the vine, he reversed his climb, but not before making a grab for Dayle. She swung away from his grasp.

Those titillating stories of white women becoming captured sex slaves were nothing but dark fantasies, Dayle knew. On the other hand, anyone who crossed the Tong ran a real risk of "disappearing" in a more permanent sense. It was said that when the Tong settled a score, they didn't even leave a body. Or, if they wanted to send a message, the body would turn up, neatly trussed, a tiny cord tied around the hands and feet and neck, the dead eyes bulging.

Newly motivated by that thought, she gathered strength, kicked against the wall, and, with a wiggle to free her skirts, boosted herself through the window, head-first, knocking the cook down at the same time. He'd been on his way to the window to check the noise. Now they rolled together over the shards of broken glass that had been scattered across the floor inside.

"What going on?" he asked before she could get her equilibrium.

"Tong," was all she answered.

Then the smell hit her. Only once before had she encountered that odor in such overwhelming concentration. Three years ago in a Colorado mining camp, a couple of her male colleagues had led her into a back

The Lady Pinkerton Gets Her Man

room behind the town's only saloon. Dimly lit like this, it had smelled the same. Back then, when her eyes had adjusted to the poor light, she saw that a woman had been painted on a wall framing an open knothole between her legs. Through the slats in the wood, Dayle saw a bucket hanging behind the hole. Half full from the night before, it was the source of the smell, and the overpowering odor had been enough to make her whole insides crawl.

Back then, she was expected to act jovial. Her companions were already indulging a bit of raw banter about the danger of getting splinters. She'd put on a good act, adding a couple of comments, all the while struggling to keep from throwing up. That in spite of the fact that she wasn't much given to the frailties of her sex.

Now the same smell pervaded everything in this tiny room. The smell, coupled with the flash of energy that had surged through her when she met the Tong outside, made her stomach roil once again. She sat up, put her hand to her mouth, and swallowed hard as she checked to see if she was still in one piece. Fortunately, her skirts and long sleeves had protected her from the broken glass. The cook wasn't as lucky. He was tying a handkerchief around a cut on his forearm.

Meanwhile, Lotta had barely taken note of them or the fact that there were Tong outside. She was kneeling beside two very young, very thin Chinese girls, talking to them softly. One had a bruise on her forehead. The other had her hair cropped short. Neither was more than twelve or thirteen. Huddled and half hidden behind a crude wardrobe, they shivered like puppies, and every time Lotta made a gesture toward them, they whimpered. One was coughing.

Dayle got to her feet. Like the painting in that mining camp, Dayle knew these girls serviced up to thirty men a night. But while the men in the Colorado camp had affectionately named their knothole "Polly

Pinetree," Dayle doubted that even the broom-brandishing pimp knew these girls' names. Or cared. She quickly checked the rest of the room. A pair of oil lamps burned near the door, giving weak light. There were a rudimentary washstand, the wardrobe, and two beds. No chairs. A curtain, patched from scraps, hung between the beds. The remains of the smashed-in window were scattered across a bare floor. That was it. Evidently, the girls were expected to sit and sleep where they worked—on mattresses soaked in that smell.

Now Lotta was here to rescue them—a fact the girls hadn't yet grasped. One had her hands over her ears. The other had pulled a ragged blanket up to her eyes. Both refused Lotta's crackers.

"What's the matter with them?" Dayle asked the cook.

He'd also gotten to his feet and was now putting his glasses back on, working the wires over his ears. "They think White Devil-Woman take them to very bad place where she roast their feet and feed them their own toes," he explained. "That's what they've been told happens to big-footed girls."

Dayle was trying not to breathe too deeply. "They really believe there is a worse place than this?"

"Always worse place."

Dayle shook her head. She'd heard that before. Any complaint at the orphanage was always met with sweet assurances from the sisters that there were "worse places." She didn't believe it then, and she didn't believe it now.

Meanwhile, her eyes darted around the room assessing the situation. She didn't like what she saw. With the balcony gone, there was only one way out. No time for crackers or coaxing.

"We have to go, now," she told Lotta as she pushed past her and grabbed the girl with the short-cropped hair. The girl gave a startled cry and struggled as Dayle swung her under her arm. Dayle wasn't big, but

The Lady Pinkerton Gets Her Man

she was strong for a woman, and the girl didn't weigh eighty pounds. She had little trouble hanging on to her. As she headed for the door, she saw the Chinese cook grab the other girl. He was having more trouble. His girl had gotten her elbow in his face.

Lotta, still down on one knee, sputtered, "Don't frighten them. Oh, please, don't frighten them. They need to know we're their friends—that we've come to save them."

Dayle wanted to groan. Fear was likely the only thing these girls understood. That's what annoyed her about rich women like Lotta who amused themselves "doing good." She didn't fault the charitable instinct, but too often it was misplaced. It was as if privileged women, like Lotta, had been the center of attention for so long they had a warped sense of reality.

On the landing outside the room, Dayle paused long enough to note the three Tong kicking down the door below. She turned in the other direction and followed the hallway to the left. Pushing through a curtained doorway, she suddenly found herself stepping over rows of Chinese men sleeping on mats. Some kind of cheap boardinghouse, she guessed.

Too groggy to give chase, the men barely blinked awake as she made her way across the room, trailing the cook and Lotta. The next room was the same, more sleeping miners. It didn't help that the girl under her arm never quit struggling. But she noticed the cook's girl had stopped flailing. She was mostly coughing.

Past the second room, Dayle came upon another landing and another staircase. She took the stairs downward thinking they would lead to the street outside. She'd had enough of rooftops and trellises.

No such luck. At the bottom of the stairs, there was no door, just a darkened hallway branching this way and that with rows of curtained rooms off each hall. Reaching a dead end and not knowing where else to go, Dayle pushed through the curtains covering one of the doorways and found herself in a tiny, unventilated cubicle lit only with the dim glow of a lamp hanging from the ceiling. The smell of opium hung in the air. Last evening's occupant hadn't been gone long, she guessed.

The cook crowded in beside her.

Lotta caught up a moment later. She entered the room, her breath quick, her face flushed despite the whitener on her cheeks, and asked, "What is this place?"

Dayle snapped the curtain shut and ignored the question. She was not in a mood for making explanations. The girl under her arm took all her strength, and she could hear the Tong coming down the hall behind them, pushing the curtains aside one after another, looking for them.

The cook had clapped one hand over his girl's mouth, quieting her coughs. With his elbow, he was feeling along the walls, looking for an opening. Dayle didn't put much hope in that. She was doing a mental inventory of the possible options. When the Tong arrived, she could give them the girls, dare them to harm Garrick Bateman's wife, or pull the gun from her pocket and forget long explanations.

She was feeling for her gun when the cook pushed on a particular part of the wall, and it slid away revealing an opening. Still holding the coughing girl, he helped Lotta through and then quickly followed himself. Dayle had to bend almost in half to get through, dragging her girl with her, but she was glad for this new possibility. She'd never been particularly good with a gun.

On the other side of the wall, she followed the cook quietly down a narrower, even darker hallway that seemed to be some kind of service area. She had no idea where they were and was beginning to think of Chinatown as an endless labyrinth.

The Lady Pinkerton Gets Her Man

In that stillness, she heard the Tong push back the sliding panel. A few moments later, she heard them feeling their way down the same hallway behind her. She was bringing up the rear now and kept imagining them drawing closer and closer. The sound of her own heart pounded in her ears until it was enough to confuse. Sometimes she couldn't tell her own sounds from the noise of her followers. That made them seem terribly immediate. She expected any moment that a hand would reach out and touch her.

Then the cook paused at a juncture of hallways. Still holding the girl, Dayle paused behind him and waited while he checked first one direction and then the other. Sounds clarified. With relief, she determined that the three Tong following them had to be farther back than she'd thought, maybe even lost, but still coming, still looking for them. Her own breath was short. She hoped the cook wasn't lost. She wanted out of here. Out of Chinatown. Out of this assignment.

Mostly, she wanted out of this assignment. There were two kinds of detectives: those who did jobs and those who solved cases. She liked to think she solved cases. She made it a habit to think and notice, always looking for the larger forces behind the surface, but the only thing to understand here was why Lotta's husband was indulging her charity, and that was a domestic matter. This was a job, a baby-sitting job. Nothing more.

Meanwhile, the cook made up his mind. He turned left and a few moments later found a door to the outside. Dayle gave a glance backward and was relieved to see the three Tong thugs hadn't rounded the last corner. She had no interest in lingering. She sprinted the last few steps, still carrying the girl.

Momentarily blinded by the outdoor brightness, she squinted as she made a quick survey of her surroundings. She was standing in a narrow street between a couple of noodle shops, a laundry, and an herb store with a sign above the door in English. It read:

> Lee Me Him Drugstore
> Broken Arm and Leg Remedies
> Medicine All Kind Very Good.

That had to mean the proprietor expected trade with white patrons and was therefore located near the edge of Chinatown, but Dayle had lost her sense of direction. She had no idea which way to go.

She set the girl down. Slight as she was, she'd become heavy. The girl looked up at Dayle, hesitated once, then took Dayle's hand. The cook still carried his girl like a sack of flour, but he shifted her from one hip to the other while waiting for Lotta to straighten her hat again.

Dayle swore under her breath. This was no place to be worrying about the angle of one's hat, and as if to prove that point, two things happened. The three Tong thugs burst through the doorway behind them just as thirty or more Chinese miners rounded the street corner ahead of them. Having finished the night shift, the miners were carrying their lunch pails and tools. Their clothes were blackened with coal dust. Their faces were still bloodless from the cumulative lack of oxygen down in the mines. That pallor was accented by the pale early-morning light.

There was a moment of mutual astonishment.

From the miners' point of view, Dayle imagined, this didn't look good—white women stealing Chinese girls. The cook must have made the same assessment. He started slowly backing away, keeping his eyes on the miners as he moved, pulling the others with him. Dayle swallowed dry spit.

She gave a quick glance in the direction of the three thugs. Like the cook, they hung back, seemingly

The Lady Pinkerton Gets Her Man

waiting to see how the miners would react, but she expected them to do something—shout an explanation, an order. Everyone knew the Tong controlled Chinatown. Surely they'd make the miners understand that they had this situation under control. The Tong kept all situations in Chinatown under control. That's what made them the Tong—feared, respected, always obeyed.

That, however, was not what happened.

One miner raised a fist, and a shout went up from all the rest. The immediate effect on the cook was remarkable. He dropped the girl and grabbed Lotta by the arm, pulling her along as he ran back toward the alley with the Tong. Too surprised to protest, Lotta merely grabbed for her hat.

That left Dayle and the two girls standing in the middle of the street. Abandoning the girls made sense. Nobody wanted the trouble they represented, not the Pinkertons, not Lotta's husband. Dayle was supposed to make sure there wasn't trouble because of this charity Mrs. Bateman had decided to undertake. That was the paramount part of her orders, and she was a Pinkerton—practical, not sentimental—but she couldn't do it. The smell of that room still clung to her clothes, and, against all better judgment, Dayle grabbed an arm of each girl and took off running after the cook.

The miners, now swinging their tools, gave noisy pursuit, shouting and banging on their lunch buckets as they came. Pigs stopped rooting in the gutters; cats yowled. Doors and windows flew open. The ruckus rivaled a fire alarm.

Dayle was not going to outrun them. That was immediately obvious. Although the girls no longer whimpered or resisted, the one with the cough was nearly doubled over trying to get her breath. She kept stumbling. Once she nearly tripped Dayle.

Still, Dayle expected the Tong to do something. To stop this. Nothing happened in Chinatown without

Tong approval. Everyone knew that. The miners behind her were supposed to know that.

But when she entered the alley, she saw the Tong thugs take to their own heels scattering in three different directions. She couldn't have been more astonished if she'd seen ghosts take flight. The Tong running from their own Chinese miners! What did that mean? But she didn't have time to puzzle the implications. At the moment, it meant she couldn't expect any help.

What was she going to do?

Turning a corner, she spotted a coal chute leading into the basement under one of the laundries. With her pursuers momentarily out of sight, she whistled for the cook while she shoved the first girl down the chute. Surprised, she uttered a tiny squeal as she went down. The girl with the short hair hopped into the chute all by herself and rode it to the bottom. Dayle followed.

A moment later, Lotta arrived at the bottom with her skirts over her head. One of her fancy petticoats had snagged the top of the chute and turned her clothes topsy-turvy before ripping completely off. The cook freed it as he came down. Then he pulled the chute away from the window and snapped it shut.

That done, he assumed his usual eyes-down, over-polite manner. Bowing, he presented Lotta with the torn petticoat while saying, "So sorry." Lotta took the underskirt, and, with a little flutter of embarrassed gestures, she rolled it up quickly and tucked it into her pocketbag.

Meanwhile, one glance told Dayle they were trapped. The only way out of this place was that coal chute. If the miners discovered them . . .

Then, as if fulfilling her worst fears, the miners who'd passed by once came back. They could be heard just outside the window, milling around, making angry noises. Everyone tensed. The cook clamped a hand over the mouth of the girl who kept coughing,

The Lady Pinkerton Gets Her Man

and they all backed against the wall directly under the window and huddled there, out of sight.

Dayle wasn't sure of the options. She felt for her gun.

The cook quietly worked a board off the side of the chute and grasped it like a club. She wasn't sure what a few bullets and a board would do against a mob of miners. Dayle searched for an alternative, a crawl space, a trap door.

The room was no more than an oversized coal bin where fuel to heat water for the laundry tubs upstairs was stored. Medium-sized lumps of the black stuff filled a third of the space, making the low ceiling even lower. They were all bent over, even the girls. Worse, the coal crunched under them every time they shifted their weight, making noise—too much noise. It was awkward to be paralyzed, bent, and huddled like that, trying not to move. The chill of the room quickly embraced them, solidifying that paralysis.

The miners outside milled, their voices grumbling louder as their confusion mounted. Half an hour ticked by.

Dayle hated waiting. To her, inactivity was like conscious death. Idleness allowed too many thoughts to circle, too many worries. And no matter how she worried this one, it kept getting curiouser and curiouser." The idea that Garrick Bateman would "arrange" to let his wife rescue Chinese prostitutes because that was a currently fashionable charity was odd enough to make no sense. Surely the man understood that no one ever really made an "arrangement" with the Tong.

In Wyoming, it was said that only electrical storms, blizzards, and other acts of God dared defy Lotta's husband. It was said the territorial governor checked with him daily. Dayle considered that maybe the man was full of himself enough to think he could tell the Tong what to do as well. If he did, he was a fool.

Dayle glanced at Lotta. She'd taken off her jacket

and was offering it to one of the girls who was visibly shivering. The girl only huddled closer to the cook and refused the coat. That obviously disappointed Lotta. Dayle watched how her long fingers and smooth hands fussed with the buttons as she put the jacket back on herself. No question, she was a fine-boned, pretty woman, but pretty women were not all that rare. What was it about her that had inspired such foolishness in a man mainly known for his ruthlessness?

Dayle looked again. Lotta was now unbuttoning the buttons on her jacket that she'd just done up. Her fingers trembled. She paused, seemed confused, started buttoning up again. Worse, Dayle noticed Lotta's breathing had become irregular, and even in dim light the contortion of her face was obvious.

The cook saw, too. He took charge of both Chinese girls while Dayle slid closer to Lotta. "Where are your smelling salts?" she whispered in the woman's ear.

Her head jerked once, a wide, unnatural movement. No other response.

Smelling salts were wrong for silent hysterics. Standard treatment was to grab the woman, shake her, slap her, if necessary, until she finally snapped out of it, usually by releasing her hysterics into a wild bout of screaming. Personally, Dayle had no use for female hysterics, silent or otherwise. She couldn't believe this. Lotta had been leaping from building to building not half an hour ago. It had gotten quieter outside, but if Lotta started screaming . . .

Dayle was trying to remember if she'd ever heard of someone coming out of silent hysterics without screaming. Dayle was afraid to touch Lotta for fear that would set her off. She did the only thing she could do. She leaned close and whispered softly. Talked. She said anything that came to her mind. Mostly, she told Lotta praising things, reassuring things. She explained several times that they needed to stay quiet because they'd almost made it. They'd almost gotten those girls out of Chinatown. All she had to do was to stay calm a little bit longer.

Ten minutes of that nonstop whispering, and Dayle's throat was beginning to feel raw, and she was about to give up when Lotta suddenly straightened and spoke one word.

"Truth?"

2

"Truth?" Lotta said again. She whispered softly enough that only Dayle could hear.

Truth? Dayle thought, and couldn't connect any meaning to the word that fit their current circumstances. At least Lotta hadn't screamed it, and Dayle noticed that the woman's hands had paused. They were no longer working her buttons up and down, up and down.

"Truth?" Lotta said once more. This time, there was an insistence to her whisper that couldn't be ignored. She expected a response.

Truth? Dayle thought again. Then it came to her. "Truth" was a game young girls played in the dark. If you agreed to truth, you agreed to answer the next question with brutal honesty.

She glanced sideways at Lotta, wondering what this was all about. "Truth," Dayle answered, agreeing to the game.

"Do you like being a Lady Pinkerton?" the other

The Lady Pinkerton Gets Her Man

woman asked with a controlled calmness Dayle found strange.

At the same time, she gave a quick glance at the cook. No one was supposed to know she was a Pinkerton except Lotta, her husband, and Dayle's boss. She doubted the cook had heard. He was listening just below the window. With reason. There were footsteps outside, coming closer.

"Do you like being a Lady Pinkerton?" Lotta suddenly insisted, her whisper becoming harsh.

"Yes," Dayle told Lotta. "Yes," she repeated, listening, watching the cook, and wanting to hold her breath—Lotta's, too.

Fortunately, the footsteps passed by.

"Yes," Dayle whispered when it was quiet outside again, and she meant it. In fact, she couldn't imagine being the seamstress she was pretending to be. As a child, she'd had trouble sitting still, going to sleep. She'd been born with too much energy and restlessness—the very thing polite young ladies had to learn to control, only she'd never been able to manage hers. Being a Lady Pinkerton gave her an outlet. She didn't know how to explain that in a way that she thought would make sense to Lotta. At a loss for words, she simply repeated again, "Yes, I like being a Lady Pinkerton."

Lotta nodded. Her whole body picked up the same motion. She rocked for a while and then whispered, "I thought so. I thought it must feel very light and airy. I mean, you can go anyplace and do anything and pretend to be anyone. Myself, I wouldn't want to pretend to be my second cousin," she added. "I'd want to be someone more exciting. Have you ever pretended to be a real adventuress?"

Dayle had no idea what to expect from Lotta or where this conversation was going.

"An adventuress," Lotta continued to whisper. "You know, the kind of woman who never gets trapped anyplace. The kind of woman who goes places like China and Africa with nothing but one suitcase. We're trapped in this place. Aren't we?"

"No," Dayle told her, thinking she sensed the problem. "We're not trapped. We're waiting. When the moment is right, we'll climb out and be on our way."

"Oh," was all Lotta answered.

A couple of minutes ticked by. Lotta's hands began working the buttons on her jacket again.

"Truth?" Dayle asked, remembering that it was her turn at the game and thinking that it was better to keep Lotta talking even if she didn't make entire sense. When she was talking, she wasn't working those buttons up and down, up and down.

"Truth," Lotta returned on cue.

Dayle was watching the cook at the window. She didn't have a question in mind, and now she had to think of something quickly. "Would you like to be an adventuress?"

"Oh, no." Lotta breathed, a startled intake of air. "That's not for me. I mean, women who are born both pretty and privileged are expected to maintain a certain level of decorum, collars clean, buttons buttoned, bows tied."

With that, she started working the buttons again.

"Who told you that?" Dayle asked.

Lotta turned her head to look at Dayle. "It's not your turn to ask a question."

"Sorry," Dayle said.

"But if you say 'pretty please,' then I'll skip my turn and answer. The rules allow that."

"Pretty please," Dayle whispered.

"It was my mother," Lotta returned. "My mother told me that. She called it 'ornamentation.' She said that women are the 'ornaments of life.' She meant that in a complimentary sense. She believed in beautifying the world. She told me that there were enough things that needed to be beautified, like window boxes and chair covers, that a lady didn't need to worry

The Lady Pinkerton Gets Her Man

herself with coarser affairs. Those matters are better left to politicians and businessmen and the like."

"I see," Dayle said, but she didn't see. She was having trouble figuring out how rescuing Chinese girls from the Tong fit into a philosophy of "ornamental women."

In another sense, she did understand. She couldn't remember a time when the whole litany of what a "lady" could and couldn't do hadn't made her a little crazy. Not as crazy as Lotta. Nothing made her that crazy. Lotta was working the buttons on her jacket again.

"My mother never called me Lotta," she was saying in a continuous flow of words that Dayle was beginning to think was the whispered equivalent of screaming. "She always called me Charlotta. Myself, I prefer the shortened form of my name, not that stuffy old matronly form. I hate being so formal, so staid, so much the social register. That's why I married my husband. He lacked such polish. He seemed more like a real person from a real place—Wyoming Territory. He came to Boston, still dusty from the West, telling stories of buffalo bones and train robbers. I thought I could listen to him forever. My other suitors, all blue-blooded Bostonians, talked only of social gossip—who they knew and what clubs they frequented. I mean, I already knew everything they said. I'd heard it all a hundred times in one form or another. I thought living with Garrick in Wyoming would be exciting." Then she paused and a moment later added, "There's no way out of this."

"That's not true," Dayle said. "I told you. We're waiting. We have to wait until the Chinese miners quit looking for us. That's all. It's getting quieter already."

"These are not ordinary circumstances," Lotta responded, and Dayle watched as her eyes wandered over the dim interior. Her nose wiggled, testing the musty air. "At home I have stacks of parlor photograph books filled with pictures of other people's

22

adventures," she went on. "I spend hours with them. I suppose that's silly, but I like looking at foreign lands and wild terrain. I don't believe anyone has ever photographed a place like this. If they have, I haven't seen such a picture. It's beyond the exotic, too real with grit and dirt. Don't you agree?"

"This is not ordinary," Dayle agreed, and wondered what was really behind Lotta's hysterics. Dayle now followed Lotta's glance as it went sideways to the girls.

"I never thought they would be so tiny," Lotta continued.

Dayle had to agree. The girls' arms and legs were stick thin. Their cheeks were hollow enough to rival their eyes. The one girl continued to cough despite the cook's stifling hand over her mouth.

"Such visible misery makes me want to hug them, stroke their hair, promise them wonderful things," Lotta went on.

"We'll be out of here soon," Dayle assured her.

"They're going to a Presbyterian mission home in San Francisco that fits girls like these for life by teaching them Christianity, English, and employable domestic skills," Lotta said in flat tones as if she were reading from a pamphlet. She looked back at Dayle. "When they understand, I hope they might remember me the way one remembers an angel—as a sudden goodness appearing out of nowhere."

"I'm sure they will think kindly of you," Dayle muttered.

It was mostly quiet outside now.

"The cook was supposed to explain," Lotta answered. "But it is probably difficult for them to understand. My husband suggested an ordinary charity. Something easier. If I'd wanted an easy life, I'd have stayed in Boston, married into an old family, and . . ." Lotta paused. She closed her eyes and leaned back against the coal bin wall.

"Are you all right?" Dayle asked.

The Lady Pinkerton Gets Her Man

She started talking again without opening her eyes. "You want to know what rich men's wives are expected to do?"

Dayle didn't care as long as this rich man's wife kept talking, not screaming, not neurotically buttoning and unbuttoning her jacket.

"Nothing." She answered her own question. "No one expects rich men's wives to do anything that matters. Certainly not save lives. We're saving those girls' lives, you know."

Dayle wasn't entirely sure of that. The one who coughed all the time probably had tuberculosis. Who knew what diseases the other one had? Nevertheless, she assured Lotta, "I know."

Lotta took a deep breath and opened her eyes. "I owe it to my children not to get killed," she said. "They need their mother."

"Of course they do," Dayle answered, because it was the polite thing to say, not because she understood what Lotta meant. "We're going to be fine," she quickly added.

"Are we really going to get out of here?" Lotta asked again.

"Yes," Dayle told her. "I think they've given up looking for us."

"Really?" Lotta asked.

Dayle nodded. In fact, she and the cook had been exchanging looks and complicated hand signals for several minutes. Now Dayle leaned closer to Lotta and explained, "We're going to split up. Together we attract too much attention. You and I will go first."

"Are you sure?" Lotta questioned, and she fussed with her buttons again.

Dayle reached over and stilled her hand with a touch.

The cook was already checking the window. He opened it, listened a moment, then replaced the chute. He listened a moment longer and then nodded to Dayle. She went first. Grabbing the edges and taking a wide stance, her feet braced against the sides, she climbed up the slippery coal slide, emerging from the ground-level window to discover that the alley was empty now except for a pig rooting near a doorstep at the far end.

Lotta followed. The cook helped her, but still she slipped a couple of times. *Better at roofs than chutes,* Dayle thought as she watched her struggle to hold her skirts out of her way.

Once they were outside in the alley, her hysterics disappeared under a calm Dayle no longer trusted. She watched while the woman looked around. Lotta took her hat off and pushed her hair back into place. The hat was smudged with black, and some of the wing feathers were bent. She brushed the dust off and straightened the feathers as best she could.

Dayle decided not to rush her. Last thing they needed now was for Lotta to become hysterical again. Instead, Dayle kept watch, in case someone decided to wander into the alley, but mostly she let Lotta fuss with her clothes and brush the worst of the black coal dust from her skirts for as long as she liked.

"Ready?" Dayle finally asked.

Lotta nodded. Then she startled Dayle by reaching over and hooking arms with her, the way women friends often do when they're enjoying an outing. Pulling Dayle's arm gently, she led. Together they sauntered out of the alley while Lotta chatted about the weather and the unexpected turns the day had taken. She phrased it politely, like that, as "unexpected turns." It was as though she was an entirely different woman.

In the time they'd sat in that coal bin, Chinatown had also transformed. The street at the end of the alley now teemed. Noodle shops had opened and were serving their morning customers on rough-hewn tables set up in the street. Fruit and meat sellers were laying out their wares. Peddlers shouldered their way through the crowd, pushing carts full of vegetables.

The Lady Pinkerton Gets Her Man

Laundry men, traveling in pairs, carried enormous baskets of dirty clothes suspended on poles that they hung from their shoulders. Everyone dodged the animals underfoot. Ducks, geese, and pigs wove in and out of the bustle, stopping only to fight over whatever fresh refuse was tossed in the gutters. The smell was overpowering, the noise raucous. Seeing that bustle, Lotta hesitated as if she had no idea how to enter the fray.

That's when Dayle took over. She pulled Lotta's arm, directing her toward Lee Me Him's herb shop. Together they made their way to the entrance, where a thin-faced Chinaman dressed traditionally in a loose blue cotton shirt and matching broad trousers had opened his shutters and was now greeting passersby. He bowed so often that the queue running down his back fairly bobbed.

Arriving at the shop, Dayle immediately bent and smelled one of his herbs. Lotta did the same and exclaimed at the wonderful smell, which pleased the proprietor. He folded his arms across his chest and bowed very deeply.

Meanwhile, Dayle glanced over her shoulder and noticed that the cook and the girls had left the alley. They were now working their way along the shadow side of the busy street. The cook held each girl by one arm and appeared to guide them rather firmly through the crowd, moving briskly in the direction of the entrance to Chinatown and the train station beyond. She was pleased to see that, and only when she was satisfied that they were safely away did she turn back to the business at hand.

"Much good medicine here," the proprietor of the herb shop was telling Lotta as she continued to exclaim over every herb he showed her.

Dayle found the man quaint. The cook had adopted a more western style of dress and grooming, no braid. Few of the miners still had queues, although most still wore the baggy trousers and traditional blue shirts. She suspected Lee Me Him maintained a more traditional look mainly for the benefit of his white customers who came to Chinatown looking for "centuries-old cures."

"Where it hurt?" he now asked Lotta. "Here?" He touched his stomach. "Here?" he asked, and touched his chest while he coughed once. "Here?" he continued, and brought a finger to his forehead.

Lotta laughed lightly. She was clearly amused at how his hands danced over his body and how his face formed itself around his questioning concern for her health.

Dayle had to admit the gestures were nice, smooth. She'd read once that in heaven everyone would speak the same language—not words, pantomime. Gestures and facial expressions were supposedly the letters of the divine alphabet, according to that author. Watching the way this thin-faced Chinaman used his hands almost made her believe that possible. He'd practically hypnotized Lotta with his motions. She could have used him to calm Lotta in the coal bin, she thought. Actually, she was pleased for the current distraction as well.

Everywhere she looked, she saw Tong.

With a fresh flush, Dayle marveled at how there seemed to be no end to this. Over roofs . . . through hallways . . . down chutes. Now it would seem they were going to have to leave Chinatown under noticeable watch of the Tong.

"Ah," the shopkeeper now said to Lotta. "Headache most very bad."

Dayle couldn't tell if he meant that as a question or a statement.

Didn't matter. Lotta drew breath and readily agreed with the man. "Yes, the headaches are very bad." Then she began to describe how sometimes the pain would start in the back of her head and move

The Lady Pinkerton Gets Her Man

forward. "The pain just pounds and pounds like a hammer right behind my eyes until I can't focus enough to read or do fancy needlework," she continued telling the shopkeeper.

He kept nodding as if he understood every word.

"We need to go," Dayle told Lotta.

Lotta refused to be hurried. The Chinaman was opening drawers and mixing herbs for her. She whispered out the side of her mouth, "I'm not going to be so rude as to leave without completing my purchase. For one thing, it would mar the deception."

Dayle didn't think they were deceiving anyone. And she'd about reached the limits of her patience with Lotta. The woman took everything to the extreme. Simple charity work wasn't good enough. She had to steal prostitutes from the Tong. Now, instead of buying a box of tea, she had to order a personalized headache powder. Next, she fully expected the woman to hold her arms wide and let the Chinaman take her twelve pulses.

Meanwhile, the Tong were on every rooftop and every street corner. Dayle had never seen such a show of force. The herb shop Chinaman knew. Even as he talked to Lotta, he kept an eye on the street. His eyes darted left and right as he mixed the herbs of her headache remedy. Lotta was the only one who didn't seem to comprehend the situation.

"Let's go," Dayle said again.

Something had to be very wrong for the Tong to need such a visible display of might.

Evidently, even Lotta knew that much. She leaned close to Dayle and whispered, "They won't bother us. Too many people would see, and everyone knows the Tong are so secretive no one is ever sure if they do a thing or not. This is not the way they work."

Dayle gave her an odd look.

But she was right. In Chinatown, the clan or *Tong* was all-powerful. They arranged every aspect of a miner's life, from assigning a boardinghouse bed to arranging, by proxy, for the miner's ancestors' graves back in China to be visited in his absence. Tong headquarters was bank, post office, and social hall. The Tong settled all disputes and dispensed swift justice from which there was no appeal. Chinese and Caucasian alike believed the Tong were everywhere and knew everything. That was the reason Dayle hadn't questioned Lotta's cook about the incident with the miners. She assumed he was Tong—the eyes and ears of the clan inside Garrick Bateman's house.

Now this.

Dayle swallowed and looked around again. If subtle fear still worked, the Tong wouldn't need men on every rooftop and on every street corner. There was no way to understand this except to assume the unthinkable—that the Tong were losing their hold on Chinatown.

That was what really made Dayle nervous.

"We need to go," Dayle said again as Lotta insisted the Chinese shopkeeper double-wrap her headache remedy because the wrapping paper was "so pretty."

Dayle wasn't worried about getting Mrs. Garrick Bateman out of Chinatown. That's why the Tong had taken up their present positions. They were making sure there would be no further incidents such as the one with the angry miners. But if the Tong were generally losing their control of the Chinese miners in White Springs, Wyoming, the result was going to be a national headache.

Like dominoes. Close the mines in White Springs, and the nation's trains stopped running. Stop the trains, and the nation's industry shut down. No exaggeration. Half the coal used in the country came from this one godforsaken alkali plateau and was mined mostly by Chinese miners. They were the key to everything. From the president of the United States on down, everyone depended on the Tong to keep the Chinese miners in White Springs, Wyoming, working.

"We need to go," Dayle said yet another time,

The Lady Pinkerton Gets Her Man

sensing the enormity of what she was seeing all around her. She was suddenly a detective working a case, a big one.

Still, Lotta took her time as she tucked her double-wrapped package of herbs under her arm and left the herb shop with such an eager bounce to her walk that it was almost a skip. "No reason to hurry," she told Dayle. "I'm sure Woo has gotten the girls safely to the train station by now."

Dayle couldn't believe the woman. She seemed to have no real sense of the situation—of any situation. Hysterical one minute, too cheery the next. This was serious. Besides their own precariousness, her husband's future was in danger. If there was trouble with the Chinese in White Springs, Garrick Bateman wasn't going to be indulging his wife's charity or anything else. The minute he couldn't keep the mines of Wyoming open, he'd be replaced.

They'd passed several more shops on their way out of Chinatown when Lotta said, "It's odd, don't you think?"

"Odd?" Dayle repeated. She couldn't help herself. She truly wondered what part of their current circumstances this other woman found odd enough for comment.

"The girls resisted our every kindness," she continued in a low voice. "I didn't expect that."

"Perhaps, they don't fully understand," Dayle offered, but she actually thought the girls probably understood all this better than their so-called benefactress.

Lotta nodded her head slowly. "We'll just have to be satisfied knowing that we did what we did for their own good. Don't you agree?"

At that, Dayle couldn't help herself. She stiffened. She hated that expression, "for their own good," and all its variations. From the time she was eight years old, Dayle had been hired out for domestic service. It was "for her own good," because work "never hurt anyone." Like Lotta, the sisters running the orphanage were so wrapped up in their own arrogant ignorance they never considered a more earthly possibility behind someone hiring a young orphan girl for "domestic service." That was the real reason Dayle hated "charity work" and the women who thought well of themselves for doing it.

Truth was, Lotta's husband looked the other way while the Tong bought girls, like these two, in China and had them smuggled into this country. He considered it business. He needed to keep his Chinese miners happy, and he didn't care what that took. Lotta's own husband! Dayle thought maybe someone ought to tell the woman that, "for her own good."

Dayle bit her tongue. In fact, it was Dayle's job to make sure Lotta didn't learn too much. She'd been assigned to her and her charity for exactly that reason. Knowing that, Dayle only muttered, "We're not out of this yet."

3

Dayle had no idea how true those words were.

She and Lotta had no sooner gotten to the train station than Lotta exclaimed, "There they are!" At the same time, she pulled on Dayle's arm and pointed to the far end of the platform.

Dayle looked and immediately caught her breath.

The Chinese girls were sitting on a huge pile of baggage at the edge of the platform. They were balanced atop that jumble of trunks and boxes with their arms wrapped around each other, their eyes big, looking for all the world like bear cubs that had been treed.

With good reason.

They'd drawn a crowd, and Dayle could tell from the cook's expression that things were not friendly. He'd positioned himself between the girls and the crowd, his arms folded across his chest, his shoulders and legs wide, his face a wall of stern determination.

"Hurry," she told Lotta.

As they made their way across the platform, Dayle

glanced around. By now, it was mid-morning. There was a chill, but mostly the weather was mild for a fall day, and other than the girls on top of the baggage, she could see nothing unusual about the train station. The depot was a low stone building with a steep roof that spread like wings over half the walkway. There were piles of baggage and baggage carts everywhere. Some of the boxes and barrels gave off whiffs of coffee beans, bananas, or pickle brine. The train platform, an expanse of raised wooden walkway, was crowded with the usual mix of people—white miners, merchants, railroad employees, families arriving, travelers passing through, kids and others who liked the excitement of trains.

Chinese were never welcome inside the train depot, Dayle knew, but usually people left them alone if they stayed outside on the platform. That, however, didn't allow for the novelty of Chinese girls and a wave of anti-Chinese sentiment that had been sweeping the nation. Within the past year, Chinatowns in both Denver and Seattle had been burned to the ground.

"They're not supposed to bring their families," someone in the crowd was saying as Lotta and Dayle approached.

The comment was correct. Dayle knew that current immigration laws forbade "Oriental females."

"Yeah, they're supposed to work and leave."

"Go back to their families."

"In China."

"Yeah, in China."

Dayle and Lotta had no sooner pushed their way to where the girls were perched than the crowd turned on them. A man in a well-cut suit stepped forward. "Are you responsible for these girls?" he asked. At the same time, his eye wandered over Lotta and Dayle's dirty clothes with obvious disapproval. It was clear he didn't understand that he was addressing Mrs. Garrick Bateman.

Dayle was about to inform him of that fact when

The Lady Pinkerton Gets Her Man

Lotta started talking. But she misinterpreted the whole situation—the man's question, the cook's nervousness. In a gush of words, she began telling the man and everyone within hearing all about how she'd saved these "poor waifs" and what wonderful charity work it was to "lift these girls above their circumstances."

Hardly taking a breath, she described the rooftops and the trellis and the Tong and how the girls were to become useful citizens at the mission home in San Francisco. It was as though once started, she couldn't stop talking. Having seen her on the edge of hysteria, Dayle now saw a touch of the same in everything the woman did and said, and for that reason, she hesitated to interfere for fear of upsetting some delicate balance. Everyone seemed to sense the same. No one interrupted. In fact, Lotta quickly became a curiosity herself, drawing even more of a crowd.

Dayle bounced up on her tiptoes and looked around, wondering why the westbound train was late. Forget long explanations, if they could just get these girls on that train and away from here . . .

Still, Lotta chattered on about the "wonderful work of reforming the downtrodden" as if she couldn't see the faces of the people in the crowd, couldn't sense their mood. When she finally ran out of breath, the same man in the fine suit slapped his leg and said, "Forget the mission home. Send them back to China. That's where they belong."

"Yeah, that's where they all belong," someone else offered, an unmistakable surliness in the tone of his voice.

Surprised by that, Lotta sputtered, "But, but, you don't . . ."

The crowd had lost patience with her.

"He's right. Missionary work is wasted on the Chinese," another man concurred.

"They don't make good Christians," someone else added.

Jerrie Hurd

Dayle could practically feel the tension mounting, the mood feeding on itself.

"Oh, but give them a bath before sending them anywhere," a woman in a gaudy hat said.

"*That* would be a 'wonderful charity,'" someone else returned, her words mocking Lotta's.

Her comment was closely followed by that of another woman, who nudged Lotta and said, "They all have lice, you know."

Dayle wanted to nudge the woman back and tell her to mind her own business. Even more than rich women with their misplaced charities, Dayle hated busybodies with their misplaced criticisms. Besides, Dayle wasn't one to take much from anyone except when she was pretending to be someone else. At the moment, she was supposed to be Lotta's poor, sweet second cousin, which meant she had to smile and apologize even for things that weren't her fault. That's how this particular role was played. Like it or not.

She hated working undercover when it meant she couldn't follow her better instincts. Yet, even disguised, she was going to have to do something before this crowd got ugly—uglier. She couldn't exactly stand there and let a riot start.

That's when Mary Stillman Davies entered the scene.

Medium height, matronly round, Miss Davies was a woman of middle years. Dowdy in appearance, she had gray hair, a soft face, and small eyes. In short, there was nothing about her that would make her stand out in a crowd, but she knew how to part one.

Swinging her cane as she went, she drove people back in all directions as she shouted above the hubbub, "The Lord's work will be done. Get out of the way of the Lord's work."

She was the missionary woman who had started the mission where the girls were going. She'd come to White Springs in order to escort the girls to San Francisco. Dayle had never met her. She'd only heard

The Lady Pinkerton Gets Her Man

Lotta talk of her, but there was no mistaking the woman. Her voice was loud and had that perfectly blended tone of pious shame and motherly scolding that almost no one enjoyed hearing. Dayle watched as a shared cringe crept across the crowd. Shoulders came up, heads turned, and a couple of people even raised their hands to cover their ears. Dayle had absolutely no use for missionary women, but she couldn't help being impressed with this one as she watched the woman clear that part of the platform with nothing more than a church voice.

"Go with God," Miss Davies called after the crowd. "His peace be with you."

When most of the others were gone, she turned on Dayle. "What do you want here?"

"No, no," Lotta now sputtered, having once again found her voice. "She's my second cousin," she explained, then paused and lowered her voice to a whisper as she added, "Actually, she's really a Lady Pinkerton. My husband insisted that I had to have a Pinkerton along with me, and it turns out that he was right. She was an immense help in getting the girls out of Chinatown. I couldn't have done it without her. We're just pretending to be second cousins, you see."

It was all Dayle could do to keep from swearing. What was it? Lotta couldn't tell a lie to a woman of the church? She had to let her know that Dayle was a Pinkerton? The cook was coaxing the girls off the top of the baggage pile, and Dayle was sure he'd heard this time.

What's more, Dayle had almost immediately noticed the brooch the missionary woman wore on the collar of her dress. It was of an unmistakably distinctive workmanship. Miss Davies had her own secrets. Dayle was sure she wasn't what she pretended to be, or at least her background was better than that of most women who took up church work. Not that she cared, Dayle told herself.

Mary Stillman Davies looked at Dayle with an

obvious new interest. Then, in a voice that reeked of righteous attitude, she said, "Well, well, well, a real Lady Pinkerton. I'd be impressed, but I have a great deal of trouble putting 'Lady' and 'Pinkerton' together, if you know what I mean."

Not one to be put off, Dayle returned, "I have the same trouble with 'Virgin' and 'Mother.'"

Lotta caught her breath.

Miss Davies, not being as easily shocked, laughed a husky chuckle. Bringing the end of her cane up under Dayle's chin, she said, "I've got no use for Pinkertons, but you might be interesting."

"I am interesting," Dayle returned.

"That's what I said."

Dayle swallowed further comment. She didn't need to know why the other woman had taken up this particular charity or where she'd come from. Thanks to Miss Davies, they'd avoided a riot. She would give the woman that much credit. The important thing now was to get the older woman and these Chinese girls on the train to San Francisco. Then Dayle could get on with her own concerns, such as reporting what had happened in Chinatown.

The missionary woman turned her attention back to Lotta. She had Lotta do a slow turn while she exclaimed at her dirty clothes and pronounced loudly that she'd been "baptized by fire" in her first efforts to "strike at the heart of this evil that kept little girls in bondage to the baser of men's desires."

That was one of the things that annoyed Dayle the most about missionary women—the way they talked. They all assumed they knew about men's baser desires or being baptized by fire. Actually, most of them didn't even know what effect their own muddling had. Their charity was rarely as charitable as they imagined.

Dayle wandered down the platform. She'd listened to enough missionary women at the orphanage to last her a lifetime. They all spoke in fancy phrases like

The Lady Pinkerton Gets Her Man

that, and she didn't need to stand there and listen to more.

Then she paused. She thought she could hear the train coming but wasn't sure. In that pause, she changed her mind.

Deep down, she knew she was being too hard on Miss Davies. Despite her annoyance with all church women, Dayle suspected Miss Davies was an exception. From what Dayle had heard, the woman had dedicated her life to saving Chinese slave girls. She'd built the mission home in San Francisco and developed an entire network of people and safe houses that spanned the western territories. Known as the "Oriental Underground," it was the equivalent of the abolitionists' Underground Railroad that had helped black slaves to freedom. When Miss Davies wasn't engaged in escorting girls along the stops, she went around lecturing and recruiting "rescuers" like Lotta. She was probably responsible for the fact that it was currently in vogue to be engaged in an "adventure charity"—something more strenuous than tea in the afternoons and shaming wealthy men into giving funds for such projects as libraries and schools. Something in that had to be respected, no matter how many overpious phrases she used.

Dayle glanced back and was startled to realize the cook was gone.

She looked up and down and all around. He was nowhere to be seen. Dayle brought her hands to her hips and swore under her breath. She had no doubt that, thanks to Lotta, the cook was reporting to the Tong that she was, indeed, a Pinkerton. She reminded herself that she needed to worry about what was happening right here in White Springs rather than worrying about Miss Davies.

With that thought, she turned and looked down the track. She could definitely hear the train coming now.

Dayle returned to where Miss Davies, Lotta, and the girls were sitting on a couple of trunks next to the

Jerrie Hurd

pile of baggage. The topic of conversation hadn't changed. Lotta, half embarrassed by the older woman's praise of her efforts, now looked up and spoke to Dayle. "They'll look quite wholesome in a few months—color in their cheeks, laughter on their lips," she said of the girls.

In better light, Dayle had to admit the two of them didn't look like much. Dirty. Too thin. Their hair matted.

"I've seen pictures of the girls at the mission home," Lotta continued. "All the girls look happy and healthy in those pictures. I imagine they're hardly recognizable from the way they were when they arrived. Isn't that so?" she asked the missionary woman.

Mary Stillman Davies assured her that was the case.

Lotta pulled the sack of crackers from her pocket and again offered them to the girls without any more luck than before. Dayle allowed herself a moment of amusement. She liked the fact that the girls hadn't ever made up to Lotta. Ladies like Lotta, dressed in their fancy clothes and matching parasols, had come to the orphanage every Easter and every Christmas, handing out brown paper bags of candy and fruit. Dayle never took one. Not once. Taking one of the bags required a smile and a curtsy. Since smiles and curtsies were all she had, she didn't give them away. Not easily, anyway. She wanted to think these girls were of a similar mind.

That illusion was short-lived.

Miss Davies thumped her cane and spoke a few words of Chinese, and immediately the girls began taking the crackers and eating them with relish.

"What did you say?" Dayle asked her.

"I told them that they belong to me now. They have to do what I say."

"Belong to you?"

The older woman shrugged. "I'm afraid freedom is

The Lady Pinkerton Gets Her Man

not something they understand. To them, not belonging to someone is to be worthless."

"That makes them your slaves?"

Miss Davies gave Dayle one of her down-the-nose missionary looks. "They're all slaves, you know."

"What do you mean?"

"Think about it, my dear. Chinese men who come to America to work are called 'sojourners.' They've never been allowed to bring their families here, and many never wanted to anyway. At most, they use a concubine or one of these sing-sing girls for a little company. They expect to 'sojourn,' not stay. In fact, it is a very bad thing for a Chinaman not to return to his ancestors' graves and tend them. Now, because of the recently passed Chinese Exclusion Act, it's illegal for any Chinese, man or woman, to come into this country."

"I know," Dayle returned. The Exclusion Act had been Congress's response to the riots in Denver and Seattle.

"Yes, but have you thought about it?"

Then Dayle really knew. "That means any Chinaman who leaves to go home can't be replaced," Dayle said with a growing understanding of what was behind the miners' anger and the Tong's problems.

"Exactly, and, in fact, none is allowed to leave. At least, not from White Springs," Miss Davies said. "These mines have to be kept open, no matter how much anti-Chinese sentiment there is in this country. Too much depends on it."

"I see," was all Dayle could manage, as her mind worked to embrace all the implications. Miss Davies obviously made herself knowledgeable about a lot of things. Dayle could respect that, too. In the midst of those thoughts, one of the girls crumbled a cracker unexpectedly, and both girls giggled—a fine sound that completely distracted Dayle. She looked around and on impulse asked, "What are their names?"

The older woman spoke the question in Chinese.

The girls' heads came up. They hesitated. Then the girl with the short hair spoke first. "Quee Sing."

The other said, "Kim Ying."

Odd-sounding to Dayle's ear. She tried the names. They came off her tongue awkwardly, and the girls giggled more. There was something about that happy sound that momentarily captivated Dayle. She repeated the names. The second time, they came out better, but not well enough to keep the girls from giggling more. It surprised her that the two of them could be so gay so quickly. They really were very young. Dayle might have continued the game and become as giddy as Lotta, but then the westbound train arrived. As it pulled into the station, she glanced up, and, as if the morning hadn't already been full of enough surprises, she was startled again.

She recognized someone.

He'd jumped from the still-moving train onto the opposite end of the platform which was some distance away, but there was no mistaking Tommy the Tube Man. He was tall and thin and had bushy eyebrows and a distinctively hooked nose. She was so surprised to see him, it took her a moment to react. Then she took a step forward and lifted her hand to wave. Tommy suddenly jumped off the platform, and, taking several running steps, he crossed two sets of railroad tracks, slipped sideways between the boxcars parked on a siding there, and was gone.

"You know him?" Miss Davies asked.

Dayle shook her head and said, "I'm not sure."

She wasn't trying to be evasive. She wasn't sure what to make of seeing Tommy. He was a performer—a contortionist she'd met while working the circus train on another assignment.

Dayle turned to Lotta. "By chance, is the circus in town?"

Lotta shook her head.

The Lady Pinkerton Gets Her Man

"Coming soon, maybe?"

Lotta shook her head again. "I'm sure I would have heard."

Dayle turned and stared again in the direction Tommy had gone. It was September, late, but still circus season. Tommy ought to be with the show. She couldn't imagine what he was doing in White Springs, and why he was avoiding her. The two of them had played cards well past midnight traveling from town to town last summer. She tried to remember whether he owed her money from one of those poker games. She didn't think so.

That trivial worry masked the deeper concern that was moving over her the way a chill moves over skin, raising goosebumps. When she could no longer avoid that larger suspicion, she asked Mary Stillman Davies, "Why was the westbound train late?"

"Someone soaped the tracks," she answered.

Dayle received that news with the silence that accompanies quick mental calculation. This was way beyond a lady's adventure charity, trouble with the Tong, or nearly causing a riot at the local train station. Soaping tracks was an Anarchist trick.

She gave herself ten seconds more to absorb this new turn. Then she cleared her throat. "The Anarchists already know about the Tong and the Chinese miners," she said, not as a question. She expected confirmation from the missionary woman.

To her surprise, the older woman sounded amused. "The Hooded Sleeper can smell when a town is ripe for the picking."

"The Hooded Sleeper," Dayle repeated, and glanced again to where Tommy had disappeared.

"Not him," Miss Davies now corrected. "I've seen him before. He hangs around where there's action, but he's not the real mastermind."

That's exactly what Dayle had concluded last summer. Not Tommy, but someone Tommy knew. Then she'd been pulled off that assignment before she'd gotten to the bottom of it.

Miss Davies got the girls to their feet, readying them to board the train.

The Hooded Sleeper, Dayle repeated to herself.

It was because she insisted on working cases, not jobs, that she'd been pulled off the circus detail last summer. Her boss wanted to uncover the kind of Anarchists who handed out leaflets, and she'd been holding out for the Hooded Sleeper. He decided she had delusions of grandeur and reassigned her to the Denver office. She could have given him Tommy but chose not to. She thought she might have another opportunity. After all, the Pinkerton detective who exposed the Hooded Sleeper would more than guarantee a career. She'd be famous.

The Hooded Sleeper was the legendary mastermind believed to be behind the current American Anarchist movement. Named after the most dangerous of mining situations, an explosive that failed to go off, this mysterious man, whose identity wasn't known even to his followers, had pulled off two of the most successful labor stoppages the country had ever experienced. If he was in White Springs causing trouble . . . She didn't even want to think about that.

She looked again in the direction Tommy had disappeared in and slowly shook her head. White Springs was supposed to be strike-proof. Nobody wanted half the nation's coal to be at risk. That's why Chinese miners made up two-thirds of the work force. They were supposed to be insurance against trouble. Everybody knew Chinese miners never joined labor unions. In fact, conventional wisdom had it that as long as the coal mines here were open, no strike in any coal mine anywhere could succeed. The modest success of the Hooded Sleeper elsewhere was all the more disconcerting for exactly that reason.

However, that conventional wisdom predated pas-

The Lady Pinkerton Gets Her Man

sage of the Chinese Exclusion Act forced on Congress by growing national anti-Chinese sentiment and the riots that had burned through Denver and Seattle and threatened San Francisco. Given that new atmosphere, anything might be possible, and all the reasons that made White Springs a bastion also made White Springs a prize, maybe the ultimate Anarchist prize. Close the mines here, and it wasn't inconceivable that the Hooded Sleeper might find himself dictating terms to the president of the United States.

Then, just as she let her thoughts peak at that pinnacle of possibilities, she paused. Tommy the Tube Man was the kind who handed out leaflets and soaped tracks, not the Hooded Sleeper. That was too obvious. Maybe she was fooling herself, imagining things.

Dayle let her gaze return to the missionary woman. "Who knows about this?" she asked.

The older woman shrugged. "Who wants to believe?"

Exactly, Dayle thought. The Hooded Sleeper could soap tracks and anything else he pleased, because no one wanted to believe White Springs was vulnerable. But Miss Davies believed, and from everything Dayle had observed, the woman was no fool.

"Soaped tracks? Is that what I heard?" Lotta now asked, entering the conversation.

Dayle had thought she was too busy with the girls to care what she and Miss Davies were discussing. She hardly noticed anything now that the girls were smiling at her. She buttoned her jacket around the one who kept coughing as she asked again, "You mean to tell me that putting soap on railroad tracks can stop a train?"

Dayle nodded. Soap rubbed on the rails at the beginning of an incline kept the locomotive from getting traction. She'd seen it once during some labor troubles outside Denver. Amazing, really. One minute, tons of steel and steam were chugging along the rail, and the next, there was plenty of steam and whirl but no forward motion.

"Someone has to put sand on the tracks to get the train going again," Dayle explained.

"Really?" Lotta asked. "But who wants to stop the trains?"

"Anarchists," Dayle said, and then told herself the Hooded Sleeper wouldn't stop a train in order simply to announce himself. There was more purpose in that action than that. She was willing to bet on it.

"Anarchists?" Lotta repeated with a definite alarm in her tone. She shivered and looked around the train platform as if she thought she might catch sight of an Anarchist slinking through the crowd.

While Lotta looked over her shoulder for the bogeyman, Dayle let her own gaze wander across the platform and the people milling there. Dayle suspected that many of them would react similarly. Anarchists had been widely denounced as "unholy, un-American, and certainly opposed to capitalism." Prominent politicians and newspaper publishers regularly fed the fear that Anarchists were secretly working to bring down the government and the whole American way of life, not to mention corrupting youth and deceiving the women who sought temperance and the vote—"un-American, socialist ideas," according to those same sources.

"Do you worry a lot about Anarchists?" Lotta was now asking. "My husband worries constantly."

Dayle shrugged. "Not really," she answered. She wasn't worried. She was sure. The Hooded Sleeper was in White Springs.

"I don't understand then," Lotta said.

Dayle nodded as if she didn't, either. Actually, she knew quite a bit about Anarchists. Besides believing that every form of governmental regulation was immoral, Anarchists believed the key to the coming revolution was to give workers a sense of their own power. They argued that the engines of commerce could be stopped like a train on soaped tracks with something as simple as a workers' strike. That's the part that worried men like Garrick Bateman, Dayle knew.

Allan Pinkerton, the founder of her company, was more fanatical. He was practically irrational when it came to the "worldwide conspiracy of Anarchists." At his own expense, he kept a significant number of his detectives constantly chasing the "elusive socialists."

That's what she'd been doing last summer when she worked the circus train posing as a seamstress repairing costumes while she tried to infiltrate a cell of Anarchists that the home office felt sure were using the P. T. Barnum Spectacular to spread their "insidious ideas" through the "innocent heartland of America." If Dayle understood what was happening here, Mr. Pinkerton's worst fears had just come true.

4

Later that same morning, Ah So, the head of the local Tong, bowed and spoke his name to Garrick Bateman's secretary, a large-bellied young man with big ears who looked surprised to see him. In fact, his eyes widened immediately.

"I—I'll get Mr. Bateman," he stuttered as he stood up from his chair, nearly knocking it over. Even though the chair stayed upright, it managed to crash into a bookcase and knock several volumes to the floor.

Ah So found that amusing. He thought it was a good thing he didn't come there often. The surprise of it was obviously hard on the furniture and the help.

It was more usual for Mr. Bateman to come to the noodle shop downstairs from where Ah So lived and eat pork-flavored noodles with him while they talked. Mr. Bateman was particularly fond of pork-flavored Chinese noodles. In fact, it had been nearly ten years since Ah So had come to Mr. Bateman's office instead of Mr. Bateman going to the noodle shop.

The Lady Pinkerton Gets Her Man

Ten years was not a long time. In China, there were ruts in roads that were older than ten years, older than everything in White Springs, Wyoming, except the coal. Ten years ago, Mr. Bateman had a different secretary, an older man less given to startle, if Ah So remembered well. Ah So preferred people who were calm.

"Is—is Mr. Bateman expecting you, Mr. S-So? Or is it Mr. Ah So?" this new secretary continued to stutter.

Ah So was beginning to think this secretary had never known calm. He probably slept fitfully. Such people were short-lived. Ah So bowed and spoke. "I am Ah So," he told the young man. "Always Ah So."

The larger truth was that it didn't matter what the young man called him. Ah So had a Chinese name as secret as the Tong he headed, but for business outside Chinatown, "Ah So" was good enough. Besides, if his true name was never spoken in America, his ancestors could not find him and punish him for wandering so far looking for fortune. The Chinese called America "Gold Mountain," because it was supposedly a land of much money. But few Chinese had actually found fortune there. Ah So was the exception. He had sent enough money back to his home province to make himself a warlord. For that, he expected his ancestors would forgive him his journey.

Soon he would return and become that warlord. Such a future required not only wealth but an ability to recognize opportunity. Ah So had acquired both in Gold Mountain. He would make a fine warlord as soon as he left Wyoming and ate enough noodles to fill out his frame. At present, the only thing that made him fat was his raccoon-skin coat.

"Mr. Bateman no expect me now." Ah So answered the second part of the young man's question. "It surprise for him. You must tell him now. Quickly now."

"Y-y-yes, yes, of course," the young man said, and

48

then led Ah So into Garrick Bateman's office before he scurried off to find his boss.

Ah So looked around. Garrick Bateman's office was a fine place with fine, smooth cherrywood furniture, a carpet, fancy wallpaper in colors of azure and gray, and cut-glass decanters that held his liqueur. It was a gentleman's place—a wealthy gentleman's place. Like Ah So, Garrick Bateman had made much, much money from running the mines in White Springs, but he was foolish. He bought fancy things and brought them to this place that would soon be a ghost town with wind whistling through empty windows. A smart man sent his money away as Ah So did. Much money belonged in a better place. When the coal was gone . . .

Ah So didn't need to finish that thought. He touched the smooth back of one cherrywood chair. He could enjoy such a piece of furniture but allowed himself only the luxury of his raccoon-skin coat.

To most of the white miners, he was known simply as "the Chineyman in the raccoon-skin coat," he knew. It was an apt description. He was Chinese, and he owned a very fine full-length raccoon-skin coat that he wore every day, year round. It was his answer to Wyoming's wind. He hated that wind. He hated it in summer when his coat protected him from the dry and the dust. He hated it in winter when his coat protected him from the chill and the snow. When he left, he planned to leave nothing of himself behind— not even his name. Maybe only his coat, he thought. He would leave it to the wind and have a better coat made in China. One with embroidered dragons.

Ah So now fingered the edge of the cherrywood desk. He noted the books in a glass-enclosed cherrywood bookcase and the bronze statue of an Indian chief that decorated the top. Garrick Bateman had fine furniture, but he didn't even know the real name of the man who had gotten his good fortune for him. Ah So smiled. Not only did Garrick Bateman not

The Lady Pinkerton Gets Her Man

know Ah So's Chinese name, but he had no idea of the name of Ah So's home province in China where his ancestors rested or the fact that he had a small-footed woman there who was his wife. The woman he kept here was big-footed and worthless. By contrast, Ah So knew what Garrick Bateman had for dinner every night and the names of his horses. He knew that he'd hired a Pinkerton to help his wife—a Lady Pinkerton. Such details were just details until the right moment.

Garrick Bateman entered his office walking quickly and heavily. His secretary followed at his heel. Garrick Bateman was a large man who obviously enjoyed more than pork-flavored noodles. He liked the gold watch chain that hung from his vest pocket and the fine polished boots on his feet. The man himself was thick-jawed and beginning to show a little gray in his dark hair. Not bad-looking by round-eye standards, Ah So thought. But he lacked lordly mannerisms. He talked too much and too jovially. Unlike the secretary, who had sensed import in Ah So's visit, Garrick Bateman gave a hearty greeting, dismissed his secretary, and sat down as if to chat.

Ah So sat across from him. He refused the drink the other man offered and waited for the conversation to turn serious. Meanwhile, Garrick Bateman talked about the weather and made general comments on the mines. Ah So nodded to these things of no consequence. To him, Garrick Bateman was like the wind that swept this place continually. The wind in Wyoming was not to be underestimated. That's why Ah So had his raccoon-skin coat, but wind was wind, not mountain.

At last, Garrick Bateman got around to business. "This is unusual. What brings you here?"

Ah So slid forward on his chair and offered half a bow. "It is no big thing to lose a couple of worthless girls. I am most happy to make the wife of an honored

Jerrie Hurd

friend smile. But I am thinking Mrs. Bateman is happy now. She will not visit Chinatown again."

To his surprise, Garrick Bateman actually flushed. "It's not possible to make that woman happy," he said in words not guarded, not carefully phrased.

Chinese did not speak that way. Nevertheless, Ah So thought the man's words were well spoken. In China, one had to be careful of fox fairies—tricksters that made fools of even wise men. Happiness was the worst of the fox fairies. It could never be trusted.

Hearing Garrick Bateman speak so strongly about his wife's discontent made Ah So hope that maybe the two of them could understand each other on this point. He was not sure. He was often not sure about Garrick Bateman. Like his secretary, he was a man without calm.

Ah So slid back in his chair to study the other man.

The wise warlord knew it was best to keep his underlings less than happy but not entirely miserable. The same was true with wives. Happy wasn't possible and tempted the fates. Misery led to rebellion. The problem Ah So faced was misery. It had become too miserable in Chinatown. He'd had to show his iron fist earlier that morning. Not good. The wise warlord was felt, not seen. In short, he needed his sing-sing girls and any other distraction that kept his miners a little bit happy. Garrick Bateman didn't need to try and please his wife so much. If they could only agree to move slowly, the current problem would be temporary. Ah So only needed a little time. He had a cousin in Canada.

"No problem with Chinese Exclusion Act," he told Bateman, switching to the larger concern they shared. "My cousin and I soon smuggle many Chinese across the border. More than enough. He have to make arrangements. It take time. It not good till arrangements are all made very good. Till then I need all my sing-sing girls."

The Lady Pinkerton Gets Her Man

Garrick Bateman laughed. "What's taking so long? That fat missionary woman who recruited my wife brags that she can get any Chinese girl out of anywhere and take her anyplace. Now you're telling me the Tong can't equal that? Are you telling me that you're no match for a missionary woman with no money, just the nickels of charity she gathers from other women at church meetings?"

"Not same thing," Ah So said.

"How is it not the same?"

Ah So shook his head. This was not the question that mattered. What Mary Stillman Davies did with the Chinese girls she stole was not important here except for the trouble it might trigger. "Why your wife need my girls?"

"I told you. She thinks she's doing the world some good. It makes her happy."

"Why you care if she happy? She your wife. She should make you happy."

"Why do you care?" Bateman returned as he fingered his fine watch chain and let his face go red. "I'm paying you three times what those girls are worth. I've never known you to care about anything as long as it paid good money."

Ah So paused to choose his words carefully.

Ten years ago, it had been different. Ten years ago, Garrick Bateman had been desperate, willing to listen to anything, do anything. A wildcat strike had closed the mines, and Garrick Bateman had to get those mines open again or lose his job. As events closed in around him, Ah So had come forward. He'd come to Bateman's office as now, but he hadn't owned his raccoon-skin coat then. That was before he could afford his one American luxury. But he knew how to help Garrick Bateman open the mines again with Chinese strike breakers. Ah So could still help Garrick Bateman with the mines if he would stop worrying about his wife and get practical.

"It is maybe a time to move slow and act deliberate."

"I'm not worried about anything," Bateman returned.

"Good," Ah So agreed. "Because you don't need to worry. You can fool the troublemakers just like that." Ah So snapped his fingers to emphasize his point. It was a trick he'd learned from watching Bateman.

"How's that?" Bateman asked.

"All you have to do is raise the wages of the white miners a little bit."

"Raise the wages?"

"Very clever. You raise the wages, and the miners stop listening to Anarchists just like that." He snapped his fingers again.

Bateman slapped the top of his desk. "There are no Anarchists in town. One set of soaped tracks, and everyone jumps to conclusions. But I'm telling you, there are no Anarchists in White Springs."

Ah So kept calm. He waited until Bateman had stopped talking and drawn a deep breath. Then he spoke. "It does not matter who is in town. Many Anarchists. No Anarchists. It is all the same. Nobody wants trouble. Mostly the white miners want more beer and sausages. Noodles are better, but if you give them what they want, we will have no trouble here from anyone. I am sure of this."

Garrick Bateman leaned back in his chair and shook his head. "You sure as hell want a lot. When I come to Chinatown, I want noodles and a few more workers. You come to my office, and you want me to disappoint my wife and raise the wages of my miners."

"I advise only. Your trouble is my trouble. It is wisdom to know how everything is connected and . . ."

Garrick Bateman hit the desk again. "That might be how things are done in Chinatown, but I'm not

The Lady Pinkerton Gets Her Man

some placid-faced Chinaman. I don't give the miners what they want just to avoid trouble. I run things here. I tell them what to do. If there are Anarchists in town and they want trouble, I'll give them trouble. You seem to forget that last time someone tried a strike here, I broke that strike, and I'll do it again, because I say what happens here."

Ah So thought Garrick Bateman was a strange man. He didn't seem to know that all of White Springs was nothing more than tents in the desert. Evidently, that impermanence also extended to Bateman's memory. Ah So remembered that he was the one who had suggested to Garrick Bateman that with enough Chinese miners he could always keep the mines open. But nothing stayed the same. What worked ten years ago would not work now.

"Trouble is like a mad dog, no good to anyone," he warned, but he knew before the words were out that it was hopeless. Bateman was possessed, his judgment given over to pleasing his wife before all else. He'd seen it happen before. With some men, nothing mattered except the one woman he couldn't have or couldn't satisfy.

Ah So stood. It was not possible to have a woman who was both pure and pouty at the same time. Chinese knew better. Wives were to show off. Concubines were to enjoy. He could not help Garrick Bateman with this woman problem. He doubted anyone could.

He bowed. It was time to go. The wise warlord knew when to move on. Besides, he had other visits to make.

Later that afternoon, after Dayle had finally gotten Miss Davies and the girls on the train and Lotta safely home, she decided to report in. That's how she came to be standing on the corner of Main and Lincoln, holding her skirts down in the wind as she let a horsedrawn trolley pass. Then she picked up her skirts and stepped over the ruts and trolley tracks on her way to the local Pinkerton office on the other side of the street.

The company's Wyoming headquarters occupied a two-story building not far from the railroad station. Gray stone, few windows, nothing fancy except the carved figures representing "Freedom" and "Progress" that decorated the top front corners of the building. One faced east, the other west. They were larger than life, half-clad female figures draped in laurel leaves and blackened with soot, perfect symbols for everything in White Springs, she thought—larger-than-life dreams dusted with the commerce of coal.

Dayle paused again before she pushed through the heavy outside door. She'd already stopped by the room at the back of Lotta's mansion, where she was staying, and changed her clothes. She'd also picked up a sewing basket. Now all she needed was to put on the demure attitude of a widowed seamstress who was returning newly mended socks and shirts to the boss inside. Even if the Tong had figured it out, she needed to keep up appearances as long as she could. Unfortunately, she didn't always find the demure part of her current disguise easy.

It was effective, though. If she tucked her chin, rounded her shoulders, and shortened her stride, she became nearly invisible. It was a simple fact of life that no one paid attention to a soft-walking, quiet-toned little woman with a sewing basket over her arm. Sometimes Dayle liked to make a game of it. She would walk down a street or through a room and count how many people never saw her at all.

Inside the Pinkerton headquarters, the main room was deep and narrow and always noisy. Agents were coming and going; news and assignments were being shouted back and forth; and whenever a train rolled by, the volume of everything went up. Tucked up small, Dayle walked quietly across the space and noticed that almost no heads turned. In fact, two

The Lady Pinkerton Gets Her Man

agents on their way out bumped into her before they saw her, and only one bothered to excuse himself.

"No trouble," she said, quietly enough that he probably didn't hear. He was already halfway out the door.

In that manner, she continued until she'd made her way to the main desk. There she set her basket on the edge and asked for Thuzla Smith, the office boss. "I have shirts to return," she added, still speaking sweetly.

"Just leave them," the agent on duty barked.

"Thank you," she answered in her sweet voice. "I don't wish to be any trouble, but I need to measure him for another order." She pulled a cloth tape from her basket and held it up as if she didn't expect him to understand anything as domestic as sewing without an additional clue.

"Upstairs," the man barked back, and waved her on.

Dayle thanked him again. Then she couldn't help herself. She mentioned sweetly how unfortunate it was that his collar seemed so "terribly frayed." Then she left him standing there, straining to check his collar while she picked up her basket and climbed the stairs.

Of the four temperaments phrenologists had identified, Thuzla Smith was the bilious type, always out of temper. He had a bad stomach and carried a bottle of patent medicine in his hip pocket which he took out and swigged regularly between shouting orders. "Keep her happy," he'd told Dayle in loud tones when she arrived from Denver for her present assignment. "Just keep her happy whatever it takes," he'd added while he put back of shot of medicine He was referring to Lotta. He really meant her husband. Garrick Bateman was the Pinkertons' "most important western client," he'd repeated at least three times while he was giving her those orders. She got the impression that keeping Garrick Bateman happy was how Thuzla Smith defined his job, which meant that her current news was not going to be well received. She suspected that no one in White Springs wanted to hear that the Tong were losing control of Chinatown or that the Anarchists were moving in.

That, however, was not the first challenge she faced. First, she had to get past the bullpen without losing her seamstress sweetness. The bullpen was a large open area at the top of the stairs where Pinkerton agents sat around a stove, chewing and spitting and telling stories while they waited to be sent out on whatever assignment came up. There were always six or seven of them in the bullpen, sometimes more, and their shared masculinity required that they never let a woman pass without comment.

"Oh-ah, lookee here, I do believe the boss is getting freshly mended socks," the first of them sang out as soon as he saw her.

"Yeah, maybe he's going to have all the buttons on his shirt for a change," another commented with a chuckle.

"Hell, if he gets too cleaned up, somebody might marry him," someone else offered.

"Oh, and that would put poor Miss Dobson out of a job," the first chimed in again.

"Not iffing she was the one to marry him?" a third suggested, and winked at Dayle.

She didn't think any of that deserved comment.

Didn't matter. One of the boys took it on himself to comment for her. "Hell, why would she want to marry Thuzla when she could have me? How about it, honey?"

Dayle pulled a face.

"Oh-ah, I can tell she wants you, all right," the first chimed in again.

"Why would she want anything from the likes of you?" another said. "She's related to the big boss's wife."

The Lady Pinkerton Gets Her Man

"Yeah, she lives in that mansion with the Batemans and everything. Ain't that right?"

Dayle shrugged.

"Guess you have to be a lady to get a lady's life," one of the younger boys added.

She really had to bite her tongue at that one. She was willing to bet not one of them had run across a roof, hung off a balcony, been chased by the Tong, or hidden in a coal bin. Hardly lady's work. And that was just her morning's adventures. Still, she managed to keep her temper down. She simply asked in her sweetest tones, "Anything exciting happen here?"

"The westbound train was late," someone offered. "But it finally made it into the station a little while ago."

"I heard about that. Someone soaped the tracks," Dayle told them, and even added a little giggle for effect. "It's the talk everywhere."

"Oh, really," the younger one said. "I thought ladies only concerned themselves with talk of the latest in fashions." With that, he set his hat at a rakish angle and got a round of chuckles from the others.

Dayle let them enjoy themselves. When they'd finished with their laugh, she asked, "Any idea who soaped those tracks?"

"Haven't you heard? That's an Anarchist trick," two of the boys answered together.

"Anarchist?" she said with mock concern. "Are you sure?"

"Yes, but don't worry. They won't be causing any real trouble 'round here," another offered.

"Really?" she asked.

"Yeah, they're spinning their wheels as sure as that engine was spinning in the soap this morning," the same guy went on.

"What does that mean?" Dayle asked. "I thought Anarchists hated everything connected to the railroad, especially Mr. Jay Gould and the other American monopolists."

"Yeah, but Jay Gould owns this town, and it's going to take a lot more than soap to change that fact."

"Yeah, I'd say," someone else offered.

"I never knew another town where one person owned practically every damned thing."

"Such language! And in front of a lady. I think you boys might give some respect."

At the sound of that voice, the men jumped to their feet, and Dayle turned.

Thuzla Smith filled the door to his office. A tall, middle-aged man, broad of shoulder, he was clean-shaven, and his hair was slicked back, but his belly had gotten soft. No prince, and yet there was no denying that even in a soft, slightly paunchy way, he was still a cut above the boys in the bullpen. Mostly, it was his piercing eyes and no-nonsense attitude that made the difference.

"You boys behave yourselves," he added, "or I'll make you catch weasels."

"Catching weasels" was the Pinkerton equivalent of "going on a wild goose chase." It referred to trying to catch con artists after they'd worked a scam and were already gone.

The boys got the idea. "Yes, sir. Sure enough, sir," they said, almost in unison.

She passed by and entered Thuzla's office.

It was a plain cubicle with a worn wooden floor, green walls, and one dirty window. There was a desk and three chairs, but Dayle's level of agitation was more than sitting would allow. She paced past the chairs to the window. Then, the moment she heard the door shut, she spoke.

"Anarchists haven't a chance in this town? Is that the general opinion around here?" she asked with a note of incredulity.

Thuzla perched himself on the edge of his desk and shrugged, revealing a cavalier attitude that really set her off

"I was just chased out of Chinatown We were nearly

The Lady Pinkerton Gets Her Man

the cause of a riot at the train station. Tensions are running that high. Do you realize the Tong had to bring out every man they had to get things quieted again in Chinatown? They're losing control," she told him, spitting it all out at once. "I don't think I have to explain what a heyday the Anarchists could have in this town if the Tong can't be counted on to keep the mines open."

An odd smile had taken over Thuzla's face.

She plopped herself down on one chair. "At one point, I thought I was going to get Mrs. Bateman killed. I thought we were all goners," she went on. "When those miners turned on us . . ."

The man started chuckling.

Dayle looked up. "Do you understand what I'm saying?"

He nodded. His odd expression became a definite grin, and he couldn't hold his laughter anymore. A raucous roar came up from his soft belly. He slapped the edge of the desk and shook his head.

"I'm sorry," he said when he got control of himself again. "Really, I'm sorry, but Mr. Ah So stopped by a few minutes ago and apologized for all that. Imagine. The head of the Tong came here and apologized to me. He had that raccoon-skin coat on and everything."

"The head of the Tong?" Dayle repeated.

"Yeah, it seems his men got carried away and 'performed too wonderfully,' is the way he explained it. He said he told his men to give the 'big boss's wife' and her friend 'an excitement,' and he felt they did too good a job. Such a good job, he had to apologize." Thuzla shook his head and let his grin grow wider. "I take it he was right. He really had you scared, huh?"

Dayle was speechless. She thought back over the morning. Had she been set up? Fooled?

"You weren't there," she said.

"No, and from the sound of it, I'm sorry I missed the action."

"Nobody was there. Nobody else saw it. Just Lotta and myself and that Chinese cook," she said, thinking out loud.

Thuzla picked up the talk. "I understand there were lots of Chinese. Ah So was quite proud of how many men he'd used to 'excite the boss's pretty wife.'"

Dayle didn't say anything. Her hands had begun to sweat. Obviously, Mr. Ah So didn't want it known that he was losing control. And who was to refute his version of things? Not Lotta. Who'd believe her? Not the cook. He was Tong. The girls were already on their way to California. That left Dayle.

Meanwhile, her boss was as pleased as he could be, perched on the edge of his desk, recounting how the head of the Tong had come to him, apologized to him for scaring one of his agents.

She was scared. She knew too well what the Tong could do to a person who knew something they didn't want known. She drew a deep breath and told herself that she might be imagining that this was worse than it really was. In any case, she wasn't going to get any help from her boss. He wasn't going to believe anything she said. He'd been flattered into thinking this was all a joke.

"What do I have to do to get out of this assignment?" she asked.

"You and I could run off to California together."

He wasn't serious, but she was. "I'd be willing to transfer back to Denver, right now."

That brought his old biliousness back. His smile slipped, his voice took volume. "Garrick Bateman is the company's best western client. If he wants his wife to have a little adventure, then the company is going to provide the best, and at the moment, you're the best we got."

Dayle closed her eyes and wanted to groan.

A few minutes later, she paused in the stairwell of the Pinkerton building and tried to think. That the

The Lady Pinkerton Gets Her Man

Tong were losing control of Chinatown and the Anarchists were already causing trouble and her own life was in danger was not a set of facts she thought she ought to ignore even if her boss wouldn't listen. Question was, who would listen?

Mr. Allan Pinkerton, the man who was already obsessed with Anarchists, she decided, and then half laughed at her own audacity. Mr. Pinkerton was in Chicago. She was in Wyoming. She'd never met him. He had no reason to want to know her. She was merely an operative, one of hundreds working for the Pinkerton Detective Agency.

A couple of minutes later, when she hadn't come up with anything better, she got serious. She told herself this was something Mr. Pinkerton ought to know—would want to know. The worst that could happen was that he'd order her dismissed as a nuisance.

It was in moments like this that Dayle knew the one advantage to having grown up an orphan. She'd learned to live with nothing, and she knew she could live on nothing again. It was the one wealth of poverty—knowing that you could walk away from anything.

From the stairwell, she went straight to the local telegraph office. She sent Mr. Allan Pinkerton, "America's most famous detective," a short, to-the-point message.

5

On the opposite side of town, Harry Bryant, an actor with a traveling troupe of Shakespearean players, looked up from where he was rummaging through his costumes and saw two beefy-looking men walk through the side stage door. They wandered in as if they owned the place, sliding a curtain aside, kicking a wardrobe trunk out of the way.

Pinkertons, he thought, and closed the lid of his wardrobe trunk.

Harry hated Pinkertons. They were nothing but hired hooligans, paid police, throwbacks to medieval times when private armies made sure certain wealthy noblemen remained above the law. Forget democracy. Here were the enforcers of Jay Gould's American fiefdom. On a more personal level, he found them damned annoying and so much a type that he could pick them out in a crowd.

The similarity was in the way they walked, arms wide, hips swinging with an almost womanly sway in order to show off their guns. This pair pushed their

The Lady Pinkerton Gets Her Man

hats back and looked the place over from the riggings in the rafters to the trunks of costumes newly stacked in the wings. Then, with a loud voice, the heavier one demanded to see the "head greasepaint."

That was Harry. He owned this traveling theatrical company. Managed it. Played in it. More to the point, he had yet to make a stop in a mining or railroad town without getting an immediate visit from the Pinkertons. They always showed up to flex a little muscle and make sure strangers knew they were in charge, not the sheriff or the mayor or the local circuit judge. In a Pinkerton town, the only law that mattered was the Pinkerton handbook.

That didn't mean Harry couldn't have fun with them.

While the two detectives continued to nose around, he finished buttoning his waistcoat. Then, picking the right dramatic moment, he whirled and sliced the air with his sword as if feeling its heft.

That sent both Pinkertons reeling back two steps.

With perfect nonchalance, Harry tipped his weapon down, planted the tip in the wooden floor, and leaned into it, striking the kind of regal pose favored for the portraiture of young nobles of the last century—an appropriate stance, he thought. He was playing Hamlet that night.

The two Pinkertons had immediately reached for their guns. Now they glanced at each other, a little sheepishly, and relaxed their arms. One adjusted his hat. Both gave Harry assessing, if somewhat careful looks. They were clearly not quite sure if Harry's swordplay had been mere playacting or more threatening. Harry wasn't sure himself.

The pair continued to eye him.

He let them look him over. He was slightly taller than either of them. His hair was sandy. His eyes were blue. His face was finely sculptured, except for his nose, which was slightly larger than perfection, he knew. He studied his face nightly as he applied greasepaint to those features. In short, he was young to be the head of a theater company and devilishly handsome, if he did say so himself, but looks in the theatrical sense could be deceiving. At the moment, he was Hamlet, the young prince of Denmark whose main fault was indecisive hesitation. Lucky for these Pinkertons, he hadn't turned and sliced the air as the tormented Richard III. In that case, he might have taken off one of their ears and not thought anything of it.

He cleared his throat. Somebody needed to say something. "Well, now, what can I do for you?" he asked, rolling his words out in his best theatrical voice, deep, melodious, and projecting broadly.

Both Pinkertons gave quick glances over their shoulders as if they thought he was talking to someone behind them. Turning back, the heavier of the pair spoke. "You the head of this troupe?"

Harry nodded.

"How long you going to be in town?"

Standard Pinkerton question. That didn't mean Harry had to give the expected answer. "As long as people keep coming to my performances," he told them, and then elaborated. "We're quite versatile as a company. We do the usual Shakespearean repertoire but also some of the lesser-known works such as *Troilus and Cressida*. That tends to extend our range and repeated appeal to the same audience. Actually, in a town like this with little else to do in the way of cultural entertainment, we could play for weeks. Personally, I like to stay in a place until we're played out, if you know what I mean."

They didn't. He could tell by their blank looks. The heavier one asked again, "But how long are you going to be in this here town?"

"Longer than usual," Harry said.

He'd given them a long answer; now he waited to

The Lady Pinkerton Gets Her Man

see how they would react to a short one. He enjoyed baiting Pinkertons, testing them, egging them on. It was a game to see how long it took until one of them shoved him against the back wall rather than try to continue a civilized conversation. He'd found that most Pinkertons couldn't sustain anything civilized.

He was just getting into that fun when Tommy the Tube Man came sliding through that same side stage door. Out of breath and in a sweat, he suddenly stopped, looked things over, and said, "What's going on?"

The Pinkertons stepped back another two steps and viewed Tommy with an expression that approximated pure astonished surprise. Tommy was that unusual-looking, and his voice was an unmodulated screech. Harry swore it sliced the air with the same effect as a sword.

"Who are you?" the heavier Pinkerton managed to ask.

"His assistant," Tommy answered, and thumbed in Harry's direction. By then, he'd obviously sized up the situation. "I used to work for the circus, the P. T. Barnum, before I came to work for him. Pinkertons guarded the train and our show. Good, reliable Pinkerton guards, yes, sir. Like they say, the Pinkertons are 'the eye that never sleeps.'"

At that, the younger of the two Pinkertons came to life. "That's our slogan," he said. "Have you read Mr. Pinkerton's detective books? They're all true stories, you know. They're all about how a Pinkerton detective always gets his man, yes, sir."

"Oh, yes, I have," Tommy told him, and clapped the young Pinkerton on his back. "I've read them all. Exciting books. Makes you want to join the agency."

"That's the reason I joined," the younger added.

"You don't say," Tommy responded with theatrical earnestness.

Harry was enjoying this again. His "assistant" had been a contortionist with the circus until he retired and came to work for Harry. Thin, pale, with a voice no one ignored, Tommy moved in a way that seemed almost spineless and yet never unsteady. At the moment, he was wrapping himself around these Pinkertons with such skill, it was as if he had to prove he hadn't abandoned his contortionist art completely.

Harry returned his sword to its scabbard.

Tommy and the younger Pinkerton exchanged a bit more banter, then the heavier one remembered the business at hand.

"How long you plan to be in town?" he asked again.

"Oh, not long," Tommy said with as much congeniality as he could squeeze out of his squawking voice. "Couple of weeks, doing shows on Thursdays, Fridays, Saturdays, and Sundays. We always make a contribution to the Pinkerton fund for widows. We never let Orientals or other undesirables into the shows. Absolutely, you won't have any trouble from us. We know what's expected."

That satisfied. The two Pinkertons glanced around one more time and then excused themselves. The younger one even waved to Tommy as he exited through the back stage door.

Harry was impressed. And curious. "What was that all about?" he asked when they were gone.

"I hate Pinkertons," Tommy snapped back.

Harry chuckled. "What else is new?"

"I don't mean those kind, I mean the sneaky undercover ones that you don't even know are Pinkertons. Lady Pinkertons are the worst of all."

"I don't believe I've ever had the pleasure of meeting a Pinkerton of the fairer sex."

Tommy shook his head. "You don't want the pleasure."

Harry knew that tone. "Who is she?"

"Dayle Dobson. She worked the train last summer

The Lady Pinkerton Gets Her Man

hunting Anarchists. She posed as a seamstress, repairing costumes. Only reason I was suspicious was because her seams didn't hold. For a while, I was worried she might get fired. Then I realized nobody cared how well she stitched."

"She's in White Springs?" Harry asked.

Tommy nodded. "I saw her at the train station this morning."

Harry shrugged. "What's another Pinkerton more or less? Lay them end to end, and you could circle this town in Pinkertons."

"She's not your regular Pinkerton," Tommy told him. "She works the way she plays poker—straight-faced, never missing an advantage. I'm quite sure she didn't expose us last summer only because she was hunting bigger prey. I think she hoped I'd lead her to you."

"Really?" Harry asked, thinking a Lady Pinkerton who could scare Tommy had to be an interesting challenge.

Tommy shot him an odd look. "You know the rule of working the road—leave the Pinkertons alone."

Harry smiled broadly. "Oh, but that's no fun."

Tommy groaned. "This is no game."

That evening, as Dayle was dressing for the theater, there was a knock on her door. She jumped and felt for her gun. Then she shook herself. It was a light knock, no reason to be startled, except that she'd been jumping at noises all evening, imagining things—the Tong. But when the Tong came for her, they weren't going to knock, she reminded herself.

The knock came again.

Dayle opened, and Lotta twirled into the room, literally making two complete circles, her evening dress flowing around her in a swirl of rustle, her voice similarly ebbing and flowing in an excited patter.

"Don't you love dressing up? It makes me feel like

royalty. Oh, no, better. I mean, I've seen pictures of Queen Victoria. Dowdy to the point of embarrassment. You'd think someone would give her a pointer or two on how to wear clothes."

Dayle was still holding the door open when the other woman struck a pose in front of the full-length mirror and glanced over her shoulder, obviously expecting some comment.

Dayle wasn't sure what to say.

Lotta had that effect on her.

Didn't matter. Lotta turned back to the mirror, brushed at a wrinkle on her sleeve, and continued, "I have no patience for those reformers who say wearing a corset wasn't good for a woman's health. Have you seen those things they call 'lady's bloomers?'" she asked, and then didn't pause for Dayle's answer. "They're ugly," she offered. "A woman needs to feel pretty. It makes all the difference."

Dayle closed the door and looked past Lotta at her own reflection in the mirror. She was wearing an Ottoman silk and velvet evening dress set off with a boa of white silk plissé shirred into ruffles. It was a nice dress, but it looked showy next to Lotta, who was wearing an embroidered surah dress with nothing more flashy than a bow on the shoulder. Like it or not, the woman had class.

Lotta brought her hands to her hips. "You don't talk much, do you?"

Dayle had thought about clothes enough to know that the sisters at the orphanage were wrong when it came to the virtue of "plain honest dress." Silk and feathers got a woman noticed. Other than that, fashion wasn't her subject.

She shrugged. "Sorry, I don't mean to be unfriendly."

Lotta now turned and faced Dayle squarely. "What made you decide to be a Lady Pinkerton?"

Same question as in the coal bin. Dayle wondered

The Lady Pinkerton Gets Her Man

at the other woman's fascination with the subject but decided on a light response. She gestured toward her sewing basket. "I don't really sew well, and let's face it, there aren't that many other things a woman can do to make a living."

"I ask too many questions," Lotta said, turning back to the mirror. "I know it's annoying. I shouldn't think so much."

"You think too much?"

"Oh, quite. It's a fault I've been trying to overcome since I was old enough to talk. Sometimes I can't help myself. I have too much curiosity. A phrenologist told me that once. My curiosity bumps are far too developed. Curiosity is a bad thing if you find yourself trying to figure out things you have no business knowing."

Dayle didn't understand that comment at all. She spent her every waking moment trying to figure things out. She'd been trying to figure out Lotta for days now. "What things do you have no business knowing?"

Lotta wouldn't answer. "Oh, nothing important," she said, and paused to push her hair up in a different style. "Ever wonder what it would be like to be someone else?" she asked.

"Who would you be?"

"Queen Victoria," she answered with surprising promptness.

"That dowdy woman you hated a moment ago?"

"Oh, not her exactly. I'd be Queen Charlotta, and I wouldn't be dowdy. I mean, if you have a chance to be a queen, then I think you ought to really be a queen, all stately and wonderful."

For all practical purposes, she was the queen of White Springs, Wyoming. There were plenty of women who envied her—imagined that they wanted to trade places with her, Dayle knew. Yet her antics had some of the flutter of flying against bars.

Dayle reached into the top dresser drawer and took out a pouch of tobacco. "You smoke?" she asked.

"Oh, heavens, no."

"Want to try? After all, this is the wilds of Wyoming."

Lotta had to think about that. "It would make my dress smell something awful, wouldn't it?"

"Oh, but the ride in the carriage on the way to the theater will surely air it out," Dayle told her. "No one will know."

Lotta scrunched her shoulders together and bit her lower lip. "Our little secret?"

"Our little secret," Dayle repeated, and rolled a smoke for Lotta.

Lotta took it, looked at it, and asked, "Do you smoke often?"

Dayle shrugged. "When I feel the urge."

Lotta handed the cigarette back. "No, really, I can't. If Garrick smelled it on me, even a whiff."

"He's not here."

"Having a fine wife is important to him. It's important to most men, but for Garrick . . ." She stopped and suddenly turned back to the mirror. "He hasn't seen me in this dress. He'll be meeting us at the theater. He has business until then. I think he'll be pleased, don't you agree? I'm talking about when he sees me in this dress."

Dayle knew what she was talking about. She agreed and was about to put the cigarette away when Lotta added, "There's another Chinese girl."

"What?" Dayle asked.

"I'm told she's kept in the back of a bathhouse, the property of the bathhouse owner. He makes her scrub tubs by day and entertain by night, if you know what I mean."

She couldn't mean she wanted to undertake another rescue, Dayle thought. Not this soon. Not after what they'd just been through. "Rescuing those Chi-

The Lady Pinkerton Gets Her Man

nese girls is a worthy cause," Dayle offered, "but, really, you can't keep doing it."

"You want to know how I got my husband to agree to let me do this?"

Dayle straightened. That was the first question Lotta had raised that really interested her. In fact, she'd wondered quite a lot on that particular point. "Yes," she answered.

"Shamed him into it. Not hard. My husband has two party brags. Actually, my husband is very good with words. Charming, like I said. He makes everything sound nice and proper, but you can be sure before this evening is over, he'll have made sure everyone knows two things: that he's such an important man nothing happens in Wyoming Territory without his approval, and that he makes his wife happy by indulging her every whim. He likes to put it exactly like that—indulging his wife's every whim."

She paused and sighed.

"Except one," she said more softly. "I started correcting him quietly. Every time he went through his party patter, I'd remind him afterward that what he said about indulging my every whim was true, except for one—he never indulged my desire to save these poor, misused Chinese girls that I'd heard were being kept against their will in Chinatown. After a while, he couldn't stand it. It's very important for Garrick Bateman never to be wrong, especially when it comes to my happiness. Do you have any idea what it's like for everyone to expect that you should be happy all the time?"

Dayle thought about that a moment. She asked, "Do you have some reason not to be happy?"

"No. My husband reminds me of that all the time. I have absolutely no reason not to be happy, because he indulges my every whim, like I said, even this one."

"Still, I don't think you can continue to rescue Chinese girls, given the current circumstances and all," Dayle told her.

Lotta immediately objected. "But you saw those girls. You saw how they lived. No one is supposed to live like that." She paused as if to catch her breath. "Doesn't it make you feel good to know you've saved them from that awful life?"

Dayle nodded. There was no arguing against the charity, and she didn't know how she could argue with someone who wanted to set a little piece of the world aright. Sending that telegram to Allan Pinkerton had been more than a little nervy. It was quite possible she was being equally naive. She imagined Mr. Pinkerton having a good laugh. After all, her message had been the equivalent of "the sky is falling."

"I don't think you understand. It's dangerous . . ."

"Dangerous," Lotta interrupted. "The only truly dangerous thing a woman can do is make her husband unhappy." With that, she plopped herself down on the edge of the bed. "If you don't mind, I think I'll have that cigarette now, because I can't think of another time when I might be offered one."

Dayle handed her the cigarette and found a match. She watched closely as Lotta's face danced through a series of expressions as she held the cigarette and tasted the smoke. Remarkably, the woman never coughed, not once.

Dayle rolled and lit her own smoke but took no satisfaction in it. She was trying to understand Lotta's "only truly dangerous" comment.

There were two places in White Springs that regularly booked traveling acts. One was known as the Recital Hall and was mainly that, an open hall with a raised stage at one end. It attracted mostly lectures. The theater was more elaborate. It was the one building in town with any architectural pretension. Three stories high, the top story was a sloping dormer with a parapet above. But mostly it was distinguished by rows and rows of arched windows, each with an

The Lady Pinkerton Gets Her Man

ornamental keystone. An awning extended over the entrance which was lit with gaslights.

Garrick Bateman's uniformed driver helped Dayle and Lotta from the carriage. They walked under the awning. A moment later, a doorman opened the theater's double doors to let the two of them enter.

"Think he smelled the cigarette?" Lotta asked as she gave a second glance to the doorman.

Dayle shook her head. Lotta had asked the same thing about her maid, the stable boy, and her husband's carriage driver.

"I almost wish he had," she answered, giving Dayle a mischievous grin. "It would have given him something to talk about."

Dayle doubted that. She was sure even doormen had more important concerns than to wonder if Mrs. Bateman had been smoking.

Inside the theater, the decor featured ferns and urns and draperies with gold tassels that matched the gilt-edged mirrors along one wall. The Batemans had seats in an exclusive box on the second level. Dayle lifted her skirts and followed Lotta up the curved staircase that led to the upper lobby. She was standing near the top of those stairs when Garrick Bateman arrived.

He was a large but good-looking man, his hair graying just enough to look dignified, but his walk was what distinguished him. It was hard to describe. His carriage suggested not so much power as ubiquity. He was this town. No exaggeration, she thought. Directly or indirectly, everyone from the stationmaster to the street sweeper owed his livelihood to Garrick Bateman. He wore that fact the way he wore his fitted jacket with the gold buttons.

More interesting was the way people flowed around him. Some got out of his way; others sought his attention; no one ignored him. Even at the edges of the room, individuals engaged in their own conversations followed his progress with quick glances. He literally left a human ripple in his wake.

Dayle had made it her business to know quite a lot about Garrick Bateman, but she'd never actually met the man. He was rarely at home and probably thought of her as no more than another member of his wife's household staff—the maid, the cook, the Pinkerton . . .

Lotta suddenly leaned close. "You're sure you can't smell any cigarette smoke?" she asked, her voice tighter, a real ring of concern in her tones.

Dayle shifted her focus to Lotta and saw her fussing with her belt, straightening what was already straight. Her face had changed from the coy naughtiness with which she had smoked that cigarette to a pinched tightness, careful, close.

The transformation was truly remarkable. In fact, Dayle was so absorbed in her study of Lotta that she almost forgot herself. Garrick Bateman strode toward her, his hand extended, his face a polite smile, and she almost didn't notice. It was the little squeaky edge to Lotta's voice as she made the introduction of her "second cousin" that suddenly brought Dayle back to attention.

He took her hand and leaned close to Dayle's ear, the way some men will when they share polite, public confidences with their wives' close relatives. But his words were not casual. "Never understood why a pretty woman would want to be a Pinkerton," he told her. That part was fine. He was letting her know that he knew who she was. Then he rocked back on his heels and let his eyes check the flow of her curves. That was letting her know that he knew who she was in an entirely other sense. Dayle straightened in spite of herself. It had been a while since a man had made her feel awkward. She hoped, at least, that he appreciated her pinched waist.

"A girl needs a little excitement," she answered,

thinking as much of Lotta smoking as her meeting his gaze. Not that looking him in the eye did any good. It was clear that he expected to own pretty much whatever he saw, and she'd just fallen into his domain.

"Excitement," he repeated. "The right man ought to be excitement enough." Then he chuckled at his own comment. There was such a familiarity in his manner, he must have thought they'd plunged past the usual barricade of polite conversation and come to complete agreement, but Dayle didn't like the undertone in his voice. He wasn't bantering. He believed a woman lived for the right man.

"Did I tell you that I know Allan Pinkerton?" he now asked. "Had dinner with him in Chicago last time I was there."

Dayle shook her head. No question, Garrick Bateman was a master at taking the upper hand. She was a local operative assigned to his wife. He was the wealthy, powerful client for whom she worked. But that wasn't enough for him. He had to let her know that he knew the founder of her company—the legendary Mr. Allan Pinkerton. He wanted to make sure she understood that. She wondered why. Surely he had more important people to impress, larger concerns. She risked a glance in Lotta's direction. She was chatting with some of the other theatergoers.

Turning back to Mr. Bateman, Dayle muttered something she hoped was vaguely appropriate and then edged away. An instinct for self-preservation had flared inside her. She didn't like this man right down to the male smell of him that still lingered near her ear.

He wouldn't let her go. He took her elbow, propelled her a step forward, and introduced her to the next person they met. He described her as his wife's cousin from Boston who was quite expert at "light tailoring and alterations." He spent the next few minutes introducing her to all sorts of people that way. She couldn't figure out why. She could only hope no one would actually ask her to do any light tailoring. Sewing was not her best skill. She'd only gotten by when she worked for the circus because costumes were rather haphazard creations anyway. The worst of it was that she hated feeling as if she was the latest bauble Garrick Bateman had gotten his wife. Still, she managed to smile and return the expected niceties.

All part of the job, she told herself.

Meanwhile, she watched Lotta circulate among the theatergoers, appearing to enjoy herself. There was a definite ease in the way she handled herself. She was the queen of White Springs, whether Lotta thought of herself that way or not.

"My wife's a beautiful woman when she's happy," Bateman said.

Dayle was startled enough to turn and engage his eye. Something in that gaze made her realize that he meant what he said. He, too, had been watching Lotta from across the room and clearly approved of what he saw: a beautiful woman laughing lightly and fanning herself with perfect ladylike style.

Dayle looked at Lotta again and wondered if Garrick had ever seen his wife when she was truly happy, not this perfected public presentation but the fuller flush with which she'd leaped from rooftop to rooftop in Chinatown. Or smoked that cigarette.

It was then that Bateman's previous words came back to her like a haunting refrain: "The right man ought to be excitement enough." And it hit her. He knew Lotta wasn't happy. By his own standards, if he was the right man, he ought to be the sum of Lotta's existence, her complete happiness. Yet his wife wasn't happy.

No wonder he bragged that he gave his wife everything, indulged her every whim, even to the point of supporting the very "lady's adventure charity" that could upset the balance of the whole territory. Dayle

The Lady Pinkerton Gets Her Man

shook her head and wondered what other lengths he would go to in order to leave Lotta no excuse for her own unhappiness.

Dayle was still puzzling that one when the play began. From what she could see, the acting troupe was an especially fine one, professional, good. The costumes were colorful, and the painted backdrops could almost transport the viewer to distant Denmark in a time long ago. But Dayle had a hard time keeping her attention on the play.

Nothing on the stage came close to the drama she was watching in the box.

Garrick Bateman continued to be solicitous of Lotta in a showy way, playing his role of the indulgent husband for the benefit of any and all who happened to glance in their direction. He hovered over Lotta, touching her shoulder one minute, her back the next. He stood for her when she stood, held her chair for her when she sat.

"Did you notice my wife's new dress?" he asked everyone who stopped by their box. "Latest in fashion, if you care about such things," he added.

It was obvious he cared. He cared even more that everyone notice.

When the play was over, Garrick excused himself to join the other men in the smoking room downstairs. At the mention of smoking, Lotta gave Dayle a silly look and giggled behind a gloved hand. It was getting late, and she'd been sipping champagne all evening from fancy glasses small enough to suggest delicacy, unless one had several. Lotta was on her sixth or seventh.

Dayle got another herself. It was turning out to be a long evening. While Lotta continued to chat with the other ladies, discussing the performance and other topics of mutual interest, Dayle drifted to the edge of the lobby.

A few minutes later, the actors appeared in the upstairs lobby to entertain the ladies, a common practice for traveling troupes. The actor who played the ghost of Hamlet's father made his way directly to Lotta. Still made-up and looking suitably ghoulish, he created a minor sensation crossing the room. It was obvious that underneath the costume and greasepaint, he was handsome, if aged, and, of course, he knew how to be charming to the extreme. He gave Lotta his rapt attention while she gushed over his performance and how "frightened" she'd been at his "perfect portrayal of Hamlet's dead father."

That's when he told her she was "far too kind" and kissed her cheek, an action that met with a little squirm of delight. Lotta actually brought her hand to the spot he'd kissed and fairly blushed with pleasure.

Shrewd, Dayle thought. A kind word from Lotta, and he and the whole troupe would become the fashion of White Springs for the next week or two. In which case his current performance was probably the most important he'd given all evening.

Having seen enough, Dayle turned and immediately bumped into the actor who played Hamlet. "Oh, excuse me," she started to say, and then realized he must have been standing there for several minutes quietly watching her as she watched the others.

Now a smile spread across his face, and she could tell he was used to getting his way with that smile. Why not? He had yet to say a word, and she was already feeling the excitement that could loosen a woman and threaten her with pure giddiness.

He sensed that, of course.

Obviously pleased with her, or maybe with himself, he opened that smile and said, "Hello."

Nothing more. Yet it was as if he'd dragged the word up from the depths of his being. His voice was deep, his eyes glimmered, he leaned closer, and Dayle knew she was supposed to stop breathing while she waited for his next utterance.

She beat him to it, dropping the tiny champagne glass over the edge of the balcony. It broke on the floor

The Lady Pinkerton Gets Her Man

below. She looked up and said, "You look like a man who wouldn't be embarrassed to share a real drink with a lady."

Not betraying a moment of surprise, he pulled a flask from his pocket and offered it.

Dayle turned away from the room and shot back a slug. It burned all the way down and felt wonderful.

"Thanks," she said as she handed him the flask.

Of course, he wasn't satisfied with that. He eyed her with a tasteful male appreciation—something much more enjoyable than Garrick Bateman's look of crass ownership. Leaning against the rail, he said, "I was watching you from the stage below."

"Me?" Dayle asked.

"You stand out in a crowd," he told her.

She laughed lightly. "I'm flattered, but I don't see why I should be of any particular interest."

He shook his head. "This is where I'm supposed to say that you're the most beautiful woman in the theater tonight. No doubt you are, but we share something else. You see, I'm quite a dedicated student of the latest in social physics—phrenology, soul semiology, anthropometry."

"Anthropometry?" she repeated. Suddenly, she was interested. Anthropometry was a system of identification based on eleven measurements. Just as tailors and hatters knew that no two human beings have exactly the same measurements, this system, developed by a Frenchman named Alphonse Bertillon, was supposedly highly accurate in identifying habitual criminals. Since making positive identification was an elusive problem in detective work, and Allan Pinkerton had rejected fingerprints as "unworkable," anthropometry had the distinction of being more promising than any other system currently available.

"How is it that you have an interest in anthropometry?" she asked.

"Actors study people in all ways."

"I see," she answered. "And how is it that you know I have a similar interest?"

"Tommy the Tube Man tells me you've read every book there is on the subject."

Dayle's heart skipped a beat.

Seamstresses, like tailors, would be familiar with anthropometry, although that wasn't her real interest. Nor was it his. At the heart of Allan Pinkerton's philosophy of criminology was the belief that criminals couldn't keep a secret, especially men who considered themselves masterminds. Like any other artist, such men wanted their work appreciated. They wanted someone who could appreciate them to know who they were. Now having met him, Dayle wondered again. Maybe the soaped tracks were nothing more than an announcement—"Here I am, try to catch me." He was that cocky.

She engaged Harry Bryant's eye.

His gaze was steady. Then slowly a smile crossed his face.

She matched it.

The idea behind phrenology, humanology, and the other sciences of social physics was that people can read character in faces; they just need to become more scientific about it. This required no science. No one survived growing up in an orphanage without honing a few instincts, and Dayle prided herself on having more wits than most. No question in her mind. The Hooded Sleeper had just announced himself to her.

6

"How do you feel about cockfighting?" she asked him. "I know where they're pitting some birds, right now."

That raised an eyebrow.

"What? You don't think it proper for a lady to supplement her purse by betting the birds?" she asked. "Hats and shoes aren't cheap, you know."

He shook his head without ever taking his eyes off her and said, "That's what I hear from the ladies in the show. They're always complaining about the price of hats and shoes. Can't say any of them have taken up cockfighting as a solution."

She was testing his limits, hoping to push him into the unfamiliar or the uncomfortable where most people revealed themselves, but she could tell immediately that this wasn't going to be easy. He was a man who was particularly sure of himself. In fact, it appeared as though he was enjoying this.

"On the other hand, I don't know," he continued.

Jerrie Hurd

"Aren't you as apt to lose money at the cockfights as make it?"

"I have a knack for betting the birds," Dayle told him. "You can put your money with me every time."

His smile widened. "Every time?"

"Every time," she repeated, and that was only a slight exaggeration.

He nodded. "I'm going to have to see this," he answered. "Nobody bets the birds with that much surety."

Dayle paused only long enough to wrap a shawl around her shoulders and excuse herself to Lotta. She might have worried about getting a jacket or something warmer, except that she knew where they were going—down by the slag heaps where there was never a chill. The slag heaps were one of the most distinguishing features of White Springs. The most menial job in the mines was shoveling out the scrap and disposing of it on those ever-glowing, huge burning mounds. The majority of what was illegal in this town went on, not under cover of dark, as in most places, but under cover of the perpetual twilight created by the burning of those slag heaps—the smoke darkening the day, the flames lighting the night, the warmth producing a little hell on earth.

By the time Dayle stepped outside the theater, he'd already engaged one of the horsedrawn carriages waiting near the entrance. He helped her in.

"By the way, I'm Harry Bryant," he said as he settled into the seat opposite her.

"I know," she answered. "You come from Pennsylvania and play Hamlet rather well," she added. "I read the program as well as watching the show."

"I'm surprised. I thought you were much too busy studying Mr. and Mrs. Bateman to notice much else."

That startled her. He hadn't been lying when he said he'd watched her all evening, even from the stage. She imagined that was quite a feat, staying in charac-

The Lady Pinkerton Gets Her Man

ter while keeping an eye on someone in the audience. He was cocky enough for it. Cocky enough to flirt with a Lady Pinkerton while he plotted bringing the whole country to a halt.

She hadn't been sure until this moment that Tommy had seen through her disguise last summer. She was sure now. Harry could have any woman he wanted, including the redheaded beauty who'd played Ophelia tonight. Instead, he'd singled her out immediately. Either he liked flirting with danger, or he thought he was too smart or maybe too handsome to get caught, especially by a woman.

"I suppose I should be flattered that you noticed."

"No, I'm sure turning heads is nothing new to you."

He was smooth. Too damned smooth. He slipped through any opening she gave him. No question. They both knew the game they were playing. She drew a breath and changed the subject. "By the way, how is our mutual friend, Tommy?"

"Apologetic. He's really sorry he didn't greet you properly at the station today. You startled him, and you know Tommy, he can be a bit temperamental at times."

Tommy had startled her, not the other way around. Still, she wasn't going to argue the point. "I know Tommy from a summer ago. How do you know him?"

"He's working for me now."

"A Shakespearean troupe needs a contortionist?"

"He's a good backstage man. Besides, he can do a great olio act if we find ourselves being pelted with vegetables because we've become overly melodramatic."

"From what I saw, you have a good company, especially Miss Valentine, the young actress," Dayle added, still testing.

He smiled. "Miss Valentine can play an equally fine Lady Macbeth, but she fancies herself to be in love with the actor who played Rosencrantz. What can I say? There's no accounting for taste."

"I suppose," was all she offered.

He let the moment linger. "If you don't mind my saying so, I think it's a little strange that Mrs. Bateman's cousin would have been working the circus last summer. I mean, a woman with rich relatives doesn't usually . . ."

"Second cousin," Dayle reminded him. "We don't know each other that well."

"That's right. Second cousin," he said, and engaged her eye. She didn't flinch under his gaze, but she did give him a point for noting that neither of their stories held up to close scrutiny.

He offered the flask again.

This time, she refused. She was going to need her wits.

A few minutes later, they left the carriage and tied handkerchiefs over their mouths and noses as they made their way between the slag heaps. Fortunately, by the time they got to the edge of the junkyard, the air was better. More wind.

The junkyard itself was an eerie graveyard of old ore carts and other metal machinery that had been cast aside to blacken with soot while rusting underneath. That eeriness was compounded by the flickering half-light and odd shadows. It was enough to disorient. She wandered a little before spotting her destination, a long, low, windowless building that had been slapped together from some of the discards. She knew it was the right place when she spotted a stocky young man with big ears leaning against the door, rolling a cigarette. He was the lookout.

For firing a gun, throwing stones, defacing a building, or cursing, a man could be fined five dollars in White Springs. But of all the crimes, short of murder, that might be committed in a mining town, "organizing" was the worst. In short, what was illegal here and required a lookout wasn't the cockfighting or the gambling or the home brew. It was a group of miners gathering in an unapproved place.

The Lady Pinkerton Gets Her Man

Miners who got together after work tended to complain, and since it was thought that complaining was the first step toward "organizing," conventional company wisdom held that miners should not be allowed to gather in unapproved places. Every man who worked underground signed a contract agreeing to that provision under penalty of losing his job and being blacklisted in any other mine. That meant that White Springs was a company town right down to the company pubs where the men got cheap beer from company bartenders while being watched by company bouncers. Of course, none of those rules applied to the Chinese. The Tong were expected to keep them in line.

Now, Dayle was about to introduce the Hooded Sleeper, the mastermind Anarchist, to the cockfighters of White Springs. Sometimes she amazed herself with her own audacity. On the other hand, she didn't know how else she was supposed to expose the man, make him show his true colors.

Dayle pulled the handkerchief off her face and called a greeting to the lookout. He immediately jumped to his feet and stuffed the newly rolled cigarette into his shirt pocket. She'd surprised him. Evidently, he wasn't expecting anyone coming from her direction, especially not a woman in an evening dress. He straightened through his hair and muttered, "Evening, ma'am," then looked past her to check Harry. Like her, Harry was overdressed for the cockfights. She saw the lookout take particular note of his fancy gentleman's shoes.

The lookout's job was to watch for police, Pinkertons, and company guards. He was also supposed to keep anyone away who might not be welcome inside. That included preachers, temperance women, and anyone deemed a "society type." Cockers tended to be a close group.

"Evening," Dayle answered. Stepping up real close, she reached into the young man's pocket and pulled out his newly rolled cigarette. "Nice job," she said as she inspected his roll. She poked the cigarette into her mouth and asked for a light.

He fumbled for a match. It was obvious his mama had taught him enough manners that he couldn't forget himself in the presence of a lady even if she'd just stolen his smoke.

"How are the birds tonight?" she asked.

"Only fair."

"Only fair" was the standard answer. Nobody ever said the fights were good. Among the men who worked the mines or in jobs supporting the mines, opinions were not offered freely. The weather was always "tolerable," the mine yield was "middling," and most didn't care enough to form an idea on much else. They might know their boss's smallest idiosyncrasy, but Jay Gould, the legendary tycoon who owned the mine, the railroad, and most of this town, might as well be God for all they knew about him. He lived in another world.

Dayle paused, giving his words enough consideration to suggest respect. Then she said, "Well, even fair birds can be interesting to bet."

He chuckled. "You must be the lady what was here the other night. I heard about you."

"Oh, really. What did you hear?" she asked. She'd come to the cockfights the first night she was in town. Less than a week ago. Not unusual. It was her experience that the men who participated in the blood sport of bird fighting generally thumbed their noses at all authority and therefore could be trusted to know what was really going on. It was the quickest way to get the real feel of a new place.

"Well, ma'am," he started, and then snorted a little chuckle. "Well, ma'am, I'd wish you luck, but from what I hear, you don't need none."

"We all need luck," she told him, and shot a glance at Harry, who was taking all this in with his own amused expression.

The Lady Pinkerton Gets Her Man

The young lookout smiled and kicked his toe in the dirt. "Before I heard about the other night, I thought ladies didn't have no luck except the kind that rubs off, if you know what I mean."

She knew what he meant. Miners were a superstitious lot. To a man, they believed in luck, the fates, devils in the tunnels. Had to. Daily, they went half a mile underground—far enough that if an accident happened, even a minor one, it was understood that the distance to the top and hope was just too far. These superstitions extended to a belief that it was a good thing to have a lady blow on your dice, hold your cards, or place your bet, but not actually play the game. It was only Dayle's obvious good luck that made her welcome, and even that was tentative.

Now the young man swallowed hard. "I don't know, ma'am. Some of the cockers were in a bad mood tonight. Problems in the mines, I hear. They told me not to let anyone new in."

She dropped some coin into the pocket where she'd found the cigarette and said, "But I'm not new. I was here the other night. You said so yourself."

He looked to Harry.

"He's not new, either. He's a traveling man. He's probably been to every cockfight in every junkyard in this country, except this one. You wouldn't want to break his record."

"That right?" he asked Harry.

The actor feigned modesty with a shrug and a coy comment. "I believe everything she says."

The young lookout hesitated a moment longer. Then he chuckled a little. "The boys are going to be real surprised. That dress alone . . ."

"I can handle them."

Harry added, "I think she can handle anything."

The bouncer chuckled more. Then he not only stood aside, he pushed the door open for her.

She was immediately greeted by the smell of sweat

and sawdust and the damp mildewy scent of the old mattresses that lined the inside walls of the shack. The mattresses muffled the crowing of the birds, and there were lots of birds. They occupied rows and rows of cages stacked four high in what was known as a "cock hotel." The light was dim except near the center of the room, which was lit by a row of kerosene lanterns hung from the open rafters. Some of the lanterns needed cleaning. They gave off smoke as well as light. Boys, too young to drink beer, had climbed into the same rafters next to the lanterns and leaned from their perches to watch the action below, while fifty or more men crowded the fighting pit in the center, slapping pants, spitting chew, and noisily calling out their bets.

They were between fights. Two handlers were standing in the cockpit showing off their birds as they drummed up business for the next match. The handlers stroked their birds and sometimes kissed their heads as they turned slowly, letting everyone take a good look. The other men shouted out wagers—some big enough to represent half a week's pay. They placed their bets on the "cowboy hat" or the "plaid mackinaw," referring to the handlers because they were more distinguishable than the birds. Then they'd look around to find someone who'd take their bet, placing an equal sum on the opponent.

In the midst of that betting frenzy, someone spotted Dayle and elbowed the guy next to him, who nudged the guy next to him. Suddenly, everyone was aware of her. A hush swept the place—not a complete quiet but a definite hesitation.

The sisters at the orphanage had not neglected the proper, ladylike aspects of Dayle's education, including how to step over almost anything without showing an ankle. They'd actually required that she practice those "skills of modesty" while balancing a glass of water on her head. Such delicacy was not the point

The Lady Pinkerton Gets Her Man

here. Knowing nearly every eye was on her, Dayle lifted her skirts deliberately high as she stepped across the threshold.

The men whistled and slapped their pants while Harry stepped aside. He clearly knew better than to upstage her at this moment. She appreciated that, because there was a whole routine she needed to go through before she could be sure they were really in, really accepted.

First, she paused, and, with a little twist of her shoulders, she acknowledged the cockers and their naughty boy antics with just the right amount of flirt in her facial expression and bosomy shimmer. Then, lifting her skirts even higher, she stepped over a dead bird that had been tossed near the doorway.

The men hooted and slapped one another.

In response to that, she dropped a mock curtsey. Giving her skirts an exaggerated swish, she sashayed up to the cockpit, turned, and ran her hand along the top edge which had been worn smooth.

The handler with the cowboy hat got so distracted that he relaxed his grip. His rooster nicked his arm with the spur strapped to its fighting leg. That drew blood and a surprised yelp. The others enjoyed that. They whooped again. Even the bird joined the fun. It stretched its neck and crowed.

"I'll bet that bird," Dayle announced. Making an exaggerated show of pulling a roll of cash from her pocketbag, she asked, "Who'll take me up on it?"

No answer.

She knew this moment. As with the entrance, there was always a pause just after she pulled her money out while the men adjusted their thinking to the idea of a woman having more than coin in her pocket. Dayle's Pinkerton wages kept her in modest style, but fortunately she didn't have to settle for that. She did well at poker and better at birds. While the men enjoyed her flirting, they respected her bankroll.

"I'll take your bet," a voice from the other side of the pit answered.

Dayle looked around. The voice belonged to John Dutton, a wide-nosed, sandy-haired man, who was one of Bateman's mine engineers—a respected job. More than that, he'd "been green," meaning he'd survived a mine explosion. The "green" referred to the fact that the gases in an explosion frequently turned men's hair and beards that color, but it had broader implications. Most men followed orders, but men like John Dutton who'd been green tended to pick the orders they followed. There was something about having been green that allowed them to get away with that.

"Thanks," Dayle said.

Dutton also gave a nod to Harry, who acknowledged the attention. Dutton's nod meant something. They were in. The noise and jostle of the fights resumed. In fact, the man next to Dayle slapped her on the back. "Good bet," he said. "I've seen that bird fight."

"Yeah, it's a ground fighter, not a flier," another added. "I much prefer ground fighters, myself."

"A ground fighter who's a cutter," the man next to him added.

That sparked a heated discussion with several other men, some of whom believed a flier had a better chance at cutting its opponent's neck and therefore was to be preferred.

Dayle took the beer offered her and stayed out of the discussion. Instead, she looked around for Harry. She didn't pick her birds by how they fought. Her technique relied on something else. It bothered her that she couldn't see Harry. She couldn't imagine where he'd gone.

She moved around the cockfighting pit bantering with some of the men, listening to others. She overheard talk of new mines opening in Idaho and good-

The Lady Pinkerton Gets Her Man

paying "sunshine jobs" down in Texas, where men were being hired to stretch barbed wire. Nothing out of the ordinary. Miners talked of other jobs, but few ever left to take one. Mining was a man killer. But some of these men were the sons of miners, the grandsons of miners. They derived their sense of manhood from knowing their backs and arms were as strong as those of the men who'd gone underground before them, never mind that they worked twelve hours a day, five and a half days a week, and were paid by the amount of coal they dug—coal weighed on company scales that the men knew were rigged. Still, they worked the mines. These were men who were proud to work beside other men.

She kept moving through the crowd looking for Harry and, at the same time, hoping to hear something useful.

The miners were mostly Cornishmen, which meant there was a surprising similarity in their height and hair color and other physical features. That carried over to a similar build of their shoulders and breadth of their stance which had been shaped by their shared occupation. She particularly noticed the men's hands.

That was a trick she'd learned working in mining towns. You could practically read a miner, like a book, from his hands. Thick with calluses and blackened with coal dust, the palms smoother and lighter than the backs, miners' hands were often more expressive than their voices. Their world was muscle and grunt. Shoulder to shoulder underground with no oxygen to spare for conversation, they gestured. Now, shoulder to shoulder over the pit, they often used the same language with surprising subtlety, and since *anarchy* was not a word that escaped many miners' lips, Dayle expected that if the socialists had been organizing in the mines, she would discover that fact first by noticing secret hand signals. That's why she was surprised to hear one young miner say with straightforward boldness, "All our troubles go away when the Chinese go away." His cohort, another young miner, quickly and vocally agreed.

Dayle paused. She sized up the pair. They both had white scarves tied around their necks, the sign of Nativists who hated all non-English immigrants, especially Chinese. Unlike Anarchists, Nativists were mostly talk—lots of talk. She questioned whether it was going to be worthwhile to join the conversation. Nevertheless, she raised her beer to the pair and said, "Couldn't help overhearing, and I wondered if the rumors are true?"

"What rumors?" the first young man asked. There was an edge of suspicion in his voice.

Dayle took a swig of beer. She wiped the foam from her lips with the back of her hand, mostly because she'd noticed the way they looked at her fancy evening attire. She wanted to let them know she wasn't as prim as she looked. She swallowed. "I hear the Chinese are getting special treatment from the pit bosses."

"No rumor. It's true," the second young miner told her. Then the two of them practically tripped over each other in their eagerness to fill in the details.

They told her about gangs of Chinese who roughed up the other miners and even stole the other miners' tools while the pit bosses turned their backs and saw nothing because the company "loved their slant-eyes." Dayle listened and found that interesting, but not exactly to the point.

"Maybe it's time to bring in the Anarchists," she offered.

"Nobody needs those Frenchies," the first told her with some feeling.

"Labor agitators are either French or Irish, you know," the second added.

"Give me Chinese before Irish," the first said with a sneer and another swig of his beer.

The Lady Pinkerton Gets Her Man

About that time, she was thankful to see John Dutton elbow his way to her side. "Does Garrick Bateman know where his houseguest spends her late nights?" he asked Dayle with a wink.

"Does he know where his mining engineer spends his?" she returned.

"I won't tell if you don't," he offered. Then his tone got more serious. "I'll double my bet if you tell me how you pick your birds."

"Woman's intuition," she answered. "You already worried about your bet? The match hasn't even started."

Dutton was not what she'd call a handsome man. He'd been in the mines too long. The color of his skin had taken on an odd translucent paleness, and his eyes were too dull. From all appearances, he'd moved beyond enjoying life, though he was still jolly enough to elbow her again and continue the banter. "Come on, you can tell me. What's your secret?"

"I look at the birds," she answered, thinking she'd never bet on John Dutton. He might have been green once, but he'd lost his fight now.

"You look at the birds?" he asked, and seemed to consider that a moment. "How do you mean, you look at the birds? What do you look for—long necks, thick legs, good eyes? What?"

She shrugged. She had an eye for the birds, that's all. There was an element of luck. She couldn't always pick the winners. But while the men boasted and bragged and spun theories about fliers versus ground fighters, she simply judged her birds the way she judged her men. Not on looks. Tall or short, didn't matter to her. Sandy-haired or dark. Small eyes or large. Foreheads that the phrenologists thought were important didn't get her attention. She noticed attitude and how they moved.

"It has nothing to do with long necks," she offered. "How do you pick yours?"

"I like long necks," he said, "and ladies with spunk. If you weren't with that gentleman, I swear . . ."

"Where is that gentleman?" she asked with a shake of her head. "I haven't seen him since we got here."

"He's in the back taking bets."

Sure enough, she found Harry in one back corner. He'd slipped off his jacket and rolled up his sleeves and was covering bets right and left. He was using a notebook. He had that much money out. He'd obviously worked a lot of cockfights.

"Keeping a theater company going is even more expensive than ladies' hats and shoes," he told her between transactions.

She didn't know what to say. This wasn't what she expected. She thought he'd use the opportunity to ask questions, plant seeds of unrest, challenge unfair mine practices, rile the men, or whatever it was that Anarchists were supposed to do. She'd given him the perfect opportunity to spread his socialist ideas with the hope that she could catch him at it.

Instead, he was making money.

She drank half her beer while she waited for a break in the talk. Then she decided that if he wasn't going to work this crowd, she would. "I hear there's been some trouble in the mines lately." She said it casually, as if she were just making conversation. "I hear the Chinese have been causing problems."

None of the men around Harry rose to her bait. The man next to her only shrugged. Another swirled the last of his beer around in his glass and said, "Just the usual from the slant-eyed bastards."

She took another sip of her own beer. Silence among miners often meant more than words. They groused loudly about small irritations but became stoic in the face of more serious difficulties. She took their brush-off as an indication that there were indeed serious problems in the mines. Everything she knew about this town indicated it was a badly mixed

The Lady Pinkerton Gets Her Man

explosive about to go off. She thought that ought to interest Harry, but he didn't even look up. He was taking bets like a common bookie. For a brief moment, she wondered if she'd misjudged him. Maybe it was only an overactive imagination that made her think he was the Hooded Sleeper.

A moment later, he leaned closer and said, "I admired the skill with which you got us in here. If you want to give up being someone's second cousin, I think you could have a nice future on the stage."

She shook her head and dismissed her doubts about him. "No thanks." Then she added, "Is there ever a time when you're not acting?"

"All the world's a stage," he quoted, and punctuated that with one of his grins.

He knew he affected her. What was it about him that John Dutton lacked, that most men lacked? She hadn't known him more than a couple of hours, and yet every time he spoke, she felt stirred.

He looked up and added, "I hope your system is as good as you say. If not, we're going to need your skill to get us out of here."

She preferred head over heart. She liked clarity, and everything about this man seemed to embody confusion—the kind of chaos that came from living by one's emotions. Yet even the head knew wisdom wasn't life, wasn't mischief, wasn't fun. She shook herself. She didn't even understand what he was doing. "I don't get it," she complained. "You're betting against my bird."

"Odds are better. You actually have quite a reputation for picking the birds. No one wants to bet the other way."

"If I'm wrong, you make a killing."

He shook his head. "If you're wrong, they'll think we're working this together."

"But if I'm right, you're out a lot of money."

"Exactly. There's nothing like losing a lot of money to make people instantly trust you. Believe me, it won't matter if we make it up later in the evening. How good *is* your system?"

She never bet a bird that was all crow. Like the man who fancied himself a lover, not a fighter, it would disappoint every time.

Men and birds of a darker, denser type were punch-drunk from having been in the fray too long. They weren't a good bet because they'd forgotten the beauty of the dance.

Nor did she care for men who thought too much or birds that took too long eyeing their opponent. The endlessly analytical were good if you wanted illumination but not if you wanted to rock the world.

Dancers were better, but not perfect. Sometimes they got so caught up in the rhythm and never got to the thrust.

The only thing close to a sure bet was the rare bird or man who arrested life with such ease it was almost as if breathing were the movement of ego. She'd underestimated Harry. He was too smart to recruit these world-weary cockfighters to his cause, but he was in White Springs, and he was the Hooded Sleeper. She knew it the way she knew he was the kind of man whose ego required breathing space—the way she knew White Springs was a prize too ripe, a challenge too irresistible.

The fight began.

The birds were bred, not trained, for the sport. Basically, a rooster would fight any other rooster it met. That was their nature. But fighting cocks were petted and pampered and then "billed" or teased ritually before they were turned loose on each other. In the tradition of the sport, the handlers held the birds in front of their chests and swayed rhythmically three times, bowing toward each other and bringing the roosters close to make them mad. For good measure, at the last moment, the handler would insert his little finger and scratch his bird's testicles. That really raised their feathers.

The Lady Pinkerton Gets Her Man

"Pit them," the crowd cried.

With that, the birds, hackles up, were set loose behind two lines drawn in the sawdust of the pit.

Immediately, the roosters flew at—and sometimes over—each other, pecking at necks, stabbing at breasts. A flash of steel and a spurt of blood meant one of the birds had found its mark. Spurs came in several styles. The ones used here were three inches long and razor-sharp. They had been fitted over the roosters' natural leg spurs before the fight. Dayle leaned over the pit. Her bird was hitting and cutting so rapidly his legs were a golden blur. The other bird was heavier. It tried once to get above. Couldn't. Instead, it went down on its tail and hooked upward. Effective. It broke Dayle's bird's wing. That wasn't good, but it wasn't fatal—at least not yet.

Any way you looked at it, cockfighting was not a nice sport. Besides being bloody, the birds died. If it didn't die in the pit, the loser would be killed by his breeder. The favored way was to tread on its head and pull up on its legs until its neck broke. A quicker way was to hold it by the head and swing it smartly around. But if it had been cut, that had the risk of covering the handler in blood.

She looked around. Many of the handlers had blood on their arms and shirts. Blood was part of the sport and probably the thing that kept most women away, although she didn't entirely understand that squeamishness. Most of these miners' wives could ring a rooster's neck, pluck it, and pop it in the supper pot without a moment's hesitation.

She swallowed. Nevertheless, she was glad she'd brought Harry to the cockfights. If the two of them were going to pursue whatever it was they were doing, it was good to keep a perspective, to understand what was at risk. This was not for the faint. The stakes were high—mines, money, power—all the things people killed or were killed for. The fact that the very nearness of this man sent a throb through her body, and he knew it, was not something she could let confuse the issue. This was deadly serious sport.

The Pinkertons had a secret bounty on the Hooded Sleeper. Any man who could annoy the agency that much had to be a worthy opponent. No question. Besides, she had her own reasons for this. Like Mary Stillman Davies, most people didn't think a Lady Pinkerton was either a real lady or a real Pinkerton. This was her chance to prove otherwise, and she wasn't about to let it slip away. Not as long as she had will and wit.

Several minutes later, both birds were exhausted enough to have lost interest in the fight.

"Handle them," the crowd cried.

The handlers picked them up and sucked at their heads to liven them up. One took scissors from his pocket and lightened his bird's plumage. He cut away most of the tail. Then they set them down again, this time on lines drawn closer together. Unless one of the birds made a killing slash, the fight would continue like that, round after round, for twenty minutes or more, until one bird refused to fight even after the handlers teased it.

The lookout had been right. The birds were only fair, and the fight was only interesting because she had money riding on it. Money and reputation thanks to Harry. The rest was easy. All she had to do was keep her head about her. Steady herself when no part of her wanted to be steady. And then get on with it.

"How are we doing?" he asked as they waited for the second round of the fight to begin.

He meant on the fight, or maybe he meant more. She could no longer tell.

"At this point, your guess is as good as mine," she told him.

7

At the same time that night on the other side of town, Daniel Suitter crouched in the shadow behind the ventilation shaft above mine number 2 and shivered. He looked over his shoulder and all around. He listened. It was a still night. No wind. The wind had died down an hour ago. Unusual for White Springs. It meant that soot from the slag heaps drifted down, teasing Daniel's nose. He rubbed it with the back of his hand to keep from sneezing.

Above him, stars dotted the sky, visible whenever the smoke drifted clear. Below him, the streets swarmed with similar dots of flickering light. Miners were on their way to work, carrying their lanterns. Daniel thought they looked like earthbound stars. He knew that they would carry the twinkle of their lights into the depths to start another shift without ever looking up. He wasn't worried about being discovered by the miners. He knew miners. He'd worked the mines all his life. Miners had a habit of not looking much beyond the ends of their noses.

At dawn, the whole town would come alive, including screeners, woodcutters, mule drivers, water carriers, loaders, unloaders, wheelwrights, coopers, carpenters, blacksmiths, and guards. Daniel hoped he and the men he was with would be through with what they were doing long before dawn. Even if not, Daniel wasn't much worried about being discovered by anyone. Except for routine maintenance, no one ever checked the ventilation shafts. In a sense, everybody in this town had tunnel vision.

Not long ago, he'd been the same. He'd worked the mines, gone to church, paid his bills. Then, one day, he woke up and knew everything was wrong, and he decided to do something about it. Having come to a life-changing conclusion didn't stop his shivers. He shivered, not because of the cold but because of the company he was now keeping.

Anarchists.

Forget rolling over, his mother was probably trying to claw her way out of her grave, spitting dirt, sucking for air, wanting to yell. At him. Old remembered ways were hard to set aside. His mother had thought Anarchists were devils, and it was hard for him not to think the same. She had been Scottish and saw devils in lots of places. Her favorite expression was, "Well, that was quite a dance with the devil." It was her way of talking about trouble. Underneath all that, she was a practical woman, who'd faced life with an unblinking sense of reality, and since she figured the devil found everyone sooner or later, she'd had no patience for anyone who caused trouble or went looking for it. Daniel had come to think of her as a good woman who'd endured too much. That's why, despite her careful training and the shivers that wouldn't leave him alone, Daniel had chosen to look for this trouble. He wanted it.

He was no Anarchist, but he'd made up his mind that he would take up with anyone who wanted to do something about the conditions underground. The

The Lady Pinkerton Gets Her Man

problem was that he knew too much. Most men only knew their own problems. Daniel knew everybody's problems.

Since he hurt his leg in an accident eight years ago, he'd taken to raising canaries for the mines. Sometimes he thought of his little yellow birds as drops of sunshine, and he wondered if they felt confused by the dark when they descended into the eternal night of the mines to serve as sentinels against the invisible, odorless, poisonous gases that could build up down there. When the canaries died, the men got out quickly. Lately, Daniel had noticed that other things had been building up in the mines, things that didn't kill his yellow birds and yet were still too deadly to ignore. That's why, three months ago, he started letting the Anarchist devils use his canary coop as a secret meeting place while he sat quietly in the back and learned about "common ownership" and "free agreements." He found the talk surprisingly fine, even interesting. He'd almost convinced himself that his mother was wrong. The Anarchists weren't devils after all. Then a couple of big organizers came to town.

The one, named Tommy, was a thin man who walked like water and talked like Daniel Suitter's canaries—high-pitched with little tweety sounds at the ends of most of his sentences. The other was always masked and wrapped in a hooded cloak. Strange and mysterious, they were like the best and the worst that he'd been taught to watch out for among hell's minions. But he'd never been sure he was in league with Lucifer until five minutes ago, when he watched that creature called Tommy turn himself into a worm and slide into the machinery that ran the ventilation fan for mine number 2. That's when the uncontrollable shivers got him.

The fact that the man-worm had been a contortionist with the circus was no explanation. It was the darkest part of the night. He would admit the light was bad, but what Daniel saw could not be explained except as some devil's trick. The creature had taken off his shoes, belt, hat, and jacket. Then the man-worm had wiggled most unnaturally, as if undoing sinew from bone. He'd literally made his shoulders fold and his hips slide past each other. He'd poured himself through the covering over the ventilation shaft. Seeing that had given Daniel these shivers he couldn't shake. But shaking or not, he was going to see this to the end.

He'd agreed to guide the man-worm and two brothers, local men who were mechanics, past the guards watching mine number 2. He'd done that. He'd gotten them around to the stairs leading up to the housing over the mine opening. He knew all the mines and all the stairs and all the guards for all the shifts, because at one time or another, he'd been to see them all. It was the nature of his business. Daniel's canaries were needed everywhere, day and night. That's why he knew too much. He'd been everywhere and seen everything.

Now he glanced all around again, looking for Pinkerton guards. He didn't expect to see any, but he was supposed to watch, so he watched. Getting four men on the roof had been easy. Pinkertons guarded the mine entrance and some streets. No one guarded the ventilation shaft. That was another reason he knew he was in bad company.

The devil never came at you where you expected. The devil and his minions knew the perfect weak point in a man or a machine. This was beautiful. When the ventilation fan broke, mine number 2 would have to be shut down. Of course, the mine owners would fix the ventilation fan, Daniel knew. He also knew that would take at least a week. To shut down one of the five mines at White Springs for a week without a single leaflet, mass meeting, or whisper of a strike was something to be admired—a real work of devilish art.

The Lady Pinkerton Gets Her Man

Daniel shivered more. Then he checked again the quickest route off the roof. Getting there was only half the job. Meanwhile, the two brothers had their mouths pressed close to the opening where the man-worm had disappeared inside. They were whispering instructions. The man-worm was supposed to find a particular rod that was about the thickness of a thumb, and then, just below where it attached, he was to file it in half. The brothers had already lowered him a rasping file.

Daniel wrapped his arms around himself and tried to stop shaking, but the more he tried, the worse it got. *Make sure you don't do the devil's work,* his mother whispered down his memory with a characteristic sharpness that made him shiver more.

"They killed Eddie," he whispered back to the darkness as if his mother's ghost could hear.

Eddie was Daniel's nephew. It was one of the quick confrontations between the Chinese and white miners that happened all too often these days. Eddie had a good room. Pay depended on how much coal a miner took out in a day. A good room meant all the difference. A couple of Chinese wanted his room. It was a strange thing how the Chinese couldn't even share the same train platform above ground, but underground they were the lords. Everyone stepped out of their way. For one thing, they were the majority underground, and they were organized. They had their own bosses and the Tong. And they knew the mine owners needed them. Eddie was too young to understand. All he knew was that it was his room. He resisted, and one of the Chinese knocked him a killing blow, and no one even asked what happened.

Daniel drew a deep breath and chanced another glance at the shaft where the man-worm had gone in. He was a clever devil. Cleverness was what made a devil. "Don't think too much, or you just might begin to believe your own devil," Daniel's mother used to tell him. But then, in another set of circumstances,

Jerrie Hurd

she'd turned around and smacked him when he didn't think enough.

Always there were dangers on all sides. In the mines, there were runaway pit cars, collapsing roofs, falling rock, flooding, suffocation, cave-ins, explosions, lethal gas. No one needed the additional hazard of gang warfare, and the Chinese had formed gangs because they were trapped themselves on this treeless plateau. The Tong wouldn't let them go, and running away was not an option. The next town was distant enough that without a horse and a map of the local waterholes, a man was sure to die of exposure before he got anywhere. It was rumored that some Chinese had already died like that. Trying to get away.

In short, if somebody didn't do something, the town and its mines were going to explode. A lot of men would die, sending shock waves out over the whole country. Daniel knew about shock waves. Literally. That's how he'd lost his leg eight years ago.

He could recall the moment with almost perfect clarity. He was loading an ore cart when he looked up and saw the swell of the explosion rolling toward him. Vivid. Time lengthened. For what seemed an eternity, he watched timbers shatter and rocks turn liquid. The sound was like the squeeze of a Scottish bagpipe. Surprising thing was that he hadn't shivered then. He'd just stood there calmly waiting for the explosion to overtake him.

Maybe that was because he hadn't had time to think. He'd thought about this a long, long time. He had other nephews and good friends in the mines. If he had to dance with the devil, he'd do it. If he had to tell his mother's ghost to go to hell, he'd do that, too. He was too old and too crippled to care about himself, but he cared about others.

Again, he listened to the night. White Springs had a mechanical hum made up of the noise of the mining machinery, the trains that came and went, and the soft whir of the air being sucked down the shaft

The Lady Pinkerton Gets Her Man

behind him. He heard the rasping file bite metal. That grating chewed its way up the shaft and blended with the other sounds. Daniel nodded with a sense of satisfaction despite his shivers. He expected that soon the whole country would be dancing with the devil, because, like it or not, he and these Anarchists had just changed the tune.

Then it happened. The rod broke. He heard the shear and the ping. Next thing he knew, the man-worm was coming up out of that shaft like smoke, saying, "Let's get out of here."

Daniel agreed and quickly pointed the way.

8

Next morning, Allan Pinkerton, a slight, aging Scotsman who still spoke with the brogue of the old country, sat at his breakfast table. He stirred his oatmeal, watched a fly circle slowly, and listened to the sound of his own voice drone on and on. He was dictating the memoirs that would become his next true detective book.

At the same time, he mentally repeated the name *Dayle Dobson* over and over. It was an exercise he did sometimes to see if a particular bit of information caught anywhere inside his head. He wasn't sure whether or not he'd ever met a Lady Pinkerton named Dayle Dobson. He couldn't remember her, but that didn't mean what it used to mean. In any case, she'd certainly sent an interesting telegram. He thought he'd remember meeting a woman with that kind of initiative.

The story he was dictating was an exciting one about how he chased Frank Reno, leader of the notorious Reno gang, into Canada. While in Canada,

The Lady Pinkerton Gets Her Man

Allan Pinkerton was nearly assassinated by a rival detective who was looking to move in on his business. He survived nearly being killed, captured Reno, and exposed his rival. Exciting, and he'd only embellished it a little. Jesse James had also stalked him once. Like an angered bear, he'd turned and begun hunting his hunter. But that was another story. He'd spin a little excitement into that tale and make it into another book. Real detective work was more a matter of tedious plodding than high adventure, but his readers didn't want to know that. That wasn't why they bought his books by the tens of thousands.

He thought Miss Dobson's information had the potential of some real excitement. Another story for his collection. He wasn't dead yet, which was to say he was glad to add another adventure to his adventures. Keep them coming.

The room was a sunny porch off the main kitchen of his Chicago mansion. It was furnished European-style in dark carved wood, the windows draped in heavy brocade. His wife's choices. He cared nothing about that sort of thing. The only decoration that mattered to him was the secretary, young and pretty. She was sitting across the table from him, and at the moment she was so intent on making quick, fine pen strokes of his words that she'd rounded her shoulders over her notebook. If he tipped his head just right, he could see down her dress and imagine the rest.

It had been a long time. He sighed. The pause was enough that the girl looked up, and her posture again became straight-backed.

"Damn," he said out loud before he could catch himself. "Sorry," he quickly added. "My oatmeal has gotten cold." He gave the bowl in front of him an exaggerated stir as if he were truly disgusted with its contents.

He was disgusted. His life had been reduced to oatmeal, long walks, cold water, and no stimulants of any kind, unless one counted the girl's bosomy prettiness. He didn't. He'd never been a window shopper. That is, until three years ago, when a stroke had left him with several annoying weaknesses. He couldn't pinch a pretty bottom, for example—not enough grip in his right hand.

"Shall I send for more oatmeal? Order a warm bowl?" she asked. Her voice was light, almost breathless.

"No, no," he said, and gave her a second glance. She was new. They'd been taking each other's measure all morning. She didn't seem to be shy. He could say that for her.

He was beginning to feel sure he'd never met Miss Dobson of the White Springs office. He remembered women who weren't shy. They were his favorites.

"It wouldn't be any trouble," the secretary continued, still talking about the oatmeal.

"No." He shook his head. "I'll just add a little of this new-fangled stuff," he told her. "That should spice it up." With that, he cut off a square of Philadelphia brand cream cheese and dropped it into his bowl.

"You put that in your cereal?" she asked with enough edge in her voice that he checked his bowl again.

The dab of cream cheese sat on top of his oatmeal, unstirred, unmelted, looking about as awkward as he felt. He'd assumed it was like butter, something to be added when you wanted a little flavor. Evidently, he was wrong. The stuff smelled like sour milk and looked like paste. He wondered what the hell he was supposed to do with it but didn't ask.

"Doesn't matter," he told the girl, and pushed the oatmeal aside. "I'm not hungry anymore." Then he made a motion with his hand to indicate that she should get back to her notebook.

"Oh, good," she said, and giggled. "It's so exciting. I just love the work." She took up her pen again. "I love your books. You've had such an exciting life."

The Lady Pinkerton Gets Her Man

Had? Had an exciting life!

Wrong choice of words, if she meant to keep the job long. He shifted in his chair and swatted at the fly with his napkin. His life *was* exciting—still. He'd founded America's first private detective agency, and now he was in the midst of making his second fortune with his books about his adventures with that detective agency. America couldn't seem to get enough of them. He'd already published twelve, at the rate of three a year, and he wasn't dead yet—a fact that his sons seemed to have equal difficulty remembering. So what if parts of his body had gone weak? His mind hadn't. He could still plot.

At the moment, he was managing several plots, and not just the ones in the novel. Besides the dictation and ruminating on how he was going to handle his sons, he was considering what he was going to do about Miss Dobson's telegram. It had come late the day before and fretted him ever since. He touched his breast pocket, feeling the stiffness of the telegram there.

What Miss Dobson reported was true. He already knew about the situation there and had taken measures. After all, he couldn't credibly claim to be "America's chief detective" if he let the whole country teeter on the brink of a disaster, threatened by a crisis in a place most people hadn't even heard about, White Springs, Wyoming.

He shook his head, remembering having made a stop there several years ago. It was hard to think that wind-whipped train stop mattered. It did. It mattered enough that he didn't think he could let one of his local operatives muddle in it, even if she'd shown initiative and he liked clever women.

His secretary shifted in her seat. He tipped his head, thinking first things first. Right now, he intended to put the better part of his mind to work on how to get his new secretary to bend over her notes again. He missed the view.

Jerrie Hurd

He started by talking faster, thinking that might encourage her to lean forward over her work, but he hadn't spoken more then a couple of sentences when his son William threw open the breakfast-room door and stood there looking over the situation. Clearly taking in the secretary's bosomy prettiness, he glanced from her to his father and back again while a knowing disgust took over his expression.

The older Pinkerton straightened. All his children sided with his wife when it came to domestic matters. That meant they assumed the worst of him. Then he chuckled to himself. Given his current weaknesses, he supposed he ought to be flattered. Thinking nasty was about as exciting as it got for him these days.

Meanwhile, William swayed slightly, and, out of habit, his father glanced at his watch. It was early—not yet ten in the morning—and his son had obviously already had more than one drink. His weakness.

William took three steps, steadied himself on the credenza, and then slapped the end of the breakfast table with enough force to make his father's oatmeal bowl jump. However, the cream cheese didn't move. It was truly paste.

"You're sending McDougal to Wyoming Territory to chase those bank robbers hiding out in the Hole-in-the-Wall?" his son asked, so loudly that the secretary cringed. "And what am I supposed to do? Drink afternoon tea with Mother? Or maybe I'm supposed to proofread your books. Oh, but you don't need me for that assignment, either. Last time I checked, we had four men on the payroll who do nothing but write those damned books for you."

Allan Pinkerton made a gesture toward the secretary. Her eyes had become round as she watched this confrontation. "Four men and a female secretary," he said, correcting his son on that point since he didn't want to admit the other one. Drinking afternoon tea with his mother was exactly what William was expected to do.

The Lady Pinkerton Gets Her Man

"Excuse me, four men and a female secretary," William repeated with an exasperated upward look. "God, when did the Pinkerton Detective Agency become a pulp fiction factory?"

The older Pinkerton poured himself more coffee. He assumed the question was rhetorical. His son was a handsome, dark-haired young man with a full mustache and good shoulders. At sixteen, he'd been a spy for the Union Army. One of the best. No surprise—Pinkerton had taught him. But since the war, nothing seemed to satisfy. Now the drink was beginning to show in the color of his skin.

Allan Pinkerton took a sip of the coffee and slowly shook his head. He'd promised William's mother that he'd keep an eye on the boy and try to keep him from the bottle, and contrary to everyone's opinion of him, he tried not to disappoint his wife in everything.

"It would make sense for me to sit around the office if I actually ran the office, but everybody knows I don't even make the field assignments, do I?" William went on.

The older Pinkerton shrugged. Another rhetorical question. Even the secretary, who was now biting her lip, knew that Allan Pinkerton, founder of the Pinkerton Detective Agency, still made the field assignments. He wasn't dead yet.

"You're the one who taught me to shoot and ride and hang around places where I might hear things—important things. Now what? That's not Pinkerton enough for you?"

The older Pinkerton sipped more of his coffee and slowly shook his head. He'd done his best to teach both of his sons the detective business, but neither had caught the vision. Robert, his younger, couldn't see past the ledger book. Accountants managed money; they didn't make fortunes. William, on the other hand, couldn't see past "law and order." He seemed to think the whole business was shooting and riding and catching criminals. If that was the case, the biggest crook in the country was Jay Gould, and they were working for him.

"You've got the whole country believing your yellow-back literature," William continued. "You ought to see the flood of romantics that apply daily wanting to be Pinkertons because of those damned books. What's the point? McDougal is the only operative who chases outlaws these days. The rest of us guard the mines and the railroads of the rich."

Allan Pinkerton had no answer for that. His son had never been poor. He'd never had to face the fact that no one made two fortunes defending the downtrodden. Didn't matter. His son was wound up to the point where he didn't require any response. He kept right on.

The older Pinkerton gave a glance to the secretary. She was a picture of pretty puzzlement. She didn't understand William as he did. William was too Pinkerton, which was to say, he was about as trigger-happy as his father. Only difference was that William wore his trigger on his hip, not in his pants. He preferred to shoot his way out of a situation. That's how he'd made a mess of trying to bring in Jesse James a few years ago. As a result, that baby-faced kid was known as the one outlaw who'd gotten away from the Pinkertons. He supposed that didn't matter now that a fellow outlaw, Robert Ford, had finally got him earlier that year—shot him in the back. But times were changing. Shooting wasn't the answer it used to be, except maybe in Wyoming Territory, and it was a fact that his son didn't seem to need the bottle when he was working in the field. He'd tried to explain that to his wife and gotten nowhere. She wanted to know that he was safe and being looked after. Safe was relative. More than anything else, William needed to be safe from himself.

Pinkerton noted the same fly as before making another slow circle. Family business was an annoyance. He could think his way through almost anything

The Lady Pinkerton Gets Her Man

but family affairs. They were always a tangle. There was no logic, and no matter what he did, it was always wrong or judged so.

"I'm better than McDougal. You know that," his son continued.

Pinkerton took a deep breath and let it out slowly. He was going to have to let William chase bandits until he got sober. He could see that. Besides, if all hell broke loose in White Springs, Wyoming, Allan Pinkerton preferred to have his son off in some remote corner of that state rather than mucking up things that required more subtlety than a six-shooter. However, first he wanted to make sure they understood each other about this current business.

When his son momentarily ran out of words, Pinkerton nodded toward his secretary, who'd lost her giggle, and said, "I dictate. She takes it down. The hired men write from her notes. Then I edit. It's the only way I know to produce three novels and a quarter of a million dollars a year from a sick old man. I won't have you disrespecting my books. Paying work is paying work."

His son sank into a chair at the end of the table and heaved a heavy sigh. "Have you heard anything I said?"

Allan Pinkerton sipped his coffee. His son refused to hear anything *he* said. The only real reason to chase a common criminal into Canada was reputation. The Pinkertons had the reputation of never giving up, and reputations of that sort had more range than a rifle. It was rumored that would-be train robbers checked on which trains had Pinkertons on board. They worried about Pinkertons even when there wasn't one within a hundred miles. Beyond that, who knew how many would-be robbers had turned to honest work rather than take on the Pinkertons?

Furthermore, his son didn't appreciate the real importance of the novels. Those books and their popularity meant Allan Pinkerton was writing his own definition of detective work and its role in modern crime fighting. Not insignificant considering that Congress had recently questioned whether or not private detective bureaus were "contrary to the spirit of republican institutions—a danger to democracy." Those fancy politicians could debate all they wanted. There was no turning back the clock.

The first armed train robbery in the United States, which happened at Symour, Indiana, on October 6, 1866, changed law enforcement forever. Crime that cut across jurisdictions required police unburdened by boundaries. From that moment on, America needed more than national postal inspectors and local sheriffs. Allan Pinkerton and his Pinkertons had stepped in to fill the void.

He had been thinking about White Springs the same way long before receiving Miss Dobson's telegram. Local strikes were one thing, but labor troubles that could take the whole nation hostage were going to require new thinking, a different response. Miss Dobson's message only made the need for that response immediate.

"We had spies and bounty hunters in this country until I invented the 'private eye.' Any respect you get for being a Pinkerton you owe to my books," he told William, not that he expected him to appreciate the depth of that accomplishment. He just hoped repeating the idea might have some effect.

William shook his head. "Yeah, yeah, I know. You've only said that a hundred times, but someone has to do the real work once in a while."

"Then go to Wyoming," he told his son. He wanted to say more. He wanted William to stop drinking and start thinking. He wanted to tell him that he loved his mother. In any case, whatever had happened between him and William's mother was no reason William couldn't be happy. Why had he taken all that womanizing nonsense so personally? But Allan Pinkerton didn't have those kinds of words in him. He never

The Lady Pinkerton Gets Her Man

even sweet-talked the ladies. He'd just spun his stories and let their imaginations seduce them. Even this giggly new secretary already thought she was a confidant who needed to protect and care for him and make sure his oatmeal was warm. How was he supposed to resist that?

"Go, then," Pinkerton repeated. "There's a train leaving for the West in an hour. Just don't tell your mother that you're going. I'll handle that."

William studied his father. He was having trouble thinking past the double shot of whiskey he'd put back before coming there. But he couldn't talk to his father like this if he weren't half drunk. Not that it mattered. Drunk or not, he'd never been able to out-talk, out-think, or out-maneuver his old man. He'd stopped trying years ago. But he wasn't stupid. His father never gave in this easily.

He looked at the girl again. He wished he knew the old man's game. He'd never tossed a ball around like a regular dad. From very early, he'd taught his sons to notice things, sneak, and spy. He made a game of it. He planted clues and dared them to discover secrets. All the while, he had to have known it was inevitable that they would discover his secrets. He didn't think it was the girl this time. She was pretty and clearly his father's type—big tits. But he suspected the old boy was finally past all that. Not by choice. He'd worn out the equipment.

No, there had to be some other reason why he wanted William out of the way. He didn't need to know why. He just needed to get out of there. Wyoming was fine. The only problem with Wyoming was that it wasn't quite far enough to get away from his father's books. They were everywhere.

He stood up from the table. "Who's going to tell McDougal that I'm replacing him?

"You are."

"Fine. Then he'll want to know if you approved. I can't give an order that's not questioned."

"Tell him I approved."

William made his way to the door. The literary reviews of his father's books were generally good. His detective ability, as described in the novels, was craftlike and admirable. However, there was never any mystery to the stories. The criminal was known from the beginning. The emphasis was on the relentless pursuit in the name of upholding the Pinkerton reputation. God help anyone who tangled with the Pinkertons, he told his readers, over and over.

What a family motto!

William paused and turned. His father was sipping coffee again. Never a big man, he seemed smaller since his stroke. Fortunately, the lasting effects had been minimal. He walked with a cane and favored one arm, that's all. His mind was certainly still keen, yet his books unwittingly created sympathy for the criminals being pursued. They became the romantic, luckless, helpless outlaws who had no hope of escape, ever. Marked men. He couldn't imagine his father making a mistake like that in his younger years. He'd gotten old.

"Say good-bye to Mother for me," he said.

"Sure, I told you I would," the old man said without looking up.

William paused and thought again about questioning why his father had changed his mind and was sending him to Wyoming, but then he didn't. For that, he'd need another drink.

That same morning, Dayle went looking for Lotta's cook. She had decided she was not going to spend the rest of her stay in White Springs jumping at every strange noise. She had to know if the Tong were after her or not.

She found Woo in the herb garden behind the

The Lady Pinkerton Gets Her Man

Batemans' kitchen. He was bent over a particular plant, picking the blossoms and dropping them into a cloth bag that hung from his waist. He brought every other handful to his nose, testing the scent, sometimes rubbing the petals between his fingers.

Dayle waited a moment. She didn't recognize the herb or what he was doing. That didn't matter. She stepped closer and was about to speak when Lotta's two children rounded a corner of the house. Fair-haired boys, ages three and five, they were chasing white-winged butterflies, a common insect. The air was fairly dotted with them. The boys' nurse, a large Italian woman, followed. She came into sight, carrying the jackets the boys had discarded despite the morning chill.

Dayle stepped out of the way. The children were that intent on their activity. The cook straightened and also watched the children. He nodded as if he found the children a happy diversion. Then he picked up a stick. Out of the corner of her eye, Dayle watched him clear cobwebs from the porch lattice work with the stick, rather deftly twirling them around the end. Then he turned and just as deftly plucked one of the white butterflies out of the air with his stick.

Its feet caught in the cobweb, the butterfly flapped its wings in place almost like a mechanical wind-up toy attached to the end of a pole. Lotta's younger son stopped in his tracks, watched the flapping of the butterfly for a moment, and then laughed an excited burst of wild merriment. The cook bowed and offered the stick with its captured prize to the child. He drew back, but then curiosity got the better of him. He took the stick in one hand and gingerly reached out with the other to touch the captured insect's wings. He laughed at the sensation.

Meanwhile, his brother complained, "Where's my butterfly?"

The cook wordlessly prepared a second stick. Only this time, he didn't catch the butterfly himself. He gave the cobwebbed stick to the older boy and pointed to where several butterflies danced in the air near a row of hollyhocks. The boy gladly ran off to catch his own.

It was a decidedly pleasant scene. Dayle took a deep breath and was filled with the smell of the garden's fall flowers and the cook's fragrant herbs. She enjoyed hearing Lotta's children still laughing from somewhere around the corner of the house. Then there was the soft whinny of a horse from the stable in back, and for an instant, it all seemed perfect.

Then she shook her head. It was all illusion. Gardens like this one didn't belong in White Springs, because White Springs didn't even have potable water. Every drop had to be transported by train from the Green River some fifty miles away. A little engine pulling four tanker cars ran back and forth, day and night. Right behind that thought came a strange sense of the dislocation that she imagined was Lotta's life. She lived in a fabricated, made-up place—a doll's house in the desert.

Dayle shrugged off those thoughts and turned back to the cook.

"That was nice—catching the butterflies like that," Dayle told him.

He bowed. "Very nice children. Boys. They come to the kitchen sometimes."

"They're very lively," Dayle commented, and then cleared her throat. "I wanted to talk to you about what happened in Chinatown the other morning."

"I only cook," he said, and bent back to his herbs without looking at her.

She took his reluctance to talk as a bad sign; still, she had to know. She tried a different approach. "Mrs. Bateman and I . . ."

Woo held up a hand to stop her.

"In China it very important every house have garden. It place where fox fairies play."

"Fox fairies?"

"The imps, the little troublemakers."

"Why would you want a place that attracts mischief makers?"

"Not attract. Fox fairies never go away. You can never kill them. You must live with them. If you don't give them garden, they live in your cupboard or under your bed. Better to have in garden."

"I'm afraid I'm not familiar with fox fairies. I was wondering . . ." Dayle stopped. "Are you saying I'm a fox fairy—not worth the trouble of the Tong's notice?"

He actually laughed. "Mrs. Bateman is fox fairy. You are worth less than the butterfly caught on the stick. We all have our places."

Dayle flushed. She didn't enjoy being compared to an insect, even if it was some relief to know the Tong didn't think she was worth choking.

"And what's your place?" she asked Woo, but he didn't answer.

She couldn't help herself. She was still feeling annoyed when she arrived at the Pinkerton office a half hour later and immediately sensed something was different. She knew it the moment she opened the door. It was enough to make her pause and shift her sewing basket from one arm to the other. The tone of the background buzz was different. There was a higher level of bustle. A couple of operatives bumped into her on their way out, not because they didn't see her but because they were in such a hurry.

Something had happened.

In the time it took to cover the distance from the front door to the main desk, she overheard enough talk to know that a train had been robbed and mine number 2 had closed down. The business about the mine didn't bother her. It wasn't unusual for a mine to close for a day or two if there was trouble in the tunnels, meaning water or gas or a minor cave-in. She saw no reason to give that talk much interest. Something about the train robbery, however, grabbed her attention. If she understood right, the San Francisco Pinkerton office was blaming the White Springs Pinkerton office for money that had been discovered missing when the train arrived there.

That didn't make sense.

The agent at the main desk was sufficiently distracted that he didn't notice Dayle for about ten minutes, which was fine with her. She stepped to the side and stood there shifting her sewing basket from one arm to the other while she listened. When she realized the men behind the desk were talking about Allan Pinkerton coming to White Springs, she couldn't help being amused, knowing her telegram had probably played a part in that decision.

"He wants to know about the Anarchists in White Springs," one agent said. "Only there aren't any."

"The soaped tracks was a diversion," another explained.

"You mean someone robbed the train while the engine was spinning its wheels? That doesn't seem sporting," a third commented.

Dayle agreed. Train robbers usually dropped a tree across the tracks and boarded with guns drawn. Soaping the tracks and simply letting the engine spin while slipping aboard seemed too easy. At the same time, she felt a certain sense of satisfaction. She'd always been sure that the Hooded Sleeper would never be satisfied simply to announce himself.

The conversation continued. "Nevertheless, that's what it was. A train robbery, nothing more."

"Certainly not the beginning of a socialist revolution," the first agent added.

"Anarchists," another returned with a tone of incredulity. "The main trouble with Anarchists is that everybody wants to blame them for everything."

Besides finding all that interesting, Dayle couldn't help noting that while the Tong didn't think she was worth killing and no one at the desk seemed to care

The Lady Pinkerton Gets Her Man

how long she stood there, Allan Pinkerton had obviously thought her telegram was worth some attention. It was with some sense of satisfaction that she thought she knew why.

The reputation of the Pinkerton Detective Agency rested on two pillars: the fact that no one ever got away with robbing a Pinkerton guarded train, and the fact that no one had ever organized a successful strike at a Pinkerton-guarded mine. If she understood the current talk, both were being threatened. No wonder Mr. Pinkerton had taken her message seriously, she told herself.

Then something about a heated argument going on in the back caught her attention.

"Things like that don't just break," someone said. He meant something having to do with mine number 2, Dayle realized, and now wondered if the closing of that mine was more significant than she'd originally thought.

"Everything breaks sooner or later," someone else answered.

"I'm telling you, it looked like someone took a rasping file to that ventilation shaft rod."

"How? A snake couldn't get down that shaft to that rod."

Tommy the Tube Man, Dayle thought.

"It's going to take two weeks to fix," the agent in the back continued. "They have to get a foundry back east to fashion a new rod and fittings."

"Mine number two is going to be closed for two weeks? Just like that?"

Without a strike, Dayle thought. Harry Bryant, alias the Hooded Sleeper, America's most wanted Anarchist, had closed one of the five mines in White Springs within twenty-four hours of arriving in town, and he hadn't even been present when it happened. He'd been with her. She couldn't help being impressed.

When the agent at the desk finally got to her, he was

in no mood to argue about anything as inconsequential as shirts. He simply told her she could go on up. She climbed the stairs to her boss's office and found only one agent sitting in the bullpen, chewing tobacco. He had his arm in a sling.

"Where's everyone?" she asked.

"Guarding every piece of machinery in town," he told her. "There's been so much excitement, I'm surprised the boss has time to worry about the repair of his collars."

"Life goes on," she answered as cheerily as she could. "What happened to your arm?"

"Dislocated my shoulder. Long story. Has to do with a mean horse."

"Sorry to hear that," she said.

"Keeps me from guarding machinery."

Thuzla Smith rose out of his chair the moment he saw her. No greeting. He started in immediately. "Who else do you send telegrams? The president of the United States? How about the ambassador to China? Or maybe the queen of England? I'm sure Her Majesty would love to know all about White Springs, Wyoming." He was so upset that he pounded his fist into the top of his desk for emphasis as he talked, and his face had taken on such a particular color that Dayle thought she ought not to aggravate him. On the other hand, she wasn't one to back down easily.

"Sorry, but I thought somebody ought to know that the Anarchists have moved in here."

"Anarchists? Forget the Anarchists. I've got a train robbery to worry about. Or haven't you heard about that?"

"I heard," Dayle told him. "I just don't understand how a train can get robbed here and nobody discover that it's been robbed until it gets all the way to San Francisco."

"Yeah, well, that's something I'm going to take up with the San Francisco office," he told her, "because

The Lady Pinkerton Gets Her Man

that's exactly true. There's no way that train could have been robbed here unless someone walked through walls or slid down a stovepipe."

Tommy the Tube Man, Dayle thought again, and suddenly she knew why Tommy hadn't wanted to see her at the train station. He hadn't gotten his nickname for no reason. Part of his circus act included "pouring" himself through successively smaller tubes. For him, a stovepipe was easy.

Meanwhile, Thuzla Smith was going on and on about her telegram to Mr. Pinkerton. That seemed to be the thing that most concerned him. "I'm sure you're familiar with the story of the boy who cried 'Wolf'?"

"What? Do you think I'm the girl who cried 'Anarchist'?"

He shook his head slowly. "Something like that. I don't know how you're going to explain your way out of this one." He paused. Then he harrumphed and added, "Well, maybe you won't have to."

"What does that mean?"

"Wear a low-cut dress," he suddenly said.

"I beg your pardon?"

"You heard me. Wear a low-cut dress. You can be sure he took your telegram as an invitation."

Dayle stiffened. She'd heard that Allan Pinkerton liked the ladies. She'd heard worse. She'd heard the Lady Pinkertons called "Mr. Pinkerton's whores." She hadn't put much stock in that. She'd heard the sisters at the orphanage called "the pope's whores" with the same kind of invective, and she'd known by the time she was six years old that wasn't possible. The pope was in Italy.

"I don't think Mr. Pinkerton has to come all the way to White Springs, Wyoming, to see a woman in a low-cut dress," she told Thuzla Smith in a no-nonsense tone.

His face reddened at that. Then he slumped into his chair and rubbed his chin. "All right, all right, but you're the one who made him believe there are Anarchists in White Springs. You got anything to show him when he gets here?"

She hesitated. If she told Thuzla about Tommy the Tube Man and her other suspicions, she doubted he would believe her. At the very least, he'd ask too many questions she couldn't answer. He'd want to know how closing mine number 2 for a couple of weeks changed anything or, for that matter, how robbing a train furthered the cause of "workers' worth." Anarchists were not usually common vandals and thieves.

"All right, you win. I think I'll wear that low-cut dress," she told her boss. But she wasn't exactly thinking about Mr. Pinkerton. Harry was the man. If she had any doubts about him being the Hooded Sleeper, they were gone now. She couldn't put it all together well enough to understand the scheme completely, but she was willing to bet when the last piece fell into place, Harry was going to have the whole country's attention. Harry was the kind of man who never did anything small. She'd done all right last night while he'd all but cleaned out the cockfighters.

"Good, but don't make it too interesting. Soon as he looks the place over and doesn't find any Anarchists . . ."

"I get the picture," Dayle told him.

9

The next day happened to be Sunday. There was a town picnic. Everyone went. Halfway into the afternoon, Harry found himself standing in the shade of a tall cottonwood with eight other men who were sharing a bottle and taking turns tossing horseshoes. Bored with the conversation, he leaned his shoulder against the tree trunk. One leg kicked over the other, his hands in his pockets, he watched Mrs. Bateman greet what passed for society in this Wyoming outpost.

More accurately, he watched Miss Dobson being repeatedly introduced to the ladies of White Springs—the ones who hadn't been to the theater the other night. After seeing her at the cockfights, he couldn't help thinking she was probably as bored as he was. Maybe more. The ladies weren't passing a bottle back and forth.

The picnic was being held near a hot spring three miles out of town. The occasion was the welcoming of a new mining engineer and his wife to the area, and since White Springs had no parks, they'd all driven their carriages out to this oasis, which was distinguished from the rest of the countryside by a patch of long grass, the smell of hot mineral water, and the shade of five trees. The only trees within miles. A small band of local musicians was playing the usual repertoire of popular tunes with a Sousa march thrown in from time to time to keep things lively.

Harry was there because he'd promised Mrs. Bateman "a little entertainment." For that reason, he'd brought two members of his troupe who didn't mind dressing as clowns and juggling when they weren't playing Rosencrantz and Gildenstern. He appreciated the members of his troupe who had versatility—something highbrow, something lowbrow. He watched as the two of them mingled amongst the ladies, attracting attention with their baggy costumes and false noses.

Mrs. Bateman also attracted attention with her every move. Not the same thing. She practically oozed that old-family Bostonian rightness that distinguished the truly elite from the would-be chic. Her husband had obviously married well. However, for originality Harry preferred Miss Dobson.

He'd been surprised by her the other night. For one thing, she was prettier than Harry had expected. More than that, he could appreciate a woman who knew her own mind and savored a little adventure. The beauty added to the sport, if *sport* described their current involvement.

Harry still hated Pinkertons, still considered them nothing more than hired hooligans, but he thought being a Pinkerton was an interesting choice for a woman. Ambitious women had to be creative in the way they made something of themselves, he knew. Being a whore was too cheap and nasty. Being a thief was rootless and dangerous. Farming a homestead was backbreaking and sucked the life out of any woman who gave herself to dirt. Being a milliner or a seamstress or a schoolmarm was too ordinary and promised nothing more than genteel poverty. Becoming a rich man's wife was the worst choice of all, if Lotta Bateman was an example. A woman might as well sell her soul. But being a Pinkerton? Well, he could appreciate the possibilities.

He watched a moment longer while Dayle made the rounds at Lotta's side, doing and saying whatever it was that "second cousins" did and said at events of this sort. He expected Miss Dobson was quite unflappable in any situation that mattered. This one didn't, and therefore he sensed a stiffness in her that he certainly hadn't observed at the cockfights. She wasn't entirely comfortable with the ladies, he realized. That amused him.

In fact, the more he watched, the more he found that awkwardness endearing, and he thought that if he was a real gentleman, he'd excuse himself and rescue her, but he didn't. He also thought it wouldn't hurt for her to be sufficiently desperate when they finally got around to each other. Besides, it would soon be his turn at horseshoes, and Harry had as good a tossing arm as anyone, if he did say so himself.

Meanwhile, Garrick Bateman was relating a joke. He was no storyteller. He rushed the punch line and then slapped the back of the fellow next to him. It was that backslapping gesture the cued the laughter. Harry only smiled. He had too much respect for delivering a good line to reward that kind of poor performance. The other men had more reason to want to flatter Bateman. They laughed and jointly commented, "Good one" and "I like that."

From his expression, it was clear Bateman believed the flattery and thought himself a jolly fellow. He was that easy to read. The man had added weight and a better cut of clothes, but he really wasn't any different from the first time Harry met him.

That was years ago. Harry had been nothing but a

kid standing in the shadow at the rear of his father's mining office when a younger, thinner version of Garrick Bateman had burst in—gun in hand, two gun-toting henchmen at his side. Harry would never forget the moment. It was the instant he first knew fear—real fear. He imagined Bateman would struggle to remember the incident, even if it was brought to his attention that he and Harry had met before. He'd been doing Jay Gould's dirty work for so long, Harry imagined that such incidents blended in his memory.

Now Garrick Bateman dressed and talked like a western aristocrat. But he still walked with the swagger of a hired gun. From what Harry had heard, he ran his town with a similar lack of finesse. Old habits were hard to overcome, Harry imagined.

Then someone called out that it was Harry's turn. He dropped those thoughts. He straightened and rubbed his hand down his pant leg, drying it. Then he picked up the horseshoe and measured its heft.

According to the Pinkerton handbook, there were two types of criminals: those who were mentally defective and therefore could never fit into the normal social order, and those who were social or gentleman bandits who came to crime by belief or circumstance. They were the more dangerous and harder to catch. The first were an aberration, the second overthrew governments. Harry represented the second type. As such, Dayle found him fascinating, especially since he'd been watching her every move from the moment he arrived at this picnic with his driver and his clowns.

His attention was enough to make her self-conscious. She found herself fussing at her clothes, straightening and smoothing, something she rarely did. Still, that would have been fine if the other women hadn't also noticed and begun to whisper.

"I believe that gentleman has an eye for you."

The Lady Pinkerton Gets Her Man

"More than an eye. He's practically ogling."

"How exciting."

Lotta was the worst. She touched Dayle the way some women do when they want to share a confidence and whispered, "He's certainly handsome."

The tone in Lotta's voice suggested more than an appreciation of the obvious. Matchmaking rolled off her words, and Dayle wondered at the peculiar leap of fancy that tempted most women to imagine attachments in even the most casual couplings. Without offering any comment, Dayle watched Harry raise his arm in triumph as his horseshoe ringed the post, and she had to admit there had been a time when she'd ached to speak the words *my fiancé, my love,* or, for that matter *my anything*. Attachments were what an orphan lacked most. Then she'd grown up and come to appreciate her lack of attachments. She was free in a way few women were.

"Don't you agree?" Lotta asked, giving Dayle another nudge. "Come on, you have to think he's good-looking."

"He's a charmer," Dayle admitted.

"Oh, yes," Lotta added too readily.

Dayle hadn't meant *charmer* in a complimentary sense. She found Harry too charming, too suave. She didn't trust him, but then she hadn't trusted Harry Bryant from the moment she first laid eyes on him, and Lotta, by contrast, hadn't stopped gushing. She still talked about his "inspired performance the other night," and she hadn't seen him at the cockfights. That was the man's real "inspired performance."

"Don't you just love his hair?" one of the other women now offered.

His hair was a little wild, meaning every strand hadn't been greased with hair oil and slicked back in what was the current popular style for men. That gave him a boyish look. However, Dayle was sure that was practiced. She suspected Harry Bryant was not a man who was casual about anything even when he seemed casual. On the other hand, she had to admit his blue eyes, strong body, and the dimple near the left corner of his mouth were hardly things a man could feign. He did have his natural accoutrements.

"Handsome and more than a little mysterious," another of the women added as if she couldn't let the subject go without comment.

"Oh, the mystery of the man is the best part," Lotta added, so quickly that Dayle gave her a glance. "Traveling men always have a delicious sense of mystery about them, as if they've seen things."

Lotta always looked as if she were posing for a portrait or some scene to be rendered by a Sunday painter. At the moment, her hands were clasped delicately at her waist, and her head was tilted to the exact angle needed to shade her face and still show off her wide-brimmed hat with its ribbons and bows.

"What do you mean?" Dayle asked.

"Oh, nothing. I imagine too much. My grandmother didn't advise travel. She thought too much travel turned the blood gypsy. That's probably just an old wives' tale, but there is something different about him, and I think it must be because he's a traveling man."

Dayle wished that the women would all go back to simpler topics, recipes, their children, the price of sausage, and leave her and Harry alone. She tried changing the subject by mentioning she'd recently read *Pinocchio,* the popular novel that was all the current rage. One of the women answered with some feeling that if lies made long noses, the lengths of some prominent protuberances would be enormous. However, when she failed to elaborate on that, no one else took up the subject.

The women were all about Lotta's age except for the young engineer's wife. She was a new bride. The others were mostly young mothers, their lives wrapped around the problems of children and husbands and households. That was the real reason Dayle

The Lady Pinkerton Gets Her Man

found it hard to talk about the same things they did. She had no experience in any of those areas. Not even childhood memories.

While the men played games, the women mostly remembered better places and fussed with the food. There was lots of food—bowls and bowls of salads and covered dishes arranged on long tables that were really wooden planks balanced on barrels and covered with cloths. A pig turned on a spit. Ice cream was being churned in a tub, and what seemed remarkable to Dayle was that none of that took care of itself. Covers had to be kept on the dishes, and flies had to be kept off the same. Servants had to be watched and children tended. Meanwhile, the women were full of advice for the engineer's new wife on how to order various household goods. None of these "high-society" families ever shopped in the local mining company stores. It was frankly admitted that the goods there were shoddy. Only miners' wives whose husbands were paid in scrip shopped there, and then only because they had no other choice.

These women had other problems. All of them were concerned with staying in fashion. Any decent woman had to get out of Wyoming at least once a year to see what people were wearing, it was agreed. Under all this conversation was the understanding that no one stayed there. White Springs was never "home" to people with enough social standing to own their own carriages and employ servants. At most, it was a necessary stop in their husbands' careers. Real society, real life was elsewhere. And, of course, none of their children ever attended school in Wyoming. Their children all went east to board for the winter months.

Even talk of Lotta's success with her latest adventure charity wasn't enough to distract. Dayle suspected it was because most of the ladies couldn't admit to an interest in anything Chinese. They much preferred discussing the prospect of a handsome traveling man taking an obvious interest in Lotta's widowed second cousin.

"Better be careful with that one. He probably leaves a string of broken hearts everywhere he goes," a woman with a wide mouth said.

"No, I think you ladies are not paying enough attention. That amount of looking is more than flirting," an older woman now said. "The man's truly smitten, I tell you." Then, turning to Dayle, she added, "You best be careful."

That was the last thing Dayle intended. The sisters at the orphanage had been telling Dayle to "be careful" or "be good" or "be still" most of her life. She'd figured out before she was old enough to look anyone in the eye that such advice mainly served the advice giver who didn't want to be inconvenienced by a girl, especially an orphan girl. As near as she could tell, there was never any real advantage to being careful, good, or quiet, and she certainly didn't intend to handle Harry with any such modesty. However, she did have enough good sense not to try and explain that.

Fortunately, the conversation flowed on without her having to say anything.

"Oh, but I have such wonderful children," the wife with the wide mouth said, "and my husband and I were very much in love once, you know."

"My Wally depends on me," another woman said. "When a woman has someone who needs her . . ."

"Oh, same with Steven. I'd follow that man to the ends of the earth," the engineer's new wife said.

"White Springs is the ends of the earth," three of the others chimed in together.

That was followed by shared laughter.

"Truth is, I wouldn't trade my daughters for anything," another suddenly added, sobering everyone again.

"Oh, me, either. My children are my life."

Dayle knew what the women meant. They envied

The Lady Pinkerton Gets Her Man

the excitement, the blush of what they imagined was new love. Didn't matter. These women could ooze as much matchmaking in their tones as they wanted; Dayle was a Pinkerton. Getting her man had a whole other meaning.

Still, having endured all that conversation left Dayle more than ready when Harry wandered over several minutes later and finally rescued her. He greeted the ladies, causing one to giggle. Then he offered Dayle his arm. She took it. Together they strolled through the tall grass toward the hot spring.

"I think I like you better at the cockfights," he told her quietly, but not quietly enough for her. She glanced over her shoulder to see who might have overheard.

"Sorry, I'll try to be more discreet. Didn't know you valued your reputation as the second cousin. Are there a lot of rules about how a widowed second cousin should act? I mean, besides not being seen at cockfights?"

"I'm sure I couldn't name them, but there are rules for everything," Dayle told him.

"Hmmm. My fault is that I assumed we weren't the sort who gave a damn for a rule if it could be avoided."

"Exactly what sort are we?" she returned.

"The sort who prefer cockfighting over horseshoes," he quipped, rounding the conversation to where they began.

They engaged in that meaningless banter, implying much and saying nothing, while making a complete circuit of the meadow, strolling arm in arm like the most conventional of couples. When they returned to the tables, most of the men had joined the women. By then, Garrick Bateman had obviously had too much to drink. His gestures had become broad, his voice too loud. Suddenly, he slapped the top of the table with one hand and shouted, "I'm going to sell that bay mare! I should have done it a year ago."

Dayle had no idea how the conversation had gotten to that subject, except that Garrick Bateman had probably picked the topic. He dominated any conversation, and from what she'd been able to observe, he had an opinion on everything. Not that anyone paid much attention. Most folks nodded at anything Garrick Bateman said and then let it go at that.

Dayle didn't imagine anyone would have paid much attention to this comment, either, except for Lotta's reaction. She gasped and brought both hands to her face. "Not Sophie," she breathed, referring to her horse by name.

That stopped conversation.

Obviously taken somewhat off guard, Garrick paused but didn't seem to think he could back down. "It's an embarrassingly mediocre horse in all ways," he told Lotta and everyone in earshot in his usual blunt fashion and too much voice, obviously expecting that to end the argument.

He didn't have enough voice to draw attention from Lotta's face. She went from being startled to being stricken. Tears welled in her eyes. "But you gave Sophie to me for our first anniversary. I love that horse."

Anyone else, even half drunk, would have melted under that tone of voice, but Garrick's pride had been touched. He turned, and, in tones that barely slid past his teeth, he told Lotta that he would not be embarrassed and it was embarrassing for him to ride next to her when she was on that horse. He ended by saying, "You can't fault a husband who wants his wife to ride in better style."

By then, the general embarrassment was such that people seemed to need to find things to do with their hands. The ladies lifted covers and checked their hot dishes; the men fumbled with hats and found places to scratch.

Lotta was holding back tears, but barely.

That's when, to everyone's surprise, Harry spoke

The Lady Pinkerton Gets Her Man

up. "I don't know. That bay mare strikes me as a fairly fine horse, maybe even a first-rate one."

The whole crowd shifted. A couple of the men stepped away from Harry as Garrick turned and gave him an odd, half-startled look. Clearly, he wasn't used to being challenged. He seemed completely unsure of how to take it.

Dayle wasn't sure what to think, either. Taking on Garrick Bateman in public was a lot different from cleaning out a few cockfighters in the middle of the night. She hoped Harry knew what he was doing.

Bateman decided to take it as a joke. He laughed. "I should have known a man of the theater would take a lady's side. But, believe me, that's not the same as being a lady's man." Then he laughed more, as if he thought he'd said something particularly witty.

Harry waited. When Bateman's humor seemed to have wound down, he said, "I'm serious. I'll wager that I can ride that bay mare well enough to beat your black in a quarter-mile race."

"You can't be serious," Bateman snapped back. "My black is from a prize Kentucky bloodline. It's the kind of horse my wife should be riding," he added in an appeal to the crowd.

Harry shrugged. "Mark out any track you want."

Dayle looked around at the other picnickers. She could tell by the looks they exchanged that most of them were enjoying this. Meanwhile, Bateman shook his head. It was because of the crowd that he couldn't walk away and simply ignore this challenge. Yet he obviously considered racing a crackpot idea.

Harry continued, "If the bay wins, the lady gets to keep her horse. It's obviously a pet, and if it wins, it's obviously a good horse."

"I tell you, you don't know horses. It's not the same as the theater," Garrick said again, trying to dismiss the whole thing. "That bay couldn't beat my black if I gave it a head start."

"Well, then, if the bay loses, you give it to me.

Jerrie Hurd

Simple. You don't want the horse anyway. Why not dispose of it with a little flair—lose it in a race. I may not know horses, but I do know showmanship."

It was obvious from the shift in his expression that Garrick Bateman thought he understood. He thought Harry was offering him a sporting way out of what had become an embarrassment. Rather than sell the horse, he would lose it in a race that would publicly prove his point—that the horse was inferior.

More than relieved, he liked the idea. He guffawed loudly and slapped several of the men near him on the back. "I'm supposed to give you the horse if it loses!"

Harry nodded, shrugged, seemed to join in the humor.

Bateman now slapped Harry on the back. "I swear, you are an audacious fellow, but I think I like you anyway." And he laughed some more.

The picnickers, now having decided how to react, joined in.

"Let's do it," Bateman announced when the merriment subsided. "Quarter-mile race, and the loser keeps the bay."

Harry gestured his acceptance with an open-handed wave toward where the horses were hobbled.

"What do you think you're doing?" Dayle asked him in a whisper.

"Embarrassing myself," he answered. "The man is that damned easy."

Sure, Dayle thought, *only who is worrying about Lotta?* The woman was fingering the fringe on her shawl the way she'd worked the buttons on her jacket when they were hiding in the coal bin. Dayle looked around, wondering if anyone else appreciated how close Mrs. Bateman was to hysterics. Dayle was sure the only thing keeping her from slipping into a bout of silent screaming was the little bit of hope Harry had offered, and Dayle couldn't stand it.

Harry was not the man to pin your hopes on. She'd watched him operate at the cockfights. No knight in shining armor, he was the gambler, ever ready to turn a quick bit of money. In this case, she figured it was by selling Lotta's horse when it lost.

Anyone could see that Lotta's overfed, overindulged bay mare was no match for her husband's sleeker, fitter, finer-bred black. Knowing that, Dayle didn't appreciate Harry making a game of dashing Lotta's fonder desires. The woman didn't deserve that.

Big surprise.

In the end, Lotta was probably the only one who was not completely astounded when Harry and the bay mare won. At which point, he presented the horse to her with all the theatrical flourish of a knight in shining armor. One look across the crowd, and Dayle could see that at that moment he was every woman's hero.

Dayle had to admit she was amazed herself. After watching the impossible happen, she found it hard not to appreciate Harry. More than that, she found herself reevaluating him, thinking she'd misjudged. She now felt fairly sure he'd planned from the beginning for Lotta to have her horse. The new question was, why?

On the surface, it was easy to understand. An afternoon spent in the company of Garrick Bateman was enough to make anyone wish for his comeuppance. He was claiming that his horse stumbled at the last minute. He told Lotta she was "lucky, that's all." No one disputed his claim, although whispered rumor had it that Bateman had been a little too drunk to ride the race well.

Dayle didn't believe the stumble or the drunk. She figured the race came off exactly as Harry had planned it. Never mind the fact that he kept shaking his head and saying he didn't know what happened. She saw through him. Underneath that self-effacing modesty, he was so satisfied with himself he fairly reeked with smugness. She knew because he was wearing the same half-smile as when he had pocketed considerable change after the cockfights.

What amazed her was that he'd applied his considerable talents to saving Lotta's horse when that meant nothing to him. He had no reason to expose himself like that. In fact, considering his larger plans, she wondered at the wisdom in his embarrassing Garrick Bateman unless smugness was his fatal fault. She wondered if he thought he was so smart he could get away with anything, including toying with his enemies. Of course, the other picnickers didn't see it that way.

The men secretly admired Harry's bravado in taking on Bateman. The women gushed at his gallantry. Dayle didn't believe in gallantry, nor was she ready to trust Harry.

When the picnic and other festivities were over, he offered Dayle a ride back to town in his carriage. Of course, she accepted. Any woman there would have walked a mile on her knees for the same opportunity. He was that much the hero, not to mention the fact that his carriage was the best that could be rented in White Springs. It was a sleek black surrey with an extended roof and fancy oiled canvas curtains that could be rolled down in rain. It had two passenger seats upholstered in the tufted, overstuffed style that was currently popular. And it came with a matched team of horses, a driver, and fancy fringed lap robes. He was smug to the point of being almost insufferable, but he knew how to do things in style.

He helped her into the carriage, and she saw the woman with the wide mouth bite her lip. So did the young engineer's wife, when they pulled away. The driver worked the horses to a nice, even trot. Harry settled back in the seat facing her.

"No one expected you to win that race," she said, thinking the obvious was a good place to start.

"His horse didn't stumble," he told her.

"I never thought it did," she answered.

The Lady Pinkerton Gets Her Man

Now that they were alone, his self-satisfaction rose to the surface like a sweat, and, to her surprise, she found that vanity endearing, even arousing.

"In my opinion, he wasn't drunk, either," she told him.

He liked that. Still wearing his funny half-smile, he studied her for a long moment.

She didn't flinch under his gaze. In fact, she reached up and undid the fastening on one of the carriage curtains. It dropped with a thud that seemed to startle him.

There was no hint of rain.

He cocked his head. "My, my, what will the driver think?"

"He'll undoubtedly assume you're getting a hero's reward," she answered.

"I'd have left earlier, if I'd known," he told her.

She doubted that. He'd enjoyed the adoring looks from the women, the appreciative nods from the men. Why not? "And missed the fun of seeing Garrick Bateman squirm? You should have seen his face when that bay mare won."

"Good, huh?"

"Good," she told him, remembering how the horses had run neck-and-neck most of the distance. If anything, the bay had been a little behind. Then, right at the end, it was as if the lighter-colored horse took wing. It leaped forward just in time to cross the finish line decisively ahead of Bateman's black. Now, she shook her head and decided it was time to up the ante in their little game. He was feeling smug enough that he might give himself away. She smiled. "I'm afraid you tipped your hand back there. After that display, you can't deny that you're a champion of lost causes."

"Lost causes?" he asked.

She nodded. "Anarchy, labor agitation, the hope of mounting a strike in White Springs. Now, there's a lost cause. No one thinks that can be done. Or what about robbing a Pinkerton-guarded train and expecting to get away with it?"

He tipped his head back and laughed. "I don't think anyone has ever accused me of championing a lost cause before. I didn't lose this one, did I?"

She dropped the second carriage curtain. "You mean to tell me you don't believe in the rights of the worker?"

"Do you?"

"I'm not the hero of the day."

Again he studied her. She felt him weighing the situation, struggling with something deeper than their banter and the heat of the moment. He shook that off with a smile, wide now, wide enough that she thought he might swallow her.

"Did I tell you that I went to school with William Pinkerton, Allan Pinkerton's older son? We're drinking buddies. His redeeming quality is that he hates his father."

"You know the Pinkertons?" That surprised her, but she tried not to show it. Garrick Bateman had also tried to impress her with the fact that he'd dined with Allan Pinkerton. She was beginning to think she was the only one who hadn't met one of the Pinkerton family. That was soon to be remedied. For now, she smiled and asked a second question. "Who else did you go to school with? Or was there some reason why you thought I'd be particularly interested in William Pinkerton?"

He chuckled and shook his head. "Oh, yes, I forgot. You're the widowed cousin."

"Second cousin," she corrected. If they were going to keep up their charade, she thought they might as well be accurate.

"Second cousin," he repeated.

"And thank you," she now said.

"Thank you for what?"

"For saving Lotta's horse. I truly wanted you to do

The Lady Pinkerton Gets Her Man

that for her. I didn't think it possible at first, but then . . ."

"Why?" he asked.

"Why what?" she returned.

"Why did you want her to have her horse?"

"Because it was hers."

"Exactly."

"What do you mean?"

He rolled his eyes upward as if the answer ought to be obvious. "Somebody needs to tell bastards like Garrick Bateman that they don't own everything. They can't buy and sell whatever they want, whenever they want."

Something in the tone of his voice betrayed more than common feeling. He was on the edge of something.

"Go on," she encouraged.

But he didn't. He paused, breathed deep, and then engaged her eye again before he told her she was a "most engaging woman."

"Engaging?" she returned. "Thank you for not insulting me with common flattery."

"Like telling you that you're beautiful or that a man could get lost in your dark eyes?"

"Exactly."

"I'll try to remember not to say anything stupid like that."

"Please," she returned, and dropped the third curtain.

He got the fourth.

The inside of the carriage took on a closeness not unlike ducking under a blanket. Same dim light. Same warmth. Same concentrated scent of just the two of them. The sway and bump of the carriage's movement made her fumble when she reached for him. She had to pause and slide forward on her seat before she could run both her hands under his jacket and down his belly, where she tugged his shirt end free.

He caught her hands in his, turned them over, and began kissing her fingertips one by one.

Enough of that.

She pulled her hands free. With one hand, she coiled her fingers into his hair, deliberately tangling as she pulled his mouth hard against hers. She wanted no tender taste of him. With the other hand, she felt for her pocketbag, where she always carried a gun and a pessary. She thought of it as being prepared for anything.

"It's all in how you ride," he whispered.

"How do you ride?" she asked.

"Simple rules, keep your balance, minimize the bounce, move with the animal . . ."

"Don't depend on the reins or grip the horse with your knees," she completed his list for him. "I know the basics. That isn't how you won the race."

He paused. By then, they'd worked past most of their outer clothes. "How did I win?" he asked her.

"With surprise," she answered. "The horses were a pair—used to being ridden together. His horse never knew it was a race until you whipped the bay mare into a lunge at the finish. It jumped ahead before the black had time to react. It was all in the surprise."

She sensed him pull back. He didn't like that she'd guessed his trick. Again, he looked at her for a long moment. She worried that maybe they wouldn't get past the sparring and initial groping. She wasn't in the habit of seducing men, but she'd gone after him because he was so full of himself, so smug and irresistible, she thought he needed to be taken down a notch. More, she wanted him to know he couldn't handle her the way he handled that mare, the way he handled most situations. This was her game, her bet, her ride, her surprise.

But something changed. It was as if when he pulled back, she was drawn in. She hadn't counted on that. Suddenly, she wanted him so much she thought she

The Lady Pinkerton Gets Her Man

might rip off the last of her clothes and beg if he didn't make a move.

Steady, she told herself way down where the quiver was growing. *Steady, steady, steady,* she hummed, because throwing herself at him wasn't the same thing at all.

When the hesitation had stretched long enough that she was sure he was going to reach for his pants, he didn't. He reached for her cheek, and she thought with some amazement that even in the tenderest of moments he challenged her.

Really challenged her. After one stroke down her cheek, he reversed himself and reached for his pants. He didn't need to tell her that he'd taken control of the situation—that he was not the kind of man who could be easily taken in. His smug smile said all that and more.

She quickly pulled on her blouse, tucked it in at the waist, and resumed her seat as if nothing had happened.

10

That evening, in the middle of the first act, Harry Bryant stepped offstage with maybe two minutes before he had to go on again and found Tommy the Tube Man waiting for him. Harry braced himself. Tommy was not the type who ever related good news.

In fact, he looked like a specter of gloom. His complexion was colorless, his eyes and hair the shade of charcoal, his nose hooked. He was wearing black pants and a black sweater and had perched himself on top of a wardrobe trunk, looking for all the world like some harbinger of the apocalypse. His high-pitched, squeaky voice only added to the effect.

"Pinkertons are the wolves of society," he said without any preliminary greeting. "Organized enforcers who hunt in packs and prey on the weak. They love to bring down the lone individual who dares cry out against the injustice of regulation. Government and its henchmen, known as the monopolists, couldn't exist without them, and, as everyone knows,

The Lady Pinkerton Gets Her Man

the female of the species is always the more dangerous."

"What are you babbling about?" Harry asked.

"I told you. She's never not a Pinkerton."

"I assume you mean Miss Dobson."

Tommy nodded. "She's searching your dressing room right now."

Harry gave a glance in the direction of the backstage area and wondered what he should do. It wasn't the first time the question had occurred to him that day. Onstage, the actor playing Polonius was speaking. Harry's cue was coming up. There wasn't time to think, much less do anything. It didn't matter, he decided.

"She won't find anything," Harry said, and picked up the sword he needed for his next appearance. "Where have you been, by the way? I could have used some help at the picnic, you know, entertaining the ladies and listening to the local gossip."

"You had too much help, if you ask me."

"What does that mean?"

Tommy cocked his head. "Everyone knows about you and Miss Dobson. You couldn't leave her alone, could you?"

Me leave her alone? he thought, and started to say as much before he caught himself. There was a time when he was thirteen years old and a neighbor girl stole a kiss when he wasn't looking. That was nothing compared to what had happened in the carriage that afternoon. But he had left her alone, not that he expected Tommy or anyone else to believe that.

"What exactly does everyone know about Miss Dobson and me?" Harry asked.

Tommy shook his head. "Oh, I suppose it's none of my business if you take up with a siren—half woman, half Pinkerton."

"A siren?" Harry asked. "Isn't that a bit dramatic?"

"More like right to the point. Men who listen to sirens forget everything else. They don't eat, don't sleep, don't continue with the cause. But don't mind me. I'm only out there twisting myself into all kinds of shapes, stealing and sabotaging and generally spreading chaos for you, the country, and the cause, while you've obviously got more important things to do, like taking your pants off."

Harry almost thought Tommy might be jealous.

He watched as the thin stick of a man slid off the trunk. He hit the floor with a soft thud. Nothing unusual, and yet he immediately doubled over and grabbed his knee. At the same time, his face became a contortion of pain.

Harry reached to help hold him up.

Tommy shook off Harry's hand and limped a couple of steps. Then he bent and rolled up his pant leg. His knee was swollen.

It was so bad that Harry looked away. Arthritis was the worst thing that could happen to a contortionist, he imagined. It was the reason Tommy had quit the circus with its twice-daily performances. But he refused to give up his other antics such as sliding down stovepipes to get inside train baggage cars where the money was. The man could have been a legend as a cat burglar if he wasn't such a devotee of Pierre Joseph Proudhon, the French philosopher who was the first to turn Anarchy into a mass movement. Tommy could quote pages of the man's writings.

"You going to be all right?" Harry asked.

Tommy rolled his pant leg down. "I'll be fine. I'm not the one who's flirting with the enemy."

"Surely you've heard the saying 'Know your enemy,'" Harry returned.

"Yeah, but do you want her to know you?"

Harry shrugged, but deep down he knew Tommy was right. He couldn't let himself be distracted. He'd known that when he drew back in the carriage that afternoon.

"She's searching my room?" he asked Tommy.

"That's what I said."

He drew breath and gave his head a little shake. For one brief moment this afternoon, he thought he'd turned things around and gotten to her. Obviously not.

Harry heard his cue. He raised his sword to effect his entrance. At the same time, he told Tommy, "I'll worry about Miss Dobson."

"Oh, very reassuring," Tommy returned. "Just remember, I'm the one who distributed Anarchist materials right under her nose, and she never knew." He raised a fist. "Property is theft," he said, repeating the slogan of the Anarchists.

Harry waved that off as he stepped onstage and again became the indecisive prince of Denmark.

"Right under my nose?" Dayle asked, stepping out of the shadow to seize Tommy by the shoulder with one hand while she pressed the shortened barrel end of her .44 against his ribs. "I think you overstate yourself."

There was no hanging on to him. Tommy immediately wriggled out of her grasp, whirled, and might have gotten away, but Dayle cocked the gun, and he'd played enough poker with her to know that she never bluffed. He also knew about her gun. Any woman who played high-stakes poker had better be armed. She'd used that gun to get them both out of a particularly nasty scrape once. He backed up until he was flattened against the theater's back wall. Luckily, she managed to keep the gun, modified to fit in her pocket and good only at short range, poked firmly between his ribs.

"What do you want?" he squeaked.

"To talk," she answered. She hadn't expected to find anything in Harry's dressing room. She had expected that Tommy would know if she showed up there, and that he would try to warn Harry. Tommy was protective of people he considered friends. He didn't have many. He could be that obnoxious. Even now, he glanced toward the stage as if he thought he might yell in that direction or something. But then he seemingly decided against that course of action.

"Talk about what?" he asked.

"Why did you want to tell him I'm a Pinkerton? I mean, where did you get such a notion? I'm sure I must have mended more trousers for you than any other circus performer in America. Costumes aren't meant to bend the way you do."

"Most women don't play poker the way you do."

"Or bet the birds," she added. "I thought we discussed that. No one can live decently on what a seamstress makes. However, it's well to appear to be gainfully employed."

He gave her a smile. "We had some good times traveling with the circus. But I'm not with the circus anymore. Got arthritis in my knees. Got arthritis everywhere, but the knees are the worst." He bent over the gun in his chest and started to roll up his pant leg again.

"I saw," Dayle told him. "Sorry about that, but I wanted to talk about anarchy. I mean, I thought we'd traveled enough places and played enough poker that we were friends. If I remember right, I've gotten you out of a scrape or two, loaned you money a time or two. Now I discover that you were holding back? You never told me how much the cause of anarchy meant to you. Enough that you're willing to steal from a Pinkerton-guarded train? Isn't that what I heard?"

Now he shook his head. "You heard wrong. It's these open rafters." He glanced upward. "All that space distorts the sound."

"Sure, and I suppose you were discussing this afternoon's picnic. I just wasn't listening."

"I was saying how the working class haven't got anything. But they got hands. All they got to do is put their hands in their pockets and they got the capital-

The Lady Pinkerton Gets Her Man

ists whipped. All the workers have to do is organize so that they can put their hands in their pockets at the same time. When they get their hands in their pockets, there won't be room for the capitalists to get theirs in there. That's what I was talking about."

"Right. Now you want me to think you're an Anarchist. I guess that's better than being a common thief."

"Besides, you saw my knee. You said you saw my knee," Tommy now complained. "I can't bend myself like that anymore. Nobody seeing my knee is going to believe I could be sliding through tubes anymore."

"Sorry about your knees," she repeated. "The thing I don't understand is why."

"Why what?"

"Why rob the train? Why break the ventilation machinery? The train robbery caused more trouble in San Francisco than here, and the ventilation fan will be fixed. What's the point of doing those things? Is it the thrill? The love of danger? I want to know why he's doing it," she said, and thumbed in the direction of the stage. "We both know he's no idealist hoping to return the world to some mythological golden age of freedom that preceded the rise of government."

"You've read Proudhon?" Tommy interrupted. His face actually brightened.

"Indeed," she returned. "But reading it and believing it are two different things, which is exactly my point. I'm guessing that Harry Bryant is motivated by something a bit more practical."

To her surprise, Tommy now smiled broadly. "You read the newspaper today?" he asked. "Not the one they print around here, but a real newspaper?"

"No, what's in it?"

"Only the usual quote from Mr. Jay Gould telling the public to be damned. He eliminated a mail train that wasn't making enough money, and when a reporter from the *Chicago Daily News* asked if the train shouldn't be run for the public good, Mr. Gould told him that he worked for his stockholders. Then he suggested that if the public wanted the train, they ought to pay for it."

She wasn't following this.

He explained. "The public already paid for that train. Taxpayers paid for every mile of track. The Union Pacific was financed by a twenty-seven-million-dollar loan from the U.S. government, not one penny of which was ever paid back."

Dayle shrugged. "I still don't get it."

"Jay Gould forced Harry's father out of the mining business. Same attitude. Didn't give a damn. Forced him to sell because you can't have a monopoly unless you own it all. His father's mine was small, but it was his father's life. He killed himself after that."

"I see," Dayle returned. Behind her, she could hear Harry delivering his lines. He was good. He could almost make her believe the problem was a mother's incestuous, overhasty marriage, not Wyoming coal mines, Jay Gould's American empire, and an arthritic contortionist who spouted Anarchist propaganda. "But you still haven't told me why you wanted him to think I was a Pinkerton? What did I ever do to give you that impression? I'm sure I don't play poker like a Pinkerton."

He was too sure of himself. "Give it up," he returned. "I knew you were a Pinkerton all the time you were working for the circus. There's always Pinkertons working the circus. I get so I can smell them. But you've met your match with that one." He thumbed in the direction of the stage. "He's motivated by something far more primal than anarchy—revenge. He wants revenge for what Jay Gould did to his father. He wants it bad enough he's waited for years, watching for just the right time, just the right place."

The Lady Pinkerton Gets Her Man

"Revenge?" she repeated.

He smiled. "Yes, revenge—one of the great human motivators. Thing is, revenge is terribly intimate. It's a lot like taking a lover. He's only playing with you. Jay Gould is his real dance partner, if you know what I mean."

11

Next morning, Harry Bryant woke with the sensation that someone was in the room. He sat up and blinked his eyes into focus, thinking for a moment that maybe Dayle had returned to search his things again.

He was a little disappointed when he found William Pinkerton sitting at the dressing table, squinting into the mirror while he smeared red stripes on his face, like Indian war paint. A saddle and a half-empty bottle of whiskey sat on the floor beside him. Spotting Harry in the mirror, he swung around and flashed the wide, engaging grin that had made him such a popular school fellow all the years Harry knew him.

"How do I look?" he asked.

He was dressed to fit his face—buckskins, a hip holster, boots, spurs. "Fine, if this was a Wild West show," Harry told him. He pushed back the bedcovers and asked, "What in hell are you doing here?"

"That's a fine greeting for an old friend."

The Lady Pinkerton Gets Her Man

Harry shook his head. "Sorry, but I can't say I expected to see you in White Springs."

"Why not? The Pinkertons have more men assigned to White Springs per capita than any place on earth. Did you know that?"

Harry knew that, but he shook his head as if amazed.

William continued. "The illustrious Pinkertons have become paid guards. We watch mines and trains and some of the best brothels in Chicago. My father takes a particular interest in those."

Harry stood and pulled on a dressing gown. William Pinkerton was one of the most affable men he'd ever known—fine athlete, good sport, loyal friend, witty jokester. He was also completely obsessed with his father, particularly his father's infidelities. William's every conversation, almost his every comment, came back to the famous Allan Pinkerton and the fact that he couldn't keep his pants on. For that reason, Harry made it a practice not to encourage the subject.

"So what's with the war paint?" he asked instead.

William looked in the mirror again and traced one long smear with his left forefinger. "Can't think that I've ever worn greasepaint or played the stage." He sat up straighter and crossed his arms over his chest in the pose photographers preferred for famous Indian chiefs. "Must be something to become a different person every night—the king, the fool, the Indian chief." He relaxed his arms and made an expansive gesture. "You like living like this?"

Harry glanced around the dressing room. It was no better or worse than a hundred others he'd known. It was the custom for traveling actors to room in the dressing area behind the stage of the local theater. That's why the dressing rooms were usually furnished with cheap beds and kerosene stoves. Harry had been on the road so long he didn't think about it anymore. He could sleep anywhere.

That wasn't what William meant, a fact he quickly

clarified. "I don't mean the room. I mean the stage. Do you like the performing life?"

Harry nodded and pulled up a chair. He liked everything from the smell of greasepaint to the sound of applause. William was right. It was never dull playing the fool one night, the king the next. Harry even liked the limited baggage that came with traveling. William's problem was that he could never go far enough to get away from his father unless it was to the depths of a bottle. He might have wished otherwise for his friend, but who was he to wish William other circumstances? Obsession with his father was what separated Hamlet from his more common friends, Rosencrantz and Gildenstern. When it came right down to it, passion, a single focusing obsession, might be all that mattered. Everything else was marking time. He was even willing to concede that it might be better to be obsessed with the wrong thing than to have no obsession at all. Much as he hated Pinkertons, he figured being a Pinkerton was what made Dayle a fascinating woman. It certainly was what made William a brave man. William had been in more gunfights with real bullets than Harry wanted to know about. With that thought, Harry reached down and helped himself to a swig of William's whiskey.

"You know, if you've had enough of playacting, I could give you some real drama," William continued. "You could join me."

"Join you?"

William nodded. He picked up a cloth and began wiping the makeup from his face. "You know, I think I was born the wrong time."

"Why do you say that?"

"The West is running out of outlaws."

Harry shrugged. "Can't say I've noticed any shortage of crooks."

"Crooks, sure, but crooks are not outlaws. Crooks juggle the accounts or figure out how to cheat the stock market. Outlaws ride horses and pack guns and

The Lady Pinkerton Gets Her Man

hole up in remote hideouts. I'm on my way to a place called the Hole-in-the-Wall. It's a red rock canyon south and west of here. Real remote. There's a gang of train robbers operating out of there. I've hired a tracker and put together a posse of men. I'm going to ride after them the way the Pinkertons used to chase robbers before they became company-paid guards." He paused and chuckled. "Trouble is, when I catch them, there's going to be one less gang of outlaws in the West." William sighed and shook his head with an exaggerated motion. "Somebody finally got Jesse James."

"I heard," Harry said.

He'd also heard about William's misadventure trying to capture the James gang. Several years ago, he'd tracked the James brothers to their mother's house and surrounded the place. Then, according to the published reports, the Pinkertons heaved "Grecian fire" through a window. Grecian fire was a smoke bomb that was supposed to force the gang out. Something went wrong. Instead of smoke, the bomb exploded. Jesse's younger brother was killed; his mother was maimed. She lost an arm. Jesse and Frank got away under cover of the explosion and the following excitement. It was said that William began drinking after that. Really drinking. Harry had tipped more than a few glasses with William back in their school days. That was not the same as showing up early in the morning with an already half-empty bottle of whiskey.

"How about some coffee?" Harry asked.

"Think I need it?"

"Couldn't hurt."

William raised his bottle of whiskey. "To coffee," he said, and took a swig.

Harry got up and lit the kerosene stove. When he turned again, he saw that William had pulled out his gun and was loading it with bullets. His friend had an inordinate fascination with guns. Harry understood.

Jerrie Hurd

Immediately after that incident when Garrick Bateman had forced his father to sell, Harry had entertained his own fascination with guns. He learned to shoot, practiced daily. He was thirteen years old and dreamed of becoming a gunslinger, famous and fast, like the men in dime novels—the mysterious ones who rode into town, set everything right, and rode away again.

It was later that he figured out that guns weren't all that effective. Kill one henchman like Garrick Bateman, and Jay Gould would hire another or maybe a whole company of thugs like the Pinkerton Detective Agency. If you wanted Jay Gould to know that he couldn't buy mines and destroy lives on a whim, you couldn't play by his rules. A person had to bring him down some other way.

Harry had tried discussing those ideas with William a couple of times when he was sober enough to understand, but he hadn't understood. He was never not drunk with his own obsession—meaning his father. William would never admit it, but he was his father's biggest fan. Perhaps more than anyone else, William believed what his father wrote in his novels—all of it, the larger-than-life adventure, the gunplay.

"Any chance you'll come with me?" William asked as he put his gun away again.

Harry shook his head. "Sorry, I got this whole company of actors."

"I know, and you don't like guns, and you don't much like Pinkertons."

"Never have."

William raised his bottle. "To actors and outlaws. I like them both." He took another swig and then capped the bottle. "I don't drink when I'm in the field. Want to know why?"

"Why?"

"Because it's hell to ride a horse with a hangover." He laughed at that. Then he opened one of the

The Lady Pinkerton Gets Her Man

drawers in the dressing table and shoved his now nearly empty bottle inside. He slammed the drawer shut. "Keep that for me, will you?"

"Sure."

William stood, shoved both his hands into his pants pockets, and moved away from the dressing table. "Wish you'd go with me. We could have a good time chasing outlaws, living on beans, sleeping in bedrolls."

Harry put the coffee pot on the stove, which was beginning to be warm. "You could join me, become an actor in my troupe," Harry suggested. "That would drive your father crazy." He knew even before he said that how William would respond. They'd had this conversation before.

Right on cue, William sighed. "You know I would, but you don't use real guns onstage."

"We use real swords," Harry offered. It was the expected next line.

"Never knew the use of a sword. I can't think of a single real-life situation where a sword would have done me a bit of good."

"Well, you know I'd join you if I could," Harry told him.

"No, you wouldn't. You hate beans, you can't abide bedrolls, and I've never known a time when you didn't prefer a carriage to a horse. But what the hell, it's good to see you," he added with a smile. "Anyway, the real excitement's probably going to happen right here."

"What do you mean?" Harry asked, suddenly wondering if his friend had a purpose other than the stated one. Did he suspect Harry?

"There's a reason for having so damned many Pinkertons in this one godforsaken place," William continued.

"And what would that be?"

"Worry," William said. He shook his head slowly.

"Somebody's worried enough to pay for all that protection. Not without reason, I understand. A strike here, and we'll all be riding horses. It would stop the trains."

"White Springs is supposed to be strike-proof," Harry told him.

"Better believe it. If all those Pinkerton guards don't work, they'll bring in federal troops. Mark my words."

Harry laughed. "This is America. No one has ever ordered federal troops to take up arms against the nation's own citizens."

"Not yet, maybe. But federal troops will occupy this town before anyone will let a strike happen here."

"Maybe cooler heads will prevail," Harry offered, thinking that was exactly why he wasn't going to try a strike. Tommy was a Proudhon fan. He wanted to mobilize the masses. It wasn't until Harry came across the writings of the Russian Anarchist, Mikhail Bakunin, that he knew how to bring down Jay Gould and his empire.

William chuckled softly. "Cool heads be damned. Big money will prevail here," he said, and picked up his saddle. "You know the difference between me and my father?" he asked, and didn't wait for Harry's response. He answered himself. "I chase robbers who steal thousands. He drinks whiskey with robbers who take hundreds of thousands."

Harry never ceased to be amazed at his friend. William understood the problem, he just couldn't let himself see it. That was probably because he knew that no one pulled a gun on Jay Gould, and he was still fascinated with guns. He still thought they were the answer.

"I met a Lady Pinkerton," Harry told him, because he never liked talking to William about his father. "Interesting woman. I didn't know you employed members of the fairer sex."

The Lady Pinkerton Gets Her Man

William looked up sharply. "I don't employ females. My father does. My mother refers to them as his harem."

Harry drew a deep breath. He should have known that was not the direction to take this conversation. Not that any direction was safe. It amazed him how William always came back to that same old subject. "Anyway, you know I'm always glad to see you," he told William, hoping simply to wind things up on a positive note. "It's not often that I get to tip a bottle with a quality bastard, especially at this hour of the morning."

At that, William brought a finger up to make a point. He said with a smile, "You forget. I'm the heir, the legitimate son. The rest of them are the bastards. And who knows how many of them there are."

They were still on William's old complaint.

Harry nodded but didn't say more.

William swung his saddle over his shoulder.

"You're right," Harry added.

"Of course, I'm right."

"I mean about the Pinkertons. They used to be famous detectives, but they've become paid guards."

"Yeah, well, and what am I to do about it?"

"Fight him."

William shook his head. "You know, I'd rather chase outlaws until there's not a damned one left." Then he laughed and gave a mock salute.

"Coffee's almost warm."

"Gotta get going," William said. "The riding will sober me faster than the coffee. Besides, I've got a hired tracker waiting on me. I'm paying him by the day. You know how it goes."

"Sure."

They clasped hands, and William punched Harry's shoulder as he went out the door.

12

Dayle was going to meet Allan Pinkerton tomorrow, and she still didn't have anything that she thought would impress him. That is, besides the low-cut dress that she was supposed to wear. Actually, she thought she would wear that dress. Why not? She had all the womanly attributes that a man found interesting. No reason not to use them.

The trick was to transform that initial vulgarity into something useful. She usually managed that with some unexpected and engaging piece of information. She thought of it as changing charm into style. Charm required knowing what to wiggle and when to smile. Style required attitude and a bit of cleverness. It was the same as the difference when playing poker between knowing the odds and knowing when to bluff. Problem was, she didn't have an unexpected and engaging piece of information or a good bluff. She had an arthritic former circus performer and her woman's intuition about Harry Bryant. That's all, and she seriously doubted that was enough to convince Amer-

The Lady Pinkerton Gets Her Man

ica's chief detective that she'd stumbled onto the Anarchist plot of the century.

She was crossing Main Street, mulling that problem, when a wagon driver yelled for her to get out of the way. Still distracted, she stepped to one side and nearly collided with a rider going the opposite direction. He swore at her as he reined his horse sharply to the left. She stumbled out of the street and swore back at him.

"Such language from a lady," she heard someone say, following that with an exaggerated clicking of the tongue

She looked around, and saw an older, thick-chested man with a block of ice balanced on his shoulder.

"What do you mean? Didn't your mother ever curse?" she asked him.

"All the time," he answered, and then nodded toward his delivery wagon. "Maybe if you let me give you a ride somewhere, you wouldn't have to annoy the town's drivers. Like me, they're just doing their job."

She shook her head, refusing the ride mostly because she wasn't exactly sure where she was going.

The ice man slammed the back of his wagon shut and carried his ice into the hotel behind Dayle. She glanced up and down the street, waiting for traffic and her thoughts to clear. Something Tommy the Tube Man said had been bothering her ever since their encounter the night before. She wanted to ask him more about what had happened between Jay Gould and Harry's father. However, she couldn't make up her mind whether to look for him in the local pool hall or at the theater again.

A cold gust of wind swirled the dust in the street and blew it into her face. She shielded her eyes and shivered. Winter was coming. She even thought she saw a few dry snowflakes dancing in the air. Everyone told her White Springs was hot as hell one moment and cold as Christmas for the next ten months. She guessed that about described it.

In fact, Wyoming's main claim to fame was terrible weather. Most Pinkertons with any ambition had gone south, where it was said that there was some "real action." She supposed there was some truth to that talk as well. Billy the Kid was killed in New Mexico a year ago. Wyatt Earp, Doc Holiday, and the Clantons shot it out in Arizona nine months ago. Add to that the recent death of Jesse James, and the dime novel writers were already lamenting the passing of the Old West. She knew what they meant. Pinkertons in places like Denver had been reduced to polite surveillance and routine guard duty. She'd taken this "baby-sitting" job mainly because it was in a place still rough enough to be called the frontier.

The ice man reemerged from the hotel. "Sure you wouldn't like a ride?" he asked again.

She looked him over. He was old enough to be her father, and his face had practically settled into the laugh lines around his mouth. She suspected that meant he was boring—the type of older gentleman who told long, repetitive stories.

"You going by the theater?" she asked.

"This time of day?"

"I used to travel with the circus. I know a member of the troupe." She didn't know why she thought she had to explain herself, though it was generally considered improper, if not outright risqué, for a woman to frequent the theater except to attend performances, and then it was expected that she be "accompanied."

"Aren't you Mrs. Bateman's relation, recently come to visit?" he asked.

She nodded. She was having a hard time maintaining her disguise. White Springs was a small place. Everybody knew everybody and everything, except what was going on in Chinatown, it seemed. Dayle tossed her head back. "Yes," she told him. "I'm her second cousin who's come to stay with her for a while, and I'm on my way to the theater in the middle of the day. Does that present a difficulty?"

"I don't have a problem with that," he told her. Then he chuckled. "I like a lady with color," he added, chuckling some more. "In fact, most of the ladies who buy my ice have strong opinions about this and that and the other."

"You don't say," Dayle returned, and let him help her up onto the seat in the front of his wagon.

The man's horses, a gray and a brown, shook their heads and harnesses. They were wearing blinders to keep them from being distracted by the hubbub of the busy streets, but they sensed her. The gray stomped one foot. The brown swished its tail. The ice man climbed up onto the driver's seat next to Dayle and calmed the horses with a smooth, soft patter about how lucky they were having a lady aboard. He chuckled about that. Then he slapped the reins over the horses' backs, and the wagon started to move.

It was just as she suspected, the ice man was a storyteller. Over the clop of the horses and the clip of the wagon wheels, he told her about the years he'd worked the mines, first in Pennsylvania, then in Wyoming. She'd discovered some time ago that men who'd worked the mines were like battlefield veterans, who, having lived with danger, hardly ever talked about anything else, as if no other part of life mattered quite as much. The ice man was no different. When he wasn't talking about his years underground, he complained about how his knees gave out. Sooner or later, either knees or lungs got a miner, he told her with some feeling.

Dayle listened politely but not with her full attention. She'd heard similar complaints. Most of the tunnels down below weren't five feet high, she knew. Besides the bad air, miners worked stooped. Ten hours a day, five and a half days a week, they swung a pick and hauled rock while bent over. That was hard on knees and left longtime miners permanently hunched. Easy enough to understand, but the driver went on and on about how he believed that weaknesses in character manifested themselves in weaknesses of the flesh. He seemed to think there was some kind of moral significance attached to which part of a miner gave out first—knees or lungs. He slapped his "no good" knees several times while elaborating his theory.

"You still have friends in the mines?" Dayle asked.

He shook his head. "Wives. I know the wives of men in every mine, working every shift. They all need ice, and they buy it from me."

Dayle nodded. "What do they complain about?"

"Not the ice," he told her. "I run a fine business."

She shook her head. "I mean about the mines. I'll bet you hear all the news about what's going on in the mines, all the gossip." Dayle gave him an elbow. "What do the women say is going on down below?"

He gave her an odd look.

"Come on, you said yourself that the women have opinions about this and that and the other. I'll bet the women know more about what's going on down under than their husbands. They talk. Compare notes. Air their complaints."

He chuckled at that and slowly nodded. "Yeah, you know that's right. They do know more."

"What do they say?"

"They're upset about the closing of mine number two. If their men don't mine coal, they don't get paid, and there's problems with water in mine number five."

"What do they say about the Chinese?" she asked.

He shook his head at that for a long time. Finally, he said, "I remember it used to be real nice having Chineymen around. They cleaned up the leavings, and they'd be the first to go in after a new tunnel was blasted. That's dangerous, you know. Now even the wives call them 'Chiney bastards.' Such language from the ladies."

"I thought we agreed. Ladies talk like everyone else. You think there'll be trouble in the mines with the Chinese?" she asked, coming back to the main subject.

He shook his head. "I just deliver ice. It's not a bad business. Did you know that ice is the main crop of New England? At least, it was the main crop until two years ago. That's when the winter was so unseasonably warm they had no ice crop at all."

"Anyone who claims to be minding his own business usually knows too much, and that's what he's mainly minding," she told him. "I take it that you think there will be trouble in the mines."

"Only a matter of time. The Chinese miners have formed gangs, and they demand the best rooms, the ones with the best diggings, but, who knows, the world might end first."

Dayle wasn't going to give up. "Are the men talking to union organizers?"

"I don't know anyone who has any use for Anarchists," he said. "Everybody needs ice, though. That's why ice is such respectable business. Do you know they ship 890,000 tons of ice from New England docks to tropical ports every year? They get fifty-six dollars a ton for it. I mean, people think regularly about tons and tons of coal being shipped everywhere, but ice? Nobody thinks of loading tons and tons of ice and transporting it and unloading it. Ice is respectable business," he went on. "Too bad the water 'round here smells of sulfur. Otherwise, when the coal runs out, I'd suggest they make ice in White Springs. Tons and tons of it. I've never known the cold to fail here."

Dayle gave up and let him talk about his ice. Still, there was no mistaking his attitude. It seemed everyone expected trouble there—everyone except the local Pinkerton office.

She could understand their reluctance. White

Springs was a world within itself. Everything arrived by train. Even the drinking water and the ice. Besides the railroad, the only other way to get anything in or out of White Springs was a rough trail fit only for mules. The water holes were few and far apart. That meant the White Springs Pinkerton office had it easy. All the agents had to do was guard the mines. There wasn't any other criminal activity to speak of. No roving outlaws, cardsharps, or pickpockets. It was too hard to make a clean getaway from this place. Given those circumstances, she thought it no wonder her boss hadn't wanted to believe a train could be robbed there or that soaped tracks were more than a prank.

More to the point, there were almost no places in White Springs to spread Anarchist literature. The company pubs didn't allow that kind of agitation. The cockfighters were even less tolerant. They didn't want any trouble that might interfere with their birds and their bets. In short, this was a town so controlled that for ten years now, there hadn't been any real trouble. Not even the usual kind.

She knew all that because she was a Pinkerton twenty-four hours a day. Once on a case, she rarely thought about much else. In the middle of the night last night, she'd gotten out of bed and slipped into the Pinkerton office through the back door, which had been remarkably easy. Actually, she imagined every locked door in the territory could be opened with common tools. She carried hers in her sewing basket.

Once inside, she'd checked the files. She'd gone through the local cases, checked the wanted posters, but quickly moved past that. Harry Bryant was not a common criminal. When she found the file on known Anarchists, the information was disappointingly dated. The most recent entry was a couple of news clippings on a huge labor rally that had taken place in New York City a year earlier. Thousands had turned out for it. Of course, there were no clippings from the local White Springs newspaper. Even the newspaper

The Lady Pinkerton Gets Her Man

was company-owned. Other than that, all she found was a couple of posters on the most notorious of the world's Anarchist leaders. They both operated out of France—the reason Anarchists were sometimes called Frenchies.

She'd been about ready to give up when she came across three pages of handwritten notes. It took her a moment to realize the notes were a memo from Allan Pinkerton himself. He was writing about the rise of "terroristic anarchism" in Russia and the Balkans. The memo was eight years old and expressed a concern that the local office "be vigilant" against this "growing menace" which advocated the "destruction of private ownership by violence and terror" and the "overthrow of governments by assassination." He speculated that this more violent form of anarchy might lead to a European war someday. Then he went on to advise against hiring anyone with a Russian or Polish accent as a Pinkerton. It seemed he was afraid the company might be infiltrated by "Anarchist spies of the worst sort." Dayle slipped the memo back into the file. She'd never known the Pinkertons to hire anyone with any foreign accent, although she understood Mr. Pinkerton spoke with a Scottish brogue.

Still, there was something about that memo that she found disturbing. She'd never heard of Russian or terroristic anarchy. It sounded like something that might equate with robbing a train or breaking a ventilation shaft rod. That as opposed to rallying the masses to undertake a strike, which was the Proudhon or French method, she knew.

She'd worked her way through the rest of the files and left without finding anything else of interest. The ice wagon driver wasn't providing anything, either. He was still going on and on about ice and the ice business. She didn't know anyone could talk that much about ice.

Other than coal and a raw frontier atmosphere, she didn't think White Springs had much to offer, either.

Jerrie Hurd

A railroad stop on a plateau of baked alkali and laterite that stretched over arroyo and ravine from horizon to horizon in every direction, the town itself straddled a wide sulfur-smelling slough that bubbled undrinkable water from a nearby hot spring. Most seasons, the stream, called Bitter Creek, was sixty feet across and barely deep enough to make mud. Spring was the exception.

There was no exception when it came to weather. The weather was wind, sometimes warm, most times cold, but always wind. Old-timers might have complained that snow never melted in White Springs, it just blew back and forth until it wore out, except that there weren't any true old-timers. The town had been built the same time as the railroad entirely of prefabricated buildings, shipped in and assembled as the tracks were being laid. Even now, some fifteen years later, the company still owned every structure, except the shacks in Chinatown, and some residential streets were hardly distinguishable from others.

With ordinary citizens as tough and dry as the town itself, brawls were commonplace and conversations predictable. Four beers into an evening, seasoned miners, who both loved and hated the place, would yell out, "What good is White Springs?"

The answer was always the same. "It holds the country together."

No brag. It was once thought that a transcontinental railroad could never be built. If you laid the tracks, how would you run the train? Fuel was the problem. There was no fuel—no wood on the great American prairie, and it was too costly to carry enough. According to some calculations, a train carrying fuel for the distance wouldn't have room for freight.

One day, a Pony Express rider, escaping Indians, took refuge under an overhang along the banks of Bitter Creek and discovered coal—one of the richest fields in the world. The rest was the stuff of story and fueled not only the railroad but the national sense of

The Lady Pinkerton Gets Her Man

destiny—God had provided for American expansion, and trains soon puffed from coast to coast, running on Wyoming coal.

"Why did you come to White Springs?" she asked the ice man when he paused long enough to allow a question.

"Restlessness," he answered. "I was younger then. I wanted to see things. I should have known that if you've seen the inside of one coal mine, you've seen the inside of them all. I don't imagine those Cornish boys working mine number three can tell Wyoming from England when they're underground."

"I suppose you're right," she commented.

"Still, there's a bit of the adventurer in all miners," he went on. "It's why miners are never really company men, if you know what I mean. We all work our own rooms and get paid on our own skill and muscle and luck. That's the main reason why no one likes the Chinese ganging up to get the best diggings," he told her. "That's not how it's done."

That was also why organizing those miners would be difficult, Dayle knew. To them, it would seem like "ganging up." Harry was smart to take a whole other approach.

Dayle left the ice man on the corner and went directly to the theater. The front doors were locked, but the side stage door was ajar. She went in and wandered around the backstage area. She found no one, and the size of that empty space, with its open rafters, amplified every swish of her skirt. Her every footfall echoed. It was enough to make her self-conscious as well as disappointed. Obviously, she'd guessed wrong. Tommy wasn't hanging around there. She should have tried the pool hall.

Never one to miss an opportunity, however, she opened a couple of the traveling trunks and poked around in them. She wasn't sure what she expected to find. It occurred to her that if rallying the masses was not your object, then you had no reason to print pamphlets. What did "terroristic Anarchists" need that might be incriminating?

Before giving up and leaving, she wandered onto the stage and looked out over the empty theater seats. There was something about standing there, center stage, that required an appropriate gesture. She looked all around and up into the balcony. Satisfied that no one was watching, she held her skirts out and made a deep curtsy.

To her utter embarrassment, that was met with applause. A single person clapping loudly. She stepped back and located the source of the sound. Looking straight up into the rafters, she spotted Harry sitting cross-legged on a narrow catwalk. He had a box of tools and a pile of rigging ropes beside him.

"Bravo," he called down, and kept clapping until she complained, saying that was enough.

She stepped back to where she could see him even better and added, "I didn't know you were up there."

"Obviously, but don't worry about it. There's something about bare boards and an empty house that's so completely unnatural, it will draw a bow from almost everyone."

"Thanks. But I think I feel foolish anyway." She glanced all around again and still didn't see anyone else. "What are you doing?" she asked him.

"Fixing the ropes on one of the backdrops. It tangled and almost didn't come down last night."

"I thought you had a crew who handled things like that."

"Well, you know how it is. If you want it done right . . . Come up, I'll show you how it's rigged."

Dayle hated heights. The rooftops in Chinatown seemed safe by comparison to the flimsy, narrow catwalk above her. Besides, the only thing she really knew about Harry Bryant was that she didn't trust him. Even worse, she'd begun to wonder what a

The Lady Pinkerton Gets Her Man

terroristic Anarchist was capable of doing. Whatever it was, she could be quite sure that it was not in his interests to allow a Lady Pinkerton to keep snooping around—a problem easily solved. All he had to do was shove her off that catwalk.

"Why don't you come down here?" she countered. "There's plenty of room on an empty stage."

"I need to finish up here," he answered. "It's tedious work. The ropes need to be measured and threaded just right—something I imagine a seamstress might appreciate, but then maybe you're not as interested in stitching as you pretend."

"Maybe you're gullible if you believe everything Tommy the Tube Man tells you."

He chuckled. "Actually, I've found Tommy truthful to the point of being blunt."

"Then I suppose it would be wise to believe what he tells me about you."

He paused. "What does Tommy tell you about me?"

Now she hesitated. If Tommy wasn't there, she thought she might as well question Harry himself, but it wasn't going to do for her to continue yelling up into the rafters at him. She needed to see his face, judge his reactions. She needed to be self-possessed and poised enough so that she could encourage him to talk, reveal himself. It was her only hope of understanding what was going on.

She glanced to where a ladder hung anchored to one wall. She swallowed. "I'm coming up," she told him.

"Good, but with a full skirt, you might want . . ."

"I know how to do it," she answered. "I didn't travel with the circus and not learn a few tricks." She shed a couple of petticoats. Then she sat on the stage and pulled off her shoes and socks. She folded the petticoats and rolled the socks and put them inside her shoes. She put her shoes neatly on top of her underskirts. Those tasks out of the way, there was nothing to keep her from the climbing.

Jerrie Hurd

She glanced upward one more time and reminded herself that a woman without courage might as well give up. Being gutsy was really the only dependable asset. Then, in her bare feet, she crossed to the ladder, took a deep breath, and climbed.

She'd watched women trapeze artists manage ladders while wearing long skirts. It required the extra motion of kicking one's leg over, forcing the fullness of the skirts behind. Without giving herself time to think or look down, she wove her legs around her skirts, and up the ladder she went.

The catwalk was another matter. It swayed as soon as she stepped onto it, and for an awful moment she froze, thinking she might not be able to move again. Harry wasn't that far out onto the catwalk. Maybe only ten steps, but the catwalk itself seemed to narrow and lengthen in her view until it might have been a circus high wire for all she trusted it.

"Gutsy," she whispered to herself. She couldn't remember when she'd first learned that word. It seemed that she'd always known it, always whispered it to herself. It was the only thing that had gotten her through all sorts of trouble.

When others at the orphanage urged her to tears, saying tears would soften the sisters, she'd refused. Tears were surrender. Stubborn, unbending gutsiness worked better. A little of that attitude, and she soon knew which of the sisters could actually mete out the punishments they threatened and which couldn't. She'd been calling people's bluffs long before she knew there was a word for what she was doing.

Meanwhile, Harry sat calmly, threading ropes onto pulleys and measuring the lengths needed to drop his backgrounds into place. When she was close enough, she allowed herself to drop to her knees and sit, her legs tucked under, her hands still gripping the railing.

He continued with his work. It was a moment before he looked up. "Gutsy," he repeated, and then grinned.

The Lady Pinkerton Gets Her Man

She looked away with a fresh flush of embarrassment.

"These rafters carry every sound," he told her, his tone dancing. He was enjoying her fluster.

She forced herself to let go of the rail. At the same time, she determined that if he tried to shove her off, she'd pull him with her. They studied each other a moment, almost as if that mutual danger was on both of their minds. Then he released a pulley rope. The backdrop unrolled with a whir, sending the catwalk swaying wildly so that they both had to reach for the railing. She hoped he was enjoying himself. She knew he'd unrolled that backdrop with more flourish than was necessary.

"That's better," he announced. "Much smoother." He meant the backdrop. Maybe he meant more. She couldn't tell.

"Allan Pinkerton is coming to White Springs," she told him, thinking to give him a return scare. In fact, he dropped one of the ropes.

"The old man himself?" he asked.

"Yes," she answered back.

For a moment, there was no sound from the rafters. Then Harry reached with a hook to retrieve the rope and asked, "Does his son William know he's coming here?"

"I'm sure I don't know," she answered.

"William stopped by this morning before he left to chase outlaws. He didn't mention his father coming. I'll bet he didn't know."

"You entertained William Pinkerton?"

"We're old school chums."

"That's right. You told me."

"He invited me to join his posse. He promised me a real adventure."

"He wanted you to go with him?"

"I told you. We're old school chums."

"Yes," was all she answered. She really didn't know

what to make of this man. Affable, well connected. His father had once owned a mine. He'd gone to school with William Pinkerton and Jay Gould's nephew. That wasn't exactly the kind of person to harbor labor sympathies. She entertained the notion that she might be wrong about him, but only for a moment. In the larger sense, she was sure Harry Bryant was a man with a purpose, a man who wanted nothing less than to get inside life and turn it out.

"Is that why you came?" he asked. "You wanted to tell me that Allan Pinkerton is coming to town?"

"No . . . yes . . . I don't know." She stopped. She couldn't exactly admit that she'd been hoping to question Tommy about him. She was saved when she heard footsteps below.

She looked down and saw a short young man carrying packages. Harry signaled her to be silent. Together, the two of them sat quietly unobserved while the young man did the same as Dayle. He looked around and even hollered once, calling into the empty theater, "Anybody here? I've got packages from the depot, freshly arrived on the train today."

Again, Harry signaled for silence. More than silence. Dayle had to sit perfectly still. If she wasn't careful, her wide skirt swept the dirty edges of the catwalk and sent dust showering downward.

When there was no answer, the delivery boy looked around once again, set his packages down, and came to the center of the stage. He bowed, not once, but three times. He paused a moment as if accepting imaginary applause. Then he picked up his packages again and exited, calling backstage, "I've got packages . . ."

Dayle relaxed. "I had no idea my reaction was so common."

"I told you, it's human nature. Everyone wants a stage."

"Why?"

The Lady Pinkerton Gets Her Man

"We all want to believe life is a well-constructed stage fantasy, because we know how such stories end—with applause."

"Is that why you play on the stage?"

"That, and the fact that I'm so damned good-looking I had to have a place to strut."

She gave him a quick glance to see if he was serious and realized she had no way of telling. He was an actor. He could be anything, generous, friendly, worldly. How did she expect to see past the practiced in him? A new wave of fear combined with her dislike of heights. She stifled a shudder.

"What orphanage did you grow up in?" he now asked her.

"Orphanage?"

"You gave yourself away when you rolled your socks. That's a neatness taught only in armies and orphanages. I doubt you've been in the army."

She bit her lip. She not only didn't trust him, she didn't trust her observations of him, yet he'd read her like a book. "Yes, I'm an orphan," she told him. "So what?"

"Nothing," he said, "except that Tommy missed that fact. Guess he doesn't know everything. So what does he say about me?"

"That you're out for revenge."

"That's all?"

"The rest of it I can guess myself."

"Such as?"

"I have good reason to believe you're an Anarchist," she said. "Maybe even a terrorist Anarchist."

"What good reason?" he asked.

She swallowed. Again, she was up against the fact that she had nothing but her suspicions. "I know you were behind sabotaging the ventilation shaft," she went on.

"Really? I thought I was with you when that happened. We were betting the birds, weren't we?"

"Exactly. Like Jay Gould, you send your men to do your work."

That hit a mark. He actually winced, which meant that his professional actor facade could be penetrated.

He turned back to his work. He clipped a rope and tossed the cutting tool into the toolbox.

She continued, "Tommy told me that Jay Gould forced your father to sell his mine."

"He's not called the most hated man in America for nothing."

"For that you're plotting his undoing?"

"Me? Take on Jay Gould? Exactly who do you think I am?"

"The Hooded Sleeper." She was going for broke.

He laughed. Not a polite chuckle but a full-bodied hilarity that gave a new sway to the catwalk.

She gripped the railing again.

He flashed his wide grin. "Hell, I must have made more impression yesterday than I knew, saving Mrs. Bateman's horse. Now you think I'm out to save the whole world?"

"Don't flatter yourself. You want to stop the world, not save it."

"I beg your pardon?"

"There's a power that comes from running things," she explained. "There's also a kind of power that comes from upsetting things—toppling houses of cards, so to speak. I think you thrive on the second. What you did yesterday with Lotta's horse was clever, even admirable, but what really gave you a boost was knowing you'd gotten to Garrick Bateman. For a moment, you had his world turned upside down, and you liked that. You really liked that."

That, too, struck close to whatever made him tick. There was a pause. She couldn't tell if he was struggling with anger, confusion, or the shared sense of their nearness. The silence denied nothing. Neither did he. When he spoke again, it was softer.

The Lady Pinkerton Gets Her Man

"Who are you?" he asked.

"What do you mean?"

She felt her insides tighten. His question was the one she was least able to answer. She didn't know who she was. If he had a father he had to avenge, that was all well and good. She had no history at all. None. If the sisters at the orphanage knew anything about the mysterious woman who had left Dayle at the home, they'd never told her.

He shook his head as if clearing his confusion. Then he tried to make light of it. "It's an actor's question," he said. "Actors study character all the time. We're always wanting to know who everyone is and why."

"Oh," she answered. "In that case, I guess I could be anyone. Who would you like me to be?"

"Not a Pinkerton," he returned.

She looked away. She was a Pinkerton because Pinkertons didn't do nice work. They uncovered secrets, exposed wrongdoing, kept company with criminals. She needed that color. With no history, no ties to anyone or anyplace, she couldn't afford to let herself be sweet and nice, like a real lady. Women who were truly ladies accommodated, blended in. If she ever let herself blend in, she expected she might disappear altogether.

"I suppose you think being someone's widowed second cousin is better."

He didn't like that answer.

"And I still think you're the Hooded Sleeper," she added.

"Well, then, at least try to think of me as a friend of the common man rather than some menace to society. Or do you have to think like a Pinkerton as well?"

"At least I think," she returned. "If you gave a thought to it, you'd know that you don't have to do anything to upset this house of cards. White Springs is going to unravel all on its own. The Tong are already losing control of Chinatown."

"I know," he offered.

"Then, for your own sake, leave things alone."
"Is that a threat?"
"Good advice."
"I appreciate that, but I've never been one to get caught with my pants down, now, have I?" he asked, and they both knew he was referring to their carriage ride.

"This isn't over yet," she returned.

13

That afternoon, Ah So wrapped himself in his raccoon-skin coat. Then he took his four armed guards and his favorite fighting cricket to the open area by the Joss House. That's where everyone in Chinatown congregated when they weren't working the mines or sitting in the baths or smoking in the opium dens. The men came to learn the news, exchange gossip, gamble. Inside the Joss House, they worshiped their ancestors, who were too far away to help them.

Deep down, the men knew the ancestors could not hear. They hoped for help anyway. Sometimes when the men were very frustrated, they went out into the desert and dug a hole, as deep as they could make it. Then they shouted down that hole, hoping the earth would carry their prayers to the bones of their predecessors. Without family, without ancestors, being Chinese meant nothing.

Some of the men who came to America lost themselves. Forgot who they were and wandered out into the desert and became truly lost—even their bones. That was only one of the dangers of coming to Gold Mountain looking for fortune.

Ah So came to the front of the Joss House a couple times a week to be sociable, to listen, understand the talk, take care of complaints. He found it made him seem beneficent if he handed out a few favors and dispensed justice with regularity. Besides, it served his purposes to settle disputes before they grew big. He never worshiped. Ah So knew too well that he could rely on no one's help, living or dead. He was on his own here. Focusing on that fact kept his thinking clear, and at the moment he needed to think most clearly.

Things were bad in the mines. Ah So's nephew had formed underground gangs. Not content to be the warlord's nephew, he had recently overstepped himself. Everyone knew it. It was the talk—how Ah So's nephew now thought he was the warlord, a bigger warlord than his uncle, the Tong leader. He and his gangs had gotten the Chinese miners better rooms to work and better tools. That made them happy. That was why Ah So had let his nephew engage in his enterprise for this long. Nothing Ah So had done lately had made his men happy.

Until Ah So worked on how to get a steady supply of new Chinese workers, he could not make his men happy. For the nephew to take advantage of that current difficulty meant he was out of touch with his family, both the living and the dead. This had made him think he was important all by himself, too important.

Ah So could no longer allow that. Everyone knew. Everyone was wondering what Ah So was going to do about his nephew. Ah So wondered himself.

As he entered the open area in the middle of Chinatown, the crowd immediately parted; conversation stopped. His nephew and several of his closest gang member friends were sitting around their cricket

The Lady Pinkerton Gets Her Man

bowls, noisily betting on their favorites. They were the last to notice. Even they fell silent as they looked up and saw Ah So and his bodyguards stride across the open space. He was still the Tong leader. They knew that. They hastily moved out of the way.

Ah So's nephew knew it, too. He came to his feet. Ah So did not bow. He didn't even nod. Instead, he flipped the back of his raccoon-skin coat up and sat down across from where his nephew had been sitting. He liked his uncle's second son, but this was Tong business. He brushed aside the current fighting crickets and set his own fighting bowl between them. He would think what to do about his nephew while their crickets fought.

Ah So knew the rules of engagement: go into emptiness, strike voids, bypass what he defends, hit him where he does not expect you. Several minutes later, Ah So looked up from the shallow red bowl where his cricket was engaged in a fierce fight and noticed the crowd of curious onlookers had grown. All of Chinatown wanted to see the outcome, not of the game but of the business in the mines.

Ah So doubled his bet. His favorite cricket was outmatched by his nephew's bigger, stronger bug, but Ah So was confident. His favorite cricket was his favorite cricket because it instinctively knew the laws of terrain: on difficult ground, press on; on encircled ground, devise stratagems; on death ground, fight.

A smooth, slick bowl was death ground.

His cricket would fight.

Meanwhile, he could tell that his nephew was feeling the slickness of the bowl of his own making. A sweat had formed on his brow, and his hands trembled when he handled the bigger bet. Ah So still hadn't decided what to do about him. It helped that the boy knew enough to be scared. Maybe there was hope for him. Maybe he would learn that he needed his uncle. One good uncle was better than a hundred gang members of questionable loyalty. In fact, his nephew's friends had all vanished, slipping away through the crowd one by one.

The crickets fought. They would continue until one cricket pushed the other over the edge and out of the bowl. When it hit the ground, its disgusted owner would stomp it into the dirt. Ah So's cricket was a fighter, never turning, never pausing. Hard to find a cricket so good. Already, his nephew's bigger bug clawed at the slick surface of the bowl with more motion than was wise. Once it turned as if it thought running was a possibility. Ah So's favorite cricket was clearly getting the advantage and was about to win, when the crowd suddenly parted again.

Ah So looked up, thinking he'd lop off the head of the man who dared interfere in this business. He even raised his hand to give the signal to one of his guards. That's when he was surprised to see a tall, light-haired man, a round-eye, approaching. White men almost never came to the cricket fights. Even fewer came to see the Tong leader without invitation.

Ah So stood.

His nephew had already jumped to his feet. He was now standing next to Ah So and breathing easier for this distraction. However, Ah So was not distracted. He noticed how his nephew scanned the crowd as if he thought he had allies. He didn't. Ah So would finish his business with him later.

First, he would deal with Harry Bryant.

He'd never met this white man, but he knew the actor immediately. His spies had been thorough in their description of him. Moreover, he knew that he was the head Anarchist come to White Springs to make trouble. One more quick glance, and Ah So determined two things: his own men were in place, and Harry was alone.

Ah So wasn't sure whether that meant Harry was courageous or foolish. He had to know that with one small signal, Ah So could make Harry disappear permanently, taking his troublemaking with him. The

The Lady Pinkerton Gets Her Man

temptation was great. Ah So didn't need trouble. And killing the Hooded Sleeper was a sure way to curry favor. The men of power in America hated Anarchists.

However, Ah So was annoyed with Garrick Bateman, and he did have his own interests to think about. He didn't need more trouble, but he sensed that things had shifted enough so that he was willing to hesitate, listen. His nephew's mischief was one thing. He sensed this was quite another.

Ah So motioned for Harry to sit where his nephew had been sitting.

Harry didn't sit. Instead, he bowed respectfully to Ah So. Then, pointing to the crickets still battling in the bowl, he asked, "What's the bet?"

Ah So named the amount.

Harry doubled it.

"You'll lose," Ah So told him. "My cricket has very nearly won already."

"Then count it as tribute to the warlord," Harry answered, and laid his money on the makeshift table.

Ah So was impressed. He returned the polite bow. "You know who I am."

"Yes, you are the 'Chineyman in the raccoon-skin coat' who just happens to control the destiny of the United States of America," Harry returned. "However, I should probably introduce myself."

"No need," Ah So answered. "You very good actor and very bad troublemaker. I know you."

With that, Ah So spread his coat and sat down. He couldn't help himself. He was more than impressed; he was flattered. He'd never had a round-eye call him "warlord." He wasn't sure many of them, including Garrick Bateman, understood his power. He preferred it that way. Hidden power was better. The man who had to show off usually had paper dragons.

Harry joined him, sitting with the cricket bowl between them. At the same time, he said, "I was once told an old Chinese wisdom: no one can cause trouble where there isn't any."

Ah So nodded. "That is a good Chinese wisdom."

"It's because of the trouble here that I've come to Chinatown," Harry continued. "I've come to ask you and your miners to flex some of your muscle. Things are bad in the mines. Things need to change."

Ah So studied the man. The message was simple, direct. The intention was not necessarily the same. Ah So smiled and nodded slightly. "An honored invitation. But we have Tong. We don't need union."

"You can't get away with being spoilers forever," Harry told him.

"Spoilers?" Ah So asked. "What mean *spoiler?*"

"Spoilers," the actor repeated. "You know. You make it bad for everyone. Your Chinese miners work too cheap and don't care about the conditions because they don't intend to stay here. They make it impossible for miners everywhere. No one can organize. No one can hope to improve working conditions. Not as long as there are the Chinese. It means that as long as you help the monopolists, you spoil things for everyone else. You can't keep doing that."

"Yes, but the monopolists pay. Miners don't," Ah So returned.

Harry shook his head. "Already the anger builds. You know about the riots in Seattle and Denver. Have you heard what happened to the hop pickers in California? Hell, you've even annoyed the Women's Industrial League. They stormed Congress and threw all the towels from the congressional washrooms on the floor of the House of Representatives because they'd been washed too cheaply at Chinese laundries."

Ah So knew that thirty-five hop pickers had been burned out of a migrant camp recently. He'd also heard about the laundry ladies. He knew there was much bad feeling all over America. But White Springs

The Lady Pinkerton Gets Her Man

was isolated. It was very far from other places. This place only needed new workers. Then the unhappy Chinese could go home, get in touch with their ancestors again. All would be fine again, even for white miners. What worried him was the fox fairy—that part of all things that was chaotic, unpredictable, and always better left alone. Fox fairy was fox fairy. With the sword, you ruled. With the fox fairy, you upset and loosed who knew what?

"I think you are the spoiler," Ah So told Harry. "Before you come, everything is good. Very good. Why you want to cause trouble? You are not miner. You make story onstage. That not good enough for you?"

"I'm giving you a chance. I'm asking you to join us before the trouble grows beyond what anyone can manage. You know what I'm talking about. What happened in Seattle and Denver is going to happen here if you don't do something—if we don't all do something."

Ah So shook his head, but he knew. Enlightened warlords paid attention to the appropriate relationships between prince and minister, superior and subordinate. Things in White Springs were out of balance. He'd tried to talk to Garrick Bateman. Tried to reason with him. Now, Harry Bryant seemed to understand the situation, but Ah So didn't really think he cared about Chinese miners. He'd come from outside the town. He had his own reasons for being there. Ah So wished he understood those reasons. He suspected that Harry was going to be more trouble than Ah So's nephew, much more trouble.

Ah So lifted his hand.

He could kill Harry, but no one killed the fox fairy. It was bad luck even to try. Besides, the man had come to Ah So, wishing to talk to Ah So. He'd even called Ah So a warlord. That was more respect than he'd gotten from his nephew.

Ah So dropped his hand, and the man at Ah So's

side pulled out a sword. In less time than an eyeblink, the ungrateful nephew's head was lying in the dust, the eyes still bright, still blinking as if trying to understand. The body spurted blood, and one arm came up as if to defend itself from the blow it hadn't seen coming. When the nephew's knees crumpled, his body tipped over the cricket bowl, forcing Harry to jump up and away. Not fast enough. Blood from Ah So's nephew's severed neck sprayed the front of the actor.

The rest of the crowd had jumped back faster and sucked air in a collective gasp. Ah So didn't care about them. He watched Harry. He saw Harry lose color and fight nausea. Stealing the train money and closing mine number 2 were clever moves, but this was not a clever business. They were talking about railroads, mines, money, power. The presidency of the United States depended on what happened in White Springs. Those were things men killed and were killed for. Ah So wanted "the Anarchist everyone feared" to know that.

While the white man was learning his lesson, Ah So bent and gently scooped his favorite fighting cricket out of the dust where it had fallen. When he straightened, he noticed the crowd thinning, moving away, as if they thought the outcome that mattered had already been settled. They didn't understand the larger picture.

"More than mining company need Chinese here," he told Harry. "We are the Great Wall against trouble here."

Harry swallowed. Ah So saw him struggle to keep from looking at the body again. His voice was weak when he spoke, but it quickly took on strength.

"Things have changed. You are not the wall. You have become the problem, and that's not going to change anything," Harry said, pointing to Ah So's still twitching nephew. "Everyone expects that from the Tong. They know how to deal with that. The times

The Lady Pinkerton Gets Her Man

have changed. It would be wisdom to change your tactics with the times."

Ah So considered those words. He sensed some truth. However, it was not wisdom to shift allegiances too quickly, and always he came back to the fact that it was one thing to steal money from a train and quite another to steal a town from the monopolists.

His own hesitancy grew from another source. He could not join Harry because he did not understand anarchy. It was a way of fighting that made no sense to him. He did not know the rules of engagement for this kind of fighting. He bowed respectfully. "Chinese do things Chinese way," he told Harry. Then, taking his cricket, Ah So left the fighting grounds.

14

At noon the next day, Allan Pinkerton, a small man with a slight limp, entered the dining room of the best hotel in White Springs. After a quick glance, he considered it adequate. The white linen tablecloths helped. His son William wore boots, rode horses, ate tinned beans, and liked roughing it. Not him. He'd had enough hard times as a child. Except when he was wearing a disguise, he conducted his business in a dark navy suit of worsted wool, black shoes, and a black derby hat. Since his stroke, he'd added a fine-crafted walking stick made of ebony tipped with gold. He liked eating at a well-laid table, and when he traveled, he preferred trains. He saw no reason why detective work couldn't be civilized. On the other hand, he knew enough to emphasize the rough, the exciting, and the exotic in his books. Different thing.

He crossed the room and was about to take a table near the window when he noticed a row of old maps decorating one wall. He examined the first, taking out

The Lady Pinkerton Gets Her Man

his glasses to give it a good look. His curiosity piqued, he walked along the wall, examining the others.

The maps, arranged in chronological order, showed the growth of the nation. Each added more and more features to the western wilderness, obviously as more and more of the territory had been explored. The map from the Lewis and Clark expedition was missing one of the West's major rivers—the Willamette. Those seasoned explorers had paddled past where the Willamette joined the Columbia and never saw it. As fortune had it, they'd chosen to travel around the wrong side of the island at the mouth of that river. Looking at the sheer size of the land mass, Allan Pinkerton thought he could have figured out that an additional watershed had to exist—without expending himself in a single day of physical hardship paddling a canoe.

Another map showed mostly blank space where Arizona Territory was. All the maps showed Wyoming Territory as flat and featureless. Hard to tell what was important from a map, he mused. White Springs, Wyoming, for example.

As expected, a few minutes later, the head of the local Pinkerton office arrived. Allan Pinkerton didn't waste time. Couldn't. He had a business to run, sons to stay ahead of, books to write, and a wife to outsmart. For that reason, he had already met Thuzla Smith earlier that morning. They'd discussed the local situation over biscuits and coffee at a restaurant near the train station. Now, he expected that Mr. Smith had arranged for Garrick Bateman to join them for lunch.

"Mr. Bateman's looking forward to meeting you," Thuzla said, obviously pleased that he'd successfully carried out his assignment. "I told him you were from Scotland. He enjoys meeting Europeans."

"I'm from the Gorbals," Allan Pinkerton corrected him. The Gorbals were the worst of Glasgow's slums—the worst in all of Scotland. He liked it known that he'd come up in the world.

That information was lost on Thuzla Smith. He either didn't know or didn't care. He was shaking his head. "I'm afraid Mr. Bateman is having a little trouble understanding your ideas on the current situation. Nothing to worry about. He needs you to explain it, that's all. I'm sure you'll do better than I did. Sometimes it takes a bit before he comes around."

"I thought you'd have it all set up," Pinkerton said.

He had a secretary upstairs in his hotel room typing his latest adventure. If he didn't get back to the dictation, that secretary would soon be out of material. Then he was supposed to meet Miss Dobson shortly after this. Actually, he was looking forward to meeting Miss Dobson. He didn't want anything to interfere with that. He thought he might even put her in his next book. He'd discovered that his readers enjoyed reading about scrappy women. Miss Dobson struck him as perfect in that regard. He thought women were amazing in the way they got a man's juices flowing, and he didn't mean just the obvious juices. It was no surprise to him that the Greeks imagined the Muses as a bevy of graceful girls.

Thuzla Smith was still making some excuse about Garrick Bateman being stubborn, when the man arrived, walking heavy, an assistant trotting at his side.

"Don't worry. It'll be fine," was all Mr. Smith offered. Then he sat back, obviously expecting that Pinkerton would take care of everything. Allan Pinkerton grunted. He'd lost track of how many people expected him to take care of everything.

Besides being stubborn, Allan Pinkerton found Garrick Bateman to be a beefy man with a big nose and big, puffy bags under his eyes. He sniffed loudly, wiggling that nose, as he came forward with his

The Lady Pinkerton Gets Her Man

purposeful stride, his hand extended. He pumped Allan Pinkerton's right arm, slapped the chief detective's left shoulder in a friendly, maybe too friendly, gesture, then turned away too quickly to seal those actions with any sincerity. Instead, he was busy pulling himself up to the table and shaking out his napkin. Allan Pinkerton wasn't sure he liked the man, and they hadn't yet exchanged ten words.

"Am I to understand that you and Mr. Gould have gotten federal troops ordered out to nearby towns?" Garrick Bateman asked, getting right down to business.

Allan Pinkerton nodded and sat down. "I thought that would be a fitting precaution."

"With all due respect," Bateman returned, "you haven't been here a whole day yet. Is that long enough to know what's going on?"

As with the maps on the wall, Allan Pinkerton didn't have to paddle a canoe across the entire Louisiana Purchase to know how many major rivers were needed to drain the western watershed, and he didn't have to smell every slag heap in White Springs to figure out this situation. He stirred his coffee and said nothing.

Thuzla Smith filled in for him. "Mr. Gould asked the president to station troops nearby, so that they'd be available if trouble starts. It's a precaution, mainly."

"What trouble?" Bateman now asked. "We haven't had any real trouble in White Springs for years."

By that time, Allan Pinkerton wondered who was really in charge there. Garrick Bateman obviously didn't have the brains. He glanced at his own employee, Thuzla Smith, but he'd already judged him to be mainly a petty functionary. Miss Dobson had put all this together quickly, according to her telegram, but she'd only recently transferred from the Denver office. He knew. He'd checked on her and already had plans to keep her distracted and therefore out of the way of his own plans. Who did that leave?

The head of the Tong.

That made sense. The head of the Tong had probably been the one who suggested using Chinese miners to break the last strike. He'd probably been running White Springs, more or less, ever since.

Meanwhile, Garrick Bateman was complaining. "I thought you Pinkertons were supposed to guard the mines. I thought that's why you'd been hired. Why do we need federal troops?"

Allan Pinkerton didn't know why the man's nerve was up. Making sure federal troops were at the ready was Allan Pinkerton's best idea for keeping the mines open. Jay Gould's interests were America's interests and had been for some time now, a fact not disputed by anyone who had more than a schoolbook understanding of politics. The president hadn't even questioned the request, not seriously, anyway. In Allan Pinkerton's mind, that was doing his job perfectly.

"I don't know," Bateman continued to say. "I don't know."

Allan Pinkerton knew. He knew Jay Gould's name would be remembered long after President Arthur's had been forgotten. Jay Gould was America's wealthiest man. Chester Alan Arthur was America's luckiest political pawn. He had been a collector for the Port of New York, and not even a very good one, from all reports. He was removed from that office in 1878 by President Hayes for incompetence. That angered the powerful Senator Roscoe Conkling. To placate the senator, Chester Alan Arthur was nominated two years later as vice president, running on the same winning ticket as James Garfield. Ironically, when President Garfield was assassinated, Conkling's man, Chester Alan Arthur, became the nation's chief executive officer. But he was still Conkling's pawn, the way

The Lady Pinkerton Gets Her Man

Bateman was Jay Gould's man. They would both do what they were told. This lunch meeting was mainly to humor Bateman.

Garrick Bateman sniffed his big nose again. "Besides, I'm telling you that there's not going to be any trouble here. I've got everything under control."

"Oh, there will be trouble here," Pinkerton said.

Bateman paused. He stared at the chief detective. "Even if there was trouble, how do we explain using federal troops to protect private mines?"

Allan Pinkerton looked to Thuzla Smith. All of this was supposed to have been explained.

Thuzla shrugged and touched the side of his head, as if to indicate what Bateman lacked.

Allan Pinkerton set his coffee down. "If there's trouble in White Springs and the trains stop, so does the U.S. Mail. As president of the United States, Chester Alan Arthur will have to send in federal troops to make sure the U.S. Mail gets through."

It took a moment for that idea to sink in. Then Garrick Bateman broke into a wide smile and a flood of excited words. "Ten years ago, we had some trouble here, and I knew I had to do something. That's when the idea of using Chinese miners came to me. Worked. Broke the strike almost overnight. But I think you're right. It's time for something else, something more American."

"You don't say," Allan Pinkerton voiced as he broke off a piece of biscuit. He was thinking lunch was going to be interminable in the company of Garrick Bateman. The main course had barely arrived.

Later that afternoon, Dayle listened to her own footsteps as she wandered along the boardwalk of a deserted street in the area of White Springs known as the ghost town. It was one of the strange anomalies of this place that while no building was more than fifteen years old, everything north of Sixth Street had already been abandoned.

Ten years ago, when Garrick Bateman replaced seven hundred striking miners with an equal number of Chinese, most of the town died. The Chinese built their own Chinatown on the other side of the creek and patronized their own shops. With fewer than three hundred white miners left, large parts of White Springs shut down. Businesses folded; houses and boarding hotels closed. Now, sand drifted against the boardwalks, shutters banged, and any paint brighter than the desert's gray had long since worn away. When the coal was gone, the rest of White Springs would suffer the same fate.

Dayle had already decided she didn't like this part of town. She shifted her sewing basket and did a half turn, looking all around. She was supposed to meet Allan Pinkerton here. She'd been told at the office that he wanted a quiet place to conduct his daily health constitutional and that he'd left instructions for her to join him here. She did another half turn, didn't see anyone, and wondered if she'd understood right.

She supposed this was a good place to take one's daily exercise if one wanted to get away from the usual horse and carriage traffic, but unlike the smoky hollow behind mine number 3, where the criminal element hung out, this was where the crazies came: miners who had been fine one day and too claustrophobic to descend the tunnels the next; halfwits who talked to themselves; loners who talked to no one.

Her head jerked at every sound. Her eyes followed every movement. She had the eerie sense that she was being watched but couldn't confirm it. What's more, she was beginning to feel ridiculous walking the abandoned street dressed in her best—silk from top to bottom and petticoats that rustled. In front of the largest of the deserted buildings, an old hotel, she paused and lifted her skirts to check what the dust

The Lady Pinkerton Gets Her Man

was doing to her best shoes. It was while she was slightly off balance, checking her shoes, that she was suddenly pinched from behind.

There were certain things a girl learned growing up in an orphanage and being sent out for "domestic service." In the right circumstances, those things became instinctive. Before she knew what she was doing, Dayle turned and delivered an upward thrust to the man's nose with the heel of her hand, a painful blow, which was usually enough. In this case, she happened to catch him as he stood on the edge of the boardwalk. He lost his balance, and her blow sent him sprawling. It was only when she'd caught her breath and had a moment to study the small man in a navy blue business suit sitting in the dust of the street that she realized what she'd done.

She'd just dropped Allan Pinkerton, world-famous detective, on his rear.

"Are you all right?" she asked, knowing better. She could see that his nose had begun to bleed. She pulled a handkerchief from her sleeve and offered it.

He took it and applied it to his nose. At the same time, he looked up and said, "By God, I do believe that was a good, firm pinch, don't you think?"

Dayle didn't know what to say. He was worried about the firmness of his pinch? That struck her as odd or maybe rude.

"It has been forever since I've been able to do a pretty bottom like that," he said, now holding the handkerchief with his left hand while he exercised his right, pinching at the air with an obvious sense of satisfaction. He gave her a sly glance and said, "I know I sound odd, but you'll have to indulge an old man's bragging."

It was only because he was an old man that she was indulging any of this. She'd already figured out that pinching was probably all the manliness he could manage. She imagined that for a man of Mr. Pinkerton's reputation, it was a serious loss.

Jerrie Hurd

"I do swear that taking this field assignment has been quite good for me. Wyoming is an invigorating place. Don't you agree?"

She mumbled something vaguely agreeable and then asked, "How's your nose?"

"Fine, fine," he said, and he removed the handkerchief to show that the bleeding had stopped.

She helped him to his feet.

He picked up his cane and brushed the dust from his suit. Then, as he took his hat from her, he said, "I assume more introduction is not necessary."

She shook her head.

"Good," he said. "You know, you handle yourself well. I never saw the dust coming until I was in it. Where'd you learn something like that?"

"Necessity," was all Dayle answered.

"Best of all teachers," he said. "Can't beat necessity. Do you know why I have such a reputation for being good at disguises?" he continued.

Dayle shook her head.

"Because of necessity. You got to be good or else. I mean, think about it, the grand acting that works on a stage is nothing compared to the fine acting required to work right under somebody's nose in a disguise. If you've infiltrated a gang of robbers who'd as soon shoot an informer as look at one, your life depends on your skill." He paused. "I did that once. I joined a gang of robbers."

He launched into a long story about that same gang of robbers, and how he'd single-handedly captured them all. A little way into the story, she recognized the incident. It was one she'd read about in an old Pinkerton file. Only he was improving on it, quite a bit.

She didn't hold that against him. She embellished every chance she got. Black stockings. Black petticoats. A little cleavage. Enough perfume to suggest the exotic. The gun in her handbag. Any woman who didn't shape her life into something larger than the day-to-day was destined to be ignored. More or less, everyone reworked the story of his or her life, repeatedly. Otherwise, it was hard to find much meaning in the rush of events.

Allan Pinkerton had simply applied good storytelling to both his detective agency and his books. In the process, he'd made himself larger than life. She imagined that presented some difficulty. Growing older gracefully was probably not easy if you'd made yourself into a living legend.

He seemed to sense that her attention had wandered from his tale. He stopped mid-story and looked her over. "You don't expect an apology, do you? I mean, putting me in the dust ought to be satisfaction enough."

She shook her head.

"Good, because it's time I got on with my health constitutional." Having said that, he didn't wait. He marched off down the street, swinging his arms with vigor.

She caught up with him. It wasn't hard. Despite his pretense of vigor, his pace wasn't that brisk, and she thought his breathing was more than ordinarily labored.

He didn't let that bother him. Seeing her, he picked up the conversation without missing a beat. "My son William is particularly good at disguises. At sixteen, he was one of the best Union spies in the war. No surprise. I taught him."

"Does he know you're in White Springs?" she asked, remembering Harry's concern.

He shook his head. "No, I don't tell William anything I don't have to tell him. He and his brother would love to take over, put their old man in a rocking chair. I don't need a rocking chair. I need Wyoming air. Look what it's already done for me." He suddenly stopped walking and started stretching. He bent over and touched the ground several times. Then he folded his arms across his chest and swung his shoulders from side to side to a count of four.

Between counts, he added, "I appreciate the dress. I noticed it right away. You're very pretty, you know, and that dress suggests the perfect amount of daring."

"Thank you."

"You're welcome." A moment later, he chuckled. "You really ought to try some of these exercises. It's very good for getting the blood to the brain and stretching the muscles. Both are required for quick responses." He stopped and chuckled to himself while he gave her another sly glance. "Of course, I don't think you lack for quick responses."

She said nothing. He thought pinching her had been clever, and she wasn't sure she agreed.

He figured that out. "You think I was rude?"

She shrugged.

He considered that a moment. "All right, I was rude, but I'm not going to apologize. My son William thinks worse. He thinks I'm a philanderer. Beyond that, he doesn't think much at all. Or at least he doesn't think about his father. But I refuse to think it's wrong for a man to admire women, and I refuse to stop. I'm not dead yet." With that, he swung his arm over his head and began some kind of reaching exercise.

She couldn't decide what she thought of him. She knew from his books that he considered himself a true detective, trusting his instincts as well as his senses. He claimed that he could read the report of a robbery, large or small, and tell at once the character of the work—the history and habits and class of the men involved. She bit her lip and mulled the possibilities. Maybe she couldn't claim to have his instincts, but she wanted to believe the man who'd founded the Pinkerton Detective Agency was capable of appreciating what instincts she did have.

The Lady Pinkerton Gets Her Man

"I think the Hooded Sleeper is in town," she told him when they began to walk again.

"That's what you said in your telegram," he answered. "No one else seems to share your opinion."

"I know, but . . ."

"Anarchists," he interrupted. "I hate them. They're all damned Frenchmen, you know, or else they've all read the same French philosophy books. The American way is hard work, frugality, and perseverance. It works. Do you know that there were twenty men who could call themselves millionaires in this country in eighteen-forty? There are now more than one hundred millionaires in America, including myself. We must be doing something right to generate all that wealth in forty years. However, White Springs is not the right kind of place to attract Anarchists. Believe me, it's too remote. Their comrades in Paris wouldn't notice their activities here. Anarchists in America always want the attention of the Anarchists in France."

"But there's an actor in town named Harry Bryant."

"Harry's in town? Hell, I'll have to catch one of his performances. I know him. He's an old school chum of my son William. He's been to our house in Chicago. You've met him?" he suddenly asked her.

She nodded. "Actually, I thought he might be involved in this."

"In anarchy? Harry? He doesn't even like to talk politics."

"He has expressed a particular dislike of Jay Gould."

"Hell, who hasn't? You know what really interests me?"

She shook her head.

"It's that meddlesome missionary woman. What's her name, Mary Something Davies?"

"Stillman. Mary Stillman Davies," Dayle prompted.

"That's the one. I can't tell you how long I've been trying to infiltrate that woman's missionary organization. That's what I want you to do—concentrate on her, win her confidence, help her with her rescues, and find out all you can about her."

Dayle suddenly remembered the expensive brooch on the woman's plain dress and her own sure knowledge that Mary Stillman Davies had a past, but Dayle had already decided she didn't care about the woman's past. The real mystery was why Allan Pinkerton was interested in Miss Davies.

"I'm afraid she already knows I'm a Pinkerton, and she didn't have much use for Pinkertons," Dayle told him, remembering her first encounter with the crusty church woman and her cane. "I doubt she'll trust me."

"Work on her. She'll soften up. It's going to take a woman to get inside that organization, precisely because she's already suspicious. Help her with another rescue. That should win her confidence."

"I don't think you understand," she said. "We nearly started a riot the other day. If Miss Davies continues rescuing Chinese girls . . ."

"Other than the Tong, I didn't think anyone much cared about a Chinese girl more or less," he interrupted. "Oh, Garrick Bateman obviously cares. His wife's charity is costing him a fortune." Allan Pinkerton chuckled at some wit in that comment that she missed. "Men will do the damnedest things for a woman," he added as if he thought that explained anything.

That wasn't what Dayle meant. "Why are you interested in Mary Stillman Davies?" she persisted.

"Not because of her girlish figure," he said, and winked.

"Fine," Dayle returned, "but exactly what is it about her that you want me to find out?"

"Everything," he said. "I want to know everything." He shook his head. "The biggest hazard in any investigation is your own prejudices—the things you don't let yourself see or think about. For that reason, it's best if you don't know what you're looking for. That way, you'll look for everything. Just observe and let me know what you learn. It'll come clear to you later."

Then, before she could ask again, he began telling a story about a gang of train conductors who were embezzling money from the railroad. "It was like discovering a whole new class of criminal," he was telling her. "Employees regularly filch from their employers," he said. "This was different. This was organized. Worse, nobody knew what to do about it. I mean, the crime wasn't even committed in one place. The trains crossed county lines and state lines. What sheriff were you going to report it to?" he asked. "That's when the railroad knew they needed Pinkertons. Same thing, you know. Miss Davies and her underground cross all lines and one ocean—clear to China. I want to know how she's got that set up and everything about what she does."

Dayle's thinking did another flip-flop. Maybe she'd overlooked something important, something beyond the obvious fact that Miss Davies had come down in life. Beyond that, no matter how she turned this new twist, she could make no sense of it.

Mr. Pinkerton had started walking again. "Forty minutes," he said. "A good, stiff forty-minute walk every day. That's the secret to health and clearing the mind. Herbal drinks are good, served warm. But baths should be taken cold. Do you eat oatmeal regularly?"

"Oatmeal?" she asked, wondering at yet another change of subject.

"Yeah, oatmeal is supposed to keep the system regulated," he continued. "I personally think oats should be fed to horses, but my doctor thinks it's wonderful. He calls it nature's food. Ask me, wine is nature's food. Wine, women, and song."

With that, he started to hum. "You can sing along," he added a minute later. "If you like, that is."

It was not a tune she knew.

15

The next morning, Dayle found herself sitting in her boss's office and listening to him retell her encounter with Mr. Pinkerton, or at least his version of it.

"He says he tests all his agents that way. Sneaks up on them. Tries out their reflexes. He believes it's important that the men who work for him have good reflexes. The ladies, too," Thuzla Smith continued.

He seemed relaxed this morning, Dayle thought. More than that, he seemed pleased that he'd tipped a glass with America's chief detective and now had an audience for the telling of it.

"Good reflexes indicate good health," he went on. "Mr. Pinkerton says he never skips his own daily health regimen, which includes stretching and walking."

"And lots of oatmeal," Dayle added.

Thuzla Smith shook his head. "He didn't mention the oatmeal."

That wasn't the only pertinent part of the story he hadn't mentioned. Dayle wondered if there was any truth Allan Pinkerton didn't improve. According to Thuzla, Mr. Pinkerton had surprised Dayle with a tap on the shoulder.

"But the best part was him describing how you landed him in the dust. I couldn't believe it. You actually had him in the dust?" Thuzla now asked.

She nodded affirmatively.

Thuzla continued to shake his head. "He says he's had more than one agent pin him against a wall, but he never had one put him in the dust. He thought you were really remarkable."

"He's not a very big man," she said, "physically speaking."

"Doesn't matter. It was all he could talk about last night."

Dayle wasn't sure how she felt about having been the entertainment that went with last evening's drinks. She wanted to get on with the matters at hand. "What do you know about that missionary woman, Mary Stillman Davies?" she asked.

Thuzla ignored her. He wasn't through with his regaling. He brought both hands up and told how Allan Pinkerton showed everyone his hat, which was still dusty from the encounter, and then a scratch on his ebony cane that he also blamed on the incident.

Finally, that seemed to cover everything he could remember or wanted to relate. He sat back and tapped the edge of his desk a couple of times while he looked at Dayle. Then he snorted a little noise of disbelief. "All that, and he thinks you're something special."

"Well, I did wear the dress you suggested."

Thuzla sat forward again. "He only mentioned that he'd given you a special assignment."

"I know. Mary Stillman Davies. That's what I came to talk about."

"He wants you to help her with her next rescue, win her confidence . . ."

"The next rescue? The last one caused such problems in Chinatown, even the Tong couldn't handle it, and when we got to the train station . . ."

"You know, I've never actually had an assignment that came directly from Mr. Pinkerton. It's always come through branch offices, other intermediaries," Thuzla was now telling her.

He wasn't going to help. In fact, he thought she should be flattered, she realized. She took a breath. "Is there a file on Miss Davies?" she asked him.

He looked blank.

"How long has she been doing her adventure charity?"

He shook his head.

"There have been Chinese miners in White Springs for ten years," Dayle continued. "Why is she only now taking an interest in rescuing the prostitutes here?"

"I suppose because Mrs. Bateman invited her to take up the work here. Nobody else was going to do anything like that. I mean, can you imagine one of the engineers' wives doing something like that, or one of the miners' wives?"

"That's because everyone knows that Garrick Bateman allows the girls to be brought here to keep his miners happy."

"Sure."

"Everyone except his wife?"

He shrugged.

"Doesn't that strike you as strange?"

"No. She's Bostonian high society. She may not know how things are done in the West. All I know is that whatever she wants, she gets. Garrick Bateman is that doting when it comes to his high-class woman. Indeed, he is."

"I understand that, but why is Allan Pinkerton interested in this? Why is it so important to him?"

"I don't know," he told her, "but don't underestimate the man just because you were able to trip him once."

She thought that was probably the first good advice he'd given her.

"Besides, most of life is knowing when to follow orders," he added.

"If you're a soldier," she returned. "I thought we were detectives. We're supposed to ask questions. Remember?"

Out in the red desert west of White Springs, William Pinkerton came across a water station. It consisted of nothing more than a water tower, a telegraph, and one old guy known as the pumper, who tended the place and pumped water into any locomotive that stopped there. It had been days since William had crossed a telegraph line, a railroad track, or any other sign of civilization. He thought he ought to check with the office in Chicago while he had the opportunity.

He and his posse rode up to the shack where the pumper lived and greeted the old guy. He told them he called himself Charlie but didn't seem very sociable other than that. William climbed off his horse and handed the reins to the Indian tracker he'd hired. He stretched his back and shook out his legs. He'd been in the saddle a long time. When he slapped his hat against his leg, knocking the dust off, his horse danced sideways. The Indian struggled to hang on to the animal.

William shook his head. The horse was a spirited buckskin with three darker stocking feet and a tendency to sidestep at every strange sound, odd shadow, or stick that looked like a snake. Not a big surprise. Every horse purchased hurriedly at some "end of the railroad" point could be counted on to have at least one bad habit. He would have preferred one that bucked, reared, or bit. Skitters were the worst.

Hired trackers were the same, unfortunately. Every one of them came with an annoying idiosyncrasy. His current tracker was a talker—a little unusual for the

The Lady Pinkerton Gets Her Man

trade. Not just a talker, he had opinions, all of them more or less centered on the same subject. Joseph Longfoot was a small man, Oxford-educated, a full-blooded Blackfoot, the grandson of a famous Indian chief. He kept saying over and over in perfect king's English that he'd gotten his "real education" from his grandfather, who read the sky, not books.

William had also gotten a European education. Not at Oxford. His had been more practical. He'd spent two years working with Scotland Yard and the French Sûreté. He'd come home with fresh ideas about the value of fingerprints and the application of science to criminal investigation, but his father had no use for "crime labs."

"The really important stuff isn't in books," Joseph Longfoot told William as he climbed off his own horse. William's father believed the same, which meant this was not a subject William cared to discuss. Besides, the tracker had said it enough times that William caught himself mouthing the words with him.

Traveling with a hired posse meant spending morning, noon, and night with your men. Under those circumstances, it wasn't long before you knew which ones had enough sense not to piss into the wind and which ones didn't. You also found out which ones loved their mothers, talked in their sleep, and farted after eating beans. Not exactly first-class living. William loved it. Even with a bad tracker and a bad horse, he liked the life. Everything was so much simpler. Even the annoyances were surface and could be mostly ignored. Better yet, you knew what you were doing and why. At the moment, he was making sure the bad guys didn't get away with robbing a train. That was the confusing part of being Allan Pinkerton's son. His father got away with everything.

The tracker talked on. "My grandfather could read volumes from the sky. What the sky didn't tell him, the land did. It's the oldest and best wisdom, you know?"

William knew that the tracker's grandfather had been shot in an uprising eight years ago. William thought he should have joined a Wild West show or taken up writing books like other famous Indians—Sarah Winnemucca, Black Elk, and Quanah Parker. Like his father. The book writers were the ones who would survive history. Biggest trick of all. In fact, most of what people knew or thought they knew of the West came from books like the ones William's father wrote—dime adventures. His father hadn't even been west that many times. There seemed to be nothing his father didn't get away with.

William asked the old guy about using the telegraph and was shown inside, where he immediately settled himself next to the one window and began tapping out his message. That done, he sat back, stared out the window, and waited.

Outside, the other five men he'd hired squatted to the ground in the shade of their horses and rolled smokes.

The tracker stood in the doorway and continued to talk.

Charlie made coffee and offered William a newspaper. He was proud of the fact that it was only two days old. The conductor on the last train to stop had given it to him.

For the next couple of hours, William read the paper, drank coffee, and swatted flies.

He'd sent his usual message to Chicago asking for news and any messages. He'd also asked if there was any report on the band of outlaws he was chasing. If they were operating anywhere close, the Chicago office would know.

That was one of the oddities of living in the telegraph age. Sometimes the office in Chicago knew more about the outlaws he was chasing than he did.

The Lady Pinkerton Gets Her Man

Telegraph wire stretched farther than Indian eyes could see. William thought about that fact as his hired tracker continued to talk and talk. After a while, William found it hard to act interested. Joseph Longfoot finally took himself outside and annoyed the other men with his talk.

Still later, William went to the door and looked out over the land. It was wide, dry, barren. Other than this little outpost, there was no other sign of human habitation except for the train tracks and the line of telegraph poles, breaking up the sky like crosses.

The response was slow in coming. William finished the pot of coffee. The men finished their smokes. They'd pulled their hats over their faces and were taking naps. The horses, too, rested on three legs, their heads down. Once in a while, one of the horses blew dust from its nostril with a loud snort. Even the tracker had given up. He sat with his back against the telegraph pole, dozing.

At last, the key began to tap. William felt for a notepad. He knew telegraph operators who could listen to the clicks and repeat the words as they came in. He wasn't that good. He had to write first, decipher later. When the key fell silent, William moved his finger across his notepad, separating the words.

It was as he thought. The gang he was chasing had struck again, robbing a bank in a town fifty miles north. They were last seen heading in his direction. That was good news. It was the first real break he'd had while chasing this bunch.

There was more to the message. His father was in Wyoming. He'd taken a train to White Springs the day after William had left. His mother wanted him to leave off his present chase and go directly to White Springs. They were expecting labor trouble there, and she wanted him to "watch out for" his father.

William knew too well what watching out for his father meant. It meant that his mother wanted him to find out what the old man was really doing. His father never left the office to go someplace like Wyoming unless he had a woman friend or wanted to annoy William and his brother or thought there was serious business to be handled.

William considered the third possibility. There were a great many Pinkertons in White Springs. He'd sensed the tension. The mines there were vital to keeping the nation's trains running, he knew. He also knew that, like it or not, his father had aged. If there was serious trouble in White Springs, there was a real possibility that his father would make it worse, not better. Lately, he had a tendency to focus on the wrong details and stir up more trouble than he solved. It was as if he thought he could move through life the way he plotted his books.

William wavered, wondering what he should do. Then he tapped out another message. This time, he directed it to the New York office, where his younger bother, Robert, worked. Robert's response arrived within the hour. Yes, he knew that the old man was in Wyoming. He understood that he'd gone there after receiving a telegram from an agent named Dayle Dobson, a Lady Pinkerton.

William was suddenly thirsty. His father was old, and he'd suffered a stroke. God's warning for the man to get his life in order, but he was obviously going to chase skirt until he dropped. It would be just like him to die in some whore's bed.

He went to the door and called to Joseph Longfoot. "The gang is moving this way after having cleaned out a bank in Hope Town. Where do you think they're going next?"

The tracker stood and studied the horizon.

That gesture was for effect, William suspected. He honestly didn't know how the sky was going to answer this question.

"Silver Gap," the Blackfoot tracker said.

"Where's that?"

"The only bar between here and the Hole-in-the-Wall. They'll be wanting a drink."

William knew the feeling. In fact, the closest bar sounded damned good to him. "We're going to Silver Gap, then," he said as he paid the old guy for the coffee and the use of the wire.

He hadn't answered Chicago. He'd let them think he hadn't gotten the message. That way, he wouldn't have to explain to his mother why he hadn't gone to White Springs. He'd known since he was ten years old that it didn't do any good to watch out for his father.

Dayle left the Pinkerton office thinking she really had no desire to find herself sitting in another coal bin under a Chinese laundry with Lotta Bateman while she was having silent hysterics. Furthermore, she was tired of pretending to be the woman's kin and carrying a sewing basket on her arm.

She wanted to walk into the nearest saloon, order a double whiskey, toss it back, and light a cigarette. She thought she might have done that except that this was White Springs, a company-owned coal mining town—very provincial. She doubted a woman would be welcomed in a bar here, much less allowed to smoke.

She settled for tossing her sewing basket into a trash barrel and taking herself to Garrick Bateman's office. She doubted she'd be welcome there, either, but it was better than going to Chinatown with his wife. Somebody needed to understand how really dangerous those rescues were, and since it involved his wife, he seemed like the right person.

Getting in to see Garrick Bateman was easier than she expected. Thirty minutes later, she swept into the man's office, giving her skirts an exaggerated swirl as she commented on the weather and the "pure beauty" of his desk. It was a truly magnificent desk. His whole office suggested "men's club" more than "working establishment."

He stood as gentlemen do when greeting a lady. His expression was startled and curious. He agreed that the wind was less cold today and seemed pleased that she'd noticed his cherrywood.

She was thinking what to say next when he added, "My horse stumbled the other day. That's why I lost the race. Dolph here agrees." With that, he nodded to a young accountant. They'd obviously been going over figures before her visit interrupted them.

The accountant was quick to agree, "Oh, yes, yes, yes. Everyone saw. The horse stumbled." He gathered up his ledgers and promptly excused himself.

Dayle agreed as well. Why not? If it was that important to him . . . She glanced around again, ran her hand over the cherrywood, and said, "Your wife does seem to dote on her horse. You were certainly a big man about it."

He liked that. "A big man, eh? I hope you're referring to more than my girth." Then he laughed while he slapped his belly.

Dayle shook her head. "I meant that everyone knows you run everything around here, everything in Wyoming, they say. No harm in a man indulging his wife if she's attached to a particular horse. However, there may be harm in her current charity. I was wondering. Has she considered other worthy causes—the miners' widows and orphans home, for example?"

"That's an ordinary charity. My wife's not an ordinary woman."

"Yes, I'm sure, but . . ."

"White Springs is a strange place for a woman of my wife's class and quality. She's from Boston, you know. She's used to having tea every afternoon and dressing for a party nearly every night. She gave all that up when she came west. Maybe I flatter myself,

The Lady Pinkerton Gets Her Man

but I think I'm giving her what the West has to offer—adventure."

That comment actually made more sense than she expected.

He continued, "Besides, she was really quite flushed after the rescue the other morning. What can I say? I know I'm indulgent. I try to be a good husband, even when I'm not allowed to give my wife a better horse than that damned bay mare."

Dayle smiled and ran her hand along the smooth edge of his desk one more time. The conversation wasn't going the way she wanted. How did she go from here to telling him that Lotta's rescues were dangerous—too dangerous? Meanwhile, she kept up the flattery. "Oh, I know," she told him. "You're a doting husband. Everyone knows that. Most of the people at the picnic think you made your horse stumble on purpose. For Lotta's sake. For your wife."

It was obvious that possibility hadn't occurred to him. Once he'd considered it, however, he really liked the idea. His face practically turned into one big smile.

She tried another tack. "What do you know about Mary Stillman Davies?"

"Not much. Why do you ask?"

"Mr. Pinkerton seems interested in her. I wondered if there was a reason for that."

Bateman laughed. "He's not interested in that missionary woman. He's interested in my wife's charity. He told me he understood about wives and their need to do good works. He thought what she was doing with Miss Davies was interesting. That's the word he used, *interesting.*"

"He told you that?"

"At lunch yesterday."

Dayle gave up. Garrick Bateman obviously had a complete blind spot when it came to his wife and her activities, which meant Dayle was going to have to

214

help Lotta rescue more Chinese girls. Lucky for the girls, at least.

On the side of town that was mostly abandoned, Daniel Suitter made the rounds of his bird coop, pulling tarps over his canary cages. The little birds fluttered their wings softly. They knew it was too early to go to sleep, but Daniel thought it was better that they roost than get overexcited, especially his nesting pairs. The slightest break in the usual routine, and his nesting birds could be nervy for a week, he knew, and it didn't take anything as grand as holding an anarchy meeting amidst their cages, either.

"Hush now," Daniel cooed to his birds, chortling soft nonsense that he hoped would calm them. In his heart, he understood why they didn't want to roost so early. He hated the dark himself. He'd spent too much of his life working the mines, descending into the tunnels before dawn, returning after sunset. Sometimes for months on end, he never saw any light but the flame of the candle attached to his miner's hat and the flicker of the kerosene lamp that lit his kitchen, where he ate his supper and changed for bed between shifts.

Not that he wasn't still a miner. Once you worked the mines, you were always a miner. There was never a night when Daniel didn't dream about being in the mines. Usually, his dreams were odd combinations of unusual images. He would be working the walls with a kitchen fork or wandering through the tunnels looking for something—his candle, his pick, his pants. Sometimes, he seemed to float through the tunnels. In those dreams, he was always asking the other miners for something—something that seemed important and was missing. On waking, he could never remember what.

Daniel had taken over an old stable in the abandoned section of town and converted it to a bird coop.

The Lady Pinkerton Gets Her Man

He'd salvaged shelves from a nearby general store, now empty, and stretched chicken wire over them to make nesting boxes. In the center, he'd installed an oversized potbelly stove, borrowed from an uninhabited hotel. His birds liked to be warm. He'd added a fourposter bed from the same hotel and a dresser. Those were in the loft. He liked living in the loft above his birds. They were smelly and sometimes noisy but less trouble than either of his wives had been.

Once he'd covered his birds, he propped the back door open and tied a neckerchief to the handle—a red one. That was the "all clear" sign. Not long after that, the men began to arrive, one by one, each with his coat turned up or his hat turned down. About a dozen in all. Different ages, different sizes, different temperaments.

Once inside the coop, the men greeted Daniel and then passed a bottle around. The last to arrive was the ice man with the bad knees. He no longer worked the mines, but, like Daniel, he would always be a miner. Daniel knew them all. To a man, they'd seen too much or heard too much or knew too many men who'd given their lives to the mines. Like the poor souls who suddenly couldn't stand the closeness of the tunnels anymore, these men couldn't take the conditions anymore. They'd begun to question the whole system of mines and miners who worked twelve-hour shifts using candles the company cut to eleven-hour lengths, expecting that the men would descend to their work in darkness and return the same way.

Daniel watched the men pass their bottle. He was feeling as edgy as his birds, waiting for the out-of-town Anarchist organizers to arrive. Every miner in White Springs had "buttons" down his back, Daniel knew, scabs that had formed over each vertebra from being repeatedly scraped against the low ceilings inside the tunnels. Got so the miners didn't trust anyone who didn't have his buttons. Daniel knew at least one of these Anarchist fellows didn't have buttons. After helping him close down mine number 2, Daniel wondered if he had a backbone. Of course, except for the mechanic brothers, none of the other men had seen what Daniel had seen. To them, that particular out-of-town organizer was just a strange little fellow with an odd voice. Maybe it was better they didn't know more, didn't know that they'd sold their souls to new devils, Daniel thought as the out-of-towners arrived.

The thin one had a satchel under his arm. With him was the masked man, wrapped in a hooded cape. Everyone knew he was the Hooded Sleeper, although no one ever said as much. The mysterious masked man usually stayed in the shadows at the back of the room. It was the thin little man who immediately stood before the group, the satchel still under his arm, and introduced himself using his Anarchist name.

Anarchists all had names like "Death's Angel" or "The Avenger." Daniel called himself "The Devil Dancer." In meetings like this, they used their Anarchist names even if they worked side-by-side with one of the others and knew his real name was John or Percy.

This was all quite usual. Still, the men shifted in their seats and glanced around at one another. They had more reason than Daniel's birds to be nervous about this meeting. Except for the ice man, they'd all signed contracts saying that they could be fired for any kind of labor agitation. Fired with no hope of ever getting another mining job anywhere, and it wouldn't matter who caught them—the company bosses, the Pinkertons, the Tong. In fact, they might be more than fired. If they were caught in the company of the Hooded Sleeper, they might be lynched.

After the little thin man had shared his name and a certain handshake, he got down to business. "I'm not here to organize a strike. Can't be done in White Springs," he told the group.

The Lady Pinkerton Gets Her Man

For a moment, the men sat stone still, the last of their liquor and the last of their banter swallowed in the same gulp.

"Yeah, well, if you're not here to organize a strike, what are you going to do?" someone asked, giving the common question a voice.

"Help the Chinese go home," the thin man answered.

That got a scattering of laughter across the room.

"I've been wanting to do that for years," someone said.

"Me, too."

"Yeah, but how we going to do it?"

A smart-ass in the back started singing a common ditty:

> "Poor Johnny Chinaman
> Sitting on a fence
> Trying to make a dollar
> Out of fifteen cents."

Daniel looked around. The thin one did most of the talking in meetings like this. Sometimes he really got wound up, going on and on about how hierarchical authority was detrimental to human potential—theoretical stuff that normally bored. Only the thin one seemed to get away with it. In an over-the-top theatrical and somewhat showy style, he entertained even when Daniel was quite sure no one in the audience had the slightest idea what he was talking about.

While he was doing that, the mysterious one watched from the back, studying the group. Daniel knew because he'd watched him watching the others. Smart. He supposed it was important for him to separate the trustworthy from the untrustworthy, the devoted from the malcontents. Plus, there were always spies who needed to be ferreted out.

"All I want to know is how we're going to make the

Jerrie Hurd

Chinese go home," one miner now called out with impatience in his voice.

"The Chinese worship at their ancestors' graves the way some of you worship in your churches," the thin one told the man. "We don't have to make them go home. They *want* to go home."

"Then why don't they?" someone else asked.

"Can't. The Tong is holding them hostage. That's why they need our help," he answered.

"Help?" another man questioned. "That'll be the day when I help a Chinaman."

"Yeah, me, either," someone else offered.

"Yeah, I've had enough of this," another said, coming to his feet. "Let's just run the Mongolians out. They've already done that in Denver."

"Burned the Denver Chinatown to the ground," someone said. "Not four months ago."

The thin one tried to ignore those comments and continued outlining the broader plan. "We're going to sabotage the tracks, damage the mine equipment, inconvenience the pit bosses . . ."

A broad-shouldered miner cleared his throat. "You're talking about soaped tracks."

"Yeah," another miner said. "I heard about those soaped tracks. Cute trick. Closing mine number 2 was better."

"Better?" someone else asked. "Who suffered? The miners who couldn't go down that mine and make their day's pay. That's who."

"It's the miners who always suffer."

"If you haven't got better ideas than that!"

Daniel Suitter slid forward on the box where he sat. He reached down. He grabbed his wooden leg and swung it around, readying it in case he needed to stand quickly. Daniel Suitter was fifty years old, and he'd known trouble, "the devil," all his life. More, even, than his wooden leg and scarred face would admit. Trouble didn't scare him. That's why he'd be on his feet telling these men to shut up and listen if he had to. It was clear to him that the thin one was losing control.

"It's going to take more than soaping railroad tracks to make a difference 'round here," one said.

"That's right."

"Damned right. This is coal country. Fancy talk and soaped tracks don't break rock here."

"We are offering more than soaped tracks," the thin one shouted above his hecklers. Then he dumped out the satchel he'd carried in under his arm. Cash spilled across the floor. Lots of money. "We didn't just soap the tracks," he told the men again. "We robbed the train."

The men looked over their shoulders to where the mysterious caped figure stood in the back. Then, wordlessly, they returned their gazes to the front again.

"You robbed a Pinkerton-guarded train?" one asked in a decidedly different tone.

The thin one nodded. "Who better to finance our plans than the eastern monopolists themselves? After all, they're the ones who have all the money."

There was a definite pause, an almost respectful hush. Everyone sitting in that bird coop knew the Pinkertons liked to brag about how no one got away with robbing a Pinkerton-guarded train. The men knew that, seemed to respect that, but it wasn't enough to swing the mood.

"The real money is in Chinatown."

"Stashed in every mattress and under every floorboard."

"I'd like some of their gold."

Daniel sensed that the out-of-town organizers had underestimated the depth of anger in these men. The White Springs miners weren't going to settle for anything short of real action, and that was exactly wrong. A riot in Chinatown would accomplish nothing.

One of the men had already grabbed a loose board

and tied an empty feed sack around one end, turning it into a torch. He was asking where Daniel kept his kerosene, so he could light it. A couple of others had pulled guns out from under their jackets. All the men were on their feet now. Shouting.

"What did Moses do when the children of Abraham were being enslaved by the pharaoh of Egypt?" the mysterious one asked from the back of the room. His voice was low and strong. It immediately silenced the others.

"Did Moses call for a strike? Maybe he could have. Maybe he should have. There were no Chinese to prevent that. Nobody had strike-proofed Egypt."

At first, the men were startled. The mysterious organizer rarely spoke. Now his voice rolled out over the room like steam coming to a head. It was a voice with authority.

Following the initial surprise, a couple of the men found what he was saying to be silly.

"This ain't church."

"What's with the sermon?"

Two or three others snickered.

The mysterious Anarchist, the Hooded Sleeper, stepped into the light. "But no," he told them. "No, Moses was a smart man. He had a better idea. Plagues. He brought plagues down on Egypt. One plague after another. What was the pharaoh to do? Was his army any good against a plague? Were his advisers any help against a plague? He even called in the royal sorcerers. No good. Nothing stops a plague. The old pharaoh of Egypt had no choice. He had to let the Hebrew slaves go."

The hair stood up on the back of Daniel's neck. He felt fairly sure most of the men in that room had no idea what this mysterious devil was talking about, but none of them resisted the spell of his talk. He now moved among the men, eyeing them from under the shadow of his hood and through his mask.

"If we're smart, we're going to do the same right

here in White Springs, Wyoming. We're going to bring one plague after another down upon this town until the pharaoh of the railroad has no choice. He'll have to let his Chinese go."

By then, only the man with the unlit torch had any fight left.

"Who needs fancy talk?" he asked. "Plagues and pharaohs?" He snorted. "What's all that? We know what we have to do"

He expected the others to agree. No one did.

For a moment, everything hung in the balance. Then one miner shuffled his feet. A couple of others sat again. The mysterious organizer had touched something—he'd won. Daniel slid back on his box and was satisfied in a quietly resigned way. He'd already seen the thin one turn into a man-worm. Now he figured he had just witnessed the surfacing of the devil in the more dangerous of the two.

16

The next morning, Dayle gave herself a good talking to. Brushing her hair with more than usual vigor, she told herself that she was a Lady Pinkerton, and as a Lady Pinkerton she had a job to do. Jobs were jobs. There were the parts that you liked and might do for no pay, and then there were the parts for which you knew you weren't getting paid enough.

She didn't think she'd ever forget Quee Sing and Kim Ying sitting on that train station platform, eating crackers and giggling. She thought every Chinese girl in every Chinatown in the West ought to have a chance to laugh like that. The excitement of rescuing the girls wasn't a problem. She thought she might get used to running over rooftops if she had some practice at it. All of that was simply part of the job.

She was a Lady Pinkerton partly because she couldn't let things alone. It was a complaint she'd heard all her life, from the sisters at the orphanage, her teachers, sometimes even her colleagues at the agency. She could never let a thing alone until she

The Lady Pinkerton Gets Her Man

understood it, all of it, every why and wherefore. It amazed her that others could live in a fog of social politeness, never wanting to peek under the veneer. It was as if they hated exposure, the way she hated heights.

She wasn't going to apologize for that. In fact, she figured it was about time she applied some of her dogged determination to the mysterious Miss Davies. Why not? Most people had secrets. No reason to avoid this feisty church woman and her past.

Dayle gave her hair a twist, pinned it up, and went downstairs to join Lotta, who was entertaining.

Besides Lotta, ten other ladies were laughing and talking excitedly as they draped the furniture of the breakfast room in linen and lace. Not furniture covers. Ladies' underwear. Piles of petticoats, corsets, and fancy underdrawers were already being strewn all around the room in gay mayhem by the time Dayle arrived.

In the midst of that excitement stood three huge wardrobe trunks, upright and open—the source of the wares being examined with such obvious enthusiasm. Stationed next to the center trunk was a prim middle-aged woman in a respectable travel dress that included enough black to suggest recent widowhood, that kind of misfortune being the only acceptable excuse for her to have taken up the genteel occupation of being a traveling undergarment saleslady.

As Dayle walked in, Lotta was holding up a particularly fine corset of yellow silk satin, a currently popular color. At the same time, she was exclaiming above the general chatter that it would look wonderful over a lace-trimmed cotton chemise. Seeing Dayle, she paused and offered a welcoming wave.

"Oh, dear cousin, where have you been? Come in. Come in. You have to see the embroidered edges on this French chemise." She put down the corset and picked up another garment, saying, "It's such fine work. Incredibly nice. Anyone who makes her living with a needle has to be appreciative of this."

That's when Dayle remembered to duck her chin, straighten her back, and greet the ladies in the proper demure and genteel fashion of a seamstress. Never mind that she'd ditched her sewing basket yesterday. She had a job to do, she reminded herself.

For the next little while, Dayle mingled, expressing an appropriate interest in the wares. She knew many of these women from the picnic. An older lady who'd been "under the weather" that day, introduced herself. Then the same woman was quick to add that she'd "heard all about it." From the look she gave her, Dayle assumed the woman meant that she'd heard all about Harry winning the horse race with Lotta's mare. That was still the main topic of conversation.

The saleswoman stepped forward with a black corset cover trimmed with tucks and narrow lace. With an apology, she explained that she had only one, but she could order more. That, of course, gave the garment an aura of being the absolute latest in fashion. It also served to focus the women back on her wares—not some four-day-old horse race.

Dayle appreciated the saleswoman. She had her act down to perfection, smiling sweetly at everything the other women said but never really joining in, as if to imply that she was consumed by a large, unspoken grief. She was dressed well but not showy. She'd even created a tattered look around her sleeve edges and hem as if to suggest that she'd known better times. That pity factor undoubtedly encouraged the other women to justify making larger purchases because they were "helping the poor woman." It was exactly the same sort of look and attitude Dayle was expected to assume as Lotta's second cousin, she knew.

In a different setting, Dayle might have tipped a glass to her. For, despite the lovely impression she was creating, Dayle doubted her history included mourning a dead husband. "There are no ladies west of

Dodge City and no women west of Denver," the saying went, and while that was rapidly changing, it was still true that only whores and rich men's wives bought fancy underwear from traveling saleswomen like this one. The rich wives could be fooled easily with a sad story, from all appearances, but Dayle knew the whores wouldn't trust any woman who hadn't experienced their life.

The other part of this scene that Dayle found amusing was the "naughty talk." The woman with the wide mouth now waltzed around the room holding up a dull red "dress improver" and said, "I knew nothing when I got married. It was all such a surprise."

"I was given a pretty pamphlet to read."

"Oh, me, too,"

"I'll bet it was the same one."

"Did it have borders with delicate flowers?"

"Oh, yes, and it was filled with poems so coy on the subject that I had no idea what it was talking about."

"Until after."

"Oh, well, surely after. That was different."

"My mother told me the real use of good underwear," another offered. There was a pause while everyone waited for her to finish. "It presents the appropriate amount of difficulty," she finally added.

That was greeted with a surprising amount of giggled agreement, which puzzled Dayle. Obviously, these women hadn't learned how to turn every layer into a tease. She glanced at the saleswoman. She knew. Then Dayle also caught the wry smile on the face of the young engineer's wife, and she immediately thought that was one woman who ought not to be left home alone.

Dayle turned her attention to Mary Stillman Davies, who was sitting quietly near the front window, sipping tea. From across the room, she was a portrait of proper ladylike decorum. Her hat removed, her skirts smoothed, her Bible open next to her teacup. Everyone had a role to play. Hers was church lady.

"You don't enjoy fine underwear?" the woman asked with her usual bluntness as Dayle took a seat across the table from her.

The maid brought tea.

Dayle shrugged and stirred in a little sugar. As a "charity case," Dayle had always worn only the finest Irish lace because of the "generosity" of women like these who bought the best and discarded last season's fashion with every spring and fall cleaning. She was grown-up before she knew that not everyone could afford the same.

"Fine underthings have their place," she answered.

"As does the natural female figure," Miss Davies retorted. "Do you know that wearing corsets is as disfiguring to a woman as the Chinese custom of binding a woman's feet?"

Dayle didn't know how to answer that. Either Miss Davies was determined to get a reaction, or she really enjoyed reading her Bible and wanted to be left alone, or she never wasted breath on subtlety. Whatever the excuse, she certainly wasn't easy.

"There are women my age who've worn a corset for so long and so tightly," Miss Davies continued, "that their internal organs have become rearranged. Now they have to continue to wear the corset just to keep themselves together. Same with the Chinese upper-class ladies. They've had their feet bound so long, they can no longer walk. But they can't take off the bindings now. If they did, they'd be in such pain they wouldn't be able to bear it."

This was exactly what Dayle disliked most about church women, missionary women, and the sisters at the orphanage. They all were too willing to spread their sanctimony—too willing to tell you what was wrong with everything. In this case, the attitude encompassed everyone from the women in this room to the wives of upper-class China.

"I don't understand," Dayle said, not because the words didn't make sense but because she didn't know

The Lady Pinkerton Gets Her Man

where the conversation was going, and she didn't know how else to respond.

"It's as if a beautiful woman isn't good enough for a wealthy man. He has to have an ideal one, a molded one," the older woman added. "Strange what we're willing do to ourselves because we think we need Irish lace."

Dayle sipped her tea and wondered what the other woman was really saying. That left Dayle studying her an uncomfortably long time until she thought to say, "Nobody needs Irish lace if you know how to walk like Irish lace."

"How's that?" the other woman asked.

Dayle shrugged. "Save your money. If you act like Irish lace, everyone assumes you've got it." Then, even though she was sitting, Dayle ruffled her skirt into place with exactly the right amount of such style.

To her surprise, Miss Davies actually smiled. "Well done." Then she tightened her expression and added, "But, of course, you know it's only women of humble origins who need to learn to walk like Irish lace. Women who are born to it learn it the way they learn their mother tongue. Where did you grow up?"

"Doesn't matter where we come from; it's where we go," Dayle said, mouthing the one platitude she'd ever found useful. At the same time, she wished she hadn't started on this subject.

"Simple beginnings are nothing to be ashamed of," the other confirmed. "Everybody enjoys a good Cinderella story, especially a true one."

Dayle didn't believe in fairy-tale endings. Even the Chinese girls they rescued would never have the kind of life they once might have dreamed of having, surrounded by their families and familiar places.

"Where did you grow up?" Miss Davies asked again.

"Doesn't matter," Dayle returned.

"Then why not tell me?"

Dayle did.

Miss Davies set her cup down. Then she told Dayle that she knew the old mother superior at St. Elizabeth's. She named a couple of the sisters and asked, "How did you come to be there? Did you lose your parents to the influenza epidemic? I'm guessing you're about the right age for that."

Dayle shook her head. "My mother left me at the orphanage and never came back," she answered, thinking that would end the discussion. Bold facts often had that effect on talk.

For a moment, it had exactly that effect. More than silence. Miss Davies's chin came up, and she seemed to catch her breath. "Do you remember your mother?" the older woman asked in a quieter tone.

For a moment, Dayle didn't know what to say. She felt overcome by a confusion that bordered on embarrassment as she realized that she'd lost track of what she remembered and what she'd turned into fantasy.

"No," Dayle managed to answer, not because she didn't remember but because she didn't want to continue this. She never talked about how she grew up.

Miss Davies sipped her tea and studied Dayle a moment. "You know, it's the Chinese mothers who sell their daughters to the Tong. They sell them knowing what will happen to them. Then they cut their hair and cry. They mourn their daughters as if they were dead."

"What does that matter to me?" Dayle asked.

"Only that I think you might try not to be too hard on your mother. Who knows why she did what she did?"

Dayle knew that.

What she remembered about her mother was that she was pretty and had long, silky hair. Dayle also remembered that for a long time, she woke every morning thinking this was going to be the day when her mother would come back for her. She had believed in mother love, the notion that mothers didn't abandon their children, at least not forever. She thought a mother would do anything, sacrifice anything, always come back. Then, one day, Dayle had figured out that her mother was too smart for that kind of sentimentality. From that moment on, she thought of her mother as strong and brave and free, riding a black horse at full gallop, her hair flowing behind, caught by the wind, her head never turning, never looking back.

In the background, Dayle heard the others talking about inconsequential things.

"I've ordered the most lovely holiday dress of pale lime silk with cream lace," one woman said.

"Oh, and I found this wonderful flowered aquamarine material . . ."

Dayle glanced in their direction because she couldn't look at Miss Davies. She'd sat down intending to probe the other woman, perhaps learn something. Instead, Mary Stillman Davies had turned the tables on her and practically laid Dayle bare. Mary Stillman Davies was something. Dayle just didn't know what, and she didn't know when she was likely to find out.

"I'm sorry, I've made you uncomfortable," Miss Davies said, and closed her Bible.

Dayle turned her gaze to the missionary woman, noting again the fine silver brooch she always wore at her neck. "Odd you should mention it. I had the impression that you enjoyed making me uncomfortable," Dayle told her, and then she excused herself.

17

Southwest of White Springs, where the red desert bumps up against a labyrinth of dry canyons and cliff-banded mesas, William Pinkerton hunkered behind a rock outcropping. There, somewhat sheltered from the wind, he held his hat against his face, protecting his eyes while a swirl of sand passed. Taking the binoculars from his hired tracker, he trained them on the collection of adobe shacks known as Silver Gap.

Not much to look at.

He lifted the binoculars to the land beyond. Even chilled and wind-weary, he never ceased to be amazed by the American West. It was a world of landforms so powerful, mysterious, colorful, intricate, and bizarre, it was as if it constituted a separate reality. William half expected the current view to slide away, like sand slipping through an hourglass, into something more ordinary—right before his eyes. It was only when he put his arms down and felt the grit in his armpits that he remembered this country could be hard as well as haunting.

The Lady Pinkerton Gets Her Man

He and his posse had ridden all morning into a nasty, cold wind. The grit was in his boots, under his belt, in his hair. The red blowing sand had stained the men's faces and made the horses look shaggy. He took a handkerchief from his back pocket and blew the sand out of his nose. Meanwhile, a fresh blast cut against his cheek. He was cold and miserable and happier than he ever was in Chicago. Here, he knew the wind would die away eventually. In Chicago, he was never sure what he could count on.

"It's them. We found them," the tracker said, directing William's gaze back to the wind-whipped town. "See the horses? The tall black one made the deep tracks I was following," the tracker went on.

Binoculars in place, William forced himself to concentrate on the business at hand. Finding a gang of outlaws was one thing, capturing them was another. He took note of the horses. Seven, mixed in size and color, all huddled in the corner of a corral behind the stable, their heads down, their tails to the wind. The tall black did stand out.

The hired tracker was still going on and on. "That's how my grandfather taught me to track whole armies. You first pick out some track, some sign that's unique, like the deep tracks that black horse makes. Then you track that one animal without worrying about how many others are marking the same trail."

William grunted. The simpler truth was that there was no reason for seven men to travel across this country together unless they were an outlaw gang or a posse. Prospectors traveled alone, settlers with a family, cattlemen with cows, sheepmen with dogs.

He turned the lenses to a sharper focus. There was a hitching post, the saloon, a two-story building with a sagging front porch which was probably the trading post, the stable with the corral in back, and four smaller buildings, probably houses. More outpost than town, the entire place was colorless except for the red earth, shapeless except for the supporting timbers sticking out from the roofs. He studied the man leaning against the outside of the flat-roofed adobe shack with the door hanging askew that announced itself on a crude wooden sign as the Silver Gap Saloon. He was smoking a cigarette, and William figured he was the lookout.

"Besides, those horses all look ridden." The tracker continued to articulate the obvious.

William wished the man had learned to sing. He knew men who could sing for hours. They'd sing all the time, marking the sway of their horse as they both walked along. Singing was fine. Singing required no response.

"Not that I needed a trail, mind you. I know this country, and I'd have come straight to this place even without sign to follow," the man continued. "Everybody's got to get a drink before heading into the badlands. Nobody goes into those canyons sober. I mean, you'll think you're drunk before you make your way through those canyons, so you might as well start that way."

William grunted again. He'd have preferred coming upon this gang of ne'er-do-wells in open country. He was getting a sinking feeling from this. It was more than the despair of knowing he wasn't likely to get anything decent to drink down there. He'd figured out that it wasn't going to be easy getting those outlaws out of that saloon.

He didn't want to wait. Under cover of darkness, it would be too easy for them to split up and slip away, one by one, into the canyons beyond. Likewise, he didn't want to set siege to the place. Adobe withstood bullets—absorbed them. If the outlaws decided to hole up inside, William and his men might fire every bit of their ammunition into those walls and never drive them into the open. Not to mention the fact that they likely had more food and drink in there than he did out here. No way to smoke them out, either. Adobe held the heat. Even though the wind outside

The Lady Pinkerton Gets Her Man

had turned cold, there was no smoke coming out the saloon's chimney. Obviously, it hadn't turned cold inside yet.

William stood. He tipped his hat into the wind and made his way back to where the other members of his posse were holding the horses on the windward side of a larger rock ridge. The tracker trotted behind him, still talking.

"What are we going to do?" he asked as William opened one of his saddlebags and pulled out a dirty buckskin jacket.

"You're going to stay here," William answered as he pulled off his mackinaw and put on the buckskin. He also found a slouch hat, which he pulled down over his ears instead of the stiffer, wider-brimmed hat he usually wore. "I'm going down alone," he added.

The tracker had to think about that. William continued to rummage through his saddlebag.

He was thirteen years old when his father taught him the value of simple disguises. At fifteen, he'd already been decorated for bravery as a Union spy in the Civil War. Back then, the Pinkertons called what they did "spying." Now they called it "detecting," because most people had an aversion to hiring "spies," including the U.S. government. In fact, government agencies were forbidden to spy unless the nation was under a formal declaration of war.

William found what he was looking for—a gun, an older, heavier model. It was the kind of gun a miner, who mainly shoots snakes, would carry. William replaced the gun in his holster with it. At the same time, he slipped his own trusted revolver into his belt and closed the buckskin jacket over it.

Meanwhile, the tracker had recovered his speech. "Why don't we just steal their horses?" he suggested.

William shook his head. He'd already considered that. There was no way to take the horses without alerting the lookout. More than likely, the only thing they'd accomplish trying something like that was to announce themselves to the outlaws. That is, unless they waited until after dark, and William had already decided that was a bad idea.

"But you have no idea what's going on down there. What if they're already drunk? What if they're busy dividing the money? In that case, they'd as likely shoot you as look at you."

There was a time for talking and a time for doing, William thought, and he mounted his horse without saying more.

He rode away alone over the ridge, around the outcropping, and down toward Silver Gap.

When he was in view of the lookout, William slouched in the saddle like some worn-out prospector who'd been stooped under a low ceiling digging for too long. There was no trouble. The lookout saw him, looked him over from a distance, looked him over again as William climbed off his horse, and all the time he never even bothered to stand away from the wall.

William tied his horse to the hitching post. He slapped the dust from his hat, taking his time, while he looked over the man and the street in front of the saloon. As near as he could tell, there were no other lookouts. That bothered him. Unless this was an unusually stupid bunch of outlaws, they had to know they were being followed, yet they hadn't taken any extra precautions that William could see. He found that about as odd as their robbing one bank or train after another. Most outlaws, he knew, spent their first loot before going after more.

William muttered a western "howdy." Then he pushed through the saloon doors, thinking he would take care of the lookout later. Inside, William paused, letting his eyes adjust to the dim light. It was as he'd expected—dirt floors, dirt walls, rough-hewn tables, a dozen chairs, a bar slapped together from an old wagon box. No mirror, no piano, nothing fancy, nothing particularly clean.

Four of his outlaws were playing cards at one of the tables. Another sat with his back to the wall, looking on. Counting the one outside, that was only six. William made a quick glance all around. The barkeep was sitting on a stool, reading a book. Some old sot with a crippled arm was wiping the counter. Nobody else, but then, before that could really worry him, the seventh man wandered in through the back door, hitching his pants, obviously having made a trip to the shithouse.

He quickly joined the others at the poker table, while William took off his hat, wiped his forehead on the sleeve of his jacket, and said, "It's mighty windy out there. Makes a man dry."

Nodding to the others, William made his way to the bar, where he ordered a whiskey. Without looking up from the book he was reading, the barkeep reached under the counter, pulled out a bottle, and poured a yellow liquid, made yellower in the light of the saloon's kerosene lamps.

"That's all we got," he said. "It ain't got a name. Just drinking hooch."

At the same time, William recognized the book—one of his father's, an old one from the looks of it. It appeared to have been passed through several hands. The title had been rubbed partially off the front, and some of the pages were wrinkled as if they'd been wet once. William swore under his breath and wondered exactly how many miles he had to ride into this wilderness before he could get away from "Pinkerton True Detective Tales."

"Our barkeep is a reading man," one of the poker players observed. "We had to threaten to shoot him to keep him from reading out loud."

The barkeep merely shifted position on his stool and turned a page. The other boys at the poker game set down their cards.

William shrugged. "No mind of mine." At the same time, he noted the two bottles on the poker table and the several empties underneath. Most of the outlaws were drunk enough that he might be able to take them right here, right now, all by himself. He was pretty sure he could do that if he stayed sober enough to shoot straight.

"You a prospector?" the same outlaw asked.

William put his glass down without tasting the liquor. The man who spoke was the leader, he guessed. However, he wasn't the one who worried William the most. The smaller, silent man who sat with his back against the wall had an uncommon keenness. He hadn't missed a detail since William walked in, including the fact that he was wearing a better gun under his jacket than the one in his holster. William knew that from the way the man's gaze had flowed over him, pausing at the bulge near his belt. At that point, his and William's eyes had met briefly.

William rubbed his nose. "I'd like to find me a silver strike. Guess that makes me a prospector, all right."

The leader grunted. "How about a book reader? You also a book reader?" he asked.

William noted the old sot was still cleaning. He glanced at the barkeep again. If this turned to gunplay, William hoped the man, his book, and his partner would take cover, but he wasn't sure he could count on that. He knew more than one good Pinkerton agent who'd gotten himself killed because he misjudged a bystander's loyalties.

"Them books are all made-up, you know," the outlaw now offered. He was drunk, his gestures wide, his words slurred. "I used to get whipped for telling lies. 'Course, I never wrote any of my whoppers down. That's probably the difference. Ask me, Allan Pinkerton is a god-damned liar, the god-damnedest."

William thought the loud outlaw would be amused to know that he shared the same opinion of his father. But he didn't say anything. He watched the silent, keen-eyed outlaw slowly draw himself up straighter, his back still against the wall, his hands now closer to his hips and his guns.

"Ask me, reading books is stupid. People what read books get poisoned by them silly words. I mean, if Allan Pinkerton says he always gets his man, everybody believes him. Why? Because he wrote it in a book. That's why. Ain't no other reason. Don't make sense. That's the same as saying a man always gets the girl or never misses a shot. Ain't true. Can't be true. Want to know the real truth?" he asked.

William shook his head. He never wanted to discuss his father under any circumstances. But the man wasn't paying attention. He went right on.

"All a person has to do is get famous enough, and then old Mr. Pinkerton will give him a Pinkerton pardon. You familiar with a Pinkerton pardon?"

William shook his head again.

"That's how you get in one of them books. First, you got to rob yourself a whole string of banks and trains, enough to get a name for yourself, so you can't just be ignored like some common criminal. Then you retire. You take the money and go off somewhere quiet, change your name, start going to church. After a while, you'll read in the newspaper about how you've been killed in some shoot-out. A little later, you'll find yourself written up in one of those books. That's as good as a pardon. Nobody is going to come looking for a famous dead man. Hell, it's better than a pardon. Why, if you was to claim you was that famous dead man, nobody would believe you. Why should they? They got Mr. Pinkerton's books."

William fingered his drink. Out of the corner of his eye, he saw the silent, keen-eyed man nudge the talkative outlaw as if he thought to quiet him, but the man obviously liked talking. William was feeling as if he'd suffered a plague of talkers lately. First the hired tracker, now this loudmouth outlaw.

"Sounds like an outlaw's wishful thinking," he suggested, mainly just so as to say something. He

Jerrie Hurd

didn't want to get the man too riled, not yet. He was still sizing things up.

The man laughed. "Oh, I know what I'm talking about. All you got to do is think about it. This is a big country. In a big country, it's a lot cheaper to say some famous bad outlaw is dead than to track him to the ends of the earth like the Pinkertons claim they do. Besides, there ain't a Pinkerton agent got the balls or the brains to track anyone to the ends of the earth, in my humble opinion. That Pinkerton stuff is all brag. Book brag."

William lifted an eyebrow.

"You don't believe me?"

William quickly shrugged. He'd heard rumors, and there was something . . .

"I tell you, a friend of mine used to ride with the Morton gang until they got their Pinkerton pardon," the man went on.

William knew his father always said there was more than one way to take care of a criminal. But his father had spent too much of his life creating and upholding that Pinkerton reputation ever to . . . William swallowed dry spit and shook his head. "I heard the Morton gang all got killed up in Montana someplace."

The loud outlaw laughed again. "Yeah, that's what you're supposed to think. Like I told you, them books are all made-up." He made another broad gesture toward the barkeep. "Them pages are lies. Why do you want to read them lies?"

The barkeep had slipped one hand under the counter, which was probably where he kept his gun. At least William was no longer worried about his loyalties. The old sot was still cleaning the same spot, which William found annoying. He wished the man would move out of the line of fire.

More annoying was the spin William's head was in, not because he believed the braggart. It was drink talking—drink and some old schoolhouse hatred of

The Lady Pinkerton Gets Her Man

books the man still carried around like a grudge. Still, talk of his father always made William feel insubstantial, somehow, as if nothing he ever did or said would matter. Sooner or later, he, these outlaws, the whole Wild West would get sucked into his father's books.

William picked up his drink and shot it back without tasting it. That was the way he usually drank when he didn't want to think about his father. That was the loud outlaw's biggest mistake. He should have waited for William to down a few drinks before he started talking. This time, William didn't even wait for the sting of the liquor to hit the back of his throat.

With the same movement that set the glass down, he reached inside his shirt for his gun. He blew open the head of the keen-eyed man with his first shot. His next two shots were economically placed. He took out the man to the keen-eyed's immediate right and then the card dealer who was next closest. That meant the loudmouthed leader had time to jump up before taking a bullet full to the chest.

The noise, of course, attracted the guard outside. William figured on that. He came around the end of the bar, kicked the barkeep's stool over, sprawling him on the floor where he would be useless, and then, dropping low, he turned and shot the lookout as he came through the door.

The old sot was now crouched behind the counter. William leaped over him. That meant he was now at the opposite end of the bar. The last two outlaws hadn't figured that out yet. They fired their only shots in the wrong direction. William changed guns and cut them both down with the "snake popper" since his own weapon was down to one bullet.

It was over in seconds.

William fired once more when the guard from outside twitched.

Nothing else moved except the barkeep.

He came up from behind the bar with his hands raised in the air. "Don't shoot," he said. "Please don't shoot. I didn't know them. None of them. They were all strangers to me."

"What you got behind the bar?" William now asked.

"Just a shotgun. I don't see well enough to shoot anything that needs aiming," the man explained. "Can't really see much beyond these books I read."

William grunted. He could hardly swallow, his mouth was so dry, but ironically he felt a sweat rising on his forehead and in the middle of his back.

Despite his crippled arm, the old sot was crawling across the floor on his hands and knees, heading for the door.

"Where do you think you're going?" William now demanded.

"He don't hear," the barkeep answered for him.

"You don't see, and he don't hear?" William asked.

"Yes, sir. That's right."

William grunted again and glanced around at the carnage littering the dimness inside this dirty saloon, and he knew he was going to have nightmares. Six months' worth. That was something else that never made it into his father's books—the nightmares that followed a shoot-out.

William picked up the glass he'd emptied less than a minute earlier. He hefted it and let it fly at the saloon door, where it smashed, spraying glass over the old sot. That stopped his crawl. He rose to his knees, shaking, his hands over his head.

William thought that was more disgusting than the blood. He wanted to shoot the old guy simply because he didn't like him. For a moment, he wavered but then managed to think better. He turned to the barkeep instead. "I got to have something better than that yellow shit to drink."

The man nodded his head fast and nervous. Then he pried up one end of the bar, pulled out two bottles, and handed them to William.

"Who are you?" he asked.

The Lady Pinkerton Gets Her Man

"William Pinkerton," William answered. "And I don't give Pinkerton pardons."

With that, he kicked over the table where his outlaw band had been playing poker. He slung the bags of money over his shoulder. Returning to the bar, he took the bottles. Then, stepping around the cowering old sot, he started through the door.

"Does that mean this here shoot-out will be written up as a Pinkerton True Detective Tale?" the barkeep called after him. "Because if that's the case, my name is Bartrum Smith, Bartrum K. Smith, originally from St. Louis."

That stopped William. He didn't know what to say. He'd killed everything in the place except the pitiful thing at his feet and his father's fan. He shook his head. Somehow, he couldn't help wondering if he'd aimed wrong.

18

Dayle went to the theater that night. All by herself. She went because of Miss Valentine. She'd heard repeatedly that Harry was often seen in the company of that redheaded leading lady. Not that Dayle cared. She simply thought she'd like to know more about her.

She reasoned that the woman was probably an Anarchist along with Harry and Tommy and likely other members of the acting company. Therefore, she required watching. Besides, becoming friendly with an outlaw's girlfriend was standard practice for a Pinkerton detective.

Allan Pinkerton believed that men tended to be indiscreet around women. They bragged, and men's bragging became women's gossip. In case after case reported in the Pinkerton files, a crime was solved when an outlaw's girlfriend talked too freely, sometimes without ever realizing what she was doing. Dayle was following a tried and true detective meth-

The Lady Pinkerton Gets Her Man

od. At least, that's what she told herself as she took a seat on the main floor near the back of the theater.

The play was *A Midsummer Night's Dream,* a mix of love and farce and miscommunication. Miss Sarah Ellen Valentine, the woman with the red hair, made a wonderful queen of the fairies—as wonderful as her equally appropriate portrayal of Ophelia the other night. And Harry made a most believable Puck—the boyish mischief maker. More than believable. Partway through the evening, Dayle was struck by the fact that Harry was a good actor. Not just good, gifted. He was carrying the play. His stage presence lifted the others to better performances no matter what roles they might be playing—Athenian aristocrats, fairies, or members of Quince's crew. They all came alive. For a while, there was no other world than the one onstage, no other problems, no other possibilities. It was enough to make her believe in fantasy or some kind of fairy world where love was all that mattered.

When the show ended, Dayle sat for a moment, transfixed, while the rest of the audience filed out. A vision of Harry continued in her mind—the light on his hair, the way he'd held his mouth a certain way, his every gesture suggestively sensual. All the devilishness of love had been captured in that performance, as if he'd become the potion himself. She'd watched the women in the audience breathe quicker and reach for their own collars, as if they felt some need to button themselves in.

Harry didn't have to play shabby towns in out-of-the-way places, she realized. He could play any stage. He could be famous, a theatrical legend. He had that much charisma.

When she assumed a disguise, pretending to be a seamstress or a barmaid, she did only whatever was necessary to get by, nothing more. He assumed the whole. He was Puck and Harry and everything he and Shakespeare knew about life and love. The difference was immense.

He obviously took pride in his work, which made her wonder why he would risk his art for something that could cost him years in prison. What did it matter to him what went on in the coal mines under this town? Did he imagine himself playing Puck to the real world, an immortal and untouchable rapscallion who could upset the plans of mere men and escape, dancing off into the woods of some loftier ideology?

She'd seen the books of spells Anarchists used. One was entitled *The Science of Revolutionary Warfare: A Handbook of Instructions Regarding the Use and Manufacture of Nitroglycerin, Dynamite, Gun-Cotton, Fulminating Mercury, Bombs, Poison, etc.* Not light reading and hardly lofty. White Springs wasn't anyone's midsummer-night's dream. She hoped Harry hadn't mistaken that fact. For, despite Shakespeare's famous line, all the world was not a stage.

Dayle lingered a little longer until most of the theatergoers were gone. Then she went backstage, asked directions to Miss Valentine's dressing room, and knocked.

"It's open," Dayle heard from the other side.

She entered and found herself blinking in an inordinately bright light. The room's gas lanterns had been turned high enough to give the small space a garish illumination, not to mention an annoying smell. The room itself was spare. The only furnishings were a dressing table, two chairs, and a screen that gave privacy to one corner of the room—the sleeping area.

Miss Valentine was seated at the dressing table, wiping makeup from her face. She looked up and caught Dayle's reflection in the mirror. "Oh, that explains it."

"I beg your pardon?" Dayle asked.

"He was a bit distracted tonight," the woman continued. "I was not sure why." She went on with the removal of her makeup.

"Distracted?" Dayle asked. "If you mean me, I'm sure you're wrong. I was in the back."

The Lady Pinkerton Gets Her Man

"He notices everything."

The woman's voice was flat. Dayle couldn't tell whether she was being matter-of-fact or annoyed.

"Mind if I turn the lights down?" Dayle asked.

"Yes, I mind. I hate the dark. I've always hated the dark," the woman answered.

"Oh," Dayle returned.

"I even sleep with them on."

"Oh," Dayle muttered again, and glanced to the screened corner.

"It's not entirely crazy. It's simply something I promised myself. I told myself that when I was grown-up and nobody could tell me differently, I was going to sleep with the lights on. Really on. And since I sleep alone, who's to mind?" She paused and looked up at Dayle again. "That's what you really wanted to know, wasn't it?"

Dayle shrugged. "I don't care how you keep your lights."

The woman snorted a little laugh. "His dressing room is on the other side," she added with a wave of her arm. "I'm sure you'll find it more agreeably dim."

Miss Valentine had hung her wig on the back of her chair. Her fairy queen dress was draped over an open trunk. She was wearing plain white underclothing made whiter by the light. She wasn't as young as she appeared onstage, or maybe it was acting lovesick and silly that had given the illusion of youth.

Dayle closed the door and crossed the room. She bent and checked her own reflection in the mirror. The bright light didn't favor her, either. The human face needed shadow, or it might as well be dead, Dayle thought. She pushed a loose strand of her own hair back into place and said, "I thought his performance was quite good, not the least distracted."

"Even on a bad night, Harry's wonderful," the woman returned.

"You're saying this was a bad night?"

"I've seen better."

The two of them searched each other's eyes in the mirror, trying to look past the wavy cheap glass and unnatural glare.

"Harry doesn't really belong to this world," the other woman said, giving up the gaze and glancing away.

"What do you mean?"

"Just what I said. Some people are too good for this world. They want too much, give too much. That's dangerous."

"How?"

"It's another form of selling your soul, if you ask me."

Dayle wasn't sure how to take that. She wasn't entirely sure what they were talking about. Harry's art? His anarchy? His charisma? She straightened and turned away from the mirror.

"You're not the first to try to save him from himself," the other woman said as she wiped the last of her makeup off.

"I beg your pardon? I didn't know I was trying to save him."

"Tame him. Capture him. Reform him. Make him a loyal, one-woman man. Whatever it is that you're trying to do, it's all the same. Personally, I got better things to do than care that much about any man."

"Better things?"

"Honey, I've been on my own since before I can remember, and rather than being a sorry case, I think I like it. Strange as that idea might sound."

"On your own?"

"I'm an orphan. Once a orphan, always an orphan, and I don't mean one of those literary orphans, either."

"Literary orphans?"

"Oh, you know, those sad books currently popular where a child of the streets, without gloves, hat, or

The Lady Pinkerton Gets Her Man

shoes, suddenly discovers after much trial and suffering that he or she is really the long-lost offspring of a wealthy duke or millionaire tycoon. Overnight, the poor dear is engulfed in the bosom of a warm family and a vast fortune."

"Jed the Poorhouse Boy," Dayle offered, naming the title of one of the currently popular books about an orphan who found his true identity. Next to Allan Pinkerton's true detective stories, those rags-to-riches tales were all the rage. She knew what the woman was saying.

"Yeah, sentimental books like that," the woman added with a little toss of her head. "Drink got both my parents, and they didn't leave a dime. End of story."

"I'm from Saint Elizabeth's in Denver," Dayle told her.

The woman suddenly turned and looked directly at Dayle. "No kidding?"

"No kidding," Dayle assured her. "I'm an orphan right down to the suppers of water and red jelly sandwiches."

The other woman groaned in recognition. "Lord, to this day, I can't eat a red jelly sandwich."

"Or plain rice with brown syrup."

"Or plain rice and no syrup."

"For which we always gave thanks."

"Because there were children who had it worse."

"In China."

"No, Africa. I grew up hearing about the poor starving children in Africa."

"Where did you grow up?" Dayle asked.

"In New York and Kansas. Lord help me. I was one of the children the New York Children's Aid Society 'rewarded' by placing me out at a farm in Kansas. Hard work, fresh air, fine family life. More like I provided the farmer with entertainment because the wife wouldn't. Then she hated me for it."

"I know what you mean," Dayle added. "We were placed out for domestic service, seasonally. Different places."

"Do you know that Kansas law acquits anyone who kills a child in the process of 'correcting'? I swear, I'll kill before I'll be that poor again."

There was a pause while that statement settled.

That's when Harry came swinging through the dressing-room door without knocking. "There's got to be . . ." he started saying, and then stopped. Seeing Dayle, his expression changed. He quickly glanced from one woman to the other. "And what are you two talking about?" he asked.

"He thinks we're talking about him," Miss Valentine said.

"Why do men always think that?" Dayle added with a shake of her head.

"Male vanity."

"Oh, most definitely."

Harry stood there a moment, disconcerted. A smile started to creep across his face, then hesitated, giving him an odd, comical expression. Speechless, which was rare for Harry, he hitched his pants and shook his head. Then he managed to articulate the obvious. "This is not a good time, I can tell." With that, he backed out.

When the door had closed behind him, Dayle and Miss Valentine glanced at each other and started to giggle as if they were old school chums sharing a secret. In essence, they did have a secret: Harry. They'd both seen his expression, and they both knew him well enough to appreciate the lack of his usual smugness.

Still wordless, Miss Valentine turned and wiped the rest of the makeup from her face.

Dayle drew a deep breath, and, looking around again, she said, "You know, you could burn the place down with these lights."

The Lady Pinkerton Gets Her Man

"At least it wouldn't be dark."

Dayle nodded. "That's true. On the other hand, there's no way to keep all the shadows away."

"I'll worry about my own craziness. You worry about yours."

"Mine?"

"We all got at least one, honey."

Dayle didn't argue.

"Harry's fine," Miss Valentine added, now standing in order to pull on a robe, "but in case you're tempted, you might want to keep in mind that he's got bigger plans than you."

"What do you mean?"

"You know what I mean."

"No, tell me."

"Some men think about getting a beer at the pub after a good day's work. That's all they worry about. Harry could tell you the price of rice in China. He thinks that broadly. To him, it's all basically part of whatever scheme he's working on, and since Tommy joined the troupe, it's been worse. Who knows what kind of grand plans the two of them are working on now?"

"He doesn't confide in you?"

"Like I told you, not since Tommy the Tube Man came around. Fortunately, that was the same time Jeremy joined the company. He's the one who played Bottom tonight."

"And Rosencrantz the other night," Dayle added, remembering Harry's comment the first time Miss Valentine had entered their conversation.

"Yeah, that's right. He's not as handsome as Harry, but he's a hell of a lot more considerate. His only bad habit is thinking he's funny. You'd groan at the jokes I have to hear." She shook her head. "But nobody's perfect. Even Harry. Now go, shoo, get out of here. I'm sure he has almost driven himself crazy wondering what you and I are doing in here."

Dayle moved toward the door. Then she paused and turned. "You have no idea what he and Tommy are scheming about?"

"Only that it's probably big."

Miss Valentine was right. Harry was waiting outside. He was leaning against the wall opposite Miss Valentine's door. No pretense of being busy or casual. No impression that he just happened to be there. He was waiting. His stance was relaxed. His expression had gotten back some of its cocksureness. However, upon seeing her, he shoved his hands in and out of his pockets in a gesture that betrayed more nervousness than he'd exhibited all night onstage. He obviously cared about what she and Miss Valentine might have been discussing. Even Harry, it seemed, had an occasional self-doubt. That was a revelation.

"What's the price of rice in China?" she asked him.

"What?"

"It occurs to me that's most likely a very important thing. The price of rice in China, I mean. It probably affects all sorts of things."

He paused, and in that pause she sensed his mind working its way around her question. He still hadn't stood away from the wall.

"It's too high," he answered. "That's why Chinese men will leave their families and come to America to work in the coal mines. Is that what the two of you were discussing in there? The price of rice?" He thumbed toward Miss Valentine's dressing-room door.

"You might say that," she told him. "Miss Valentine seemed to think that you'd know the price of rice in China. I wondered if she was right."

"So you were talking about me."

"As a subject, you did come up. On the other hand, you might be surprised how much Miss Valentine and I have in common. Besides knowing you, we're both orphans."

The Lady Pinkerton Gets Her Man

He nodded, said nothing.

"All in all, I found Miss Valentine quite interesting. I'm glad I met her."

He nodded again, said nothing.

Dayle wondered if he was being obstinate or careful.

"More interesting than meeting Allan Pinkerton?" he finally asked.

She shook her head. "Surprisingly similar, actually."

"Similar?"

"They're both opinionated on certain subjects. She grew up as an orphan. He grew up poor. Underneath, I doubt they're all that different."

"Are you sure you met the real Allan Pinkerton? You know, short, slight, an egomaniac with an eye for women."

"Well, I must admit he wasn't what I expected, but interesting men rarely are."

"And how do you define an interesting man?"

"Define him? Words are a poor substitute for life. I simply know one when I meet one. Trust me."

He laughed and then cut that merriment short as if he didn't really trust her cleverness or his response. She found both reactions flattering. She enjoyed knowing she'd managed to both irritate and puzzle him.

He stood away from the wall. "Want to go to Chinatown?" he asked.

"Chinatown?"

"Tonight. Right now. There's nothing like a bowl of Chinese noodles after a show. Ever taste fresh ginger?"

She shook her head.

"Wonderful. It engages both the mouth and the nose in an absolutely balanced sensation."

She was a little startled. The only reason she knew for anyone to go to Chinatown after dark was to smoke a little opium. She shook her head slightly.

"Most women would assume the worst of such an invitation."

"What? That I'm trying to tempt you to your destruction? My guess is, you don't need any help with that. On the other hand, if you've missed the experience of fresh ginger, you've missed one of the great pleasures of life."

"Is that so?"

"I know you think I'm consumed by politics, anarchy or something like that. Truth is, I'll take pleasure first any day." He held the side stage door open for her. "Coming?" he asked.

19

Ah So came straight up from his chair. He couldn't believe what his guard was telling him. He couldn't believe that actor had come back to Chinatown. Didn't the man realize how close he'd come to having his head chopped off?

Worse, he couldn't imagine what he was doing with that Lady Pinkerton. He should have chopped both their heads.

Miss Dobson was the only person outside Chinatown who knew how close Ah So and the Tong had come to losing control the other morning. The Tong were not supposed to lose control. Knowing what she did, if she decided to team up with that actor who was really an Anarchist, there was no telling what mischief the two of them might cause.

Ah So drummed the top of the table with his fingers while he tried to think his way through this new development. No matter how he thought about this, he couldn't help feeling that the two of them coming there together was an insult, an obvious flaunting of Ah So's current weakness. His first inclination was to slit their throats and let them learn good manners in some other lifetime. However, the last thing Ah So needed right now was more trouble, and, unlike with Chinese, killing Americans usually meant creating more trouble, not less.

The Tong guard from downstairs, a man with a crooked nose that twitched when he talked, was taking some pains to describe the situation in detail, including how Harry Bryant and Dayle Dobson had come into the noodle shop and ordered pork-fried noodles and fresh ginger. It was late, near midnight. Most white people who came to Chinatown after dark came to smoke dope or gamble. The guard couldn't understand why these two were eating noodles—only noodles.

Ah So understood. He knew the actor. He wasn't an opium smoker or much of a gambler. He was a dreamer, and dreamers were worse than gamblers. Dreamers thought they could ignore the odds. That thought only made Ah So drum the table all the harder. Clearly, something had to be done about Harry Bryant and his equally meddlesome female friend.

Ah So reached for his raccoon-skin coat.

He'd been studying his account books, trying to tell himself that he'd accumulated enough wealth, that it was time he returned to the village of his birth. Unlike the actor downstairs, who wanted to use White Springs to change the course of history, Ah So had no real interest in the troubles of this wind-blown desert, where the houses would soon be empty, just as this land had no real interest in him. The Chinese were never going to be a large part of America's history. That had been decided when Congress forbade their immigration. No matter. No self-respecting Chinaman wanted this land. It would take too many bones

The Lady Pinkerton Gets Her Man

of too many generations to bless it. With that thought, Ah So closed his account book and locked it in the drawer.

Maybe he was just tired of worrying about large things, like mines and railroads and miners whose coming here was complicated by laws. Sorrows came from seeing too much, he knew. Life taken in entirety rose out of the landscape like impassable mountains, beautiful only in their enormity. Joy, the only possible happiness, was found in the simple, everyday pleasures—a warm bath, a raccoon-skin coat, a fine fighting cricket. He closed his eyes and shook his head.

He would go home soon, he decided, but first there was this business downstairs to take care of. For a little while longer, he was the Tong leader in this outpost, and anyone who thought differently was going to have to think again.

He squared the coat on his shoulders.

He could have had the woman killed the other morning, but killing a white woman was a particularly tricky business. Besides, he hadn't thought anyone would believe her, no matter what she said. As an extra precaution, he'd taken the trouble to explain things in a way he knew others in White Springs wanted to understand. That should have settled the matter.

Now this.

The main thing was to move slowly, he told himself. He didn't need to get the better of Harry or the woman. All he needed was to stall them long enough to get things back into balance. As soon as his cousin got him a supply of new miners . . . Ah So paused in the middle of that thought. Smuggling was easy. Chinese pirates had been smuggling everything large and small for thousands of years. Chinese pirates were legendary. It was said that a good Chinese smuggler could get anything, anywhere, anytime. Ah

Jerrie Hurd

So had no doubt his cousin could smuggle all the miners anyone could ever want as soon as he got things set up.

Stalling was a different matter. It was never easy to steady events—marking time, waiting. It was even harder when someone else, in this case the actor downstairs, was determined to take advantage of the situation, twisting the flow of events to his own advantage.

Ah So slipped a knife into the sleeve of his coat.

The real question was why? Why was Harry doing this? Did he think he was going to become rich or famous or become a warlord for his efforts? Ah So did not think so, and that was why he could not understand anarchy. It was nothing. It got nothing. In a larger sense, that was the fault of all Americans. They seemed to think freedom was precious. Chinese knew better. Chinese knew order was the antidote for too much freedom. Order was old. Order was good. Ah So made order for the Tong. The Tong made order for the mines. The mines kept the trains going. The trains kept America going. Who did not want that?

The Tong guard from downstairs was now repeating himself. Ah So silenced him with a gesture. The man's talk stopped, but his nose continued to twitch. Ah So found that unaccountably annoying. He wanted to tell the man to cut off his nose if he couldn't control it. Instead, with another gesture, he sent the man back to his post.

Then Ah So went down to meet his guests. The back stairs were narrow and wooden and made one turn. Near the bottom, as was his custom, he paused long enough to put his eye to a peephole. What he saw gave him even more pause. Lots more pause. He didn't know when he'd seen such an obvious infatuation between a man and a woman.

The Lady Pinkerton Gets Her Man

He flipped off the gaslights illuminating the stairway. Then, standing in the dark, he looked again. No mistake.

Harry and Dayle were sitting opposite each other, leaning across one of the noodle shop tables, their faces close, the conversation obviously intense. The tension suspended between them was as palpable as the fine-flavored noodles that hung from the chopsticks they shared. Ah So could hardly believe what he was seeing.

This was reckless. He was an Anarchist who wanted to stop the world. She was a Pinkerton who wanted to stop him. In fact, the woman was so single-minded, she'd refused to abandon those two worthless Chinese girls the other morning, even when thirty miners and three Tong enforcers chased after her.

Ah So leaned away from the peephole. He fussed with the knife in his sleeve, rubbing the smooth handle between his fingers as he toyed with the possibilities. He sensed opportunity. Not the kind of opportunity he'd expected. That was fine. It was one of the tricks of the fates that nothing ever moved straightforward, not even time. Like fox fairies, the illogical popped up everywhere. For that reason, the wise warlord knew how to bend even the fickle and freckled to his purposes.

Love, he knew, could expend hours exploring the tiniest of pleasures, like noticing the feel of the woman's hair. Not all her hair—the fine strands next to her face and along the back of her neck. In short, love required time—the very commodity he needed.

In that case, he thought he'd be a fool not to use it.

With that thought, Ah So shoved the knife farther up his sleeve and snapped a flap over it. He went to the kitchen, a place crowded with sides of pork, boxes of vegetables, and the steam that rose from the noodle pots and hung in the air. The night cook stirred one of the pots while his assistant scrubbed a counter with a piece of pumice. Both looked up, and, seeing the Tong boss, both immediately stiffened. The assistant dropped the pumice. The cook bowed deeply as he apologized for the younger man's clumsiness. The assistant, taking that as his cue, wordlessly picked up the pumice, and then, more than bowing, he practically bent himself in half.

Ah So acknowledged the bows. Then he ordered the assistant to build up the fire in the fancy guest room upstairs. He went on to describe exactly how he wanted the chairs uncovered and the pillows on the bed fluffed. From the cook, he ordered a plate of sweets and a bottle of fine liqueur. He requested that they be sent to the same chamber with crystal glasses and fine china plates. And napkins. Americans liked napkins, he remembered.

These orders were unusual enough that Ah So caught the assistant glancing sideways at the cook, as if he thought the older man might offer some explanation, some shrug or meaningful gesture. That amused Ah So. He liked to create confusion whenever possible. It made his men wonder what the warlord might do next. When the young assistant hesitated longer, Ah So raised his voice. That sent him scurrying.

When he was gone, the cook glanced once at Ah So and then reached for the poison he kept on a shelf above where he chopped his vegetables. Ah So stayed his hand. With a little encouragement, he figured the man and the woman would be their own poison.

Harry looked and saw the Tong leader coming out of the back of the noodle shop. Before he was halfway across the room, all the miners eating noodles in the same shop found they were no longer hungry and

The Lady Pinkerton Gets Her Man

hastily left, causing such a commotion with their going that Harry felt a sudden confusion himself as he wondered what was going on.

Wanting to talk to the Tong leader was the real reason he'd come to Chinatown tonight, or, at least, he'd thought that was the real reason until he saw Dayle taste ginger for the first time. The taste of fresh, thinly sliced ginger had teased such a mix of surprise and pleasure from Dayle's expression that he'd become aroused, his whole being focused on the idea that he'd be a happy man if only he could keep causing that same mix of surprise and pleasure in her.

Unfortunately, that was exactly the moment when Ah So decided to make his appearance, wrapped in his raccoon-skin coat and his wide smile. Now everyone else was leaving. No one had scrambled away from the cricket fights when he'd shown up there wanting to talk to the Tong leader. How was this different? All he wanted to do was leave a warning. After the Anarchist meeting the other night that nearly turned into a riot, Harry knew that things were far worse in the mines than anyone was willing to admit. Even Ah So.

Reluctantly, Harry put down the chopsticks, slid the noodle bowl back, and struggled to bring his full attention to this new matter, which was important and maybe dangerous considering how quickly the room had cleared.

First, he chanced a glance at Dayle. The surprise that the fresh ginger had created on her face had now shifted to an alertness—her professional Pinkerton alertness. He recognized the look and wanted to swear. For one brief instant, he'd penetrated past that. He shook his head and then shifted his attention to the Tong leader. Harry stood to accept Ah So's greeting. He introduced Dayle.

The Tong leader nodded to her. "White Springs

Jerrie Hurd

Chinatown have many wonders—fine herbs, fine noodles, fine smoke. All much better than coal bin." At that comment, the man chuckled, making an odd nasal noise which he suddenly cut short with a snort.

Harry had no idea what the man was talking about. Dayle obviously did. He watched her level her gaze. Looking Ah So straight in the eye, she said, "Last time I was in Chinatown, I found your hospitality lacked a lot."

Harry caught his breath. No one talked to the Wyoming warlord like that. Maybe Dayle didn't understand who he was. Then Harry dismissed that thought. Everyone knew "the Chineyman in the raccoon-skin coat."

Fortunately, the Tong leader decided to take her comment graciously. He pulled up a chair, spread his coat, and sat down. "I apologize. Obviously, I must do better. It is not good to have a poor reputation for hospitality." He indicated the freshly sliced ginger. "At least my root spice is good. Most fine root spice anywhere in Wyoming."

"Yes, it's very good," Harry hastened to agree. He also sat down, wondering how he could turn this conversation to what he needed to discuss.

Ah So continued talking to Dayle. "Your friend like Chinatown very much. He like to visit here day and night. Perhaps I should be flattered."

Dayle glanced at Harry. "You really come here that often?" she asked.

Harry shook his head. "Our host exaggerates. I came to bet on the cricket fights a couple of days ago and lost."

"It never wise to bet against the Tong leader."

"Everything changes," Harry continued. "What was a sure bet once may not always be a sure bet."

"All the more reason to move slow, avoid trouble, pick your enemies carefully."

"Your enemies? What about your friends? Do you pick your friends with equal care?" Harry asked. "It's a friend who tells you the truth, not what you want to hear."

"What is the truth I do not want to hear?"

"Things are not just tense, they're explosive. Sitting on White Springs and doing nothing is like sitting on sweating dynamite. You need to do something, or it's only a matter of time until it all gets away from you."

"Time?" Ah So repeated, and for a moment Harry had hopes the Tong leader might listen. Then he shook his head slowly. "No, I am right. Friends add spice. No more. Enemies matter. It is one of the hazards of engagement that you will become like your enemy. You will mirror him. Americans don't understand this. They run here and there, doing this and that, making many enemies and much chaos. Chinese wait. Much wiser."

"I'm trying to tell you that you don't have time to wait. You already have too many enemies—the entire Congress of the United States and their Exclusion Act, every non-Chinese miner in this town, half your own men. My offer stands. You can join your friends and make things better, or . . ."

What offer? Dayle wanted to know. Her mind had been working every possibility, trying to make sense of this exchange between Harry and Ah So. She should never have come to Chinatown, not for the adventure, not for Harry, not for any reason. She knew too much. Ah So had taken some pains the other morning to make sure no one believed her. She had no idea what he might do if he thought Harry believed her.

"You don't really have a choice," Harry was saying.

Ah So shook his head. "In my village back in China, very little changes."

"You see, that's what we Americans do best," Harry

continued. "We change. We adapt to new ways in a new country."

"To not change is good. When you return, it is all the same," Ah So continued. "That is most good."

To Dayle, it seemed as if the two of them were talking about different things. She didn't care. She wanted to leave, get out of there. She couldn't understand why Harry was even trying to reason with the Tong leader. In her mind, that was the very definition of futility.

The Chinese who came to work the mines could come and go, spending a third of their lives in America, and never really leave their home province. Few Chinese learned English, fewer adopted western dress, almost none lived outside the Chinatowns that dotted the landscape like transported villages complete with the exotic sounds and smells of the Orient. Hadn't Harry looked around? She'd inventoried all the possible exits, every window, every door.

Meanwhile, Harry and Ah So continued sparring until Ah So slapped the table with both his hands and exclaimed, "Enough! Enough of this. Miss Dobson is right. My hospitality is lacking. This shop is no place for honored guests to eat ginger and noodles. You must be my guests in a finer place upstairs."

Instantly, two Tong guards appeared.

Harry glanced from one to the other and sat straighter. "Your hospitality exceeds itself, but we need only these few noodles. Then we will be going."

His words had taken on a nervous edge, Dayle noted.

"Besides, it's late. We need to go." He grabbed Dayle's hand and rose out of his seat as if he thought he might flee, dragging her after.

It was too late for that.

Ah So slapped the table again, and one of the guards pushed Harry back into his chair. At the same time, the young man who'd served the noodles

The Lady Pinkerton Gets Her Man

stepped forward, bowed, and presented Dayle and Harry with silk robes.

They took them reluctantly.

"You will be my guests for the night. It is a very special room. Best hospitality. Enjoy yourselves. Only enjoy." With that, the Tong leader bowed once and left.

When he was gone, the guards stepped back, and one held open the curtain to the back stairs. Harry came to his feet. For a moment, she thought he meant to resist. That would be foolish. He obviously came to the same conclusion. Instead, with a little laugh and a shake of his head, he tried to make light. "I believe we're going to get more adventure than we bargained for."

What could she say? Trying to match his light tone, she muttered, "Indeed, things have turned interesting."

At the same time, she couldn't help wondering what Ah So wanted more than he wanted them dead. She was still asking herself that question when she entered the room at the top of the stairs.

Not large, the room was overly warm and too heavily scented for her taste. She rubbed her nose, trying to clear it of the sandalwood incense, while she made a slow turn, examining these new surroundings. She couldn't help feeling even more disoriented than she'd been downstairs.

The room was so Chinese, she thought she might have crossed an ocean, not a threshold. The furniture, consisting of a large bed, a small table, and two high-backed chairs, was all carved and lacquered. The walls were hung in red velvet. The bed and chairs were piled with matching pillows. A pair of golden dragons were painted over the fireplace. Some strange fanged creature had been carved into the door posts. Two large porcelain Foo dogs guarded the table, where sweets and drink had been laid out on fine dishes and cut crystal. It was seeing the drink and sweets that finally made it all make sense.

She turned one more time, taking in the luxurious closeness, the dim light. She started to laugh, then stopped herself. She realized that in the relief of knowing she was not about to die, she could quite quickly become hysterical. This was the last thing she'd expected, and yet there was no mistake. This was clearly the Chinese idea of a boudoir.

Her mind settled on that point, she flung herself onto the bed, giving herself over to its rich, velvety softness, sinking deeply into the pillows. From that vantage point, she watched Harry's continued confusion. He circled the room like a caged animal. He checked the window, which was locked and barred, at least three times. He opened the door twice, only to be greeted by the two guards and have to close it again. He paced, checking every corner, every wall. He studied the ceiling, obviously looking for some escape.

That's when she finally let herself laugh.

"What's funny?" he wanted to know.

"This," she answered.

"This?" he questioned. "What part of this amuses you? There are Tong guards outside the door."

"Doesn't matter. I don't think you really want to insult the Tong warlord's hospitality by leaving too soon, anyway."

"His hospitality?"

"This is his best room. That is his best liquor." She pointed to the table. "He said so himself."

Harry turned once more, seemingly to take in the ambience of the room for the first time. She knew the moment the meaning of all the red velvet and sweet scent hit him. He was embarrassed, she realized. Tongue-tied. Suddenly unable to look at her.

It was rare to have Harry Bryant at a disadvantage, and she'd managed it twice in the same evening. She

The Lady Pinkerton Gets Her Man

couldn't help herself. She had to rub it in. "I believe our host wants us to enjoy ourselves. Really enjoy ourselves."

"Don't be ridiculous. Why would he want that?"

"How would I know? Haven't you heard? The Chinese are inscrutable."

Harry turned and looked at her. He still had nothing to say. He just stood there studying her for such a long time, she grew self-conscious and wished she hadn't thrown herself onto the bed with quite such abandon. Nestled in the red velvet, she imagined she must look the temptress, the femme fatale tainted with Eve's evil.

She sat up and pulled her knees under her chin.

Harry turned again and poured himself a drink. "Want some?" he asked.

She didn't answer. She was churning inside. She'd brought to this tournament of wills all her instincts of observation and an absolute determination to know this man and all his secrets because she was a Pinkerton, and because she believed anarchy was evil. She still had no use for anarchy. Try as she might, she could not imagine a nonviolent, nonhierarchical, nature-loving world where workers sang at their jobs because they knew their labors were for the benefit of all mankind. That was nonsense. Her job was to enforce the law, but having come to know Harry, she was beginning to think there ought to be a law against a nation waking up its dreamers.

Her problem was that she'd seen too much of life, before she was five years old, ever to be starry-eyed. That had left her with a fascination for the dark side of humanity—its secrets, its crimes. It had also left her with a tendency to analyze rather than feel. This moment being the perfect example. What other woman could sit here amid Ah So's rich velvet, coolly working on some understanding of the situation while she waited to see if he ever turned around, ever looked at her again?

She tipped her head back and stared at the ceiling, trying to imagine what kind of woman Harry really wanted. Not that she thought she could change to become that woman. What choice did she have? If she ever denied her restless curiosity, it would consume her. Her fearlessness and audacity were the things that had kept her alive all those years in that awful orphanage. They were also what kept her too independent. Yet if she tried to be otherwise, she suspected she would become too ordinary to appeal to a man like Harry. Her paradox.

She broke the silence because continued thinking was going to drive her crazy. "I don't know why you tried to warn him. The Chinese never join causes. They don't need anything. They're terribly self-sufficient, you know."

He finally turned. "Rather like you in that regard."

"I beg your pardon?"

"Is there anything you need? Any cause you'd join—besides the Pinkertons, of course. I don't count the Pinkertons as a cause."

"I don't understand."

He rolled his eyes as if he thought he'd made his point. She didn't think he needed to be so smug. She slid off the bed and poured her own drink. Standing next to him, she realized his breathing was labored. She chanced a glance at his face, wondering if he was experiencing the same emotional churning. His expression was pained in a way she couldn't understand.

He spoke. "What if I told you this was the last chance?"

"The last chance?"

He nodded. "The last moment when we might save White Springs. I meant what I told Ah So. This place is going to explode, and I . . ."

"Hush," she whispered, putting one finger to his mouth. "It's late, and nobody saves the world after midnight."

The Wyoming warlord had given her this one night,

and she was prepared to beg if she had to, but her single touch was enough. Like a coiled spring that had just been triggered, he grabbed her and threw her onto the bed with enough force that the wind whooshed out of her lungs, leaving her open-mouthed and fighting for air. Then he paused. He lay on top of her and worked his jaw, the way he did when he was looking for words.

"I'm afraid," he whispered.

"Afraid?" she breathed back.

"Don't you know? Love like this is always tragic."

"Hush," she said again, now covering his whole mouth. "Nobody quotes Shakespeare after midnight, either."

Still, he hesitated. There was an awkward wordlessness, not from any question of what either of them wanted. It was more that what they wanted was so large neither of them knew where to start.

She kissed him first, and from the way his shoulder instantly melted around her, she knew he loved her. That, too, was dangerous. There was nothing worse than an idealist in love, she thought. A man like that might think anything was possible, might expect to discover the ideal. Not in her. She didn't care. None of that concerned this one night, she told herself, while at the same time marveling at how even in the spin of her own desire, her mind wouldn't let loose. Her body did. She felt her limbs become pliable under his touch.

He kissed her ear, her cheek, the hollow of her neck. Love was the ultimate illusion, she realized. It made you want to believe nothing else mattered, and when his hand found its way up her thigh, she knew nothing else mattered. She'd faced Tong hoodlums, angry Chinese miners, and Lotta's hysterics without panic, but this . . . She was suddenly awash in the realization that this could conquer her. Harry. His mouth. His hands. His face in her hair. Their voices reduced to animal sounds. She wanted to be full of him. She wanted him to plow her with all the anarchy in his being, drive it through her like a stake piercing her Pinkerton soul.

Afterward, they were both so spent neither spoke for a very long time. One of the candles went out, darkening the room.

He whispered, "You asleep?"

"We're the eye that never sleeps."

He groaned.

She knew the Pinkerton slogan was not what he'd wanted to hear, but she couldn't help herself.

A moment later, he asked, "Ever think about running away?"

All her life. That had been her daily fantasy when she was growing up. She'd imagined hundreds of ways to run away. She'd worked out elaborate plans, clever escapes. She'd imagined wild, free escapades, but she'd never gone. It wasn't that she couldn't leave the orphanage. That was easy. It was that she didn't know where to go. Destination was always the downfall of her schemes.

"Sure," she answered.

"Good, because I can't see myself becoming a Pinkerton, and you're not likely to become an Anarchist. Our only chance is to run away."

"But where would we go?"

"Does it matter?"

That was a novel idea. She wondered why she hadn't thought about that. Anywhere could be a destination. All you had to do was go and keep going. She had to admit there was an unmistakable seduction in that idea, but she didn't trust it.

"Where?" she asked again.

"Any place. Patagonia," he answered. "We'll go to Patagonia."

"Patagonia? Where's Patagonia?"

"It's this perfectly marvelous wild prairie in South

America. The explorer Magellan described it as a country of black fogs and whirlwinds located at the end of the inhabited world."

"Oh, please," she groaned. "Not another White Springs."

He sat up in the bed. "You haven't caught onto the spirit of it. Patagonia, like Mandalay and Timbuktu, is a real place. You can buy a sailing ticket and actually disembark there. It's also one of those places that has invaded the imagination. Patagonia is the farthest place one can go, the point beyond return." There was a pause. "Will you run away with me?" he asked, his voice now low and serious.

She looked at him. "To Patagonia?"

"Yes," he breathed.

Maybe it was the room with its exotic decor or the incense. Whatever the reason, she caught the vision. She imagined herself shipboard, Harry by her side, facing into the wind. Waves slapped the hull below, sometimes spraying upward, sea birds screamed above, and everything smelled of salt.

She amazed herself. She wasn't sure how she'd put that fantasy together. She'd never seen the ocean, never seen a sailing ship. Just pictures. Just books of sea adventures.

He was right on one important point. It was the only hope the two of them had to love, really love, in the sense of endless adjustments and readjustments, rage and loyalty, and the blind tenderness of growing old together. She let him talk, spinning plans. He told her how they would go to San Francisco and book passage from there. He was still talking when she drifted off to sleep, her dreams weaving images of his words, filling her with visions of a strange, flat, endless land where even the mud was wet with sky.

Sometime later, she woke with a start, and for a moment she couldn't remember where she was. Then she felt Harry sleeping beside her, and it all came back—the fresh ginger, the Tong leader, loving Harry. Mostly loving Harry. She closed her eyes and listened to the rhythm of his breathing. Maybe if she'd been born in Patagonia and grown up on whirlwinds at the end of the world, she might have stayed. Unfortunately, she knew the dark side of this fantasy.

She and Harry weren't the kind of people for whom love would be enough. She could only imagine the horror that would follow if she tried to become the sole focus for Harry's enormous utopian ambition.

If that wasn't reason enough to leave, she also knew Lotta was planning to rescue another Chinese girl that morning, and there was no telling the trouble that woman was likely to get herself into.

When she was done dressing, Dayle paused a moment longer to listen to Harry's sleep. He seemed so peaceful, she wanted to brush his cheek and leave him a kiss. Instead, she fluffed a pillow, placed it beside him, and pulled the cover up. She hoped it would give him some comfort if he didn't miss her the moment he woke.

Harry woke with the first rooster crow. He glanced at the sleeping form next to him and reached out to touch Dayle, then thought better and pulled his hand back. If she woke, he would have to explain too much.

He hadn't lied. He'd meant everything he said about running away with her—all the way to Patagonia. But even Patagonia wasn't going to be far enough away if things turned nasty here. He feared bloodshed and people dying. He didn't think he'd ever be able to forgive himself if he didn't try to do something to stop that.

Dayle was an uncommon woman, but it was his experience that even an uncommon woman had trou-

The Lady Pinkerton Gets Her Man

ble understanding how she could be the center of the universe by night and second to his current concerns by day.

He pulled on his clothes, quickly, quietly. Then he tiptoed out into the hall, leaving her sleeping form tucked into bed.

20

Harry didn't get halfway down the stairs before he ran into Ah So coming up. The Tong leader was followed by four Tong guards who bumped into each other, one after the other, when their boss stopped short. That created a moment of confusion as feet stubbed stairs and elbows bumped walls. Harry took one step backward and had to catch his own balance in the dim, narrow passageway.

"They send for soldiers," Ah So said without preliminaries. "They want trouble. They expect trouble. They have many, many soldiers waiting for the trouble they expect."

Harry had no idea what the Tong leader was talking about. He finished putting on his jacket while he tried to understand Ah So's agitation. He'd never seen the man rock from foot to foot or move his arms while he talked. And if he didn't keep his voice down, he was going to wake Dayle. Harry glanced over his shoulder and upward in the direction where he'd left her sleeping.

The Lady Pinkerton Gets Her Man

"Woman gone," Ah So told him. "She go two hours ago. She make the trouble that bring soldiers. You must stop this trouble. Stop soldiers. Very important."

"Dayle's already gone?" Harry asked.

"She help boss woman."

Harry had to think about that. He turned and climbed the stairs again, taking them two at a time. He burst back into Ah So's Chinese boudoir and ripped the covers off the bed—pillows. He swore and punched a fist into one of the bedposts while his mind wrapped itself around the fact that Dayle was not a woman easily wooed.

One part of him admired the fact that she'd seen through the fantasy to the larger truth that neither of them was the type to traipse around Patagonia or any other place without purpose. Another part of him wanted to think that for one brief, shining instant she'd tossed all reason aside and gone with him to the ends of the earth.

"She make the trouble now that make the soldiers come," Ah So was saying again. He and his guards had followed Harry up the stairs. "When soldiers come, we all have much trouble."

Inside his head, Harry still had a vision of Dayle's long legs stretched across the bed. They'd banged their heads together in the wild twist of trying to mix themselves, he remembered, and somewhere near the roof of his mouth, he swore he could still taste her. At the same time, he knew that Ah So expected him to say something, respond somehow. "Soldiers?" he mouthed. "What soldiers?"

"American soldiers. The U.S. Army is coming here. Soldiers will keep mines open, not Chinese."

"What?" Harry asked.

Ah So reached behind and took a newspaper from one of his guards. He thrust it at Harry. It was a *New York Times* folded with the front to the inside.

Harry opened it. The date was a week earlier. There

was something about a fire at a harbor warehouse and something else about the world-famous circus elephant, Jumbo, being killed in a train wreck.

Ah So grabbed the paper again. He turned it to the back page and pointed to a small item near the bottom.

Harry eyed the Chinaman. Then he took the paper, smoothed the page, and read. The story was less than three column inches. A notice, nothing more. It simply said that Brigadier General Oliver Otis Howard, commander of the Department of the Platte, had ordered four companies of the Seventh Infantry to Laramie, Wyoming.

"Where did you get this?" Harry asked.

"I have friends," Ah So said. "Friends in New York City who understand what they read. They sent me this immediately. There's more." He shoved a second newspaper into Harry's hands.

This time it was an edition of the Chicago newspaper, similarly folded, dated a day after the first. This time, the item of interest leaped to Harry's attention. Six companies of the Ninth Infantry under the command of Colonel Alexander McCook of Camp Murry, Utah, had been ordered to Evanston, Wyoming, to "insure the uninterrupted delivery of the U.S. Mail."

Laramie was a hundred and fifty miles east. Evanston was roughly the same distance west. If he believed what he was reading, White Springs, a waterless half-abandoned coal camp in the middle of the high alkali desert was currently surrounded by ten companies of the United States Infantry, but his mind balked at the idea. No one had ever ordered federal troops out to stop a strike or, in this case, the mere threat of a strike. State militia, yes. Pinkertons, yes. He'd counted on the fact that Wyoming had no militia and Pinkertons were expensive. There was a limit to the number of Pinkertons even Jay Gould could afford.

Now Allan Pinkerton and Jay Gould had upped the stakes. The real bad guys in this, they weren't about to

The Lady Pinkerton Gets Her Man

let go of their stranglehold on America's engines of commerce—the coal mines and the railroads. They were even prepared to mock the constitution of the United States of America. In Harry's mind, that wasn't very different from a military coup.

He shook his head. "This is a democracy, for God's sake. We don't turn our own military against our own people. I don't think that's even legal."

Ah So shrugged. "Democracy. Anarchy. Nobody talks philosophy once the soldiers start to march."

Harry knew Ah So was right. More important, from what he'd said, it was clear that Ah So had figured out that having soldiers in town was not going to work in his favor. The Chinese had become a political liability. That meant that once the soldiers were brought in, the Chinese miners would be phased out, replaced with white miners who'd work nearly as cheaply under near martial law conditions. In short, Jay Gould and company were switching soldiers for Chinese, but the result would be the same. White Springs would be strike-proof—secure as ever—and Harry had no idea how to prevent it.

Ah So had waited too long to switch sides. Anything the two of them did now would only serve as an excuse to have those soldiers ordered in and play out the scenario according to Allan Pinkerton and Jay Gould's plan.

Harry swallowed. "But they have to have some reason. They can't just march soldiers without justification."

"Nothing must stop U.S. mail," Ah So said, and pointed back at the newspaper page.

"It doesn't say that," Harry objected, and then remembered that it did. "Hell, that's no excuse. Everybody knows Wells Fargo does a better job of delivering the mail," he complained. Yet even as he said that, he knew none of this had anything to do with the actual delivery of letters. He just hadn't thought that any president, much less the indecisive, incompetent, weasel-faced Chester Alan Arthur, would dare use federal troops to keep mines open—privately owned mines. The man might as well loan the U.S. Army to Jay Gould, which, obviously, he just had.

Ah So, sensing that Harry now understood, began rocking on his feet and waving his arms again. "Yes, yes," he said. "Yes, yes, yes."

By contrast, what was going through Harry's mind was a chorus of "no," because he realized he'd played right into this scheme. Jay Gould and all the rest of the moneyed heads of this country must have been frantic wondering how they were going to keep White Springs secure. Given the growing national anti-Chinese sentiment, they had to know it was becoming increasingly unlikely that they could continue to count on mining coal with Chinese miners. Martial law was probably always their first choice as a solution, but that was a little difficult to manage inasmuch as no one, not even the president of the United States, could order an army into White Springs to secure the mines unless there was trouble first. Harry had provided the trouble or, at least, the threat of it.

"You're right," Harry told Ah So. "This is a time to move slowly and pick your enemies carefully." In fact, the slower they moved, the better, he thought. As he saw it, their one hope was not to trigger the trouble Jay Gould and his henchmen were expecting. Without any actual trouble, they couldn't send in the soldiers. What's more, if the soldiers stayed in Laramie and Evanston long enough with no apparent purpose, that might become an embarrassment in and of itself. All he and Ah So had to do was keep things quiet. Very quiet.

Ah So shook his head. "No, you right. Chinese have no friends. But now is too late. Already trouble. The Lady Pinkerton and the lady boss . . ."

Harry turned. "Dayle? What's she got to do with this?" He remembered her complaining last night

The Lady Pinkerton Gets Her Man

about being expected to help Lotta Bateman rescue another Chinese girl. How could that . . . ? Then he knew.

Worse, he felt as though he'd been shorn by a Delilah. She'd teased him, tempted him, tantalized him into thinking she was the danger, when, in fact, the real hazard had always been the larger forces at work in this town—Jay Gould, Allan Pinkerton, and others who'd do anything to keep the coal flowing out of this place.

"The devil take Jay Gould," Harry let slip.

"Yes, yes," Ah So said with some excitement. "Now you understand."

"Understand? Me understand?" Harry asked, drawing a deep breath. "I think I was the one who told you the Chinese couldn't count on anybody," he started. "No, but you don't listen. You're still lopping heads off like it was last year or last decade . . ."

"Yes, yes," Ah So said. "You come now. You must help the Lady Pinkerton before she cause much trouble, too much trouble."

Dayle's skin crawled.

This was wrong. She sensed that everything about this was wrong and felt for the gun in her pocket, while Lotta squealed with delight, singing over and over again, "Can you believe it? Can you believe it? Look at this. Can you believe it?"

Dayle couldn't.

At first, Dayle had been relieved. They hadn't climbed over a single roof. Instead, Lotta's Chinese cook, carrying a lantern in the predawn, had led the three women—Lotta, Mary Stillman Davies, who had made a big deal of the fact that she hadn't been on a "real rescue" in years, and Dayle—to an unremarkable door in an alley on the northernmost edge of Chinatown. He'd paused, looked around. Then, with a grunt, he'd kicked the door in.

Instant mayhem ensued.

As the four of them rushed in, Chinese men jumped up from couches, tumbled out of sleeping berths, and made every effort to rush out. At the same time, Chinese girls screamed and clutched their clothing. Bongs hit the floor. One broke. All in all, there was such a general confusion that it took Dayle a full minute to realize the cook had kicked open the door of a Chinese brothel, not the cheap crib they'd found before but a fancy bawdyhouse, probably as fancy as any to be found in a Chinatown. In fact, the rich red velvet decor and gold trim rather uncomfortably reminded her of where she'd spent her own previous night. Same lacquered furniture. Same porcelain Foo dogs.

That, however, was not what made her skin crawl.

By contrast, Lotta's skin had a rosy glow. She whirled and clapped her hands and practically danced around the room, even as the Chinese men, eight or ten in number, were still clearing out. "It's a miracle," she exclaimed, and kept gushing. "One girl. I thought we were going to rescue one girl who was being hidden in a bathhouse. Now look! I declare, we may have halted Chinese slavery in White Springs. Don't you agree? Oh, you must agree."

That last comment was addressed to Mary Stillman Davies, who, like Dayle, was too dazed to answer. It was only when Lotta added that she was "purely excited" at their surprising good fortune and hugged the older woman that Miss Davies finally came to herself.

"The Lord be praised," she muttered. "Yes, the Lord be praised."

They'd stumbled into what was basically a single room, not large, about three times the size of Ah So's guest quarters. The center was some kind of Turkish delight piled with pillows, while along the walls, arranged three high, were sleeping berths. Each was curtained. Ladders of polished wood ran up the sides of the walls to the top bunks. Paper lanterns hung from hooks outside the occupied spaces. The lanterns gave only a dim light. There were two windows, both shuttered. A fire burned in a stove in one corner.

Besides the alley door, there were two others—the front door that the spooked customers were scrambling to get out and another on the back wall, close to the alley door. It led to a kitchen, Dayle guessed from the smells coming from that direction. She assumed it also led to stairs going up to the living quarters on the second floor. Any Tong guarding this place would come through that door, Dayle knew. Gun still in hand, she kept her eyes on that exit while she jammed the latch on the alley door.

By then, Mary Stillman Davies had taken charge of the rescue. "Gather the girls," she said to Lotta. "Quickly. We need to get out of here."

Dayle's exact sentiment. She expected Tong any second, not to mention that as soon as the surprised customers came to their wits, they were likely to have second thoughts about letting three white women run them out of their pleasure palace.

Meanwhile, Lotta pushed back curtains and lifted bedcovers, uncovering one girl after another. She found one who'd climbed into a laundry basket, another who'd crouched behind a screen. Most, having been told hideous stories of white women who were really witches, had hidden themselves. Still worrying about the door to the back, Dayle lost count. There were thirteen or fourteen. Not one coughed. Fourteen healthy girls.

That was what made Dayle's skin crawl.

They weren't supposed to have found this place. This hadn't been arranged, not in the same sense that Garrick Bateman had "arranged" the last rescue. These girls were too valuable and too many. Yet Lotta's cook had led them right there, no roofs, no lattice, no balcony.

No cook, Dayle suddenly realized.

Lotta gathered the girls in the middle of the room,

where they sat on a rug, shoulder to shoulder, wide-eyed. Mary Stillman Davies stood over them, looking like Queen Victoria—same stern expression as in the queen's portraits. The only difference was that Miss Davies held a cane instead of a scepter. She rapped the cane on the floor every time she spoke, and every time she spoke, the girls quivered in unison. If Miss Davies looked like the queen, then Dayle thought the girls looked like a flock of birds huddled together waiting out a rain. Only this was no rain shower.

"Have you seen the cook?" she asked Miss Davies while still keeping her eye on the back door. This place would be guarded, well guarded, she knew. It shouldn't have taken the Tong this long to react.

The older woman shook her head. "Haven't seen him."

"I don't like this," Dayle admitted.

"A pox on Allan Pinkerton. May the devil play music on his ribs."

"Mr. Pinkerton?" Dayle asked.

The older woman nodded. "He wants to ruin me."

"Ruin you? Unless I'm mistaken, this is probably the biggest rescue in the history of your mission."

"Exactly."

Dayle caught the older woman's eye. Usually, there was no way to read Miss Davies. She was as tightly controlled as the hair she pulled back and wound into a bun without a stray strand ever working itself loose. This was the exception. This time, the woman's glance flashed such fierce anger that Dayle took a step back as if she'd bumped unexpectedly into something dangerous.

"I-I don't understand," Dayle said, and that was the other reason her skin crawled. Not only didn't she understand Miss Davies, she didn't understand any of this.

"He's hoping I won't be able to handle fourteen girls the way I handle two or three. He thinks if he overwhelms me, he'll be able to trace me, trail me,

The Lady Pinkerton Gets Her Man

expose my method for rescuing these girls and getting them away. Well, he won't, because I won't let him."

Dayle studied the woman, the shape of her nose, the way her mouth worked as she spit out those words, and Dayle absolutely couldn't figure out what she was talking about. There was no mystery about where she took these girls, no reason to trace her or trail her. What was Mary Stillman Davies's obsession with Allan Pinkerton and his with her? Surely she understood that the immediate danger was not America's most famous detective. It was the Tong.

Any thoughts that ran in that direction only deepened the enigma of Mary Stillman Davies. Why, Dayle wondered, did the woman care about Chinese girls in particular? There were all kinds of charities— prostitutes of every race and age in every town in the West, not to mention the hundreds of girls trying to grow up in orphanages all over the country, most of which were little better than this place. Why didn't the woman rescue some of those unfortunates, occupy herself a little closer to home?

Dayle shook herself. She didn't have time for those thoughts.

"Where's the cook?" Dayle asked Lotta.

No help. Lotta looked up as if missing him for the first time.

"Never mind," Dayle answered. Then, with a gesture toward the girls, she added, "Find them some more clothes. It's cold outside."

Miss Davies answered that comment. "Won't do any good. They deliberately see that they don't have any extra clothing or shoes. Keeps them from running away."

Dayle paused and gave a glance at the girls' bare feet. The first two girls had been barefoot as well, Dayle remembered, but she and the cook had carried them most of the time. "Gather blankets, then, anything."

She decided she couldn't wait any longer. While the

others were finding blankets, Dayle opened the back door and entered the hallway leading to the kitchen. Her fear was that the cook had gone to secure that way and met with Tong. Either way, she had to know. Last thing she wanted was to walk into a Tong trap with Garrick Bateman's wife and the West Coast's most famous woman crusader.

She let the door close behind her. Then she stood in the half-dark, listening. There were faint sounds, but nothing that seemed alarming. Gun in hand, she moved forward slowly, feeling her way toward the lighted room in front of her. When she got to the end of the hall, she paused again, listening more. She entered, waving the gun in every direction as she shouted, "Hands up! Don't move!"

No one. On the counter next to the sink, vegetables and a half-plucked duck had been abandoned. The faucet dripped. The back door had been left open. A screen banged once.

She noted the one window, a pantry door, a second door she assumed led upstairs, and a half-high door that was probably the entrance to a cellar. She dropped a bar across the door going upstairs, and then, noting the pantry door was slightly ajar, she moved in that direction. By then, her skin more than crawled, it could have walked on its own.

She knew how to handle being scared. Senselessness was what drove her over the edge, and none of this made sense. She could understand the customers getting out. Whatever the trouble, they'd figure they were better off avoiding it. But the Tong pimps who ran this place? Why had they been so quick to run?

As she passed the sink, Dayle picked up the butcher knife that had been left next to the duck. She slipped it inside one of her high-button shoes and looked around for anything else she thought might be useful. It was with the idea of finding useful items that she opened the pantry and discovered the cook.

His throat had been slit.

The Lady Pinkerton Gets Her Man

She didn't scream. She couldn't remember when she'd last screamed. Very young, she'd learned to take being beaten or used without ever uttering a sound, until it was no longer in her to make noise when she was hurt or horrified. In fact, in such situations, she usually had to remind herself to breathe. In her effort not to make noise, she'd forget that the rush of air down her own throat was a necessary sound and not nearly as loud as it might seem.

She had less control of her thoughts. Her mind tumbled in a wild flood of images. She remembered the cook catching butterflies on a stick and how he had been worried about letting fox fairies into his kitchen. She was quite sure it wasn't a fox fairy that had gotten him in this kitchen, and in the midst of that thought, she realized that she had no idea what a fox fairy looked like or what a fox fairy might be capable of doing. She suddenly wondered if seeing a fox fairy would be better or worse than meeting a Tong. At the same time, she remembered Woo laughing and telling her that she wasn't worth the Tong's trouble. She never wanted to believe that more than at this exact moment.

Somewhere in the midst of that confused swirl, she found the strength to reach over and slam the pantry shut. She jumped at the noise that made and began to shake.

She could handle anything except uncertainty. In this case, she was faced with utter uncertainty. She could make no sense from anything. She didn't understand what had happened to the cook or why he'd brought them there. She didn't get Mary Stillman Davies or Lotta's fascination with this charity, let alone Garrick Bateman aiding her efforts. Most of all, she couldn't figure out why there were no Tong. This combined ambiguity had overwhelmed her usual good sense so much that she couldn't move except for the shaking. She couldn't move because she had no idea what to do.

She jumped again when she heard something behind the cellar door.

That might have been the last straw for someone else. To Dayle, it was salvation. It was exactly what she needed to beat her shakes, because suddenly she knew what to do.

She crossed the kitchen in five quick, quiet steps. Then she turned, and, putting her back against the wall next to the cellar door, she concentrated on holding her gun steady while she waited for the door to open.

A moment later, Ah So emerged from the cellar, brushing cobwebs from his raccoon-skin coat. With cool determination, Dayle lowered the gun against his head and said with perfect calmness, "Don't move."

He froze. His hand stopped exactly where he had been brushing at the cobwebs, and his face lost expression until he was jostled by Harry emerging from behind him. Then he looked worried.

Harry was obviously confused.

"What the . . ." he started to say, and then slowly raised his hands as he stepped aside to let the four Tong guards out of the same cellar.

They had their hands up before they entered the room.

That's when Harry tried his wide grin. "I'm glad to see you. Where are the others? We've been worried . . ."

Dayle's mind seized on "We've been worried," and her confusion threatened to be too much again. What did "We've been worried" mean? And why was Harry climbing out of the cellar with the Tong leader? Had the two of them joined forces? Had they always been working together?

"Shut up!" she told him, and cocked the gun in case he was of a mind not to take her seriously. This was simply too much to think about.

Harry didn't hush. "Dayle we don't have time for this," he pleaded.

The Lady Pinkerton Gets Her Man

"Time for what?" she asked. "What is this?"

"We've come to help you get the girls out of here. I know you may have other orders from Mr. Pinkerton, but you've got to think broader than that. People are likely going to get killed, and I don't believe you really want that to happen."

Dayle's mind flashed to the bloody cook inside the pantry, and a delayed nausea left her unable to say anything. She let him talk.

"We'll take them back through the cellar. It should be safe that way . . ."

Her mind raced until it snagged on something Harry had said. *What orders from Mr. Pinkerton?* She had no orders from Mr. Pinkerton except to try and find out more about Mary Stillman Davies. She didn't see any reason why that would concern Harry or the Tong leader or why that would have anything to do with this.

She pushed the gun tighter against Ah So's head. "You want me to believe that you're letting fourteen girls go? You want them to leave? You're helping them leave?"

She watched the Chinaman swallow. "Mrs. Bateman must be most happy. Happy news, only happy news must be reported from White Springs. It is happy place. No sing-sing girls. Only work and much, much coal coming out of here—four hundred and fifty train carloads a week. No trouble."

Dayle shook her head. "Nobody wants Mrs. Bateman to be that happy."

"Chinese know that winning one hundred victories in one hundred battles is not the highest of skill. To subdue the enemy without fighting is the highest skill."

"What the hell is he talking about?" Dayle appealed to Harry.

"The soldiers," he said.

"The soldiers? What soldiers?"

"Don't tell me you don't know about the soldiers."

"What soldiers?" Dayle repeated.

He paused and looked at her. "You really don't know, do you?"

"What soldiers?" she asked for the third time.

Harry turned and paced to the sink. He stood there a moment and then slammed the edge of the counter with the heel of his hand. "We've all been used. Damn it. We've all been used."

"What soldiers?" Dayle insisted.

It took him a moment to turn. When he did, he leaned back against the sink and looked at her for the better part of a minute before he said, "We should have run away to Patagonia. We should have just said to hell with everything and gone."

"Well, we didn't," she said. "Now, what soldiers are you talking about?"

He drew a deep breath and shook his head. "This town is going to be under martial law so tight no one will sneeze without getting shot," he told her, and then continued. When his explanation finally made sense down to the Tong pimps killing the cook because he'd betrayed his own and then clearing out because they knew Ah So wanted no trouble, Dayle lowered the gun.

Harry's own understanding was focused on wanting to stop a riot and the knowledge that he was running out of time. Even while he was in the kitchen explaining the situation to Dayle, Chinese miners began rattling cans and pelting the front of the brothel with stones and garbage. As soon as he'd satisfied Dayle about what was going on, Ah So ordered two of his guards to lead the women through the cellar, showing them the way out. At the same time, he and Harry went to see what they could do about the mob.

When Harry opened the front door, things were already bad enough that he and Ah So had to duck

The Lady Pinkerton Gets Her Man

their heads and throw up their shoulders to ward off the hail of objects flying through the air. Mostly, the men were throwing mud balls they'd formed from the muck that ran along the side of the street. These splatted against the side of the brothel and dripped down. One particularly messy mud glob hit Ah So square on the front of his raccoon-skin coat, sticking the fur with a nasty, foul-smelling mess. Ah So immediately looked down and started to brush it away, but it only smeared and stuck to his hand.

The pelting halted. Not the tension. That hung in the air like ozone after a lightning strike. But the men waited. Ah So was still the Tong leader, an unmistakable figure from any distance in his raccoon-skin coat. Therefore, the audacity of someone splatting the man was enough to halt the mass madness, at least momentarily. In fact, some of the men were stepping back, starting to drop away.

To his relief, Harry watched the crowd continue to break up. He was about to reenter the brothel, thinking that if he hurried, he might catch up with Dayle. As he started to turn, he sensed something.

At first, he wasn't sure what. A new sound? He listened again. Yes, it was definitely a sound, a low rumble. He looked up the street in the direction of the noise and saw nothing . . . nothing. He was about to excuse the feeling as nerves when he looked again and noted the sky was lighter in that direction. It was sunrise, but he wasn't looking east. A moment later, a mass of white miners rounded the end of the street carrying torches. Their number was enough that the march of their feet rumbled through the earth. That was what he'd heard or sensed, he realized.

Ah So's Chinese miners, who had been on the verge of dispersing, now closed and raised the sticks with which they'd been rattling their cans. Harry watched one individual break off a railing and test its heft.

All the while, Harry was anticipating what he knew he had to do. Someone was going to have to march out, meet this mob, and turn them back. He figured he was that someone. Never mind that he wasn't a Tong leader or any kind of leader. To most of these men, he was nothing more than an actor, and acting was a suspect occupation. Real work, as far as these miners were concerned, involved getting one's hands dirtied and callused. Then there was the fact that he was an outsider who'd only been in White Springs a week. Worse, he would be coming down the street from the Chinese side.

There were, however, advantages to being an actor, he told himself. An actor knew the value of audacity. Harry tossed aside his hat and started down the street. Despite the chill, he pulled off his coat as well and dropped it. Then he stripped off his shirt.

At the same time, he studied the mass of miners, trying to figure out who might be a leader. He considered a tall fellow who walked with a certain unmistakable straightforwardness. There was another older man who carried himself a step ahead of the others. However, Harry's eye kept returning to a thin man in a plaid mackinaw. There was something about him that seemed familiar.

"Out of our way!" the man with the straightforward walk shouted.

Harry was no obstacle. Nevertheless, the mob slowed, and every man in the mob eyed Harry.

"Go home!" Harry shouted back. Holding his shirt above his head, he let it flap in the chill breeze. He wanted the angry miners to wonder what he was doing. "Go home," he said again. "Everything is fine. There was just a little misunderstanding. That's all."

"We want the white women they're menacing!" another man in the crowd now yelled.

Harry wanted to say, "What white women?" But he knew better. The mob had been worked up by someone who'd told them about Mrs. Bateman and her charity, probably before the white women had actually discovered the Chinese girls.

The Lady Pinkerton Gets Her Man

Harry glanced in the direction of the man in the mackinaw. He remembered now. The man was a Pinkerton—a favorite of old man Pinkerton himself. He was the same man who'd caused trouble in the Pennsylvania coal fields several years back. Harry had no doubt the man was the source of this mischief as well.

"The women are fine," Harry told the crowd. "They're probably at the train station already. Everything's fine."

"Yeah, and what are you doing here? This is a long way from the theater."

"I'd say," another offered.

"Entertaining the Chinese, are you?" someone else wanted to know.

"Yeah, and what's with flying your shirt in the cold wind?"

Harry hopped onto a vegetable cart parked at the side of the street. "Glad you asked about my shirt, because I wanted to ask about yours. Who would you rather give the shirt off your back? The Chinese over there or Jay Gould? The Chinese over there work hard and take care of themselves. So what if they never say howdy or tip a beer like a regular fellow? Jay Gould ain't never going to give you a howdy, and he's too good to drink beer. He drinks the fancy stuff. More important, he probably thinks he already owns your shirt. He thinks he owns your skin and the muscle and the bone you use to hold the picks that dig his coal out of his mine. That's the trouble with monopolists. They're never satisfied until they've got it all. But hell, all you got to do is take your shirts back," Harry told them as he put his own back on. "He can't mine this coal by himself. He needs you. You are the key to his wealth."

He had the crowd's attention, but he sensed that he was no more than a momentary distraction. He was up against ten years of these men watching their town die around them while Chinese miners, loved by the boss and protected by the Tong, worked all the best jobs. That anger had worked itself into their souls the way coal dust had worked its way into their lungs and had begun to bleed them from the inside out.

Now, on top of that, these hardworking, God-fearing, no-nonsense miners had been led to believe that those same Chinamen were now threatening white women, polite-society white women, the boss's wife. As he spoke, the enormity of what he was up against grew on him like fear, like the fear he'd first learned on that day when he watched his father sell out to Jay Gould at gunpoint and, as a young boy, could do nothing except be scared and wait for the scare to pass.

Not this time, he told himself. Somehow, he had to make these men realize that what they were doing would only make conditions in the mines worse, not better. They were being used as pawns.

"Mining was my father's life," he now told the men, because he didn't know what else to say. He went on to tell them how his father discovered the coal and opened the mines at Red Road, Pennsylvania—two mines producing fine, soft coal, the kind steel mills needed to make coke.

He explained the fight his father had to put up before he got a railroad spur built into those hills. Otherwise, he wouldn't have gotten that coal to market at a competitive price. "Those mines became my father's whole life," Harry told them again, because he knew there was a reason why generations of men, even whole cultures of men, such as the Cornish, descended together into the mines. Grandfather, father, son, and grandson all took up the same trade, even though they knew mining killed. It killed more than the men who died with cave-ins and faulty explosives. It sucked the life from lungs and knees, creating cripples who died wheezing. Still, they willingly descended into the depths and pecked at the earth because they belonged to a fraternity. Deep

The Lady Pinkerton Gets Her Man

down in the caverns of their souls, these men preferred to die as part of something rather than live alone.

"My daddy worked the mines at Red Road," one of the miners now called out.

"Mine, too," someone else shouted. "He ran the lift at the South Red Road Mine."

"But they closed that mine," another speaker called out. "Just closed it one day with no notice."

"Yeah, my daddy couldn't get no more work after that."

"I heard it was mined out."

"Hell, that was a huge lie. My daddy said there was plenty of coal left."

"It wasn't mined out," Harry answered, sensing the shift in mood and his own acceptance. He had them now. He really had them. He came forward, balanced himself on the edge of the vegetable cart, and finished the story. He told them how his father lost the mines at Red Road.

"Jay Gould wanted to limit the amount of coal coming out of Pennsylvania," Harry said at the end. "That's why he closed the mines."

"Why would he buy something to close it?" another miner wanted to know.

"That don't make sense."

"Yeah, a man can't sell what he don't dig."

"No, but he can raise the price of what he does dig," Harry answered. "You have to think like a monopolist, like Jay Gould, who only cares about himself."

For a brief moment, the men understood how their lives fit into larger patterns and that solving the present frustration might require them to think differently. He could see it in their eyes and in the way they now leaned forward, listening. Given a chance, he thought he might have more than turned the situation, he might have won the men to the cause, but he wasn't given the chance.

Two shots rang out.

Two of the men in the front of the mob slumped to the ground, dead.

Instantly, guns were drawn, and men scrambled for cover.

While Harry was delivering his speech, the Chinese had taken refuge in the brothel. That was good. It got the men off the street and out of sight of the white mob. However, once inside, some of the Chinamen had thrown open the window shutters and taken up positions there, armed. They were now returning the fire from the white miners who were shooting at them from doorways and alley entrances.

Harry jumped down and took cover behind the vegetable cart. With two of their colleagues down, Harry knew the white miners blamed the Chinese for starting the gun battle, but he wasn't sure.

It had happened fast, but it seemed to Harry that the two men had fallen wrong for being hit in the chest. One lay in the street, not far from Harry. Picking his moment, Harry darted out, grabbed the man's leg, and pulled him behind the cart. First, Harry checked to make sure he was really dead. He was. Then Harry rolled him over. The bullet had gone clear through the man's chest, bloodying him both front and back, but Harry had seen other shot men. He knew. This miner had been killed from the back by someone in the same mob.

Harry searched what he could see of the nearby alleys and doorways, looking for the man in the mackinaw. He didn't know if he'd fired the shots, but he suspected as much. He located the man standing in the shadow behind a rain barrel. He was watching Harry, and Harry had the sense that he'd been watching him all along. Realizing he'd been discovered, the man turned and disappeared down the alley.

The gun battle still raged. One more man was down, across the street. He had a bullet in his leg. A couple of shots had pinged into the vegetable cart at

The Lady Pinkerton Gets Her Man

Harry's back. The shooters on both sides were miners, not marksmen, not that lacking gun skill lessened the damage when one of their shots did hit something.

Harry waited until there was a lull in the firing, then he ran for the alley. Bullets immediately sprayed the dirt behind him. He tripped as he ducked behind the same rain barrel. He rolled over, picked himself up. Then he looked right and left, searching the crowd, trying to find the man in the mackinaw. If Harry was right, he'd murdered two men in cold blood. He hurried farther down the alley, still searching, but the alley branched, and there was confusion everywhere.

The gun battle was only a small part of the chaos. Chinatown was being sacked. Every direction, every street, every alley, Chinese were fleeing ahead of mobs of white miners who had turned nasty and were now tearing through the tarpaper and tin roof buildings, tossing furniture and clothing and everything into the street. The men were turning out trunks, slashing mattresses, and throwing boxes out upstairs windows.

"Find their money piles!" someone yelled.

"They don't trust banks!" The shout was on every side. "They hide their money."

"Not money—gold. Celestials keep gold. Only gold."

In a stupor of disbelief, Harry stood near the front of the noodle shop. It was the same one where he and Dayle had eaten earlier. He couldn't believe that was only hours ago. He let himself be jostled from one side and another as he tried to wrap his mind around the mayhem. The only solid sensibility he could grasp was the horrible sure knowledge that it was going to get even nastier.

It's only the beginning, he told himself.

The legendary "piles" that everyone was shouting about were just that—legendary. Chinese miners didn't spend money, because they sent it back to China. When the white miners didn't find anything of any worth, their fury was going to turn on the Chinese themselves.

Harry gave up looking for the man in the mackinaw. No doubt, the man would get away with murder, and no doubt, the soldiers, all ten companies of them, would be arriving soon in White Springs. There was no stopping that now.

Harry worked his way back through the milling mob. He headed in the direction of the gun battle that he could hear still raging. He wondered what he should do. He wanted to leave, forget everything except Dayle, and go someplace far away. *Patagonia,* he thought, only the thought wasn't amusing. He wanted to pretend none of this had happened.

At the end of the alley, he ducked behind the rain barrel again. From that vantage point, he surveyed the continued conflict. The men in the street were still pinned down. The Chinese had thrown open more shutters. They were now firing from the second floor of the brothel. But no matter how many shutters the Chinese opened, they had no place to go, either.

Harry shook his head, wondering how all this would end, and then he happened to catch sight of seven white miners jumping from roof to roof. They were headed in the direction of the brothel, and they were carrying axes, kerosene cans, and torches.

His first thought was that it was full daylight now. They didn't need the torches. Of course, deeper in his mind, he knew exactly why they needed the torches. He was trying to avoid knowing, but he couldn't. They were planning to set fire to the shabby brothel. Worse, he knew that it would go up like a tinderbox, cooking all the Chinese inside.

There were probably sixty Chinamen inside, including Ah So.

Harry wasn't sure what to do. He couldn't shout. He was too far away, and he wouldn't be heard above the gunfire anyway. There wasn't time to circle

The Lady Pinkerton Gets Her Man

around to the back or climb over the roofs himself. His eyes returned to the street in front of him. There was almost no cover except for the vegetable cart and a doorway he thought he might make if he ran hard enough.

Like raindrops, Harry told himself. Running through gunfire was probably like staying dry in a rainstorm. All you had to do was walk between the raindrops.

21

When Dayle saw the Chinese brothel burst into flames, she knew Harry and Ah So had failed to prevent the worst. Her first instinct was to leave Lotta and the girls with Miss Davies and return to Chinatown and find Harry. She wasn't sure why, or what she would do when she found him, but she knew what it meant for him to have lost control of the situation.

Everything he cared about . . . She stopped that thought and wondered when she'd started hoping for him. She supposed it was when she realized she'd been set up. Somebody had arranged for the white miners to show up when they did. No question, she'd walked into a trap. It had cost the cook his life. Who knew what it was going to cost her or Harry or the rest of the town.

Thing was, Harry was supposed to be the Anarchist, the troublemaker. Only this wasn't trouble he'd caused, she knew. It was trouble he was trying to stop. She doubted anyone had wanted this to get out of hand, but that's what had happened. She wondered what Harry and Ah So would do now. She had the same problem. She was standing midstream, ankle-deep in the sulfur-smelling mud that was Bitter Creek, trying to decide what she should do.

Obviously, everything had changed. She wasn't even sure what side she was on anymore.

The real problem was more immediate. Earlier, she and the others had decided to wade the mud creek when they realized that crossing the bridge would mean encountering gangs of white miners going in the opposite direction. That was before they realized the difficulty of wading. It was impossible to keep their skirts above the muddy mess and nearly impossible to walk. Most of the girls had fallen at least once. That meant that most of them were covered in the foul-smelling muck, and unless they kept moving, the ooze threatened to suck them deeper than their ankles, making walking entirely impossible. Even as she watched the flames, Dayle held her shoes shoulder-high and worked her feet up and down, treading the mud. There was no way any of them could stand still.

Meanwhile, the flames had an effect on everyone.

Lotta began breathing in short gasps as she exclaimed over and over, "Oh, my! Oh, my! Oh, my!" The Tong guards shouted something in Chinese and took off, immediately abandoning the women to go back to Chinatown. The girls started whimpering. A couple of them started crying hard enough to sob.

Dayle looked around for Mary Stillman Davies, thinking she might say something in Chinese to calm the girls. She spotted the older woman near the rear of the troop. She was bent over, helping a girl who had fallen. Maybe it was the light, or more likely the exertion of treading the mud, but when she straightened, Miss Davies looked older and more frail than Dayle had noticed before. Again, Dayle felt a surge of uncertainty, wondering what they would do.

At the same time, Chinamen began to burst out of

Jerrie Hurd

Chinatown, fleeing in every direction. Some plunged into the creek mud. More headed for the hills. Realizing there was no time for calming words or anything else, Dayle did the only thing she knew to do. She grabbed the arms of the two girls closest to her. Pulling them along, she made for the White Springs side of the creek as fast as she could move, hoping the others would follow. They did.

But there was no way to move fast through the mud. Several minutes later, Mary Stillman Davies slogged to the front of the little troop. She was puffing heavily. She walked beside Dayle for a minute while she caught her breath enough to be able to speak. Then she said, "We've got to get them to the train station before they take it into their heads to run off like the guards. Anyone who goes back is going to get killed."

"Well, then, talk to them, not me," Dayle returned, wondering what the older woman expected. Saving Chinese girls was her crusade. Dayle had never wanted any part of it. However, she'd no sooner said that than she relented, took a deep breath, and added, "Tell them it will be all right."

"Will it?" Mary Stillman Davies asked, and pointed to the stream bank in front of them.

Dayle had been so intent on getting through the mud, she'd put her head down and not noticed that a crowd of onlookers had begun to gather there. Women. Children. Whole families. Some had climbed onto the railroad cars in order to get a better look at the excitement that was going on across the creek in Chinatown. A few had begun to cheer, urging the rioters on. Dayle suddenly stopped and wondered if the crowd was likely to let her little troop pass. That was obviously Miss Davies's concern. The mood was nasty. A single glance at Miss Davies, and she knew the other woman was more than concerned. She was scared.

Dayle also noticed that more and more men, on their way to the melee, crowded the plank bridge

The Lady Pinkerton Gets Her Man

upstream. Where before they'd carried hatchets, clubs, and knives, now they had guns, mostly Winchester rifles. Not just miners, either, but railroad workers and anyone else with a grudge against the Chinese or a taste for violence. That's when she knew this was not just an unfortunate incident. This was a full-scale riot.

It was at that same moment that the fire bells sounded. Dayle made a full turn, taking in the whole scene, and she wanted to laugh, maybe hysterically. Who thought that those bells would rouse any volunteers interested in putting out the flames? Dayle chanced another look at Miss Davies.

"This is serious," the woman muttered.

Dayle swallowed and offered an assenting nod. Then, although it involved slogging through more mud, Dayle abruptly turned and led the little troop downstream past the worst of the crowds before she let them leave the wet and scramble up the stream bank. In the time it took her to get the girls out of the creek, the hill east of town literally turned blue with a swarm of Chinamen who'd escaped the riot wearing only the characteristic peasant shirts of that color. Not just on the hill, everywhere there were fleeing Chinese. They fled west toward mine number 3, north toward the bottom of the rock butte. A few, under the influence of rice wine or opium, stumbled in dazed confusion. However, the majority went southeast, through sagebrush and greasewood to the plateau and the alkali desert beyond. Some carried what they could in a bedroll or bandanna. Most carried nothing at all.

That was wrong, Dayle thought, deadly wrong. None of them would survive a night on that cold, wind-swept expanse without warm clothing, without shelter. Dry flakes of snow already danced in the wind, announcing a coming storm.

"We've got to keep moving," Mary Stillman Davies now told Dayle.

Dayle knew that. They had found momentary shelter behind a water tank on the White Springs side of the stream. Out of the wind, they'd paused to wipe the mud from their feet and put their shoes back on, but Miss Davies was right. They couldn't stay there. The train station was still their destination, but she wasn't exactly sure of the best way to get there. She was figuring this out, moment to moment.

Dayle signaled for the others to wait while she checked the street beyond. Circling around the water tank in one direction, she encountered a white woman, a laundress whom Dayle remembered having passed on the streets of White Springs more than once. Large and loud, the woman's talk was always the same. She complained about the Chinese laundries, and how the "coolies" in them used cheap soap and dirty water. She bullied her customers with guilt and the idea that they ought to support "a real American," meaning her and her laundry. Now, to Dayle's astonishment, the woman was standing at the edge of the stream bank with a rifle, taking shots at the fleeing Chinese as if she were hunting sage hens on a Sunday outing.

Dayle gave a glance over her shoulder. Her first responsibility was to the safety of her little group, but she couldn't let the woman continue to shoot at unarmed men. Dayle checked in both directions, making sure the woman was alone. Then, picking her moment, Dayle quickly stepped out of the shadow of the water tank and shoved the woman from behind, making her lose more than her aim. She lost her balance, slipping down the bank into the mud below, her gun getting wet in the muck. Not waiting for her to recover, or to discover who'd pushed her off the bank, Dayle stepped back into the shadow of the water tank and tried the other direction.

On that street, she encountered a group of young boys. One had a pig tucked under his arm. The other two were chasing a goose. The pig was spotted, a

The Lady Pinkerton Gets Her Man

breed the Chinese favored. No doubt, the boys were carrying home the spoils of looting and had momentarily lost the goose, but at least they weren't shooting anything. Dayle motioned for the others to follow her that way.

With only one bridge into Chinatown, most of the activity was concentrated on the streets leading to and from the bridge. Dayle kept her group to the side streets. She used alleys whenever she could. Still, twice they had to turn and retrace their steps in order to avoid marauding mobs.

In one alley, they encountered a Chinaman bleeding from a bullet wound in his thigh. The bullet must have also broken the bone. Unable to walk, he was trying to scoot himself along, moving in the same direction, heading toward the train station. While Dayle stood watch, Mary Stillman Davies bound the man's wound with strips of a blanket. Lotta wrung her hands and paced back and forth, saying, "Oh, my. Oh, my." Once, she grabbed Dayle's arm and asked, "Did we start this? Do you think we're the cause of this?"

Dayle shook her head, not because she didn't think they had some responsibility but because she figured everyone had some responsibility. This had been waiting to happen for a long time. It might have happened without any prodding, although she was sure it had been more than prodded. It had been planned. Now, the important question was not how it had begun but how it was going to end. Not well, she feared.

Although they could no longer see the flames, Dayle and the others could still hear the roar of the fire. The increasing sound made it clear that larger and larger portions of Chinatown were going up in fire. From time to time, an explosion rocked the air. Dayle assumed that happened whenever the flames found one of the kegs of gunpowder most miners stored in their cabins. Bits of wood, crockery, metal, and glass descended in a soft hail that caused most of the girls to cringe but seemed to affect Lotta even more. She wrapped her arms over her head and moaned louder, "Oh, my. Oh my." A black cloud of smoke had almost obliterated the sky, turning the daytime to twilight, and still the fire bells continued to toll.

When Miss Davies had bandaged the Chinaman, two of the older girls got under his arms and helped him to his feet. Half carrying him, they all continued together. The wounded man slowed them, but, working together, the girls seemed to cling closer and whimper less. In fact, they seemed to have a better grasp of the situation than Lotta.

"How much farther?" she asked, and kept asking every time they paused or turned a corner. "Is it much farther?" She insisted that she had to know, as if she weren't familiar with White Springs and couldn't answer her own question.

Dayle answered over and over, "Soon, we're getting closer." She spoke the way she might have talked to a child, because she sensed the edge of Lotta's hysteria, and the last thing she needed was for the woman to slip into a silent fit. She wished the woman would hang on to herself.

She hoped, too, that Harry and Ah So were right and there were soldiers on the way. She wondered how long it might take them to get there. She didn't like martial law any more than anyone else, but she didn't know how else things were likely to be brought under control, and people were dying. As she and the little troop of women slowly worked their way through the streets, dragging the wounded man, Dayle's hope turned to a firm belief that, like it or not, the soldiers were the answer. The soldiers would stop this.

Unfortunately, when the group emerged from the last alley in the circuitous route to the train station, it wasn't soldiers who had secured the station. The stationmaster was riding a horse back and forth in front of the platform. He was carrying a rifle and

The Lady Pinkerton Gets Her Man

shouting, "No quarter! Shoot them down! Give them no quarter!" It took Dayle a moment to figure it out.

He meant the Chinese, any Chinese, who, like Dayle and her troop, were trying to get to the train station. For the most part, these were poor souls who'd managed to grab something of worth and now hoped they might trade their goods for a ride out of town, but the stationmaster was letting no one pass. He had men, railroad employees, positioned all around. They were armed and obviously meant business.

Remembering the reception she and Lotta had gotten the first time they'd shown up at the station with Chinese girls, Dayle wondered if some kind of mob mania had infected the man, making him insanely determined that no Chinese would set foot in his station regardless of the circumstances. The fact that he might kill over something like that seemed incredible, but perhaps no more incredible than the laundress who'd been shooting Chinamen from the stream bank. A sick, hollow sensation found the pit of Dayle's stomach as she realized there was no possibility of reasoning their way out of this. It was all madness.

"What's the matter?" Miss Davies now asked.

Dayle shook her head. "We need the soldiers. I wonder how long it will take for them to get here."

"Soldiers? What soldiers?" the older woman wanted to know.

"Oh, I know about the soldiers. Many soldiers. They're coming from everywhere," Lotta now suddenly said.

"You know about the soldiers?" Dayle asked her.

"Oh, yes. It was Garrick's brag last night."

"His brag?"

She nodded. "You know. He likes to have a new brag. One that tops all the others. He starts at the beginning, and he builds his brags until he gets to feeling manly enough that he can... Well, you know."

If Dayle couldn't believe what she was seeing, she certainly couldn't believe what she was hearing. Garrick Bateman's bedroom sweet-talk consisted of bragging!

"What soldiers?" Miss Davies asked once more, because that was the important question.

Dayle shook her head and explained briefly. She added, "I'm not sure how long we might have to wait for them."

Miss Davies listened. Then, with all the single-mindedness of every religious crusader Dayle had ever known, she dismissed everything else in favor of her own purpose. With a little snort, she picked up her cane and said, "I don't care how many soldiers they think they're bringing in here. That's the westbound train over there." She pointed across the platform to the passenger train standing on the tracks while it took on water. "And I intend to get these girls on that train."

Before Dayle could argue otherwise, Miss Davies exited the alley, full stride, her skirts slapping against her ankles, her cane raised above her head. She shouted, "How dare you stand in the way of a noble Christian work?"

The stationmaster turned but had no chance to respond before Mary Stillman Davies was beating his horse with her cane while she continued to berate the man with her tongue. "Haven't you heard of the higher moral law?" she continued. "Don't you know that you'll have to answer to that? No one stands in the path of righteousness."

There was a tense moment when Dayle thought the stationmaster might shoot the woman crusader. Given the way his horse was dancing sideways, trying to avoid her continued blows, he might have missed, except that the range was close. But he didn't shoot.

The Lady Pinkerton Gets Her Man

At the last second, he raised his gun in time for the charge to go off in the air. At the same time, his horse, still trying to avoid the blows from Miss Davies's cane, reared, lost its footing, and fell backward onto one haunch, spilling the rider. The stationmaster was thrown against the wooden boardwalk. The horse immediately got to its feet, unhurt. The rider let out a yell and rolled in the street, clutching his arm in agony.

The horse was promptly captured by an enterprising young Chinaman, who darted out of a doorway, grabbed the animal, pulled himself into the saddle, and rode off to the delight of the wounded Chinaman in Dayle's group, who yelled a cheer and raised an arm to the young man.

At the same time, a surge of Chinese pressed forward from every doorway and nearby street. With the stationmaster incapacitated, they rushed the station in such numbers that it created a new confusion, as they came from everywhere, running forward and grabbing on to the sides of the train. They piled into empty baggage cars, frightened the passengers by crowding into the passenger cars, and, when those were full, climbed onto roofs. The first ones up turned to help the others.

The stationmaster's men, mostly ticket clerks and baggage loaders, fired a few shots, but there were too many Chinese, and it was clear that the railroad men didn't have their hearts in killing. They quickly fell back.

Meanwhile, Mary Stillman Davies bent over the stationmaster, who was still rolling in the street and screaming with pain. She stamped her foot once and told him to "shut up." Then she checked his injuries. A moment later, she pronounced that his arm was broken and that he'd live. Then she walked away, leaving him to take care of himself or appeal to someone else for help in getting out of the street.

When she'd finished with the stationmaster, she

beckoned for the little troop to follow her. Dayle believed that Mary Stillman Davies might have gotten those fourteen girls onto the westbound train in spite of the mobs of Chinese miners who'd already grabbed every available space, if Garrick Bateman and several of his men hadn't suddenly ridden up and blocked the way. More than blocking the way, three of Bateman's men blocked the tracks and pointed rifles at the engineer of the westbound. He and his crew climbed off the train with their hands in the air in what looked like a train robbery. Common sense told Dayle that no one in his right mind would stop a train at the station in broad daylight. Further, Garrick Bateman was not a likely train robber. She did sense, however, that Lotta's husband was a desperate man. Never mind that he'd dismounted and handed the reins of his horse to an attendant and was now taking off his gloves as if he hadn't a care in the world.

"There will be no trains leaving White Springs until things are under control again," he announced.

All this time, Lotta had been at the rear of the group, helping with the wounded Chinaman. Now, seeing her husband for the first time, she suddenly exclaimed, "Oh Garrick! Oh Garrick!" the way she had been saying, "Oh, my! Oh, my!" Continuing with a flood of words, she left the wounded man and rushed forward, saying, "I'm so glad to see you. Oh, you can't imagine. They're killing them, shooting them down, burning them out. You have to stop it!"

At the sound of her voice, Bateman turned. Seeing his wife's muddy clothes, he stiffened and said, "You're filthy. Where have you been? I've had men out looking for you. Men that I need for other things," he added.

"Oh, you wouldn't believe where I've been," Lotta continued. "We had to cross the muddy creek and sneak through the alleys and back streets. We almost didn't . . ."

"I'll have someone take you home," he interrupted.

The Lady Pinkerton Gets Her Man

"You need to get cleaned up." He turned and was about to give the order to his secretary, a large-bellied young man, but Lotta objected.

"We have a wounded man with us," she told him. "I can't just leave him and these frightened girls. The man needs a doctor and a blanket."

"Get home," he told her again. "Your children need you."

Mary Stillman Davies touched Lotta's arm. She spoke softly. "We'll manage here. Perhaps it would be better if you went home. Your children may be as frightened as these girls."

Bateman then turned on Miss Davies with a curled lip. "How dare you compare my children to those whores? There's no comparison. None. Further, I can take care of my own affairs," he told her. "Nobody needs your meddling. Nobody has ever needed your meddling."

Dayle figured that wasn't exactly true. He and whoever else was behind this mess had needed Miss Davies when they thought her charity might trigger enough trouble to get the soldiers brought in. But someone had miscalculated. Badly miscalculated. Miss Davies, no doubt, had figured that out by now as well. However, the older woman was wise enough not to contradict Lotta's husband. Dayle, too, kept her mouth shut.

Lotta, however, lived on a delicate edge, where her survival required that she not know things that she couldn't help knowing. For that reason, she had embraced a blindness that left her breathlessly unsure of everything, including when she might misstep and stumble on the very reality she was trying not to touch. This was one of those missteps.

Obviously relieved to think that her husband was there to take care of things as he usually did, Lotta kept talking when she should have kept quiet. Since she made it a habit not to think too much, she was putting the pieces of the current situation together even as she spoke, and before she knew it, she'd let her words lead her to the raw claw of too much truth.

"But if you stop the trains, what's to keep all the Chinese from being murdered?"

That was the ugly, unspoken truth. Garrick Bateman needed his Chinese miners in order to keep the mines open. He wasn't letting them escape, no matter what—at least not yet. That was painfully clear.

It was equally clear from the shift in Lotta's expression that she understood what she'd said as soon as she'd said it. Her face drained of color, and she ended her words with a little gasp that brought her hand to her mouth.

At the same time, she immediately began a breathless repetition of "I'm sorry, I'm sorry, I'm sorry," and began to back away. "I'm sure you know what's best."

Too late.

Garrick Bateman turned and grabbed Lotta by the neck. He literally picked her up by the throat and threw her against the train station wall. Still choking her, he spoke, his words sliding past his clenched teeth. "You can't ever shut up. Why is it that you can't ever shut up?"

Lotta wasn't breathing, and although her mouth opened and her eyes bugged as she struggled for air that she couldn't get, she resisted remarkably little. She didn't kick or raise an arm. She seemed to be suspended. More than hanging from his hands, her feet off the floor, she seemed to have suspended all her animation as if waiting for this to pass. That's how Dayle knew that it wasn't the first time something like this had happened. Lotta was experienced at the passivity necessary to survive her husband's anger.

Dayle couldn't help herself. She looked away, and then, seeing the young Chinese girls cowering together, Dayle suddenly understood Lotta's fascination with being able to rescue someone and send them away to a whole new life.

The Lady Pinkerton Gets Her Man

She turned back when she realized Garrick Bateman's rage might have gone too far this time. He was still speaking a stream of invective into Lotta's ear. "I'll teach you. I'll show you how a wife should act and what she should say," he went on. Lotta's face had turned blue, and her eyes had begun to glaze. Dayle took a step forward, but Mary Stillman Davies had already raised her cane.

"Stop it!" she said now, pounding Bateman's back the way she'd pounded the stationmaster's horse. "Stop it. She can't hear you. You're killing her. How are you going to explain that to your children? Is that what you want?"

At first, Dayle was worried that Miss Davies's blows were going to be countereffective. The man seemed to choke harder under her barrage. Then, as suddenly as he'd grabbed Lotta, he let go and turned to knock Mary Stillman Davies aside with the wide sweep of his arm and the full focus of his anger. She fell at his feet, her cane rolled out of her reach, and when she scrambled to her knees, he kicked her flat again before she could reach the cane.

Dayle didn't move. Instinctively, she knew that, as a woman, if she interfered, she'd only make matters worse. It was the young, large-bellied secretary who stepped forward. He pushed Garrick back before he could kick Miss Davies again.

"That's enough," the secretary told his boss. "We've got to get ready for when the soldiers get here. That's what's important now—getting the soldiers here. We've got to get those soldiers sent in here and soon."

Garrick Bateman seemed to come to his senses. He shook himself free of the secretary, and then, squaring his shoulders, he said, "Wives are like mules. They go stubborn on you if you don't keep them whipped."

The young man, obviously not inclined to argue with his boss under most circumstances, now nodded and said, "I've heard that's often the case. I'm not married, myself." At the same time, he glanced back at Lotta, clearly worried about her.

She'd slumped to the platform floor. Dayle had already studied her as closely as she could without going to her. She was pretty sure the woman was breathing, although she didn't seem to be fully conscious. Miss Davies remained on the platform floor herself. With one arm, she was holding her ribs where Bateman had kicked her. At the same time, however, she'd managed to get her other hand on her cane. Dayle remained immobile and waited while the secretary continued to talk to Bateman, calming him, shifting his attention to the soldiers.

She knew the secretary was doing all that could be done. She didn't want Garrick Bateman to walk away from this. She wanted the man strangled, beaten, knocked senseless. She wanted him to feel the frustration of having someone do something like that to him and not be able to do anything about it. No wonder Lotta seemed half crazy at times. What other refuge did she have?

Dayle closed her eyes. That didn't help much. Violence and a feeling of mob madness hung in the air as palpably as the smell of smoke and the incessant tolling of the fire bells. Still, she had to do something to keep from reaching into her pocket, pulling out her gun, and killing Garrick Bateman, not only because of what he'd done to Lotta but also because of what he was doing to the Chinese and the town. She told herself that the only reason she didn't shoot Garrick Bateman was that shooting him was too good, too quick.

Men like Garrick Bateman needed to be strangled slowly. They needed to feel the helplessness and the slow dying. They needed to know that life squeezed out of existence in any form was life squeezed out of themselves and everything else. This wasn't just domestic. If a woman couldn't count on kindness from the hands of the man sworn to love her, then there

The Lady Pinkerton Gets Her Man

was no hope for the rest of the world. Sooner or later, it would all be strangled, burned, and beaten.

"Some mules require more whipping than others," Bateman was now saying. "My wife's family spoiled her. They treated her like something fancy," he continued.

Dayle opened her eyes and wondered if he'd ever looked back to check the condition of either of the women he'd knocked down. The secretary did. Several times, he looked back as he kept nodding his head and agreeing with everything his boss said. He guided Bateman back to his horse and helped him mount. Then he climbed onto his own horse. After Garrick Bateman had given orders to the men with the rifles to "hold the train, no matter what," the two of them rode off.

As soon as they were gone, Dayle bent and lifted Miss Davies to her feet. They both went to Lotta, who was now fluttering her eyes and breathing in the short, panting gasps that Dayle recognized as one sign of her silent hysteria. At least she was alive, Dayle thought, and reached out to touch Lotta's shoulder. At that touch, a quiver went through Lotta that infected Dayle.

She suddenly drew back, realizing she was near hysteria herself. Garrick Bateman had come close to killing his wife, and she hadn't been able to do anything. As a Pinkerton, she took some pride in the fact that she always got her man, but the Pinkertons never sent her after wife beaters. That wasn't even considered a crime.

Dayle looked at the woman crusader. Most of the time, Mary Stillman Davies was an officious old busybody who couldn't be bothered about anything but her charity. Yet she was the one who'd managed to do something. Very likely, she'd saved Lotta's life. She left and returned with some water for Lotta. Dayle shook her head. "Take care of the others," she told her. "I know how to handle this."

Jerrie Hurd

Dayle spread her skirts and sat on the floor next to Lotta. She began talking to her softly, knowing, since that morning they'd shared in the coal bin, that soft talk seemed to help when Lotta was breathing like this and acting nearly stupefied.

For a long time, Lotta said nothing. In fact, it was long enough that Dayle began to worry that this time she might not come out of her rigid state. At one point, not knowing what else to do, Dayle reached over and pulled up Lotta's collar, half hiding the red welt on the other woman's neck. Then she changed her mind and uncovered the mark again, thinking the world ought to see, ought to know.

Meanwhile, Mary Stillman Davies had practically turned the train station into a field hospital. She'd broken into the storeroom and found some supplies. Then she'd organized the Chinese girls into a nurse brigade. They'd found a barrel of lard which they were applying to burns and some yard goods they were tearing into bandages. Some of the passengers from the westbound had also joined in. The others had stormed off to protest the delay. More and more wounded kept arriving at the station. The worst of them were being carried. Miss Davies directed them to the benches in the waiting room.

Dayle leaned her head against the wall. She remembered Lotta asking over and over, "How much farther? How much farther?" as if she'd thought the nightmare would be over as soon as they arrived at the train station.

All of a sudden, Lotta heaved a single loud sob and then began to mutter something between softer sobs. Remembering how the woman had eased out of her silent hysterics in the coal bin, uttering bits and pieces of nonsense until finally a coherence set in, Dayle took her words as a good sign and leaned closer to listen.

"My babies," she was saying. "I've got to stay alive for my babies."

The Lady Pinkerton Gets Her Man

Dayle agreed with that.

Then Lotta suddenly half lifted herself from the floor and grabbed at Dayle's arm as if to pull her up, too. "I've got to get my babies. You have to help me find them and bring them here. My babies."

Dayle gently tugged on Lotta's arm until she sat back down. "Your children are fine, I'm sure," she told her. "They're at home. That's the safest place they can be right now."

Seeing Lotta stir, Mary Stillman Davies returned and bent over both Dayle and Lotta, asking, "How is she?"

Dayle caught the older woman's eye. Whatever else there was about this Christian crusader that annoyed Dayle, she had to admit that Mary Stillman Davies didn't lack a certain competent gutsiness. Dayle struggled, thinking she wanted to say something about that, but somehow the words didn't come.

"How are you?" Dayle asked instead.

The woman snorted. "The day I can't take a beating and give as good as I get, I hope they put me in a wooden box." Then she started to ask again about Lotta, only to stop when she heard Lotta's muttering.

"What's she saying?" she asked.

Dayle shrugged. "She wants me to go and get her children. She'll be all right. I've seen her like this before. She seems to sort of mutter herself back into sanity."

"No, she's exactly correct. You must go and get her children for her."

Dayle didn't know what to say. It crossed her mind that maybe Miss Davies had taken more of a blow than either of them realized. She was making less sense than Lotta.

Dayle slowly shook her head. "I don't think that would be wise."

"We're not talking about wisdom. We're talking about necessity. It's absolutely essential that you go and get her children," the older woman insisted, bringing her hands to her hips.

Worse was the look in her eyes. It had narrowed to the same deadly seriousness with which she and her cane had taken on the stationmaster and then Garrick Bateman. Crazy or not, she meant what she was saying—she expected Dayle to go and get Lotta's young boys.

22

Dayle couldn't believe she'd agreed to go after Lotta's children. It made no sense to bring these young boys to the train station in the middle of a riot. This, however, had not been decided on the basis of any kind of common sense. Lotta's silent hysterics had turned into louder and louder muttering, all of it centered on her "babies" and how she had to have her "babies." That, coupled with Mary Stillman Davies's stern insistence, had finally left Dayle feeling trapped and willing to do almost anything as long as it got her out of the train station and away from the two of them.

As a result, Dayle was now sitting in a canopy-top wagon with Lotta's children, their Italian nurse, and two wounded Chinese, whom the driver had stopped to pick up on a street not far from the Bateman mansion. One of the Chinese was bleeding badly enough that the nurse was on her knees between the carriage seats, pressing a petticoat against the man's stomach and trying to stop the flow of blood from where he'd been shot. From the time he'd been lifted into the carriage, he had drifted in and out of consciousness, sometimes babbling, sometimes writhing.

The second wounded Chinaman sat on the floor of the carriage near the head of his companion, holding his own hurt arm. When the more seriously wounded man babbled, he leaned close to his companion's face as if trying to understand what he was saying. It seemed that he wasn't always successful. After most such episodes, he leaned away again and shook his head. It was while he was bent over his companion one time that the badly wounded man suddenly looked up into the other man's face and then convulsed, arching his back and flailing one arm. His eyes lost focus and rolled into his head. Blood ran from his mouth.

At that, the younger of Lotta's children, who was sitting in Dayle's lap, began to whimper and ask for his mother. Dayle gently turned the boy's head away from the scene and whispered quiet words in his ear, including the promise that they'd soon find his mother, not that the boy's mother could do anything about the newly dead man or the riot that had killed him, but then she didn't imagine that was what the young child wanted. He simply wanted Lotta's familiar warmth and comfort. It was all anyone wanted in times of trouble, Dayle knew, and she held the child closer as he continued to whimper.

"He's still a baby, you know," the older boy now offered as an excuse. He wasn't crying, and although he was sitting on the same seat as Dayle, he had maintained his distance.

"You're not frightened?" she asked.

"I've seen dead things before."

"Not a man, surely?" The sight of this newly dead Chinaman had haunted Dayle with her memory of finding the cook. That unbidden remembrance had been enough to leave her feeling shaken, more shaken than she wanted to admit.

The Lady Pinkerton Gets Her Man

"Gary likes to talk tough," the nurse now added. "He thinks he's his father already."

"How would you know?" the boy asked in a defiant tone.

"Been your nurse since before you could talk," she answered. "Since before you could walk."

"I don't need a nurse," he said, but Dayle noticed that his eyes never left the face of the dead man, even as the nurse tore off a second petticoat and put it over him, creating a lace and ruffles shroud. The older boy's look was intense and unwavering to the point that Dayle wondered if he'd inherited some of his mother's tendency to silent hysterics. She wanted to reach over, slide him closer, and put her arm around him, but she knew he'd resist.

Meanwhile, the "baby" snuggled closer. Dayle stroked his hair while she studied his brother and wondered which was worse, crying or refusing all comfort for fear that it might be false. She knew children at the orphanage who never cried. Never loved, either. Even the other Chinaman had turned his head away by now.

The nurse boosted herself up from the floor where she'd been trying to help the dead man. As she took her seat, she reached for the older child. Grabbing one arm, she pulled him against her. He acted annoyed but didn't resist too much. He finally turned his head and gazed out the carriage.

Dayle wondered about the Italian woman. She was clearly the practical sort. She had immediately taken charge of the badly wounded man and now wasn't taking any nonsense from the older of Lotta's children, yet when Dayle arrived at the house and said they needed to take the children to their mother who was at the train station, she'd asked surprisingly few questions. She was the one who'd sent for the driver and the carriage. Dayle wondered if she was now having second thoughts. There was blood on her shirt and her hands.

"We should be there soon," Dayle offered.

The woman seemed startled at Dayle's comment. She suddenly began wringing her hands. She glanced from the boys to the dead man and then outside the carriage. When she finally responded, it was to ask, "Where will she take the children?"

Dayle didn't understand the question.

She must have returned a puzzled look, because the nurse quickly continued. "I know she won't be able to afford a nurse, but I love these bambinos like they were my own. I know she has to go. Actually, I've been wanting her to leave, hoping she'd go. She's right. This is a good time. In the midst of all this trouble is good. He'll have to worry about the mines first, if you know what I mean." She nodded toward the children, indicating a reluctance to speak any more plainly.

Dayle understood. She'd understood when it happened that the incident between Lotta and Garrick at the train station hadn't been the first. This only confirmed that. Dayle glanced again at the children. They had to know as well.

"I even put a little something in the bottom of the valise," the nurse now added. "It's not much, but it'll help her. I suspect."

Dayle shook her head. Lotta wasn't running away. Lotta could never run away. The wife of a poor man might manage to disappear, but not Lotta. Her husband had means enough to have her tracked down no matter where she went, and no court in the entire country would uphold a mother's claim on her children over a father's claim on his heirs, especially his namesake heir. Dayle brought her eyes back to the older child, the one called Gary, the one who was already struggling to act like a man.

Dayle didn't try to explain any of that. She simply shrugged. "No one is going anyplace. The trains aren't running."

"The trains aren't running?"

The Lady Pinkerton Gets Her Man

There was such a note of incredulity in the nurse's voice, it made Dayle want to laugh. Why was it that nobody in White Springs believed the trains could stop running? Jay Gould and the Union Pacific Railroad were not God, even if they had created this town.

"Mr. Bateman stopped the trains. He doesn't want any of the Chinese miners to leave."

The nurse considered that a moment. "Well, that one left," she said, pointing to the dead man. "That one got away," she added, her voice flat.

With a chill, Dayle knew they weren't necessarily talking about the Chinaman. They were talking about Lotta, and what might be her only escape.

Before more could be said, the carriage lurched to another stop. It was with some relief that Dayle handed the younger child to the nurse and climbed out to see about this new delay. She didn't like discussing situations she knew couldn't be changed. She preferred moving, doing. She'd left the orphanage at age sixteen vowing she'd never find herself without options. It was living in the orphanage that made her decide that love was a woman's worst option. Too often, love, even the natural love of one's children, became a woman's worst trap. She preferred the gun in her pocket and being a Lady Pinkerton. In fact, in time, she'd become grateful for her lack of human entanglements. Having never had any attachments made it easier to avoid them, although she had to admit Harry had nearly gotten to her.

Nearly, not quite, she repeated for her own sake.

There were more wounded Chinese lying at the side of the road. By the time Dayle climbed out of the carriage, Lotta's Chinese driver was already bent over one of them. She joined him and quickly determined that none of these three Chinese was as badly hurt as the dead man in the carriage had been. Relieved by that, Dayle straightened and stepped back. With the three wounded men were several healthy Chinese miners who'd been attending their compatriots. At the driver's instructions, they now prepared to lift the wounded into the wagon.

Since the driver seemed to have things under control, Dayle walked up a little rise to see what she could see. Although the Bateman mansion was some distance from Chinatown, the carriage was now fairly close to the town side of Bitter Creek. They were still somewhat upstream from the plank bridge, which meant the wounded they were picking up had already been carried a great distance by their friends. When she thought about it, she knew that meant the Chinaman with the wounded arm had shown remarkable loyalty. Injured himself, he'd managed to carry his companion across the muddy stream and up the steep bank and partway into town before they'd found them and stopped for them with the carriage. All that, and still his friend had died. She thought it was too bad that kind of courage hadn't been better rewarded.

As she crested the top of the stream bank, she realized the drama she'd witnessed inside the carriage was minor in comparison to what she was seeing now. Half of Chinatown was in flames. Even though it was some distance away, she could see huge piles of bedding, clothing, and furniture littering the streets. Dogs and pigs rooted through those piles. Or, more correctly, they rooted through the piles that were merely smoldering, not burning. The animals would have to hurry if they hoped to find anything, she thought. For at the same time, she noted the gangs of men going street to street with torches, setting fire to anything that was left.

She thought again about Garrick Bateman. Desperate men did desperate things. Lotta said it right. Stopping the train made no sense, but what else could he do? There weren't enough guards or Pinkertons to stop this. It was futile even to try. It was futile anyway. No matter how determined he was to hang on to his Chinese miners, it was obvious the rioters

The Lady Pinkerton Gets Her Man

didn't intend to leave the Chinese anyplace to return. They wanted them out of White Springs, maybe out of Wyoming. She only hoped the soldiers arrived before the rioters got to the train station.

She looked around again and saw that the driver almost had the wounded loaded into the carriage. The train station was going to be overrun, she knew. That's where she was taking Lotta's boys, and that's where the driver wanted to take the hurt men. Sooner or later, that's where all the Chinese would come looking for a way to leave White Springs. When the soldiers arrived, they were going to be faced with an interesting dilemma. Protecting the Chinese wouldn't be enough. How would they shelter them? Feed them? If defending Chinamen was politically distasteful, she couldn't imagine what would happen if some photographer sent the eastern newspapers a series of pictures showing soldiers building shanties for Chinese miners. She shook her head. Whatever else happened there, she suspected the days of the Chinese mining coal in Wyoming were over. Bateman was finished, he just didn't know it yet.

She again remembered Harry. If the possibility of organizing the town was lost, at least he was going to see the end of cheap Chinese labor. Maybe he would count that a partial victory. At the same time, she knew better. Harry never did anything halfway. That was what made him both charming and exasperating.

Once, last night, she'd tried to get up for some water because the room was overly warm, and they were both so dry-mouthed they could taste each other's thirst, but she couldn't. They'd loved each other that much. She'd tried to get up three times and each time collapsed back into the bed. Naked, her skin to his skin, and unable to rise, she'd been reduced to laughter as the only thing either of them had left to release.

She'd looked at him and laughed. After that, whenever either of them looked at the other, they both laughed. That went on until their sides ached, and then even laughing wasn't possible.

At last, Harry had rolled out of the bed and crawled to the table, where a pitcher of water had been left beside the washbasin. He had drunk some and then brought the pitcher to her. She'd taken it from him and drunk thirstily. She was still drinking when he fell asleep next to her.

She suddenly wondered where Harry was and what he was doing in the middle of all this mess. The sensible thing would be for her to find him, and then together they could leave White Springs to its own problems and go . . . where? If they couldn't make love like ordinary people, she seriously doubted that they could ever live that way. She couldn't imagine Harry keeping a regular job, and she knew she was not the kind of woman who was likely to settle for a little white cottage with a Singer sewing machine in the parlor.

What would they do?

Things were bad by the time Dayle and the others got to the train station. Displaced Chinese were clogging the roads and camping along the side of the train tracks. They'd abandoned the westbound train and instead filled the station platform with their hurt and dying. Dayle climbed down from the carriage and helped the children out. Then, leaving the nurse and the driver to care for the wounded, she took the boys inside.

The moment the younger one spotted Lotta, he ran to her. The older boy acted as if seeing his mother was nothing special. Dayle had watched him take in the whole scene, the streets full of Chinese, the depot full of wounded. He never showed emotion, but his head turned when a man moaned loudly from a corner near the ticket booth. Still, he said nothing. Like Lotta, he

The Lady Pinkerton Gets Her Man

looked and then held what he saw in suspension. It wasn't until they were less than five steps from his mother that he finally broke and ran.

As Lotta drew him to her, she looked up at Dayle. "Thanks," she said.

Dayle nodded. She didn't think going to Lotta's house, gathering her children, and bringing them there in the midst of a major disturbance that threatened to engulf the whole town and maybe the whole region was covered by a single *thanks*. On the other hand, she didn't know what else there was to say. She was glad to see Lotta was past her hysterics and didn't seem to be any the worse for her experience at Garrick Bateman's hands, and she didn't know how to express that, either.

"They're fine children," she offered, and then excused herself to find Mary Stillman Davies.

Dayle found the Christian woman crusader in the station storeroom treating a miner's badly burned arm. She was too occupied to look up. Dayle had to clear her throat and say, "I brought Lotta's children here. They're fine."

"Good," the woman grunted, and still didn't look up. "Now, if you don't mind, could you see to that man over there?" She waved in the general direction of another Chinaman with burns.

Dayle couldn't help herself. Anger welled up. She didn't really have a knack for nursing, but more than that, this do-good church woman had sent her on a senseless mission and then didn't even have the sense to comment on it. Not even so much as the thanks Lotta had offered. Nevertheless, Dayle managed to steady herself. "There are bigger problems than the ones right here under your nose," Dayle told Miss Davies when she had enough control to keep her voice level.

The woman finally looked up. "What bigger problems?"

"Dozens, maybe hundreds of miners outside with

no shelter. It's going to be snowing by midnight. Some of them will be frozen by morning."

"I know," the older woman said. "That's why I got the stationmaster to open the empty boxcars."

"Boxcars?" Dayle asked.

"Yes. There are some thirty empty boxcars parked on a siding outside. I know it's not the best shelter, but . . ."

"Wooden boxcars," Dayle now asked as another worry claimed her attention. The memory of the mobs she'd seen systematically burning Chinatown, building by building, rose like a specter.

"Yes, I suppose they're wooden," the older woman repeated. "Why does that matter?"

"Who's guarding those boxcars?" Dayle insisted without answering Miss Davies.

"I don't know. There's a Chinaman in some kind of fur coat who seems to be taking charge."

"Ah So! Ah So's here? Is Harry here also?"

"Harry?"

"Yes, Harry Bryant, the actor."

"I don't know. Is that important?"

"Very," Dayle answered, and left immediately.

Outside, Dayle had to step around the hurt and the sick who were hunched or lying on makeshift pallets scattered across the train platform. She was bumped and jostled as she entered the crowds that were everywhere else. She looked for Ah So. She pulled herself up on her tiptoes and scanned over the milling masses. She worked her way past the main tracks and the roundhouse to the siding, where a long row of empty boxcars stood.

In the end, she smelled Ah So before she saw him. She didn't know it was the Tong leader she was smelling. She just knew her nostrils were being assaulted by a noxious burnt-smelling odor that couldn't be ignored. Turning to try and find the source of that annoyance, she spotted Ah So and immediately called to him.

The Lady Pinkerton Gets Her Man

It was then that she noticed how his raccoon-skin coat was singed on one side. The hair had been almost completely burned off the shoulder and was blackened near the collar. It was his burned coat that she'd smelled, and it was truly foul. When he turned, she saw that the hair on that side of his head was also burned and his eyebrow was completely missing. That gave him an odd, damaged look, but he didn't seem to be hurt otherwise, just singed.

Obviously also concerned about securing the area, he was busy directing men with rifles to the tops of every other boxcar. She knew in an instant that wasn't going to be enough to hold back the mobs. Getting more men was no problem. They needed more guns. She tried to think where they might get more rifles but couldn't concentrate for being more and more conscious of the foul smell coming off the Tong leader's burnt coat.

"How can you wear that thing?" she asked as soon as she was close enough to say something.

In some ways, it was a stupid question. It was cold and getting colder. He was probably the only Chinaman in the vicinity who had anything warm to wear. However, she didn't think that was enough excuse to continue enduring the putrid smell of burnt hair and singed skin coming off that article of clothing.

Ah So clearly thought differently. He immediately drew himself up taller and pulled the coat tighter around his shoulders. "I am the Chinaman with the raccoon-skin coat," he told her. "This is no time to be mistaken for anyone lesser."

Dayle got the idea. Truth was, the coat wasn't the worst thing she'd experienced lately, just the worst-smelling thing. "Where's Harry?" she asked. "I'm sure he must have an opinion on all this."

Ah So was suddenly silent.

"Where's Harry?" she repeated.

"He very brave man," Ah So now said in a different tone of voice. "Most men talk very big. Then, when trouble comes, they run. It is difference between the warlord and the foot soldier. Warlord know what he has to do, and he do it. Foot soldier don't know, and he don't do it."

Dayle had no idea what Ah So was talking about. She hadn't asked him for a lengthy character assessment of Harry. If she'd wanted that, she'd have taken Harry's photograph to a phrenologist, although she suspected she knew what the phrenologist would say. He'd no doubt note the high forehead as a sign of intelligence and the strong jaw as a sign of determination. She personally liked Harry's well-turned ears and the tiny scar next to his lower lip.

Ah So continued talking on and on about how the fates favored the brave. Under the best of circumstances, Dayle had trouble puzzling meaning out of Ah So's talk. It didn't help when he got philosophical. She also knew from experience that it didn't help to interrupt or hurry him. Dayle shifted her weight and wished he'd get to the point. Either he knew where Harry was, or he didn't.

"Cowards no understand. They expect the fates to ignore them," Ah So went on. "It not that way. All the universe likes courage, bravery and courage." Ah So paused to shake his head. "Harry outran the bullets to his back. The fates liked him. Harry dodged the bullets coming from his front. The fates liked him. He jumped through the window and knocked down my man. He fine. He warn us about the fire on the roof."

Somewhere in the curl of Ah So's words, Dayle began to get a bad feeling. "What did Harry do?" she asked, not sure she understood.

"He save my life. He not save my coat, but he save my life. He save that man's life." Ah So pointed to the guard on top of the closest boxcar. "He save that man and that man." Ah So continued pointing to his guards, one by one. Dayle recognized the man atop the first boxcar. He had been one of the guards who'd escorted Dayle and Harry into Ah So's Chinese

The Lady Pinkerton Gets Her Man

boudoir, but remembering that detail was avoiding the larger truth she now knew was coming.

"What did Harry do? Where is he?" Dayle asked again, her voice taking an edge.

"He died a brave man," Ah So finally said.

Dayle felt as if she'd fallen through a nightmare into some world where everything churned and bumped together—present events, old memories, details, lots of details. It was as if time no longer mattered, only the tiniest of remembered details. She wondered for a moment if all of life and living ultimately came down to those tiny remembered details that we all gather like lint in our pockets.

Her breathing quickened, and her mouth went dry. She wanted to run, but she was paralyzed as Ah So continued his story.

"As I told you, the fates remember the brave. Cowards die. Not the brave. The large forces in the world, the fates, are controlled by the ancestors. They know. They see what we do with courage. It is why Chinese never go far from their ancestors. It is not good to be alone with no one to watch for you. But now, the fox fairies don't care about anything. Harry finished his bravery. The fates are pleased, but the fates looked away, and the fox fairies, those no-good, senseless mischief makers, got him."

"The hell with fox fairies," Dayle suddenly spit past her dry mouth. "What happened to Harry?"

Ah So stood for a moment stone-faced and still. "It was stray bullet. Stray bullet hit him in head."

Dayle started to go. She turned and started to walk away, thinking she didn't care anymore. She didn't care about anything or anybody, but she didn't get far before she knew that wasn't true.

"It's not over," Dayle said, returning. "When the mobs finish burning Chinatown, they're going to want to burn these boxcars next," she said, although her words sounded distant even to herself.

"Maybe soldiers come first," Ah So suggested.

"The soldiers will never come," she answered. It was a truth that had been forming in the back of her mind with growing conviction.

If the soldiers were coming, they'd have been there by now. More, she thought she knew why they weren't there. She suspected President Arthur had changed his mind. Perhaps he hadn't fully understood. Whatever the reason, he must have realized and reversed himself. It was said that Horace Tabor in Colorado lost a bid for election to the Senate because he'd supported Chinese miners. Given the current feeling, it was political suicide to send soldiers to protect Chinese miners.

"There won't be any soldiers," she repeated, and then said it again, knowing as she spoke what it meant: more would die, maybe lots more.

23

Dayle went to find Allan Pinkerton, because somebody had to do something. If the soldiers weren't coming, that meant the Pinkertons were the only ones with enough men and guns to help. If Allan Pinkerton ordered his agents to guard the train station instead of the mines, there might be a chance of ending this short of a complete massacre. She had no idea whether he'd actually agree to do that, but she had to ask.

As she entered the Pinkerton office, she was struck with how deserted it was. No bustle, no jostle, no loud talk. It was almost as though the building had been abandoned. Everyone had been sent out, she realized, and her spirits sank. Even if Mr. Pinkerton gave the order to protect the station, someone would have to gather the men. That would take time. She wondered if she was being too hopeful. Maybe this was beyond what anyone could solve.

As she approached the main desk, she realized that besides the agent on duty, the only other person in the office was Mr. Pinkerton himself. He looked up and saw her.

"Well, now, Miss Dobson," he exclaimed, and looked her over as if no crisis was large enough to stand in the way of his appreciating a woman of comely form.

Dayle wondered what it would take to make him think of something else first. Then, deciding this was not the time to be timid, she put a little swish in her skirts. If that's what it took to get the man's attention, then that's what she would give him. She didn't stop in front of the desk, either. She swished around, saying, "The Chicago fire must have been awful."

He seemed puzzled.

She continued, "I was trying to think of things that were worse than this current situation, and then I remembered that you lived through the Chicago fire. That must have been absolutely awful."

"It was," he offered, and then offered no more.

She'd hoped to trigger his retelling of that event. The Pinkertons had lost the home office to that fire, including a roomful of files on habitual criminals known as "the most extensive rogues' gallery in the world." Mr. Pinkerton had referred to that loss as "irreplaceable." It was after the Chicago fire that he took up writing detective novels.

She tried again. "This town is not as big as Chicago, but I couldn't help wondering what would happen if the mobs spread the flames from Chinatown to the main part of White Springs, say, maybe the train station. If a fire at the train station spread, all of White Springs might be engulfed. Who knows? The fire might not even stop at the edge of town. Whipped by the wind, it could spread across the prairie. It could take out miles and miles of telegraph poles. I understand that a prairie fire can sometimes get into the railroad ties under the tracks and smolder for days. No one would even know the track was on fire until a train came along and was derailed."

The Lady Pinkerton Gets Her Man

"Why would the mobs start trouble on this side of the stream?" the on-duty agent asked. "They live here themselves."

She nodded. "You're right," she answered the agent while keeping an eye on Mr. Pinkerton, trying to judge his reaction. "You're right, unless the mob gets carried away, as mobs sometimes do."

"The important thing is to get those soldiers sent in here," the agent said, and he might have said more if Mr. Pinkerton hadn't raised a hand to stop him.

"I'll take care of Miss Dobson," he said.

"Yes, sir," the agent returned.

Mr. Pinkerton motioned for Dayle to follow him.

Together, they crossed the room and climbed the stairs. When they were halfway up and out of earshot of the other agent, Mr. Pinkerton cleared his throat.

Dayle braced herself. She expected to be reprimanded for overstepping herself. If not that, she expected him to say something about the riot. He didn't.

"What have you managed to learn about that missionary woman?" he asked.

Dayle didn't know what to say.

"They tell me you're a good detective. Surely there must be something about Miss Davies that has piqued your curiosity."

Dayle still didn't know what to say. No question, a curiosity about Mary Stillman Davies had possessed Dayle from the moment she first met her, and yet she couldn't believe Allan Pinkerton was asking about a missionary woman in the middle of this riot. Unless . . . Dayle suddenly wrestled with the thought that Mr. Pinkerton might know things about Miss Davies that she only suspected.

"I want you to go with her when she takes those Chinese girls to San Francisco," Allan Pinkerton now told her.

"I beg your pardon?" Dayle returned, thinking that

maybe this was more a case of his thinking in a straight line—never wavering from some purpose once he was set upon it. "No one's going to San Francisco. The trains aren't running," she added.

"Well, that's not a permanent condition," he told her, and tipped his head in a rather obvious attempt to see down her dress.

She straightened and stepped back.

He shook his head and said, "Bateman will get the trains running again and soon. You can count on that. When that happens, I want you to stay with Mary Stillman Davies. Follow her."

"You don't believe this whole place is in danger of burning to the ground?" she asked.

"Whether it does or not, some things can't be helped."

"Or won't be helped," she returned.

He didn't like that barb. "Don't get idealistic on me. Pinkertons are not policemen. We're hired guns. Sometimes it pays to keep that fact in mind."

When she offered no response, he shook his head again and changed the subject. "I understand you grew up in an orphanage."

Dayle nodded, wondering how he knew. More than that, she wondered if he was trying to connect her background to his interest in Miss Davies. She considered the possibility that he knew more about both of them than he wanted to say. Why, she still didn't understand.

"I grew up poor myself," he said as they resumed their climb up the stairs. "The poorest, worst section of Glasgow. I was working in the textile factories by the time I was eight. Half the kids working at those factories never saw their sixteenth birthday." He paused long enough to wiggle his fingers in her face. "I never even lost an appendage. I was determined I wouldn't fall victim to my birth."

She shook her head. She hardly thought this was the time or the place for a long reminiscence.

The Lady Pinkerton Gets Her Man

He sensed her thought. "I'm telling you this because I expect you to understand. People who grow up poor know about raw necessity. How many children died in your orphanage? What was it called?"

"Saint Elizabeth's," she said.

"That's a nice name. Sounds like a nice Christian charity. How many children died in that nice Christian institution?" he asked again.

"I don't know," Dayle answered.

"You don't know, or you don't want to tell me?"

They'd reached the top of the stairs. Mr. Pinkerton paused again to catch his breath.

"I don't know," Dayle said. "I wasn't exactly keeping count."

"Was it half? A third?"

"More like a third," she said.

"Better odds than where I grew up," he mused, and then, having caught his breath, he continued on, leaving her to follow.

"What does my childhood have to do with anything?" Dayle wanted to know. If he knew something, she wanted him to say it.

He entered Thuzla Smith's office as if he owned it. "Nobody cared, did they?"

"I beg your pardon?"

"The children died because nobody cared. One less orphan meant one less mouth to feed, one less expense. In fact, I'm willing to bet that if we opened the account books of your Saint Elizabeth's, we'd find that they needed to lose exactly a third of the children to stay solvent. No problem. The sisters managed as best they could. They probably never admitted even to themselves that their level of neglect exactly matched the shortfall of their funds."

"I don't understand." Whatever point he was making, it wasn't what she expected.

"I told you. I'm talking about raw necessity, and we both understand. We both decided to live in spite of it. Am I right?"

Dayle couldn't answer. She was suddenly a churn of emotion. She knew what he was saying. It was a truth she'd avoided more than all others. He was right, but this was not a subject she cared to discuss. She didn't even like thinking about it. What could she say?

She crossed to the window as she always did when she came into this room. She liked looking out, especially when she was feeling agitated and needed a distraction.

"Where's Thuzla?" she asked, wanting to change the subject. Besides, she found it was strange to be in his office and not see her boss's red, blotchy face.

"They're all out guarding whatever needs guarding," he answered as he sat behind Thuzla's desk and tested the turn of his chair. "Every Pinkerton in White Springs is out on guard duty except you and I and that man on the desk downstairs."

Then she said it. "You're not going to help the Chinese, are you?"

Mr. Pinkerton grunted. "That's what I'm trying to tell you. This is a terrible situation, and you're right, it'll probably get worse before it gets better. But you and I grew up poor. We understand that some things are beyond hope, and the best thing is to look out for yourself."

Dayle stared out the window and bit her tongue, trying to keep herself from saying something she knew she'd regret. Besides, she didn't need to ask, she knew. Allan Pinkerton had set her up, walked her into a trap, and nearly gotten her killed. There was a riot going on outside because he'd miscalculated. At the last moment, the president of the United States saw through his scheme and refused to order the soldiers into White Springs. Now, the old man seemed to think he could excuse all that with a few platitudes about the raw necessities of life. Worse, he didn't even seem to be worried.

She shook her head. "Garrick Bateman doesn't understand. He's finished," she said.

The Lady Pinkerton Gets Her Man

"Worse than that. Garrick Bateman will take the blame."

That's when she understood his calm. He'd messed up, but he was covered. Bateman was going to take the fall. And when things got bad enough, the president would have to send in the troops anyway—like it or not. All Allan Pinkerton had to do was sit there and wait for things to get bad enough. He still expected to win. Never mind the bloodshed—the "raw necessity," as he liked to call it.

She shook her head again. "And Bateman has no idea."

Mr. Pinkerton chuckled. "I'm afraid he hasn't the intelligence."

She wished Allan Pinkerton would give her credit for intelligence, because as she continued to stand there staring out the window, she'd noticed the layout of the train station below—really noticed. She saw the water train pull into the station and begin to pump out its tanks. Life went on, and in a town with no potable water, the water train, at least, couldn't be stopped.

"What made you become a Lady Pinkerton?" he asked.

She was seeing details that she'd never noticed before. Details that suddenly seemed important—like how the siding sat on a little rise and the way the tracks could be switched. For that reason, she didn't answer at first.

"There must be some reason why you decided to become a detective, especially since they tell me you're very conscientious. That's rare."

She turned away from the scene outside the window long enough to look at him, to wonder at his almost inhuman detachment. "I read about Kate Warne in a school primer and knew I wanted to be a Lady Pinkerton from that moment on," she answered.

"Really? Kate's story is being read by schoolchildren? I'm not sure how she'd feel about that. Kate was a woman with plenty of opinions, most of them surprising. Rather like you in that regard. For example, you don't like what you're seeing out that window, do you?"

Dayle glanced back at the window. "Actually, from this distance, it all looks quite simple."

"Exactly," he said, and leaned forward over Thuzla's desk.

He was a small man and surprisingly less formidable than her regular boss, but she knew he was not a man to be underestimated. She wondered what he might do to a Pinkerton who betrayed the company—who betrayed him.

"Exactly," he repeated. "Not many of us rise above the fray. Somebody has to. Kate did. What story did you read in that school primer?"

"The one about how she saved President Lincoln's life."

He laughed louder. "I'll bet it didn't tell how she seduced the colonel of the Maryland militia right in his own house in order to accomplish that feat, did it?"

Dayle shook her head. "It told about how she uncovered a plot to assassinate the newly elected Abraham Lincoln, and that if she hadn't warned him, he might never have been inaugurated, never have become president. In that case, history would have been different, very different."

"Well, I guess that's a fair enough account. But if you ask me, history leaves out all the interesting details. Maybe I'll write you up in one of my true detective novels," he told her with a wink. "I think I'll call you the Denver Doll."

She knew she was supposed to be flattered, but, in fact, she was feeling repulsed.

"I could call you something else," he offered.

"No, that's fine. Very fine, thank you," she said, expecting that he would call her a great many other things before this was through.

The Lady Pinkerton Gets Her Man

"You'll be famous," he added.

Or infamous, she thought, and then questioned what she was about to do. What made her think she could outsmart Allan Pinkerton? It was said that he could solve a crime without ever visiting the scene. He'd ask to be given the details, and from a very few facts, he could describe the criminal. He was right about the orphanage, St. Elizabeth's, down to the worst of the details. No question, he was good, and he knew her weak point—knew what she wanted.

The reason the story of Kate Warne had become fixed in her mind was that a Lady Pinkerton was somebody. She was nobody, an orphan who didn't even know her real name. She'd spent most of her young life aching to be somebody like Kate Warne, somebody important enough to be written up in a book.

For a moment, she studied the older man. She wondered what Kate Warne had seen in him. Deep down, she thought she knew, but it wasn't there anymore. She wondered if Allan Pinkerton had lost himself when he had his stroke or before that. Maybe when Kate Warne died. Rumor had it that they were lifelong lovers.

"Your son's friend Harry Bryant is dead. One of the casualties of this necessity," she told him.

He appeared startled. "How did that happen?"

"He was in Chinatown when the trouble started," she said, and felt almost as removed from her words as she was from the scene below the window. Harry had gotten to her last night. There would come a moment when she'd have to deal with his dying, but not yet. There was still too much dying all around for her to absorb any of it.

Allan Pinkerton shook his head. "That's too bad. Life is messy. No use denying it."

She knew. Usually, she liked her life messy. She was attracted to the unruly because the unruly wasn't as likely to absorb a person into some kind of bland, solid sameness. She'd counted on Harry for that. She'd dared love him because she knew he was one of the chronically discontented who had to live on the edge. Trouble was, if you lived that way, you ran the risk of dying that way.

As she was considering those thoughts, she was also considering again the scene outside the window, the layout of the station, the signal house, the siding. She went over her plan one more time. If someone were to . . .

She closed her eyes at what was an impossible idea. She was all alone.

"Come away from the window. Forget what's going on down there," Allan Pinkerton was now telling her. "When the trains start again, go with Mary Stillman Davies. Believe me, that's your best chance to get ahead in this business."

She heard him, but she didn't answer. She checked out the window one more time, memorizing the details.

"Did you hear me?" he asked.

"Yes," she answered. "Only you've never exactly explained your interest in Miss Davies."

"Oh, but that's the fun part. You're a Pinkerton detective. Remember? Figuring it out ought to be half the pleasure." Then he winked at her. "I think we're a lot alike, you and I. We both grew up poor and know how to make the most of an opportunity, even one born of necessity."

She glanced once more out the window. She might have taken his advice and done as he suggested, except for that view.

"I don't intend ever to be poor again," Allan Pinkerton was now telling her.

She walked away from the window, thinking he'd forgotten the real advantage of growing up poor. A person who remembered how it was to be poor could operate on guts and nerve alone, if that's all she had. Allan Pinkerton could stop the coming massacre

The Lady Pinkerton Gets Her Man

without ever leaving this room. He could do it with an order, which was simpler and a lot less dangerous than what she had in mind. She wondered how he could live with himself knowing he could stop it and not stopping it. She knew she couldn't. No matter the cost. In fact, to do nothing was to become like him.

"Perhaps you're right," she said.

"Of course, I'm right," he answered. "It'll all work out for the best. You'll see."

At the door, she paused. Before she did something desperate, she had to know. "Any chance the soldiers will arrive before . . ." And then she couldn't finish the sentence, couldn't actually say it.

"Before they kill half the Chinamen in town?" he asked.

She nodded.

He shook his head. "Like I said, you can't help some things. You have to do what you have to do."

"Exactly," she answered.

At the same time, she reminded herself of the consequences. Rather than becoming a famous Lady Pinkerton, written up in one of his books, she was about to ruin any chance she had. That didn't strike her as being smart, but it did strike her as being more in touch with reality than the elderly detective ducking his head to one side and hoping to catch a look at her ankle as she turned to walk out.

If Dayle was going to pull off a bigger rescue than Mary Stillman Davies ever imagined, she was going to need an engineer. Fortunately there was a man who hung out at the cockfights who she thought might be a candidate. She didn't know him. She only knew that he was called Bald-head Ted and lived in one of the abandoned hotels on the far side of town.

He was a black man, well respected. It was said that he was the best locomotive fireman anywhere on the line. Some of the men at the cockfights liked to tell the story of how Bald-head Ted bragged so often and so long that he could shovel coal into a firebox faster than any newfangled mechanical stoker that someone finally took him up on it. They staged a contest. At the end of the story, she was always warned not to bet against him.

Now she was hoping he'd bet with her.

She found the hotel and knocked on the door.

No one answered.

She knocked again.

Still no response. She shook her head and wondered what had made her think Bald-head Ted would be at home. For all she knew, he was out with the mobs, burning out the Chinese with the rest of them. Still, she couldn't make herself give up.

She knocked again and then tried the door. It was open. She stepped cautiously into a cavernous room that had once been the hotel's lobby. The place was empty. Her footsteps echoed, even the swish of her skirts rolled around the space and returned like a whisper. It was enough to spook her.

She hollered up the stairs. "Anyone home?"

No response.

She looked around the empty lobby. It was clean. Floors swept. No dust. Even the high ceilings were clear of cobwebs. She noted that an American flag had been tacked to one wall. There was a rocking chair near the front window.

She tried calling again. "Anyone here?"

A cat answered. Meowing, it curled its way down the stairs, rubbing against the stair posts as it came. It was a large tortoise-shell cat with mismatched eyes. When it got to the bottom of the stairs, it walked all the way around Dayle and then jumped onto the sill of the front window and seated itself there while it licked a paw.

That's when Dayle noticed a photograph, not large, hanging from a single hook near the same window.

The Lady Pinkerton Gets Her Man

The picture was hanging high. She had to take it down before she could examine it. The image was of a handsome couple, well dressed. They were posed in a simple but old-fashioned style, the woman standing behind the man. His fine, high hat covered part of her chin, even though she'd cocked her head to one side.

"Can I help you?" someone behind her asked.

She jumped and turned, nearly dropping the photograph.

Bald-head Ted was tall, thin, and very smooth on top. Even in this half-light, his head glistened. He was standing at the bottom of the stairs, a rounded wooden stick hanging from one hand.

Dayle noted the stick. However, she didn't take his attitude as particularly menacing.

"Handsome couple," she said, and replaced the photograph. "The man's hat is particularly fine," she added as she turned again to face him.

"My father," the tall man told her. "The hat cost him a week's wages. He was as bald as me, but he was a lot more vain. He liked his fine clothes, and he wouldn't have no picture taken without his hat."

"And the woman must be your mother?"

He nodded. "She was a long-suffering woman. Her revenge was that she outlived my father. I come from free people living in Philadelphia since before there was a United States of America. Got folks living there still."

Dayle looked over her shoulder at the photograph again. She wasn't sure how to begin her business. "I apologize," she said. "I didn't mean to enter your place uninvited. No one answered, and the door was open, and . . ."

The cat had left the window and was now rubbing Bald-head Ted's leg, but he took no notice. He continued to stand straight, unmoved, the stick still at his side.

She swallowed. "And I hear you're the best fireman working the rails."

"That why you come all the way up here to this old hotel?"

She told him, "Yes."

He shook his head. "I can't say I've had many fine ladies take an interest in my ability as a fireman, especially not white ladies with guns in their pockets."

That startled Dayle enough that she immediately checked her weapon.

He laughed. It was a deep, gentle chuckle. "It only makes a tiny little bulge. Probably no one else would notice, but I've learned it's wise to know where the guns are. Not many women carry guns. I wasn't sure about you until you gave yourself away."

"Oh," was all Dayle could say. She was fully chagrined.

"Smooth moves," he said. "Never move fast. Move slow. Move sure. My father taught me that."

"He a fireman, too?" Dayle asked.

"Fighter and gambler," he told her. "Unbeaten at boxing and rarely beaten at cards. It was those smooth moves. Now, why did you really come here?"

"I came because I know every fireman hopes someday to get promoted to engineer, and I've got an engine I need you to drive."

Bald-head Ted had started to set his stick down. He stopped and looked around at her as if she were crazy.

This time, Dayle chuckled. "Smooth movements are fine, but it also helps to get your opponent's attention."

"My, my," Bald-head Ted said as he continued to look at her. "You are a most surprising visitor. Full of vinegar, as they say. Full of vinegar." He lowered himself to one of the steps and rubbed his knee. "Where you going to get this engine you want me to drive?"

"It's the water train. It's the only thing running right now, and I have this idea about using that water train engine to get those boxcars parked on the siding

The Lady Pinkerton Gets Her Man

all the way to Evanston, the next stop. I mean, things are bad. Somebody needs to help the Chinese get out of town."

He laughed. "If I was to do that, I'd never have me another railroad job. I'd make the blacklist, I would."

"But nobody has to know it was you," she told him. "Just before you roll to the next station, you could jump off, hide out for a day, and then hitch the next train coming back here. I'm sure you know enough about hoboing to do that."

"Like the phantom brakeman," he said with a little chuckle. "I'd be the phantom engineer, and nobody would know it."

"You'd know. You'd know you drove your own engine once."

He considered that a moment. They both knew that as a Negro, he'd never be promoted to engineer, no matter how good a fireman he was. That's why she'd come to him. She didn't know who else would be willing to take the chance.

Bald-head Ted rubbed his knee some more. He turned his head one way, and then he turned it the other, as if chasing a thought back and forth. "That there water train engine is so small, even her crew calls her the 'cabbage cutter.' That engine ain't going to pull nothing to Evanston, not even something as lightweight as them boxcars full of them slant-eyed fools."

"Why's that?"

"Because it's basically a yard engine, and an old one at that. They only use it to haul the water because that's a short run, ten miles, no more. Back and forth, back and forth. That's all it's good for."

"I don't believe it."

"You don't know much about trains, do you?"

"I know I like to ride trains better than horses," she returned.

He chuckled. "Me, too. But I'm telling you the gospel truth. The problem is water. You gots to fill that engine all the time because it don't carry much, and it leaks. You should hear the crew on that run complain. There's not enough water stops between here and Evanston to make it with that old rusty bucket."

"Can't we carry extra water?"

"How? You going to have time to outfit that engine with an extra tank?"

"Why don't we take one of the tanker cars with us?"

"Sure, and out in the middle of the desert, how you going to pump water from the tanker to the engine?"

"So it can't be done?"

"The way this problem is usually handled is that when the water sinks too low, the engineer will unhook his drag freight and then run the engine to the next water tower, fill up, and come back for his load. In this here particular situation, I don't think that's going to be too practical, either."

"Most engineers," Dayle said.

"What about most engineers?" he asked.

"You said that's how most engineers handle a problem like this. What does the exceptional engineer do?"

He chuckled. "I figured you'd be asking that 'cause I knowed this one fellow. He was one hell of a train driver. He knew his engine the way some men know their horse, and he was a real highball artist. He loved to make those fast runs. He didn't never dally at the stations, coal chutes, or water towers. They say he never once left his drag freight on a siding while he went for water. No, sir, he considered that way too slow a way to do his business. He knew just how to suck enough juice out of his engine to get it where he wanted it to go, no matter what, but he was driving a real engine, not a roundhouse switcher."

"How far do you think you could get before you sucked that cabbage cutter dry?" Dayle asked.

"I don't know. I don't know how bad it's leaking."

"Close enough? Could you get those Chinese within

walking distance of Evanston? I mean, those Chinese are going to get killed if they stay here."

They looked at each other a moment. She felt him test her determination. She didn't waver. The sisters at the orphanage had drummed into her the fact that a woman could only be ruined once. They'd meant something else, but Dayle figured the idea applied. If she was going to ruin her career, she might as well make the event memorable. Bald-head Ted looked away first.

"There's no way I'm going to drive that engine and not get caught. We best be clear on that point, but I tell you, I don't envy those poor Chinamen," he added.

Dayle nodded. "I heard you were a good man."

"Yes, ma'am, I am."

"Can you get them close enough, then?"

"I'll try, ma'am."

"You'll need a crew."

"I know a man who'll shovel coal for me."

"What about a brakeman?"

"Don't need no brakeman," he told her. "There ain't going to be no slowin' on this run."

That settled, Dayle needed someone to throw the switches, someone with exactly Tommy the Tube Man's peculiar skills. At the theater, she found the troupe packing as fast as they could throw things into trunks. She spotted the redhaired actress first. She was rolling wigs in towels and shoving them into a box while she sniffled into a handkerchief. Dayle figured she knew why. Miss Valentine had heard about Harry.

Dayle drew a deep breath. She watched a moment and then pointed out the obvious. "No reason to hurry. No one's leaving town right now. The trains aren't running."

The redhaired actress shrugged and continued to gather up props and scripts. "That's what a company of actors does, you know. When there's trouble, we pack. Most of us ran away from home or a husband. We can't handle trouble."

Dayle didn't say anything to that. It was more than she wanted to get into at the moment. "Where's Tommy?" she asked instead. "I need to talk to Tommy."

The redhaired actress straightened and brought her hands to her hips. "Follow the noise," she said. "Just follow the noise."

At first, Dayle wasn't sure what the woman meant. The whole place was a jumble of sounds. Then she heard it, a sucking, sobbing sound.

"What is that?" Dayle asked.

"Tommy," the woman told her, and pointed in the general direction of Harry's dressing room.

Dayle found Tommy sitting at Harry's dressing table, sobbing those loud, sucking sobs and drinking Scotch from a bottle. He looked up, saw her in the mirror, and immediately started talking. "He played the greatest Hamlet I ever saw. It made me cry to watch him. He was not a man who did anything shoddy. He knew how to put himself, all of himself, every bit of himself, into what he was doing. It made him an artist, not an actor. Do you know how rare it is to meet an artist? Actors we got. This whole place is full of actors, scared actors, who want to leave town now that they can't depend on Harry. But an artist, a believer, a visionary, we don't have enough of those. Never enough, if you know what I mean."

Dayle knew what he meant and suddenly had to wrestle with her own feelings again, being in Harry's room, seeing his clothes. That was no condition for her to be in if she was going to do what she knew she had to do.

She poured water from the pitcher on the washstand into the basin. She carried the bowl to the dressing table, cleared aside the greasepaint with her elbow, and plopped the basin and its cold water down

The Lady Pinkerton Gets Her Man

in front of Tommy. Then, before he knew what was happening, she pushed his head into the water, turning his sobs into a bubbling gurgle.

He struggled, but he was too drunk and too surprised to resist effectively. His limbs flailed such that he never did get his feet on the floor under him. She held his face in the water until his struggling shifted from a surprised flailing to a more serious grasping of the table and the chair as if he expected those objects to hold him up, lift him out of the water as he began to fear she might drown him.

There was nothing like nearly dying to sober a person, she knew.

When she let go, he pulled back so hard he toppled his chair, making enough noise to bring several of the others running to see what was the matter.

"She's trying to kill me!" Tommy sputtered from where he lay on the floor, but no one believed that. A moment later, they'd all gone back to their packing. Tommy rolled off the chair and got to his knees, wincing at the soreness of his arthritis. He wiped the water from his eyes, and then, looking around at her, he snarled, "What did you do that for?"

"I need you to finish what Harry started," she told him. "Harry died trying to save the Chinese miners, only he didn't quite get them safe."

24

Back at the train station, Dayle found Mary Stillman Davies on her knees, bent over the injured foot of a Chinaman who'd fled without his shoes. Dayle asked to have a word with her. Miss Davies spoke briefly to the man in Chinese. Then, as she stood up and straightened her back, she started relating how the man with the injured foot had been forced out of his bathhouse at gunpoint. He'd arrived at the station without clothes as well as shoes, just a small rug that he'd found someplace and wrapped about himself.

About the time she began to moralize about the "true necessities of life," Dayle interrupted. Everyone had a story, this day especially, and while this man's naked plight was mildly amusing, Dayle had more important things on her mind, such as saving his life, not to mention the fact that she never had time for moralizing. She got right to the point.

"Do you think you could get the wounded onto those boxcars outside?" Dayle asked her. "It would need to be done quickly and quietly."

The Lady Pinkerton Gets Her Man

"Wha-what?" the older woman sputtered, and then screwed her face into an expression of surprise. "Why would I want to do that?" she asked. "The shelter's better here." Without waiting for Dayle to offer any kind of answer, she immediately went on to object. "Some of these men can't be moved. They're hurt too badly."

"Leave the ones you can't move," Dayle told her. "I imagine Lotta and her children's nursemaid can look after them. I have someone who's going to get those boxcars out of White Springs and as far as the next stop, but we've all got to move quickly. When things start to happen . . ."

The woman's expression slipped from surprise to doubt. "Get the cars to the next stop? How are you going to do that?"

"It's a little difficult to explain completely," Dayle said. "You'd have to examine the railyard and see how it's laid out to understand, and time is important. Can you trust me and get the wounded on board?"

"What about the men Garrick Bateman left guarding the westbound train? What are you going to do about them?"

That was one of the real beauties of Dayle's plan. The Pinkertons and most of Garrick's men were guarding the mines, not the railroad. That meant there was almost no one to stop what she was about to do.

"Just move them quickly and quietly. Even if the men notice, I don't think they'll care. If one of them asks, tell him you need more room in the station or that you're moving the wounded to where you think they'll be safer. I know you can be convincing when you want to be."

That compliment was enough to squeeze half a smile from the older woman and a quick agreement. "Oh, yes, yes, I can be most convincing. I've heard that said before." Then she looked Dayle over with an expression that wavered between curious and skeptical, and for a moment, Dayle had the distinct impression that the older woman wasn't sure she believed Dayle. The idea that anyone could get the Chinese, wounded and all, out of White Springs did seem far-fetched. Who else would dare anger both Garrick Bateman and Allan Pinkerton? She'd be lucky to take in laundry after this. At the same time, Dayle wondered what she'd do if Miss Davies refused to help. Leave the wounded?

Then the older woman made up her mind. "We'll have to leave a few," she said, looking around the room. "It's going to be crowded on those boxcars." Mary Stillman Davies's voice had assumed its usual no-nonsense tone. "We'll leave the Batemans' nursemaid to care for the worst of them, because we have to take Lotta and her children with us."

It was Dayle's turn to sputter. "Take-take Lotta with us? Why?"

"Why?" the older woman echoed. "Were you planning to run off with half of Garrick Bateman's miners and then leave her to face him alone?"

"He'll come after her," Dayle countered.

"He's going to come after all of us."

"It'll only make things worse," Dayle returned. "If she goes with us, he'll blame her. He'll think that somehow she's at fault, that maybe it was all her idea or something."

"Which is exactly the reason we can't leave her," Miss Davies said. "You saw him. He's the kind of man who thinks everything is his wife's fault and makes her pay for it."

Dayle had no answer for that, because she knew it was true. Still, she didn't need this complication. She was trying to save hundreds of Chinese, and the last thing she wanted was to get tangled up in Lotta's domestic situation, too. While it was probably true that Garrick Bateman would come after them anyway, having his wife and children along only meant that he'd come after them with a vengeance.

The Lady Pinkerton Gets Her Man

Then Dayle shook her head. On second thought, she didn't know what difference it would make. Garrick Bateman was going to want to kill them all anyway. She heard herself agreeing, "All right. All right. Bring her."

Dayle found Ah So out by the boxcars. He was practically holding court. Someone had found him a wooden folding chair and an empty crate where he could rest his feet. He was sitting at the side of the tracks, wrapped in his smelly, half-burnt coat, his feet up, his head held high. Several Tong thugs were in attendance. They demanded order and a proper amount of respect from the line of petitioners waiting to have a few words with the Tong leader.

Dayle was taken aback by the scene enough that she paused a moment and watched. As near as she could tell, Ah So was assigning places on the boxcars. She hadn't known those empty freight cars were his to allocate, but then she didn't understand a lot about how the Chinese did things.

As she came forward, the others stepped aside. Facing Ah So and fortunately standing upwind of his coat, she began to explain. She knew the exact moment when Ah So caught on to the main points of her plan. His feet came off the crate, and his eyes widened.

A moment later, he was standing. Waving his attendants out of his way, he went to the nearest boxcar, ducked low, and looked under it, sighting along the tracks. That didn't seem to satisfy. He shook his head and trotted down the line of boxcars until he got to the end one. Dayle and several others followed close behind. Crossing the tracks, Ah So looked from the signal tower to the desert beyond. He still didn't seem to be satisfied. He shook his head more. "Hill not very high," he answered. "Maybe cars not roll so good."

From the Pinkerton second-story window, the first

thing Dayle had noticed was how the boxcars were sitting near the top of a gently rolling hill. Someone had built an extra-strong bumper at the end of that siding or "house track" for exactly that reason. More than the bumper, she saw that if the switch were thrown and the brakes released, it wouldn't take much to start those boxcars rolling away from that bumper and the station. At some point, they would pick up enough momentum that they'd roll right out of town, five hundred tons or more, picking up speed as they went. She thought it likely that the runaway cars would get three, four, maybe five miles out onto the alkali flats before they slowed again.

Her first thought was simply to roll the boxcars away from the station. She doubted any mob, no matter how bent on mischief, would brave the wind to march clear out onto the plateau in order to set the cars afire. With her next thought, she knew that was false hope and knew why that idea wasn't good. The wind blew in that same direction. All the mob would have to do was set the prairie afire, and the wind would carry the flames to the boxcars. The worst of it was that even without fire, the cold wind would get the Chinese. By morning, she expected many would be dead of exposure. Some were likely to die in those boxcars even if they remained in the shelter of the train station. It got that cold in White Springs when the sun went down. That's when she saw the water train chug into the station, and she thought getting the boxcars five miles down the tracks was only a beginning.

Ah So was still shaking his head and repeating, "This not very big hill." Obviously, he hadn't seen what she'd seen. She pointed to the top of the closest boxcar. "Look from up there," she told him. "You'll see."

He hesitated while he looked all around at the crowd that had gathered. To her dismay, Dayle realized the Tong leader didn't like taking orders from a

The Lady Pinkerton Gets Her Man

woman, a white woman. Especially while there were others watching. She saw him scan the crowd. Then, as if to put her in her place, he stripped off his half-burnt fur coat and handed it to her, obviously expecting her to hold the stinking thing while he mounted the railroad car.

She took it and stood holding the coat at arm's length from her own clothes while he climbed. With his arms free, he went up the side of the boxcar, quickly. Pulling himself onto the roof, he scanned the horizon, walked to the other end of the car, looked some more. She knew he'd decided in favor of the adventure when he paused and turned the brake wheel, loosening the brake on that car, before he climbed back down and took his coat.

"First we shoot guards," Ah So said flatly.

Dayle was so taken aback, she didn't know what to say. "Shoot the guards?" Same as the argument she'd used with Mary Stillman Davies, she didn't think the men Garrick Bateman had left behind would be any problem. Any activity around the boxcars wasn't likely to be noticed, or if it was, she thought it likely the men would dismiss it as the Chinese doing whatever the Chinese did.

One of the things she knew the Chinese did was set derailed cars back on the tracks. She'd watched a Chinese road gang do that once with nothing more than muscle and two long steel poles. She imagined that starting the cars moving ought to be easier. She didn't know why it couldn't be done without drawing attention.

"You can't shoot the guards," she told him.

"Must shoot guards," Ah So said. "Best way. Then no cause trouble."

Dayle couldn't help herself. She counted the guards. Five. She knew that more than five men had already died that day, and more, lots more, would die if they didn't get the Chinese out of White Springs, but she'd never considered the possibility that her plan would require shooting somebody. She didn't understand it. Everything had seemed so clear and so easy from the Pinkerton window—start the boxcars rolling, grab the engine off the water train, go.

With her next thought, she knew exactly why killing the guards was a terrible idea, and Ah So knew it, too. In fact, he and his armed men could have overwhelmed those five guards anytime they wanted. They could have commandeered the westbound train and headed for San Francisco long before now. There was nothing stopping them but good sense.

If word got passed down the line that the Chinese of White Springs had turned on the mine guards and shot them, they'd be met at the next station with a lynch mob worse than the one torching the Chinatown here. He'd already figured that out. He was testing her.

"No," she told him. "You can't shoot the guards. That would make this war, and I'm not going to let you turn this into war."

Ah So tilted his head as if to study her mettle.

Dayle set her jaw. At the same time, out of the corner of her eye, she saw the first of the wounded being helped across the train station platform on their way to the boxcars. *Trust Mary Stillman Davies to get things going,* Dayle thought. At the same time she never flinched under Ah So's gaze.

"No," she repeated. "You can't kill the guards. It will only make things worse, and you know that."

The Tong leader squared his shoulders inside his stinking coat, and, for a moment, they were engaged eyeball-to-eyeball until he turned and mumbled something about being a warlord, not a fox fairy.

"I make war," he told her, "not mischief."

Dayle didn't understand fox fairies or the male need to demonstrate a certain amount of bravado. He never meant to harm those guards, but somehow he felt he had to pretend otherwise. She didn't care as long as they got on with this. And they did get on with it.

What followed next was a flurry of activity. The boxcars had been anchored by hand brakes, a brake per car. A couple of Ah So's men climbed atop the cars. Then, jumping from car to car, they released the brakes, except for one. The brakes on one boxcar wouldn't let go. Stuck, maybe rusted, the clamps wouldn't come off the wheels.

Someone found some grease. That didn't help. The car with the stuck brakes was three from the end. Ah So suggested unhooking it. They would leave the last three cars behind.

Dayle didn't like that idea. The problem was the guards again. She didn't expect them to notice right away if the whole string of cars started to move slowly, inch by inch at first, but if part of them began to move away from the other part of them—that would be hard not to see. She tried to think where they could find a mechanic or a blacksmith. Perhaps in the roundhouse, but how would they explain the need for his services?

Ah So, having the same idea, sent his men car to car looking for a particular Chinaman. When they found him, he examined the mechanism from up top, shook his head, climbed down. He searched the ground around the tracks until he found a certain size rock. He slid under the car, wrapped his shirt around the rock to muffle the noise, and pounded on the brakes where they'd clamped the wheels. At the same time, the men above tried again to turn the brake wheel. When the brake broke loose, it released with enough force that one of the men lost his footing. He dangled for a moment from the brake wheel before his companion pulled him back onto the roof.

Meanwhile, Mary Stlllman Davies and the Chinese girls were helping more of the wounded onto the cars, and others of Ah So's men had found some old sections of rail that they intended to use as levers to help them get the cars rolling. When the problem with the stuck brake was solved, everything else was in position.

While Ah So and his men started the boxcars moving, Dayle walked down the tracks until she was in view of the switching tower. That was her signal to Tommy. Suddenly, the tracks switched under her feet. She was expecting it, and yet it still gave her the same kind of start as discovering a snake in the grass. That start was followed by a wave of relief. Obviously, Tommy the Tube Man had gotten himself into position.

She looked back at the boxcars that hadn't started to move yet, at least not perceptibly. She chanced a glance in the direction of the five guards. A couple were smoking as they lounged near the big engine hooked to the front of the westbound. The others seemed equally relaxed. Some had their backs to the siding and its string of boxcars. Next, she checked the water train and its engine now sitting in the station—four driving wheels in back, four smaller ones in front, a cowcatcher, a smoke stack, a large box headlight nested into its base, and brass trim all around.

It was late afternoon, the light was low. The sky was overcast, partly from the smoke in the air and more from a coming storm. There was a chill but no smell of moisture. She doubted the clouds obscuring the sky would yield more than a swirl of dry snowflakes. She was glad. She'd thought earlier that a big storm was on its way. More important, this was the moment when she knew her plan was going to work.

The devil's in the details, she remembered the sisters at the orphanage repeating. She wasn't done with this yet, but it was as if she felt events switch in her direction at the same time as the rail moved. Holding on to that sense of suspension, she made a

The Lady Pinkerton Gets Her Man

complete turn, slowly taking in everything, until she realized the boxcars were moving, really moving. Obviously, getting them started had been easier than anyone expected.

She gave another quick glance at the guards. They still hadn't noticed. Glancing all around, she realized that no one had, but they would soon. Too soon, if she didn't get going. She picked up her skirts and hurried down the tracks to the back of the roundhouse, where she found Bald-head Ted waiting for her. He'd brought a friend. The two of them had already seen the boxcars begin to move.

"This here's Daniel Suitter. He'll be my fireman," Ted told her without taking his eyes off the boxcars.

Dayle couldn't take her eyes off Daniel Suitter's wooden leg. She didn't know how he was going to shovel coal with a wooden leg.

As if reading Dayle's mind, Ted said, "Daniel's a hard worker. Used to be a miner until he lost that leg. Now he raises canaries and has his mind set on mischief, which is to say he doesn't much like things the way they are. He'll be a good fireman."

Dayle decided this was not the time to argue. The boxcars were picking up speed.

Ted whistled softly. "That's going to make some commotion," he added. "Some real excitement. Any moment now. Any moment now."

That's when Daniel Suitter seemed to size up the situation for the first time. "If them cars are already moving down the track, how we going to get the engine 'round in front to pull them?"

"We going to push them," Ted told him, never taking his eyes off the boxcars.

In fact, Dayle noticed the muscles in his neck and arms tense and relax, tense and relax, almost as if he were pushing the cars himself. At the same time, she couldn't help noticing that his friend didn't like what he was seeing. He was digging his wooden leg into the dirt.

"The devil does things backwards," he said.

"What you mumbling about?" Ted now asked.

The older, one-legged man shook his head. "Nothing. Only how we going to watch for something on the tracks? That there cowcatcher ain't no good in the rear."

"We going to pray and never slow down," Ted told him. "We're going to go so fast our own whistle ain't going to catch up with us."

"That's dangerous."

"That's how legends are made."

"I'm not going on no dangerous ride," Daniel now complained. "Some engine jumps the track, and it's always the fireman who gets scalded—scalded to death."

"That's only if you got some bad engineer. I'm the engineer on this run."

Daniel shook his head. "I don't know," he began to whine. "I don't know."

Dayle tensed. She wished Bald-head Ted would try to be a little more persuasive with his friend. The boxcars were really beginning to move, and they weren't going to manage without a fireman.

Then it happened, the boxcars broke loose—a wild runaway. Seeing that, Dayle felt such a surge of excitement, she looked at Ted, who looked at his friend Daniel.

"You going to make me miss my chance?" he asked.

His friend worked his mouth and then said, "I just wish we didn't have to run it backwards. I like to see where I'm going, especially if I'm going to hell."

"It's the good Lord who don't want us to see where we're a-going. We all driving our trains by faith, blind faith."

Daniel seemed to consider that a moment. Then he gave his wooden leg a hitch and nodded his assent.

Meanwhile, all hell had broken loose.

Someone in the roundhouse had blown the alarm, a series of short, sharp notes meant to wake the whole

The Lady Pinkerton Gets Her Man

town. The guards had grabbed their guns. That amused Dayle. No one was going to stop a runaway freight train with a rifle. In fact, no one seemed to know what to do. Those who had come running in answer to the alarm whistle were now mostly standing around watching the boxcars pick up speed as they raced away. Some of the Chinamen began to wave from the open doors. They sent up a shout. Hanging off the last car were six Chinamen, the last of the men who had been pushing the cars before they took off on their own.

In that confusion, the water train's regular fireman and engineer swung down from the cab to see what was going on. Dayle and her new train crew were waiting. They came up from behind. In no time, they had them tied, hand and foot, and gagged. They left them kicking by the side of the tracks.

The little engine had already been unhooked from the tank cars and turned. It was ready for the return run. Dayle, Bald-head Ted, and his friend climbed aboard. It was surprisingly small. The cab roof was low enough that Ted had to lower his head or stick it out the window, and Dayle had trouble keeping out of the way as the men got down to work.

They worked; she worried. She shifted her weight from one foot to the next and tried to keep from saying anything, but she couldn't keep quiet when Ted asked Daniel to check the water for a third time.

"We need to go," she said.

Ted gave her a quick glance and muttered, "When you work with a steam locomotive, especially an old one, you tend to worry a lot about leaks."

Then it happened. Her worst fear. Someone from the roundhouse noticed something amiss. "Hey, what's going on there?" he shouted.

Dayle felt for her gun. It was small and no good except at close range, but she knew Ted wasn't armed at all, and she doubted Daniel had a weapon. However, she underestimated Ted's charm.

Jerrie Hurd

With a winning grin and a cocksure wave, Bald-head Ted yelled back, "Somebody's got to go after those runaways."

Then, before the other man could think about that, Bald-head Ted swept open the throttle with his right hand. With his left, he eased the air brake. Daniel bent to his work. Ted blew the whistle, two long, ear-splitting wails, the "leaving town" signal. If the man from the roundhouse had any further questions, his voice was drowned out by that whistle and the start of the engine.

Then, just as the train began to pick up speed, Tommy the Tube Man grabbed hold and swung himself up. With another hop, he boosted himself to the edge of the tender and took a seat there, shaking his head and complaining nonstop. "I got to get a regular job. My knees, it's my knees," he went on. "I can't do this circus sideshow stuff anymore. It's killing my knees."

Dayle was glad to see him. She gave him a thumbs-up sign and let him keep mumbling. On the other side of her, Bald-head Ted had begun to hum as he and Daniel settled in like a regular crew—Bald-head Ted on the right, Daniel working from his left.

Dayle had to admit Daniel seemed to be doing fine, wooden leg and all. "I raise canaries," he told her when she asked where he'd learned to shovel coal. That made no sense, but she didn't question him further.

Instead, she leaned out the back of the cab, letting the cold wind whip at her face as they picked up speed. It was bracing enough to make her cheeks tingle with the bite of the cold. She didn't care. She liked the way the air felt as though it had substance. She felt she could almost grab hold and hang on to that breeze. It was full of sound and smell and cold. It passed by her with that much body.

A mile out of town, Bald-head Ted pulled the whistle and let out a yell. "Hoo-oo-rey!" he ex-

The Lady Pinkerton Gets Her Man

claimed. "We high-stepping tonight!" he called out even louder than the train whistle's wail.

Dayle knew how he felt. She wasn't sure how to explain it, but she imagined that on her deathbed, when she thought about being alive, it would be this moment she would remember.

25

When Allan Pinkerton heard the alarm, he hurried out of the Pinkerton building as fast as he could. He half expected to see the train station in flames. His heart was pounding, partly because of the exertion and partly because he was worried that Miss Dobson might be right after all. When she'd warned him about the whole town possibly burning down, he'd thought she was overwrought from having been caught in the middle of the riot when it started. Now he was sweating, imagining the worst.

He'd lived through one town-destroying fire. He'd watched the wind whip the flames, watched them leap from building to building, sometimes moving faster than people and horses, and that wasn't the worst of it. He'd felt helpless. He hated feeling helpless. He prided himself on the belief that he could turn any situation to his advantage. However, he was getting older. Being older hadn't slowed him mentally, but physically, moving around had become more difficult

363

The Lady Pinkerton Gets Her Man

since his stroke. He was pretty sure he couldn't outrun a fire, not this time.

When he got outside, he didn't see any flames, but there was lots of smoke. The problem was, he couldn't tell where the smoke was coming from. He grabbed a young boy coming down the street and offered him a dollar if he'd run ahead and see what the trouble was.

"Quickly," he emphasized.

The kid hesitated and looked at him oddly. He didn't understand that. It was unlikely that the boy's father made more than twenty dollars a week. He was offering him a whole dollar for five minutes' work. Finally, the kid shrugged, grabbed the dollar, and ran. He called over his shoulder, "Everybody knows already. It's them Chiney bastards. They're riding a runaway train."

Allan Pinkerton didn't know if he believed the kid. He wanted to know how the boy had heard that and how something like that could be possible. But the kid was gone.

Allan Pinkerton picked up his pace until he was puffing and his right leg began to pain him. By the time he got to the station, he'd stopped enough different people and gotten enough details that he was no longer surprised by this turn of events. When he finally got to the station platform, he pulled out his folding spyglass and put it to his left eye. Sure enough, he saw the little engine running backward down the tracks, its smoke curled over it like a squirrel's tail. Ahead of the engine, the boxcars were traveling even faster. Even at this distance, he marveled at how they swayed on the tracks. He figured the Chinamen were getting some wild ride.

That's when Garrick Bateman arrived. He rode his horse right up onto the platform. He climbed down, took the spyglass from Allan Pinkerton, and had his own look. He swore loudly and asked, "How did this happen?" He looked around for someone who could

Jerrie Hurd

answer that question. When no one did, he asked another. "Who's driving that engine?"

"A Negro fireman," one of the men he'd left to guard the westbound offered.

"A Negro fireman—no engineer?"

"There wasn't time," the same man ventured to explain. "Somebody needed to go after those cars and quickly. I mean, them Chinamen must be scared out of their wits."

Allan Pinkerton was already suspecting worse. As soon as Garrick Bateman had grabbed the spyglass, he'd looked around the station, and he didn't like what he was seeing or, more accurately, what he was not seeing. Things were too quiet.

While the men Garrick Bateman had left to guard the westbound tried to tell him that all the excitement was no more than an accident, soon fixed, he hobbled to the door of the station and looked inside. It was as he expected. The waiting room was nearly empty. There was only one large woman with fewer than a dozen wounded. That didn't fit with the reports he'd been getting that Mary Stillman Davies was running a field hospital out of that waiting area. Further, he didn't like the idea that he didn't see Miss Davies. He'd learned long ago that it was a good idea to keep track of that woman's whereabouts.

When he returned, the guards were still trying to tell Garrick Bateman that everything would be fine when the water train engine and its fireman engineer caught up with those runaway cars. Allan Pinkerton didn't believe it. There was more going on. The evidence was all around if Garrick Bateman would stop looking through the spyglass and focus on more immediate matters.

"There are no Chinese anyplace," Allan Pinkerton commented.

"No Chinese?"

"That's right. Yes, sir," one guard was now offering. "They all got on the boxcars."

365

The Lady Pinkerton Gets Her Man

"Why?" Bateman asked.

"Why, sir?" The guard looked at Allan Pinkerton oddly. "That's where they were told to go. We don't let Chinese wait at the station."

Allan Pinkerton couldn't contain himself any longer. "You're saying that every single Chinaman who could walk, hop, or crawl is on that runaway?"

The guard puzzled the question, but Allan Pinkerton couldn't help noticing how Garrick Bateman's expression changed as some understanding began to dawn on him.

Then, before the guards could make any more lame excuses, the regular crew of the water train came running up. With them were the railroad men from the roundhouse who'd found them and untied them. Together they told quite a different story. This time, it was Pinkerton's turn to be surprised.

"A woman?" he asked, and made them describe her again. He wouldn't have been surprised except that the description fit Miss Dobson, not Miss Davies. He could believe Miss Davies would do something unexpectedly desperate. He'd given Miss Dobson credit for more sense.

Garrick Bateman, now recognizing the same description, turned on Allan Pinkerton. "Why would Miss Dobson think she needed to concern herself with this unfortunate accident?"

Allan Pinkerton never ceased to be amazed at the larger man's stupidity. He'd already figured out that the runaway cars were no accident. In fact, he thought he had the whole scheme figured out. Now he was wondering what he was going to do—how he was going to turn this to his benefit.

Meanwhile, Garrick Bateman was questioning everyone within earshot, trying to understand what was "really going on."

Allan Pinkerton took his spyglass back and watched the action on the desert. At the same time, one of the roundhouse men was describing the Negro fireman as

366

someone "nobody bets against." Allan Pinkerton was beginning to think the same of Miss Dobson.

"Unhook the engine from the westbound. We're going after them," Bateman ordered.

"Can't," someone else said.

"Who are you?" Bateman demanded.

"The switchman," he answered. "Only I don't have any switches anymore."

"What?"

"Somebody threw them and then filed them so they can't be thrown back."

"That's impossible. You'd have to practically crawl inside the mechanism to do something like that."

The switchman shrugged.

Bateman sputtered and shouted, "Get someone out on the tracks and move those switches manually, then."

"Won't do any good," another of his men offered. "By the time we get that done, we're not going to have any water on the westbound. Someone quietly turned a couple of screws into the bottom of the water tank and then pulled them out again, leaving two holes the size of fingers. That engine's not going anyplace but into the roundhouse for repairs."

"What else have we got? There has to be something!" Bateman shouted.

"There's a couple of handcars."

By that time, Allan Pinkerton was enjoying himself. He tried to imagine Garrick Bateman working a handcar, pumping it up and down as he rode off after his Chinese miners.

"Our Miss Dobson seems to have thought of everything," Allan Pinkerton told him.

Garrick Bateman wasn't amused. In fact, he turned and grabbed Allan Pinkerton by his lapels. He practically lifted the little man off the ground as he breathed through his teeth. "I hate Lady Pinkertons."

"So does my son William. If it's any comfort, I'm

The Lady Pinkerton Gets Her Man

sure there won't be any Lady Pinkertons once he takes over."

That wasn't exactly the answer Bateman expected. He gave Allan Pinkerton an odd look as he let go of him and said, "I'm not beat yet. I'll wire ahead and have someone blow up the tracks."

Allan Pinkerton already knew that Garrick Bateman was finished. Blowing up the tracks only suggested that the man had even lost his good sense.

"You don't want to do that," Pinkerton now told him. He knew Mary Stillman Davies and how she worked. "Your wife and children are on that train. If you don't believe me, ask your nursemaid. She's inside."

Garrick Bateman looked over the top of Allan Pinkerton toward the station. "That can't be true."

Yet Allan Pinkerton could tell by the tone of his voice that even he suspected it was the truth.

"I'm afraid so," Pinkerton said.

Then the larger man turned on him again. "How could you let this happen? You're paid well to keep these mines open. How did you let this happen?"

By that time, a couple of Pinkerton agents had arrived. They now grabbed Bateman and shoved him off their boss.

Allan Pinkerton straightened his jacket. "When you start playing games with mines and railroads and hundreds of lives, the outcome is never exactly certain—never entirely predictable. The trick is to turn what happens to your advantage. I'm not licked yet. Believe me, this isn't over."

Pinkerton could tell by Bateman's expression that he had no idea what to make of that answer. All he had in him was bluster. "She can't get away with this," Bateman declared. "She can't get away with this."

Allan Pinkerton wasn't sure whom he meant— Miss Dobson, Miss Davies, or his wife. It didn't matter. "No one gets away with anything, ultimately. It's one of the things you can count on as a detective," he told Bateman. "However, in this case, everything has changed, and the only choice we have is to play by Miss Dobson's rules."

At heart, he actually found that prospect amusing. He enjoyed interesting, challenging women. *Not since Kate,* he thought. He only wished he were young enough to enjoy Miss Dobson fully.

Out on the prairie, Dayle and her train crew passed a pile of something lying beside the tracks. It looked like a metal jumble of some sort.

"What's that?" Tommy the Tube Man asked, and pointed, but not in time for anyone else to see. "There's another," he called out, but they were still moving fast enough that it was hard to distinguish what had caught his attention. Then there was a third and a fourth sighting.

"Tools," Daniel said.

"Mining tools, too heavy to carry," Bald-head Ted added.

He'd no sooner said that than they rode the engine over the next little rise and encountered the first group of Chinese miners, twelve or fifteen in number, marching along beside the tracks. Bare-chested, they were wearing only pants, shoes, and their mine hats with the candles attached.

"Where did those poor bastards come from?" Tommy asked. Then, when Ted threw him a look, he suddenly muttered an apology to Dayle for his language.

No apology needed. She was wondering the same thing.

"They were working the shift," Daniel now offered.

That made sense. Most men worked underground without shirts, Dayle knew. Until now, she'd thought only of Chinatown and what had happened there. She

The Lady Pinkerton Gets Her Man

hadn't thought about the men who were down in the mines when the trouble started. Obviously, the riot had spread quickly, forcing these men up and out onto the prairie without even giving them a chance to stop where they piled their shirts and kept their lunch buckets. No food, no water, no shirts, and too far to walk. She wondered if they knew how hopeless their situation was.

And these were the lucky ones. They'd at least found the railroad tracks. Probably they hoped they could flag down a train or grab on to a freighter as it came along. She looked down the line. Similar groups dotted the distance for as far as she could see, maybe seventy to a hundred individuals altogether, and she couldn't help wondering how many more were lost in the rolling hills, wandering without direction. With the sky overcast and the light dimming to evening, there was no way to know east from west or any other direction. Other than the train tracks and the telegraph wire running alongside, there were no landmarks.

Obviously entertaining similar thoughts, Daniel muttered, "I hear there's wolves out there."

"There's no water out there," Tommy the Tube Man said. "That is for certain."

As soon as the half-naked miners saw the engine, they stopped. They shouted and waved. They'd no doubt already watched the boxcars roll by and knew that something was happening.

"We have to stop," Dayle said, grabbing Bald-head Ted's elbow. "We can't leave them here."

Ted shook his head. "Where they going to ride?"

"How far ahead do you think the boxcars have gotten?"

"There's a little hill not three miles away. Them runaway cars ain't going to make it past that rise."

"Slow down enough to let me jump off," Dayle said.

"You sure?" he asked.

Jerrie Hurd

"I'll gather them up and march them as far as the boxcars."

"I don't know," Ted complained. "I don't like leaving you all by yourself."

"I'd do it," Tommy said, "but my knees aren't going to make a three-mile hike."

Ted half covered his ears, annoyed at Tommy's voice. "He always talk like that?"

"I'm afraid so."

Ted shook his head more, but he applied the air brake.

Dayle tied up her skirts and hung out the side of the cab, waiting for the train to slow enough. That's when she knew she'd spoken too soon. Although the engine was not far from the ground, the motion gave a sense of height. For one anxious moment, she was afraid she wasn't going to be able to do this.

"Now!" Ted called. "I don't want to lose more speed than this."

She hated heights, and this was worse. She couldn't get a fix on anything solid because nothing was solid. It was all moving.

"Now!" Ted called again.

She hung one more moment, and then she did the only thing she could do. She twisted around and threw herself off backward, tucking her arms as she fell. The falling was mercifully short. The landing was unmercifully hard, not at all softened by the fact that she landed squarely on her fanny. She sat there stunned for a moment before she gathered enough wit to wave, letting the others know she was fine or would be.

A couple of minutes later, she rolled onto her knees and stood. There was a certain stiffness. She sensed that she was going to ache in some unmentionable places, but after a few steps, she was fine. She couldn't say the same for her skirt. The bottom ruffle was torn loose. She had the choice of tearing it off or tripping on it. She ripped it off.

The Lady Pinkerton Gets Her Man

Looking up, she saw several of the Chinese miners trotting down the tracks, catching up to her. When the first arrived, he bowed.

She returned the gesture.

He bowed again.

She returned the gesture and pointed, indicating the direction they needed to continue.

By that time, most of the others had caught up with her. They were also bowing and nodding. To a man, they all had their arms folded across their chests, their hands tucked in their armpits as if holding their own warmth. She didn't blame them. Now that she was no longer next to the engine's firebox, she realized how fast the temperature was dropping. Soon it would be dark. They were going to have to keep moving, and that meant more than this bowing exercise. With the full extension of her arm, she again pointed the direction. Then she started marching that way. The others quickly fell in behind.

As luck would have it, the march turned out to be longer and colder than Dayle had anticipated. She gathered more and more men as she went, including three she found already sitting on the ground, so shaken with shivers that at first they refused to walk farther. Some of the others helped them up and forced them to move.

Someone started a song. The Chinese words meant nothing to her, but the rhythm helped the walk.

When it got dark, the miners lit the candles on their hats. But because of the wind, the men had to shelter their little lights next to their bare chests. Sometimes when she looked back, she had the eerie sensation that she was being followed by a line of floating illuminated faces.

As they got closer, the engine's headlight spread illumination across the desert and down the tracks, creating two shimmering ribbons, beckoning them the last few steps. At that point, most of the Chinese ran ahead, and there followed an explosion of chatter as

Jerrie Hurd

they greeted the others who were already on the boxcars.

She was too tired to run. In fact, she was so tired that she had resorted to counting her steps. Ten more, then ten more after that.

As she trudged the last little way, she watched Ted and Daniel and Mary Stillman Davies move in and out of the light. They were directing the miners she'd gathered onto various cars. She was still counting her steps and watching that activity when she first noticed another figure, who, like Ted and Daniel and Miss Davies, was busy getting everyone on board.

At first, there was no recognition, just a general sense of someone else, someone she knew she ought to be able to name. Then she stopped, and for a moment she thought the light was playing tricks on her or that she was more exhausted than she wanted to admit. She stood there at the edge of the light, unable to move, while she studied the figure with the bandage around his head. She wouldn't let herself believe. She looked for something unfamiliar in the too familiar movements.

Turning, he saw her and came forward into the bright light. There was no mistake. He paused. Obviously reading her expression, he flashed his wide smile and said, "Yeah, I know what you mean. For a while, even I thought I was dead."

26

At first, there was no time for lengthy explanations. They needed to get the last of the Chinese on board and get on their way. That was fine. From the time she'd left that upstairs window knowing what she needed to do, she'd worked her way through this, one step at a time, continually amazed at the twists and turns. Finding Harry alive was only the most amazing one.

Still, she couldn't help herself. More than once, she reached out to touch him—brush his elbow or rest her hands lightly on his shoulder. She had to assure herself that there was a solid reality to this last, most fantastical of the twists.

So much had happened since she'd left Harry in Ah So's boudoir and slipped out into the dawn to help Lotta that she was having trouble remembering, much less comprehending it all. Now that Harry seemed to have things under control, it was easy to let herself slip into a daze of exhaustion. She'd gotten them this far. Now she was only too happy to let someone else worry about the final details.

Only once did she focus clearly enough to interrupt with a question. She wanted to know what they'd do if they found more miners farther on. That had suddenly seemed important because it was dark now, and she didn't think they'd be able to see the miners in the dark.

Harry assured her that they'd gathered all the miners who'd made it as far as the tracks. He'd already sent men ahead scouting for others. He'd done that while he was waiting for her to arrive with her group. His men had found a few more, not many. This seemed to be about as far from White Springs as anyone had gotten on his own.

There were, no doubt, others lost on the prairie, beyond help. Harry assured her that he didn't think there were many. He explained that they needed to take care of the men they had—get them off this windblown plateau before they all froze. She didn't argue.

Then all the bustle of the loading, all the shouting and sliding of boxcar doors stopped, because it was finished. It was time to roll. Ted and his friend climbed aboard the cab of the engine. Dayle and Harry and the others got into the first boxcar. All except Tommy the Tube Man, that is. He balked. First, he wanted to ride on top. Harry wouldn't hear of it. It was too cold. Then Tommy whined that he was sure Ted and Daniel needed help in the cab.

"The workers of the world need to stand elbow-to-elbow with one another," he told Harry.

When Harry wouldn't go for that idea, the truth came out. Tommy was particular about the tight spaces he was willing to occupy. He didn't mind pouring himself through a stovepipe or worming his way into the inner workings of complicated machinery, but he couldn't tolerate the idea of sitting inside that crowded boxcar full of people.

The Lady Pinkerton Gets Her Man

Harry shoved a railroad lantern into Tommy's hands. Then he told him he could have the corner, where he could touch the sides of the train car whenever he got feeling crowded. Surprisingly, that satisfied. Tommy got on the train.

Dayle joined Mary Stillman Davies and Lotta and her two sons near the same corner. They were huddled around another railroad lantern, which they had to steady as the train started to move. Soon they were clicking along at a respectable pace.

The car was crowded, as were all the cars. Except for a few wounded who couldn't sit up, most of the Chinese squatted shoulder-to-shoulder, their knees under their chins. Some rested their heads on their knees, trying to sleep, but the ride was too rough for more than light sleep. Every time the car swayed, it was impossible not to knock into the next person.

Nor was it quiet. The rails outside clicked past. Inside, the humanity sighed and talked in two languages.

When everything was settled, Harry, Ah So, and a couple of Ah So's Tong guards joined them. Mary Stillman Davies couldn't stand the smell of his burnt coat any longer. She complained. Ah So took it off, folded the fur to the inside, and sat on it. Then Harry invited two Chinese brothers to join them. They were the laundrymen who'd saved him. With Mary Stillman Davies translating, they helped him tell his story.

The stray bullet that Ah So thought had killed Harry had actually only grazed his head. Wounds on the scalp often bleed profusely, and this one was no exception. It had produced enough blood to look more serious. It had also rendered Harry unconscious for a time. Harry was bleeding and limp when Ah So and his men pulled him out of the burning brothel and in the ensuing confusion left him on the stream bank, thinking there was nothing more they could do for him.

"The first I knew I'd been shot was when I woke up

inside a laundry basket, swaying back and forth as it was being carried along. I couldn't figure out whether I was dead or dreaming," Harry told the group. He touched his hand to his head and shook it carefully, expressing his confusion.

The laundry basket was one of the large wicker and wooden hampers that Chinese laundrymen carried suspended between two long poles that they rested on their shoulders as they made their rounds gathering huge piles of dirty sheets and shirts. These two were beginning their rounds that morning when the riot started. When they happened to find Harry on the stream bank and realized he wasn't dead, they used one of the shirts to bandage his head. They lifted him into the basket and carried him with them as they fled White Springs ahead of the mobs.

If worse came to worse, they expected to be able to barter a white man for their passage—especially a white man they recognized as having come to Chinatown to talk to the Tong leader. That had to mean he was an important person, even if he was trouble to carry.

When Harry first came to and tried to stand up, he nearly toppled the brothers, basket and all. They considered that part of the story funny. They got excited, and Harry got frustrated. He didn't understand where they were taking him. They couldn't understand what he was saying. Every time he tried to walk on his own, however, he got dizzy and would fall down. Finally, realizing he didn't have much choice, Harry let the Chinese brothers put him back in the basket and take him wherever they wanted.

The rest of the story was fairly simple. The brothers happened on a Chinese vegetable seller who still had his cart. Harry was moved onto the cart. Then the brothers and the vegetable merchant took turns pulling. They followed the tracks out of town. Maybe because they had the cart, they were among the Chinese who'd gotten the farthest when they looked

The Lady Pinkerton Gets Her Man

around and saw the runaway boxcars coming down the tracks and knew that something was going on.

The Chinese laundrymen brothers then launched into a long discussion of their theory of luck—their good fortune in finding Harry, their good fortune in meeting with the vegetable seller and his cart, their good fortune at being in the right place when the boxcars came rolling down the tracks. The fact that Mary Stillman Davies had to translate their words only served to slow what Dayle thought was an already tedious discussion. It was Dayle's observation that past luck had no charm. It was the hope of good fortune that focused interest.

She sensed that Harry felt the same. He was sitting next to her, close enough that she felt him twist and fidget as the talk got long. She found his impatience endearing. He was the luckiest of them all.

She leaned close and whispered, "Does it hurt much?"

"Remarkably little," he whispered back. "Once the initial dizziness passed, it hasn't bothered me much at all."

She wanted to believe that. She wanted his extraordinary luck to follow him everywhere and forever.

He wanted her to tell him about the train. "The Chinese laundrymen brothers are right," he whispered. "It isn't an ordinary thing to look up and see twenty-eight boxcars full of Chinese miners coming down the tracks."

Dayle was tired. How they got there didn't seem important, only that they were there—all of them. She shook her head and let Ah So and Mary Stillman Davies tell most of the story. Somehow, that only added to Harry's discomfort. As the two of them filled in more and more details, he became more and more agitated. She wondered if he was hurting and not admitting it. Finally, he couldn't seem to sit any longer. He started to stand, but the car was too crowded, the swaying too erratic. He was forced back down.

"Are you all right?" Dayle asked.

"No," he said. "No," he repeated with even more expression.

Ah So was in the middle of describing how it felt to ride the boxcars as they picked up speed. Now he stopped.

"No," Harry said again. Then his voice took on an accusing tone. "Don't any of you understand? Don't you realize what Allan Pinkerton is going to do to her?"

Vaguely, in the back of her exhaustion, Dayle knew what he meant, and it did strike her as an odd quirk of their luck that while he was now safe, she wasn't. She wondered what the Chinese laundrymen brothers might have to say about that. She wondered if this was what the Chinese called "meeting the fox fairy."

His words sobered everyone. Dayle suspected that they all knew and had always known the consequences. Lotta was the exception.

"What will Allan Pinkerton do?" she asked.

It took a moment for him to respond. When he spoke, the edge was gone from his voice. In its place was a tone of resignation. "The Pinkertons have a reputation to uphold," Harry told her. "It's said that they will chase a train robber to South America if they have to. They never give up. No one ever gets away with robbing a Pinkerton-guarded train."

"That's exaggerated," Mary Stillman Davies said. "I happen to know that neither Allan Pinkerton nor any of his agents has ever chased anyone farther than Mexico."

"But this is a special case," Harry returned. "This time, a Lady Pinkerton, one of their own, has stolen the whole damned train and half the miners needed to keep all the other trains in the country running. If that isn't something Allan Pinkerton is going to make an

The Lady Pinkerton Gets Her Man

example of, then this bullet must have knocked the sense out of me."

"You don't know that I'm a Lady Pinkerton," Dayle objected.

To that, Harry only grunted. He was having none of their previous games. "Allan Pinkerton doesn't have a choice," he went on. "Otherwise, the Pinkerton reputation becomes a laughingstock, a national joke."

No one answered that, and Dayle didn't try to say anything. She'd always known what was at stake. She'd always expected that after this adventure was over, there would be no place for her to go except to jail. She'd grown up in one institution. She thought she could handle living in another.

Of course, when she'd made that decision, she'd thought Harry was dead. She paused in the middle of that thought, because it occurred to her that it didn't matter. Whether Harry was dead or not, from the moment she knew there was a way to save the Chinese, she'd never had a choice. What kind of person would she be if she knew she could save hundreds of lives and then did nothing?

Last time she saw Allan Pinkerton, he'd asked her why she'd become a Lady Pinkerton. It was because she'd needed some way to describe herself.

Who are you?
A Lady Pinkerton.

That thought almost amused her now, because she knew something more important about herself. She knew that she had the guts to do whatever she had to do. She imagined there were people, important people with proud names and long genealogies, who couldn't say as much about themselves.

"Miss Dobson can come to China with me," Mary Stillman Davies offered.

Harry dismissed her with a grunt. "China, South America, there's no place he won't follow. Our only hope is that he's getting old. He can't be relentless forever."

"No," Ah So said. "You listen. She speak very true."

Harry turned his attention back to the missionary woman.

"Nobody has ever found a woman I've taken to China," Mary Stillman Davies now told him with a tone of pride. "Nobody," she repeated. "I'm taking Lotta there, and nobody will find her or her children. Believe me."

It took a moment for Dayle to figure out what the missionary woman was talking about, and then she knew. She knew it all—why Allan Pinkerton was obsessed with Mary Stillman Davies and her missionary work, why Lotta and her children were on this train . . .

Suddenly, she was glad she'd gone and gotten Lotta's children when Miss Davies insisted, even though it hadn't made much sense at the time. Lotta wouldn't have left without them. Now she was going to escape to a new life. She was going to be rescued, like the girls she'd rescued.

She couldn't help herself. She wanted to laugh. She'd thought the only person with a plight worse than hers was Lotta. Then the larger irony added to her amusement as she realized all those parlor stories about women disappearing into the Orient, never to be heard of again, were true. Only in a different sense.

She couldn't help being pleased for Lotta. Dayle had been genuinely worried that Mrs. Bateman might not get out of this alive.

At the same time, her admiration of Mary Stillman Davies soared. Harry was right. Stealing this train meant that Dayle had managed to embarrass Mr. Pinkerton beyond what he could tolerate. Mary Stillman Davies, however, had managed to make herself a continuous embarrassment. If what she was saying was true, she'd used her underground railroad to rescue more than Chinese girls. She rescued wives like Lotta, and Allan Pinkerton, America's most famous detective, hadn't been able to recover a single one of those errant wives. Dayle could only imagine the snide comments he'd had to endure in men's clubs from New York to San Francisco as a result.

"Not one?" Dayle now asked.

"Absolutely. You'll be safe," Mary Stillman Davies assured her.

Dayle shook her head. She didn't need assuring. She wasn't thinking about herself. She was still struggling to understand the scope of Miss Davies's accomplishment. She looked to where Lotta's children slept with their heads in her lap and wished them well. She was enormously pleased and relieved for them.

"I'll go with you," Harry now offered.

"What, and become a missionary?" Dayle asked. "If I remember right, Anarchists don't have any more use for religion than for government."

"Oh, but you never proved that I'm an Anarchist," he reminded her.

She returned a short laugh. "I didn't have to prove it," she told him. "I always knew it. You're the chief Anarchist—the Hooded Sleeper."

"Still, I'll go with you. We'll figure out something. At least we'll be together," he continued.

She shook her head. She appreciated the offer. She was happy for Lotta, but when she thought about going to China herself, an undeniable repulsion rose in her like bile coming up her throat.

Mary Stillman Davies was a remarkable woman. There was no escaping that fact. She was, no doubt, the exception among Christian crusaders. Unlike the hundreds, maybe thousands, of Temperance Union women from England to Australia, who had stood in front of saloons, pubs, and bars, speaking and singing and praying against the "evils of drink," which was really only a polite phrasing of the real problem— men who beat their wives—only Mary Stillman Davies had actually done something. She'd created an escape, a haven, and at the same time effectively thumbed her nose at Allan Pinkerton and the irate husbands he couldn't help. Dayle admired that, but she didn't want to do the same.

The idea ran counter to every bone, every sinew in her body. It made her blood recoil. She thought she'd rather die than become a missionary woman. However, she knew of no way to express that. She'd sound ungrateful, maybe even spiteful. After all, Miss Davies had just saved her from jail.

Suddenly, it didn't matter how crowded it was in that boxcar or how rough the ride, Dayle had to have some air. She stood and steadied herself as best she could.

"Are you all right?" Harry asked.

She lied. She told him she was fine. Then, with a calmness that surprised even her, she suggested that he and Ah So plan what they would do when they got the miners to Evanston or as close to Evanston as Bald-head Ted managed for them. Excusing herself, she stepped over and around the Chinese miners while she made her way to the door of the boxcar.

Once there, she cracked the door open enough that she could stand in it and watch the treeless, rolling hills slip by. She closed her eyes and leaned her head against the door frame, where she not only listened to the clack of the wheels, she felt the vibration. She hoped Bald-head Ted was enjoying his ride into story and song. This was a tale that needed to be told with exaggerated romance and a happy ending.

A few minutes later, she glanced back and saw that Harry was engaged in a close discussion with Ah So. That's what he did. He was an organizer—a man of words and ideas and big plans. He didn't belong in China any more than she did.

She also saw that Mary Stillman Davies had gotten up and was checking some of the wounded. She was having trouble keeping her balance in the rocking car, even using her cane. Nevertheless, she managed her rounds. A moment later, she joined Dayle in the open

The Lady Pinkerton Gets Her Man

door. She planted her cane in the door jamb and looked out over the same nighttime landscape.

"You'll like China," she said.

Dayle didn't think so, but she kept that thought to herself. The train was slowing. Obviously, they'd gotten as far as they were going to get.

Miss Davies spoke again. "China is a wonderful place. The scenery is like nothing you've ever seen. Day or night. Do you know that in some places, the hillsides are completely terraced? You look out a train like this and see stairs going up the sides of every mountain. There's also a kind of tree there that's like nothing else."

Dayle didn't say anything. She didn't know why she wanted to worry about exotic trees and hills covered in stairs. She'd never even seen the ocean. Yet another part of her knew Miss Davies was right. She ought to view this as an adventure, a chance to travel. Few people who grew up in an orphanage in Denver, Colorado, ever got to see China.

While the other woman talked on, Dayle wrestled with her real feelings about this woman, which she could no longer deny. She wondered less about the marvels of the Orient than about Miss Davies. She started to ask, "How many . . . ?" Then she stopped herself, because that wasn't the real question. There was something else she wanted to know but couldn't bring herself to ask.

Miss Davies anticipated the half-stated question. "I've lost count," she volunteered, and something in the tone of her voice suggested that she was pleased at Dayle's interest. "I used to keep a little book where I listed the names of the girls and women who'd been helped through the mission. Then, one day, I decided it was better to let the angels record."

That wasn't what Dayle wanted to hear. She had no patience for angels. She didn't believe in miracles. She'd given up waiting the day she threw away the only thing her mother had left with her, never mind that the sisters at the orphanage assured her that her "souvenir" from her real family indicated she was from fine folks.

Dayle swallowed. She'd known the truth from the first time she saw the brooch Miss Davies always wore.

"Why didn't you ever come back for me?" Dayle asked, finally getting the words out. "You rescued all those others. Why not me?"

Now Miss Davies had nothing to say.

Dayle continued. "I threw it away, but I had a bracelet once that matched the brooch you always wear."

Miss Davies's hand rose to the pin holding her collar together. Her hand covered the garlanded lion design.

"It's an uncommon pattern. I'm sure I've never seen the like anywhere else. Nor do I expect I ever will again."

"I wondered," Miss Davies said softly.

"You wondered?" Dayle asked.

"I wondered the first time I met you," Miss Davies replied. "Somehow, you remind me of my own mother—your grandmother. Remarkably so. I wondered again when you told me the name of the orphanage, and how you were left there."

"That's all? You wondered?"

Miss Davies took hold of the edge of the door. "That was all I could do, but I did it all the time," she replied. "There was never a day when I didn't wonder about you, wonder what you were doing, wonder if you were all right. Why do you think I took up this work? Every time I helped someone, I hoped that it would make up for what I did to you. I hoped that the angels were watching and would send someone to help you, because I couldn't."

"You couldn't?"

"You were the only thing that was keeping me alive. When my life was like Lotta's, there was no place to run, no place to hide. I knew your father would kill me unless he needed me alive for some reason. You were the reason. As long as he didn't know where you were, he needed to keep me breathing. He had me followed. For years, he had me followed, hoping I'd weaken and go for you, reveal where I'd left you. When he died, you were almost grown. By then, I figured it was too late. By then, I was sure you hated me."

Dayle didn't say anything.

"I guess I was right," Miss Davies added. "You do hate me."

Dayle wasn't sure. She believed that Miss Davies, or whatever her real name was, had done the only thing she could do, but that was what annoyed her about women who became Christian crusaders. They always settled for second best, make do. No matter how much good they did in the world, it was always too little, too late. What Mary Stillman Davies wanted was to stop men like Garrick Bateman from beating their wives. Instead, she'd settled for hiding them. Remarkable as that was, it was still second best, not that Dayle knew how to do any better.

She swallowed. The train was definitely slowing. Soon they were going to have to worry about the miners again and how they were going to get them the rest of the way.

At the same time, she realized she didn't hate Miss Davies. In some ways, she was exactly the woman she'd imagined in her fantasy—her mother, riding away on a black horse, her hair flowing behind, always free. But in this case, she was riding a train and thumbing her nose at the likes of Allan Pinkerton. Not bad. The fact that it wasn't enough to change the world wasn't her fault, but it did make Dayle reconsider. Maybe Harry and Tommy were right. Maybe what was needed was a complete revolution. Anarchy.

"Why Saint Elizabeth's?" Dayle asked. "There are better places."

Miss Davies shook her head. "Believe it or not, I was a lot like Lotta then. I simply didn't know better."

To that, Dayle nodded. "I understand."

"Thank you," she returned.

A moment later, Dayle added, "I'm sorry."

Miss Davies reached over and squeezed Dayle's hand. "Oh, but when we get to China, we'll make up for lost time," she promised with a little catch in her voice. "I can't express how grateful I am. The good Lord has answered my longest-asked prayer. His angels be blessed. His goodness be praised. His wonder and might be . . ."

Miss Davies didn't get to finish that thought.

Suddenly, a boot kicked the door wide open, and three men swung from the roof into the car. They knocked Miss Davies down and sent Dayle reeling back, nearly stumbling over the miners sitting everywhere. She barely got her balance before she looked down the barrel of William Pinkerton's gun.

27

Dayle's first reaction was gratitude. She wasn't going to have to go to China. Her second thought was alarm. Harry was going to get shot after all.

He'd jumped to his feet and was coming straight at William Pinkerton as if he didn't see the gun, or maybe it was that he didn't see the look on his old school friend's face. William Pinkerton meant business.

The other two men also had guns, but they seemed more nervous than determined. They swung their arms side to side, trying to keep everyone covered. That seemed to work. No one had moved since the three of them dropped through the door.

Except Harry.

William had one of his guns pointed at Dayle. The other was pointed at Harry, and, as near as she could tell, he hadn't blinked since his feet hit the floor.

She stepped sideways, hoping to get between the two of them. It was too far, and there were too many Chinese sitting in the way. She reached with one arm and managed to spread her palm across Harry's chest, staying him momentarily.

"No, please don't," she said.

She wasn't sure whom she was addressing with those words—William, hoping he wouldn't shoot, or Harry, hoping he wouldn't get shot. All she knew was that there had been too much killing already and none of it for any good reason.

Harry felt Dayle's hand hold him. He halted. "What do you think you're doing?" he now asked William.

"Stopping a train robbery," William answered.

Harry half laughed. "Look around. There are wounded here and women. Is this what you call a train robbery?"

"Just because the circumstances are a bit out of the ordinary doesn't make something right. Stealing is stealing. If you think about it, this is stealing on a grand scale, and frankly, I don't want to know how you're involved in it."

"He's not," Dayle quickly said.

Harry tried to shush her.

She wouldn't be quiet. "He was shot. Some Chinese laundrymen found him and brought him along with them when they escaped White Springs. He just happened to be with them when we found them walking beside the tracks. He had nothing to do with any of this."

Now William half laughed. "I think you protest too much," he said. "I've known that Harry has been mixed up in all sorts of things that I've chosen not to know. I never wanted to have to come after him." Then, shifting his look to Harry, he repeated, "I never wanted to have to come after you."

Ah So now stood, making one of the other men nervous enough to cock his pistol. "No. She speak true. I help steal train. Not him. He only actor who

The Lady Pinkerton Gets Her Man

got in way of bullet. Very bad luck. You can deport me. I go home to my ancestors."

"That's not the story the darkie and the guy with the wooden leg tell," William returned, and shook his head. "I couldn't believe it. I'm following the tracks back to White Springs, and what do I see? A backwards train. Now, that's something that begs to be investigated. I notice the train is already slowing, so I ride up alongside, climb on board, and I'll be damned if that engineer isn't proud of himself. He thinks folks are going to sing about him. He thinks they'll be singing about him a hundred years from now. What's this country coming to?"

"What's the harm in a song?" Harry asked. He knew William always wanted things to be the way they were "supposed to be," meaning a father who was supposed to be faithful. However, he could usually be won over with reason.

Not this time.

William's knuckles became white where he gripped his guns.

Harry pushed Dayle's hand out of the way. He took a step closer to his old friend and a different tone. "No, maybe you're right. The wrong tune can be damned annoying."

"I just shot the hell out of a whole gang of outlaws who thought that if they got famous enough, it wouldn't matter what they did," William told Harry. "Just because you do something bigger and better and wilder than anyone else doesn't make it any less wrong. Nobody steals a train and gets away with it."

"Fine," Harry agreed, "but that's not the main problem. You've got twenty-eight boxcars full of Chinese miners who've been run out of their homes and driven out of the mines. Some are wounded. A couple might not live. What are you going to do with them?"

"I'm going to order an engine out of Evanston and push these boxcars back where they belong."

"What if the miners don't want to go back there?"

"I no want to go there," Ah So told him. "I want go home to my ancestors."

William seemed to look around for the first time. "They're supposed to be in White Springs working the mines," he muttered, then stopped. "What's that smell?"

Ah So was putting on his burnt coat. "I am Tong leader. Train stopped. Now I take my men back to the ancestors." With that, he gave a signal, and all the Chinese who weren't hurt stood at once.

The two men with William suddenly backed themselves to the door and seemed undecided about what to do next.

"William, you can't stop this," Harry now said in a low, sincere tone. "It's gone too far to turn it back."

"But it's not supposed to be like this. You aren't supposed to get away with doing whatever it is you decide to do. There are rules." Then he swallowed and shifted his attention. Looking over his shoulder and all around, he finally agreed. "All right. Let them go. But not her." He turned both guns on Dayle. "She doesn't get away with this."

Dayle agreed. "Yes, get them out of here," she said.

Harry looked from her to William. The other thing he knew about his friend was that the mere mention of a Lady Pinkerton was enough to make him livid. He wasn't sure how he was going to talk William past that, but first things first. He signaled for Ah So and Mary Stillman Davies to gather the wounded and go. William's men stepped aside, and everyone immediately started climbing off the car.

Most of the Chinese were off when another of William's men rode up beside the door and shouted, "You got to see this!"

"See what?" William called back.

"It's a wagon train."

"A wagon train? There are no wagon trains anymore."

"I don't know what else to call it."

The Lady Pinkerton Gets Her Man

Obviously annoyed by this news, William shifted his weight and called back. "You have to be crazy."

"Not crazy enough to imagine this," the man answered.

"How close are we to Evanston?" Harry asked.

"I don't know," William answered. "Maybe five miles. I mean, I can't believe that engine got this far."

"It wasn't the engine. It was the engineer," Dayle corrected.

He didn't like that. "Shut up," he told her.

Harry added his own whispered "Please." He wasn't going to be able to handle this if Dayle didn't stay out of it.

"You got to see this," the rider insisted. "There must be forty wagons if there's ten."

William Pinkerton seemed to consider his options, then, pointing to Harry, he motioned him toward the door with one gun. "You go first."

Harry did. Dayle and William Pinkerton followed. Outside, a new day had dawned. The sky was getting lighter by the minute, and when you looked west, there was an unmistakable line of wagons coming over the horizon, all kinds of wagons, fancy wagons, farm wagons, oxcarts. Harry couldn't make any sense of that. Neither could anyone else. Then one of William's men, who'd ridden ahead, returned with the news.

"You're not going to believe this," he said as he rode up and whirled his horse around, raising a little cloud of dust.

"I already don't believe this," William answered. "Tell me the rest."

"They say that because the trains have all been stopped in White Springs, there wasn't an engine to send. So the mayor of Evanston rang the fire alarm bells, woke people up, and organized this wagon train to come and get the Chinese miners. They want to help the poor bastards 'return to their ancestors.'

More than that, the mayor and everyone else wants to meet the ingenious Miss Dobson who freed them."

"Freed them?"

The man nodded. "Your father has wired every train stop down the line and every newspaper in the country telling them how Miss Dobson freed these Chinese so they can go home."

"Give the public what they want," Miss Davies now commented. "I think even I'm going to have to give your father credit for this one. Who'd have thought he could turn this to his advantage?"

William was in no mood. "The public be damned. My father has only one interest. He'll do anything for one of his precious Lady Pinkertons—even make her famous. Never mind that she's a train thief and probably a whore."

The man on the horse didn't get it. "That's right," he answered with too much cheer. "The mayor says he never met a Lady Pinkerton, much less a famous one."

Harry knew that to William's way of thinking, this was probably the worst news. In fact, Harry couldn't read the successive series of facial contortions that gripped the younger Pinkerton's expression.

Except the last one.

He understood that one too well. William meant to kill Dayle.

She, too, seemed to sense that. He saw her visibly stiffen.

That's when Ah So turned to the closest telegraph pole, lifted his arms to the wires overhead, and bowed as if it was an act of worship. "Very clever," he said loudly. "Mr. Pinkerton is the warlord of the most difficult of wars. Very clever."

That seemed to shake William out of the moment "What's he talking about?"

"I haven't the slightest idea," Harry said. He also didn't have the slightest idea what to do next. He

The Lady Pinkerton Gets Her Man

knew that when William got muddled, his solution was to shoot first and ask questions after. On the other hand, he found himself wishing Ah So would keep on. He'd managed to distract William, at least momentarily.

"We Chinese know there are five kinds of war," Ah So said. Then he proceeded to name them: "Righteous, Aggressive, Enragement, Wanton, and Insurgent."

By then, Harry noticed that while the gun was still on Dayle, William's attention was divided.

"The first is war to quell disorder," Ah So continued. "The second is war of conquest. The third happens when troops are raised to satisfy a ruler's personal vengeance. The fifth is when the people overthrow corruption. But this—this is the fourth kind of war, Wanton War, the war of greedy lords."

William appealed to Harry for an explanation.

Harry shrugged. He was beginning to hope that the more confused William got, the more likely it was that he'd give up and head for the nearest bottle.

"Each of these fine wars is fought very differently," Ah So continued. "Wanton War is won by the side with the best agents of deception. No question. Mr. Pinkerton is the Warlord of Wanton War."

"I have no idea what you're talking about," William complained directly to the Tong leader.

"I no understand myself until now. Words can be weapons. I know this. But I did not know that words could be the whole army. Mr. Pinkerton say right words, 'protect the U.S. Mail,' and he almost get soldiers sent. When that not work, he make up story like he put in book and send it down the wire. Everyone believe. War won. I didn't understand the power of this. I didn't know words by themselves could win the Wanton War. Mr. Pinkerton is smart man. I bow to him as the new Warlord of Words." With that, Ah So again lowered himself in front of the telegraph pole. "It is new age—the age of wires that move lies like armies."

Then he turned and marched westward along the train tracks, passing under the telegraph poles, heading home. As he marched, the other Chinese fell in behind him.

Harry ran his fingers through his hair and took his own glance upward at the telegraph wires overhead. He couldn't help himself. The more he listened to Ah So, the more sense that Chinaman seemed to make. He rather hated to see him leave. At the same time, he stepped in front of Dayle and reached for William's gun. "You got a bottle in your saddle bag?" Harry asked. "I think it's time we shared a drink."

Still, William wavered. "I'm not letting a train thief go."

"Nobody but you thinks she's a train thief."

"But she is."

"She is," Harry agreed. "Only now the mayor of some nondescript, windblown train stop in this Godforsaken country wants to meet her, and you and I need to go get drunk because what else are we going to do?"

William wavered a moment longer and then gave Harry the gun.

In the next hour, Dayle told her story so many times, even she lost track of what was truth and what was tale. She was praised and congratulated. She had her hand shaken more times than she could count and had more hats tipped in her direction than she could remember.

All the Chinese had gotten into the wagons and started west on their way to Evanston, when Harry finally showed up again. He simply walked up behind her as she was wishing Lotta well and said into her ear, "Come away with me."

He said it as if he thought it was that easy.

The Lady Pinkerton Gets Her Man

"Where's your friend, the young Mr. Pinkerton?" she asked.

"Far enough into the bottle, he doesn't need my help anymore. Come away with me," he asked again.

She thought about that.

"Come away with you?" she echoed, because she wanted to absorb the words. She wanted to believe all this could end with her and Harry riding off into the sunrise.

Harry had gotten to her in more ways than one. He'd given her back her hope. He'd actually made her believe there could be a better world where men like Bald-head Ted ran the trains and Tommy the Tube Man fixed the machinery.

She wondered where they would go. She had unfinished business with Mary Stillman Davies. She still found missionary women damned annoying, but she and Miss Davies were the only people who'd ever stymied Allan Pinkerton. That wasn't a bad family heritage. She wasn't exactly sure how she wanted to explore that. She knew she wasn't going to go to China, but she thought she might like to go to San Francisco. She could visit her mother's mission and see the ocean.

"I knew you didn't want to go to China any more than I did," she told Harry. "I always know when you're lying."

"I want you to come away with me," he said again. "Is that a lie?"

"No," she returned.

"Well then?"

"What as?" she asked.

"I beg your pardon?"

"What as? Your wife? Your paramour? Your partner?"

He gave her a confused look. "As anything you want, I suppose."

"But would it be as exciting as being a famous Lady Pinkerton?" she asked.

"You can't be serious. You want to continue to be a Pinkerton after this? For one thing, I can't believe Allan Pinkerton is entirely pleased with you."

She shook her head. "Once Allan Pinkerton makes someone famous, he considers her his creation. I know it's hard to understand, but I suspect it's an old man's remaining pleasure. In short, I expect he'll feel protective toward me from now on. Besides, that's who I am. I'm a Lady Pinkerton—a *famous* Lady Pinkerton like Kate Warne, who was the first. I'm sure you don't understand."

He snorted. "You're right. I don't. I've never had any use for *any* Pinkerton."

"Nor do I have any use for the kind of anarchy we experienced back in White Springs."

"I didn't start that. You know I wasn't responsible for that."

"I know. But it's all the same, isn't it?"

"No. Nobody should get away with what happened back there. This isn't over."

"Nothing is ever over."

"I'm serious. Someone needs to upset the order of things, make things right."

"Within the law, maybe. I mean, what gives you, or anyone else, the right to work outside the law?"

"You think stealing a train was legal?"

"I always meant to give it back. Besides, we both know that's small compared to what you want to do."

He touched his bandage and shook his head as if trying to clear some confusion. "What exactly are you saying? That you'll come after me if I carry through against Jay Gould and his like?"

"You're charming, but you're not above the law."

"You can't be serious."

"One misstep and you're mine."

"I don't believe this."

"Better me than William Pinkerton."

He paused. He glanced in the direction of his old

The Lady Pinkerton Gets Her Man

school chum. He worked his jaw the way he sometimes did when words failed him, which wasn't often.

She didn't know what to say either. He could philosophize all he wanted, but the end did not justify the means. It didn't matter who was responsible. Loosing chaos on White Springs, Wyoming, had accomplished nothing, except get a lot of people killed. That wasn't the answer.

He tried again. "Of all forms of caution, caution in love is the most fatal to happiness," he whispered.

No good. She and Harry were the sort who'd drive themselves crazy if they tried to live on love alone. Like it or not, they'd both embraced a larger world than their own self-centered satisfaction. It was the reason neither of them would have gone to China . . . or Patagonia.

"Does this strike you as the cautious, the safe way to go?" she asked him.

"No," he admitted.

"Good, because I never figured us for being the cautious sort."

Their eyes met. It was a gaze that might have transported, except that they both knew, both understood. This wasn't the end. Likely they'd be bound forever in this war of wills. They both knew the world needed to be different, but how to accomplish that was another story.

He looked away first.

A moment later, he asked, "Exactly what do you suggest we do?"

"Wave," she answered, and pointed to where Tommy the Tube Man was entertaining Lotta's children. He was wrapping himself into some kind of human knot.

Stef Ann Holm

Nominated by Romantic Times for a Best Historical Romantic Adventure Award, Stef Ann Holm is renowned for her vivid depictions of love and adventure, with a gift for storytelling that allows her to summon the images and textures of a bygone era.

Crossings 51047-9/$5.99

Weeping Angel 51045-2/$5.99

Snowbird 79734-4/$5.50

King of the Pirates 79733-6/$5.50

Liberty Rose 74125-X/$5.50

Seasons of Gold 74126-8/$5.50

Portraits 51044-4/$5.99

Forget Me Not 00204-X/$5.99

Harmony 00205-8/$5.99

Available from Pocket Books

Simon & Schuster Mail Order
200 Old Tappan Rd., Old Tappan, N.J. 07675
Please send me the books I have checked above. I am enclosing $_____ (please add $0.75 to cover the postage and handling for each order. Please add appropriate sales tax). Send check or money order--no cash or C.O.D.'s please. Allow up to six weeks for delivery. For purchase over $10.00 you may use VISA: card number, expiration date and customer signature must be included.

POCKET BOOKS

Name _____
Address _____
City _____ State/Zip _____
VISA Card # _____ Exp.Date _____
Signature _____ 1176-04

Let
Andrea Kane
romance you tonight!

Dream Castle 73585-3/$5.99

My Heart's Desire 73584-5/$5.50

Masque of Betrayal 75532-3/$4.99

Echoes In the Mist 75533-1/$5.99

Samantha 86507-2/$5.50

The Last Duke 86508-0/$5.99

Emerald Garden 86509-9/$5.99

Wishes In the Wind 53483-1/$5.99

Legacy of the Diamond 53485-8/$5.99

The Black Diamond 53482-3/$5.99

Available from Pocket Books

Simon & Schuster Mail Order
200 Old Tappan Rd., Old Tappan, N.J. 07675

Please send me the books I have checked above. I am enclosing $_____ (please add $0.75 to cover the postage and handling for each order. Please add appropriate sales tax). Send check or money order–no cash or C.O.D.'s please. Allow up to six weeks for delivery. For purchase over $10.00 you may use VISA: card number, expiration date and customer signature must be included.

POCKET BOOKS

Name _____

Address _____

City _____ State/Zip _____

VISA Card # _____ Exp.Date _____

Signature _____ 957-08

An All-New Collection of
Heartwarming Holiday Stories

UPON A MIDNIGHT CLEAR

Jude Deveraux

Linda Howard

MARGARET ALLISON

STEF ANN HOLM

MARIAH STEWART

**Available in Hardcover
From Pocket Books**

POCKET BOOKS

1405-01

NEW YORK TIMES BESTSELLING AUTHOR

JULIE GARWOOD

☐ HONOR'S SPLENDOUR	73782-1/$6.99
☐ THE LION'S LADY	73783-X/$6.99
☐ THE BRIDE	73779-1/$6.99
☐ GENTLE WARRIOR	73780-5/$6.99
☐ REBELLIOUS DESIRE	73784-8/$6.99
☐ GUARDIAN ANGEL	67006-9/$6.99
☐ THE GIFT	70250-5/$6.99
☐ THE PRIZE	70251-3/$6.99
☐ THE SECRET	74421-6/$6.99
☐ CASTLES	74420-8/$6.99
☐ SAVING GRACE	87011-4/$6.99
☐ PRINCE CHARMING	87096-3/$6.99
☐ FOR THE ROSES	87098-X/$6.99
☐ THE WEDDING	87100-5/$6.99

<u>THE ROSE TRILOGY</u>

☐ ONE PINK ROSE	01008-5/$2.99
☐ ONE WHITE ROSE	01009-3/$2.99
☐ ONE RED ROSE	01010-7/$2.99

AVAILABLE FROM POCKET BOOKS

Simon & Schuster Mail Order
200 Old Tappan Rd., Old Tappan, N.J. 07675
Please send me the books I have checked above. I am enclosing $_____ (please add $0.75 to cover the postage and handling for each order. Please add appropriate sales tax). Send check or money order--no cash or C.O.D.'s please. Allow up to six weeks for delivery. For purchase over $10.00 you may use VISA: card number, expiration date and customer signature must be included.

POCKET BOOKS

Name _____
Address _____
City _____ State/Zip _____
VISA Card # _____ Exp.Date _____
Signature _____

811-14